TREACHEROUS

TREACHEROUS

GRIFTERS, RUFFIANS AND KILLERS

SHORT STORIES

GARY PHILLIPS

To Arnold Hano, the storyteller

Contents

Acknowledgments

- "The Performer" originally in *Orange County Noir,* Akashic, 2010
- "The Kim Novak Effect" originally in *Ellery Queen Mystery Magazine,* November 2008
- "Swift Boats for Jesus" originally in *Politics Noir: Dark Tales from the Corridors of Power,* Verso, 2008
- "Roger Crumbler Considered His Shave" originally in *Los Angeles Noir,* Akashic, 2007
- "The Man for the Job" originally in Dublin Noir: *The Celtic Tiger vs. The Ugly American,* Akashic, 2006
- "Ther Investor" originally in *Damn Near Dead 2: Live Noir or Die Trying,* Busted Flush Press, 2010
- "The Snowbirds" originally in *Once Upon a Crime: An Anthology of Murder, Mayhem and Suspense,* Nodin Press, 2009
- "Sportin' Men" originally in *Full House,* Putnam Juvenile, 2007
- "Beginner's Luck," originally in *Shades of Black: Crime and Mystery Stories by African-American Writers,* Berkley Prime Crime, 2004
- "Branded" originally in *Flesh & Blood: Erotic Tales of Crime and Passion,* Mysterious Press, 2001
- "Black Caesar's Gold" originally in *The Heroin Chronicles,* Akashic, 2013
- "Can't Be Satisfied" originally in *Too Much Boogie: Erotic Remixes of the Dirty Blues,* LL Publications, 2011
- "Incident on Hill 19," originally in *Retro Pulp Tales,* Subterranean Press, 2006
- "Disco Zombies," originally in *The Cocaine Chronicles,* Akashic, 2005
- "Rio Blanco" originally in *Guns of the West,* Berkley Books, 2002

- "House of Tears," originally in *Black Noir, Mystery, Crime and Suspense Stories by African-American Writers*, Pegasus, 2009
- "Chatter," originally in *Plots With Guns: A Noir Anthology*, Dennis McMillan Publications, 2005
- "Masai's Back in Town," originally in *Send My Love and a Molotov Cocktail: Stories of Crime, Love* and Rebellion, PM Press, 2011
- "The Counterfeit Comrade," originally in *Measures of Poison* Dennis McMillan Publications, 2002
- "The Measure," originally in *The Blue and the Gray Undercover: All New Civil War Spy Adventures*, Forge 2002
- "The Calling," Akashic's Monday's Are Murder (online), 2013

Praise for Treacherous

"Treacherous: Grifters, Ruffians and Killers by Gary Phillips isn't a book you'd want to give to your best friend who loves cozies, as the subtitle indicates. In fact Maureen Corrigan said on NPR that some of these stories 'would make Nancy Drew faint facedown into her cucumber tea sandwiches.' I didn't know that Ms. Drew was into cucumber tea. Or maybe I'm reading the sentence wrong. At any rate, this is a collection full of the real hardboiled thing."—Bill Crider, *Mystery Scene Magazine*

"Phillips obviously loves his anti-heroes, as the stories' major characters are all, as the subtitle promises, grifters, ruffians and killers. You may not be on their side, but you can't help but be fascinated by their escapades… Phillips unfaltering ear for contemporary urban dialogue and patois, relentless pacing that grabs you from the opening sentence—oh, and plenty of sex and violence, too."—Alan Cranis, bookgasm.com

"Those looking for a fun romp amid crime and killers will be satisfied."—*Publishers Weekly*

I

GRIFTERS

The Performer

Avery Randolph finished the stretched-out riff of Billy Joel's "Just the Way You Are," hoping his playing covered the unintentional flattening he gave the last lyrics. He meant to take his voice up a notch, not down. The throat was the second thing to go. There was polite applause from the Seaside Lounge crowd, and Randolph nodded slowly while noodling the keys jauntily.

An aging couple, both in bright attire, their matching sterling gray hair arranged just so, walked by the piano, hand in hand. The woman, peach-colored lipstick gothically enticing in the bar's subdued lighting, dropped a five into the large brandy snifter for tips. She smiled. Randolph smiled. The man gave a quick wave to a short-haired woman at a table near the window, and the two departed. The man let his hand glide down and, briefly and tenderly, flutter against the woman's backside.

"This is for Emily," Randolph announced and began a leisure intro into "Straighten Up and Fly Right," channeling Nat "King" Cole, letting it build while several patrons bopped their heads and tapped their feet to the rhythm.

"Cool down, Papa, don't you blow…your…toppppp," he finished in the key he meant to, and this time the applause was more heartfelt. He stood and bowed and blew a kiss to Emily, the one the man had waved to, sitting at her usual spot next to the window overlooking the medical center down below. For sixty-three, Randolph reflected, she looked good, handsome in her dark blue dress and diamond broach, an ever-present martini glass near her steady blood nailed hand.

She lifted her drink and toasted him with a sip and a toothy grin.

Randolph finished his set with an instrumental rendition of Fats Waller's "Ain't Misbehavin'" adding, "Don't forget the sand dab special, folks, Rene swears they are to die for." That got a few chuckles, and he did a wave on his way to the bar. Among those sitting there was a National Guard trooper in his camouflage, his combat service badge dully gleaming over his flapped breast pocket. He was drinking a beer from a pint glass and was having an animated conversation over his cell phone. He turned his body away and hunched over some as Randolph perched on the opposite end.

Carlson, the head bartender, came over with his Jack and Coke. "You tinkled them good tonight," he commented, setting the squat glass on a napkin with the Lounge's name on it.

"Thanks, man." Momentarily, Randolph watched the logo become distorted by the wet bottom of the glass, then took it to his lips.

"I guess you have to go easy on that stuff, don't you? Or does it help your playing?"

Randolph looked over at the woman who'd sat beside him. She was young, that is, younger than him. In her late twenties, he figured, jeans and some kind of loose faux suede top. Not too much make-up, Rite Aid earrings. Pretty, but not overwhelmingly so. He sized her up as the wife or girlfriend of some soldier or marine over in Iraq or Afghanistan. Lonely. Bored. There was a lot of that in Los Alamitos.

"Everything in moderation," he said. He didn't offer to buy her a drink, making sure he kept his eyes on her face and not down on that alert swell beneath the top's material. The bare arms, though, impressively toned.

"I used to play guitar in high school," she continued, "even had us an all-girl band for a while. But you know how it goes," she elevated a shoulder.

"Not the next Bangles, huh?" She frowned.

"Before your time," Carlson piped in. A not so subtle reminder that Randolph was probably a decade and half older than her. Randolph resisted a remark. Goddamn Carlson was older than he was but worked out on the weights and had bragged about getting pectoral implants. "So I can pick up more pussy easily," he'd cracked to Randolph and Rene Suarez, the chef.

"Can I have a gin tonic?" the woman asked, looking from Carlson back to Randolph.

"Yours to command," the bartender said and went to prepare her order.

"What do you do now?" What the hell, Randolph concluded, no sense making it easy for Carlson. Besides, he was just making with the chit-chat, no more, no less.

She jerked her head and said, "Work at the PX on the base. Original around here, right?"

Carlson returned with her drink. "Me lady."

"Shit fire," the soldier engrossed on the phone swore as he threw the thing across the bar top. It slid into another customer's glass, the drink's owner glaring at the Guardsman. "Aw, hell, here we go. Another old lady done told her hero boy bye-bye." Carlson, himself a vet, double-timed to cool out the serviceman.

"Your husband on his second or third tour?" Randolph asked the woman. They both watched Carlson putting an arm around the soldier's shoulders, his head down as he mumbled words of self-pity.

"He was killed about half a year ago. Roadside bomb hit their convoy coming into Pakitka Province." She drank some. "Jeff was Army, then after he rotated out, he wanted to do something about what he'd seen over there. Something different." She shook her head. "Jeff's a…sweetheart. He worked for CARE International delivering food and relief."

She put the gin down quietly. "Damn. Sure sorry to hear that."

"Lori. My name's Lori." She offered her hand, and he shook it, smiling crookedly at her.

He told her his name, and for several minutes, they sat side-by-side in their shared silence. Carlson returned after escorting the soldier outside.

"Sorry, folks, I'm back," he announced and got behind the bar to fulfill his enabling duties.

"Hey, look," Randolph began, "let me get your second G and T, okay? I'm not, you know, trying anything funny."

"Thanks, but no thanks, Avery." She'd turned her body toward him slightly and touched his arm. "I better get going. Inventory tomorrow, so I've got to be in early." She got off the stool, and the young widow strolled out of the landlocked Seaside Lounge.

"You get her number?" Carlson asked when he came over to Randolph.

"Kind of," the piano player answered, looking off, then readying the order of songs in his head for his next set.

A week later, he was finishing off a loud and lyrically incoherent sing-a-long version of "Volare" when Lori returned to the bar. She was wearing a modest skirt, shirt, and sweater top combo, and earrings that sparkled in the low artificial light. Randolph banged the keys with his heel a la Little Richard for the climax, everyone clapping and laughing. He stood, breathing heavy, pumping both fists in the air to more acclaim. A patron shouted, "Right on, baby," above the din.

"Glad you came back," he said to her. She lingered on the side of the piano, her purse atop the instrument. Normally, he'd say something about that but didn't want to break the mood—his, at least. People came by and gave him pats on the back and shoulders. The brandy snifter was brimming with bills tonight.

"Want to go somewhere, have a sandwich or something? I'm hungry."

She leaned in closer to him. "Hungry for what?" Her smoke-colored eyes remained steady on him.

"There's a little hole-in-the-wall place over on Cerritos," he answered neutrally, but not breaking his gaze from hers. "They have great vegetarian burritos with fire-roasted peppers. *Magnifico.*"

"I like meat alright."

They grinned at each other like over-heated teenagers as Randolph collected his tip money. Over in the corner at her customary table, Emily Bravera sipped her martini carefully as if testing the stuff for poison, watching the couple over the rim of her glass.

Randolph and the woman descended the outside stairs from where the Seaside Lounge was on the second floor of an aging '80s-era strip mall. Down on the parking lot asphalt, he became aware of a familiar odor and looked up to see Carlson, the bartender, taking one of his Camel breaks. He leaned on the railing, the unfiltered cigarette smoldering in his blunt fingers. Lazily, he looked at them. The two men then nodded briefly at each other, and Randolph walked the woman to her eight-year-old bronze Camry with a dark blue driver's door. He gave her the directions to where they were going, standing near her and pointing off in to the near distance.

"See you there." She gave him a peck on his cheek, her fingers holding onto his upper arms. Her hair was freshly washed and smelled of blueberries and mint.

At Agamotto's Late Nite Eatery and Coffee Emporium, they ate and talked. Lori McLaughlin was originally from Buffalo. She'd met her late husband Jeff, a local boy from Long Beach, when she'd come out to Southern California four years ago, winding up working at a dog food manufacturer.

"That's a trip," Randolph remarked. "Like big vats where the meat and whatnot is all mixed together?"

"This place, Emerald Valley, is like the Escalade of dog food makers," she said, biting into her barbecue meatloaf sandwich and chewing. She then pointed at the sandwich. "Good cuts of meat like this, natural ingredients, grains, they make a high-end product selling to trendy pet stores in West LA and further down in the OC like Newport Beach and Lake Forrest."

"But not for us peasants here in Los Al." They both chuckled.

Randolph asked her, "You have family back in Buffalo?"

She had some of her beer and dabbed a napkin to her mouth. "Let's just say there's a reason I came out here to put as much distance between me and that so-called family." Still holding the napkin, she squeezed his hand. "Okay?"

"Okay."

The lanky youngster in the stained apron behind the counter gave them a grunt as the couple left. He returned his attention to a news item on the small TV he watched, an image of Long Beach police personnel leaving a burglarized condo in Belmont Shores from earlier that day.

Out in his car, after she had him pull behind a closed liquor store, they made out. There was a bare bulb streaked with an oily substance over the metal back door of the establishment, and slivered fractions of that light filtered into the car's interior and over their grasping forms. Randolph had his hand over her sweater, cupping one of her breasts as they kissed. He moved his thumb across her hardening nipple. She placed one of her hands on his zipper and rubbed.

"That feels good," he murmured.

"This'll feel even better." She tongued his ear and unzipped him. Involuntarily, he sucked in his stomach. "I didn't catch any hairs, did I, Avery?" she asked in a concerned voice.

"No. Light-headed is all."

"Mmmm." She worked his shaft and then bent down.

Randolph leaned back, eyes fluttering, noting he needed to clean his headliner. Try as he might to fixate on prosaic matters to prolong the sensation, he soon wheezed, "Hey, careful, I'm…I'm about to come."

She gave him a lingering lick along his penis, returning to the tip. "Uh-huh." And she let him climax in her mouth.

"Sweet mother of mercy," Randolph exclaimed, grinning like a goon.

From her purse, Lori McLaughlin produced a half pint of Jack Daniels and, breaking the seal, had a swig and handed it across.

"Remember your motto," she said as he had a taste, "everything in moderation."

"Most assuredly," he retorted.

She took something else from her purse and, palm up, presented it to him. "Because you're not through, piano man. You have encores tonight."

He took the offered orange oblong tablet of Cialis. "I'm not that old, you know."

"I know, darling." McLaughlin had pulled up her skirt and, using her middle finger, pleasured herself. He stared and said nothing. She continued this for several moments, then took off her light blue panties and pressed them into his face. He breathed in deep, then popped the Cialis in his mouth, not bothering to wash it down with the booze.

Early that morning, at her three-and-a-half-room apartment not far from the Joint Forces base, Randolph pulled on his cigar-smoking Woody Woodpecker head boxers and went into the kitchenette in search of juice or cold water. On the counter, he spotted a past-due notice from SoCal

Edison.

On a book ledge crowded with perfunctory knick-knacks was a picture of a square-jawed, handsome Lance Corporal he took to be the late husband. He picked it up to see it better by the moonlight. The confident look of the soldier reminded him of the photo of his father, a decorated combat captain who died in Vietnam. A man he never met and only knew from Polaroids and letters his mother kept. He sighed inwardly, put the picture back, and traipsed to the refrigerator. Inside, he found an open can of Diet Pepsi and straightened up, holding it. One hand on the open door, the light from inside the refrigerator casting its glow about the compact space, Randolph looked at a print of a leafy country lane hung on the wall. It wasn't anything special, like the kind of mass-produced reproduction demonstrating the virtues of the frame you came to buy.

Guzzling the soda, looking sideways at the lane, cold air blowing against his lower legs, he suddenly had a massive, pulsing erection.

"*Magnifico*," he said, proudly stalking back into the bedroom, moving his hips to let his member swing from side to side. He hummed "Rocket Man" and sent up a prayer of thanks to the horny bastard who cooked up the orange wonder.

In the morning, Randolph stretched, scratched his side, and rubbed his whiskered face. In the other room, he could hear Lori McLaughlin talking on the phone.

"…no. You listen to me, Karen, that's not going to happen, you understand? I won't stand still while you try that kind of shit with me."

He got up and used the bathroom. When he stepped out, McLaughlin was sitting on the edge of the bed in her cloth robe, hunched forward, arms across her upper thighs like a player waiting to get called back in the game. He sat close, putting an arm around her shoulder.

"Can I help with anything?"

She made a sound in her throat. "I could lie to you and tell you it's nothing," she began, "but you might as well know now as later." She regarded him for a moment and said, "I was talking to my wonderful ex-mother-in-law. A woman who would make Big Bird slap the shit out of her." She chuckled evilly at the mental image.

"This involve a child?" he asked, having also noticed last night an assortment of toys in a cardboard box in a corner of the living room.

"Yes. My daughter Farley."

"Farley?"

"Jeff had a good buddy who lost his legs over there." She's just two and a half, and, well, you can see I'm not exactly living the OC lifestyle."

"Who is around here?" He gave her a squeeze.

She jutted her chin in a westerly direction. "Over in Rossmoor, they are. Them and their wall."

"Screw 'em," Randolph said. "They think they shit gold." She snuggled closer to him, putting a hand on his thigh.

"Jeff's mother, Karen, has recently stepped up her campaign about how she knows it's tough for me to get by alone and be able to feed and raise Farley. How she can provide for her and all that. Her third husband, not Jeff's father, owned a firm that supplied some kind of guidance system for missiles. Anyway, he dropped dead of a stroke and left her sitting pretty in a mortgage-free McMansion in Irvine. That's where Farley is now."

She rubbed his thigh and eyeing him said, "I didn't plan on seducing you, Avery. But Karen suddenly showed up yesterday when I went to pick up Farley from the sitter after work. And, well, she demanded time with her granddaughter. She lords it over me what with her paying for the child care and other things for Farley."

She scooted over to her pressed board nightstand, and opening a drawer, took out a digital print. She handed it across to Randolph, who smiled at the photo of a bright-eyed toddler held aloft by her beaming mother. She took it back, lingered in it, then replaced it in the drawer.

"So I was just a way for you to blow off steam? A revenge schtup aimed at your mother-in-law?"

She shoved him playfully and clambered on top of him as he lay on his back, enwrapping her in his arms. "How observant of you, Dr. Phil." They kissed eagerly as he undid her robe.

On a Thursday evening several days later, they lay in bed in Randolph's apartment near the race track. Intermingled yells of delight and disappoint-ment could be heard through his cracked sliding window over his bed as the last race finished.

Randolph dialed the radio from the news on the rock station McLaughlin had put on to the jazz station from the college campus in Long Beach. "Suddenly," a McCoy Tyner number was in mid-play. He let his mind drift as the pianist-composer did his thing.

"You bet much?" she asked, lying partially on him, his finger gently following Tyner, stroke for stoke, on her shapely butt.

"Now and then I go over there, but I play the ponies like I know poker, not too damn good." He stopped playing and began kneading her flesh, getting aroused.

She nuzzled his neck. "What if you could make about thirty thousand on a sure thing?"

"You know a horse doper?"

"I know where to get sixty, maybe seventy thousand tax-free dollars. Half for you and half for me, Avery. Between your couple of nights a week at the Seaside and substitute music and civics teacher, you're not living *la vida loca* either."

He stopped rubbing and focused. "What are you talking about, Lori?"

"Remember I told you about Emerald Valley?"

"The dog food company."

"The owner, Brice, he's an old hippie, still smokes marijuana, gives his money to saving the rain forest and all that crap."

"Okay. But I'm not comprehending."

"He has a safe in his office. He's still down with the people, don't trust the system, so he's always kept cash around, different places, you see? One of them is his office 'cause he's always got some burned-out acid head or old surfing bro falling by for a touch." She paused, placing her hand firmly on his chest.

"Even gives it up to an ex-employee or two," she continued. "I had to go see him for a loan, and he's always had a thing for me. Gave me a handful of those Cialis pills, saying to leave a trail of them through the forest, and he'd find his way to me. Laughing and having a good time." His tone frosted.

"This about keeping Karen at bay?"

"She's told me she's going to initiate, her word, legal action. If I just show her I can afford a lawyer, she'll back down. I know how her wormy mind works. She's cheap in so many ways."

"Why not ask Brice for the loan? Sounds to me like he'd do it for you and not sweat when you couldn't pay him back. The good fight and all that."

She pulled slowly on his limp penis. "Because he'd want something in return, Avery. Brice is a freak, get it? He's been in trouble in the past for beating off in his office in front of females. He'd want me to do kinky things to him regularly for repayment. Do you want me to do that?" She started to stroke him slowly. His breath got short as he got hard. "I might be willing to be a thief, but I'm no ho."

She continued with her hand job. "Unless you're going to bitch up. Turn your head when I have to shove a studded dildo up his ass and hear him scream 'Mommy.' Make like I'm not your woman." She took his balls in her hand.

"Not likely," he groaned as he put his fingers to her throat and applied pressure. She gasped, and he leveraged her under him.

"Fuck me rough, baby," she demanded—and he did.

The plan wasn't elaborate. It was straightforward and textbook efficient— if it was a chapter from a manual on thievery. Emerald Valley Premium Dog Foods was in a seventeen thousand square foot, one-story landscaped building on the cul-de-sac end of an industrial park not far from a 605 freeway off-ramp. Lori McLaughlin had made a Sunday after-hours rendezvous to get the money from a thrilled Brice Hovis. McLaughlin told Randolph he'd insisted that she think of the loan as a long-term investment in her and her daughter's futures and to come by his office to finalize the deal he'd said.

McLaughlin knew the layout of the factory, and once she got Hovis wound up, she'd said with a sneer, she'd leave a side door that let in from the parking lot, used by employees when they had to work overtime, unlatched.

Dressed in overalls obtained that day from a thrift store and wearing rubber dishwashing gloves, Avery Randolph gained access to the facility at the appointed time. Inside, he easily spotted the thin strip of light coming from the slightly ajar office door at the far end of the plant. He eased forward on tennis shoes also obtained at the thrift store. His outfit would be burned afterward.

Randolph passed belt feeders, tall stainless steel devices that had large conical-shaped vats atop them, automated packaging stations, and long, heavy-looking machinery bolted to the concrete floor with drive shafts that led to partially encased circular rotors he took for chopping and grinding up the meat Emerald Valley turned into dog food. Stilled circulation fans were set at various strategic locations in the ceiling.

McLaughlin had explained to him the business, like a lot of pet food manufacturers, bought rendered meat from elsewhere and this was shipped to them as were grains and cereals from other suppliers. Randolph was pleasantly surprised the air in here smelled like cheeseburgers.

Coming to the end of a large box-like machine on stout legs, a dryer he could tell from its stamped label, he was near the office. He halted, shutting out all distractions, getting it together for his performance. It's all about the in-between, man, a jazz guitarist reminded him on a studio gig.

He heard Hovis moaning in pleasure between whaps. The tang of marijuana cut through the burger aroma.

"Goddammit, yes, oh yes, doctor."

Randolph stepped into the light to see Hovis leaning over his desk in a stripper nurse costume, short skirt up over a thong, with high heels and a red-haired woman's wig lopsided on his bald head. McLaughlin, in her underwear beneath an open lab coat, was holding a dog hair brush, the kind with short wire bristles. She'd been using that side on the man's tenderized rear end. There was a strap-on dildo and a plastic enema bottle filled with s clear liquid occupying the paper-laden desk.

Hovis straightened up and stammered, "Who, what is this?" There was a good-sized alligator clamp dangling from his encased penis.

By then, Randolph, trying not to giggle too much, had covered the distance between them and squirted liberal amounts of pepper spray into the man's eyes.

"This is not safe," the dog food man blurted, hands grabbing at his face while he did a run-in-place dance of pain in his night nurse uniform.

McLaughlin slugged him over the head with a smoking bong, shattering it. Hovis ran and crashed into a tall file cabinet, knocking it and him over.

"Don't either one of you fuckin' move," Randolph blared. He quickly tied a handkerchief around the downed man's tearing eyes, and McLaughlin made sounds like she was being manhandled. Randolph tied Hovis up with cord he'd brought along and got a ball gag strapped around his mouth. He writhed and whimpered on his side on the floor, then lay still.

"Where is it, bitch?" Randolph growled, giving it his best Steven Segal guttural rasp.

"I don't know what you're talking about." She slapped her thigh for effect and grunted.

"We'll see about that. Come here, let me show you what me and that dildo are gonna do to you." He marched her out of the office and, after a suitable period, returned and began tearing up the office. He knew where Hovis kept the money from McLaughlin but had to sell the search.

He kicked over a surfboard leaning in a corner. Above that, in a compartment Hovis had installed, was the cash hidden in the ceiling. "Well, what do we have here?" He walked over to Hovis and kicked him. He got a stifled yell for a response.

"Clever cocksucker, aren't you?" Randolph said to the trussed-up owner. "Your girlfriend held out but it's a good thing for both of you I got eyes." He placed a chair under the area of the ceiling and, pushing up on the acoustic tile, revealed a large fishing tackle box. He took this out, assessed the contents, and exited the office.

Hovis didn't know that McLaughlin knew where he kept the money. She'd spied once when she'd worked at the company. Though naturally, he'd suspect her, there had been an employee she told Randolph he'd fired a few months ago and she'd make sure to subtlety train his suspicions in that direction. Or so she'd said.

On the darkened factory floor, he removed his disguise of bushy afro wig, false goatee, and Halloween rubber nose. McLaughlin, in her bra and panties, stilettos off so as not to make noise, came over to him, and gave him a passionate kiss. He rubbed his hand between her legs.

"Better get going. I'll meet you back at my place, Avery."

"I like it when you say my name," he whispered back.

"I know."

He punched her hard, twice, in the face, reeling her back while she held onto him for balance. Like a boxer clearing their vision, she shook her head and then broke one of her heels off. She put the shoes on and wobbled into the office while Randolph turned toward the way he came in.

"Brice, Brice, are you all right?" she screamed, running into the office. McLaughlin's face rearranged itself from mock concern to icy resolves. "Briiice," she drew out, hand beside her mouth but barely saying his name. "Briiiice, my demented shithead, can you get up?" She guffawed and removed a dagger-shaped letter opener from a pen caddy on the desk. The blade was in the style of a medieval knife, and she withdrew it from its sheath. She sauntered over and cut Brice Hovis' legs loose and removed the ball gag and handkerchief. His hands remained bound.

"Oh my God, are you all right, Steph?" His eyes were red and wet. He looked from her to the open ceiling and back.

Her fingers trilled the tip of the letter opener. "I'm fine, Brice. Real fuckin' good." She flicked the blade and nicked his thigh. Crimson ran behind the black mesh stocking material.

"Hey," he said, backing up, "this is no time for that. Untie me, would you?"

Swaying her body, she stepped closer, waving the letter opener around like a drunk musketeer. "And what if I don't, Brice? What if I take it too far this time?" She took another nick out of him, this time from his chest.

Brice looked about panicked while backpedaling in his heels and skirt. "Quit fucking around, Stephanie."

"I'm serious as a fever, Bricey. Come on, beg for your life." She placed her hand on her mound. "It makes me wet." She lunged forward and tackled Hovis, who went over, McLaughlin straddling him.

Down on the floor, he squirmed and bucked but ceased when she put the tip to his throat, letting it sink in a centimeter.

"Why?" he pleaded, "why are you doing this?"

"Because I can, cunt." She made another cut, and Hovis' eyes fluttered, his breathing shallow. A tsk-tsk sound came from her, and she made to backhand him awake.

"Yo, Steph, is it?"

The woman, who went by two names, looked up to see Randolph, his disguise back on, standing in the doorway. She chortled. "Yeah, so? What're you gonna do about it, homeboy?"

"This," he said calmly, shooting her in the mouth as she laughed at him.

The woman's body tumbled off of Hovis, her heelless shoe laying across his leg. Randolph bundled the terrified exec again.

"There's something like ninety thousand in here," a woman's voice said behind him. He turned to Emily Bravera, who was in slacks and a striped shirt. She was on one knee, having counted the contents of the tackle box. She relatched the lid.

"Not bad," Randolph said. "Plus, Hovis can't squawk to the law since he was hiding it from the IRS."

"Well, he does have some explaining to do in that get-up of his and two bodies sprawled out." Her arm in the crook of his, him holding the strong box, the two strolled out to the parking lot. Laying dead on the uneven asphalt was the bartender, Alfonso Carlson. He'd been in wait for Randolph to ambush and kill him. But Bravera, a one-time investigating officer with the Criminal Investigation Command of the Army, had done the bushwhacking. Inside was his daughter, Stephanie Carlson. The Command's motto was "Do What Has to be Done."

Before they departed, Bravera put her face close to Randolph's, squeezing his cheeks in her blood-nailed fingers, her tan prominent against his burnished copper skin. "You liked fucking her, didn't you?"

"Just doing my job, Cap'n."

"Just remember, Thelonious, I know how to use a rifle with a scope."

"I keep that information uppermost in my mind."

"See that you do." She kissed him deep and long.

* * *

At the Seaside Lounge, Avery Randolph began a mournful rendition of "On Green Dolphin Street." At her table by the window, Emily Bravera sat and drank sparingly, appreciating his handling of the tune. The two had been working this area for more than a month now, pulling off several lucrative burglaries from Long Beach then south along the Orange County coast. Jewelry, a few telling homemade DVDs, cash, and even gold bars horded against the next meltdown. For it wasn't only old hippies like Brice Hovis who didn't like reporting all their income.

The front they'd constructed involved Bravera being a general's widow living in Rossmoor. Real estate being what it was these days, the realtor was happy to rent to the widow on a month-to-month basis. She was personable, knowledgeable on a variety of subjects, worked out at the local gym, and managed to get herself invited to this or that soiree or club event, thus being able to scope out various domiciles.

Bravera had knowledge of security systems, and Randolph knew a thing or two about safes. For him tumblers or electronic lock sequencing were different sets of notes to master—particularly when you employed certain tech to aid in the stealing effort and revealing pesky nanny cams. Tomorrow, they were going to take down the beach house of the matching-haired couple. Yes, they'd agreed; he and Bravera had one sweet hustle going.

When the supposed Lori McLaughlin came on to him, the possessive Bravera did some checking and found out that she was Carlson's daughter. Randolph and Bravera didn't know what the pitch was, but figured the two were setting Randolph up for an Oswald—be the fall guy. The piano player had hinted to the bartender he'd beat out on a dope charge in Baltimore. That was a lie, just part of the dodge like his funky apartment near the track. But the Carlsons must have figured a footloose brother hiding out in the OC, wanted on a criminal charge elsewhere, was a good fit for a robbery-murder here in town.

Randolph and his older lover and partner, not wishing to pass up an opportunity for enrichment, had let the scheme unfold. In another month or so, not foolish enough to push their luck, they'd move on.

"Like Duke said, man, you gotta play with intent to do something," the pianist said sotto voce then hummed and teased the keys, ending the extended version of "On Green Dolphin Street." There was sustained clapping, and several patrons rose and dropped larger denomination bills in the snifter. Randolph had announced he was taking up a collection to bury father and daughter. Bravera put in a fifty, smiling at him. He lifted the glass with both hands, bowing slightly to those gathered from his piano seat.

* * *

"The Performer," *Orange County Noir*, Akashic Books, 2010, GP, editor.
Reprinted in *Between the Dark and the Daylight*, Tyrus Books, 2009, Ed Gorman and Martin H. Greenberg, editors.
Reprinted in *The Interrogator and Other Criminally Good Fiction*, Cemetery Dance Publications, 2012, Ed Gorman and Martin H. Greenberg, editors.

The Kim Novak Effect

ere I was running a sweet little hustle, not really hurting anybody, and yet I found myself strapped spread-eagle, chest down, across a piece of three-quarter-inch plywood plunked across two sawhorses. My pinpoint Oxford Raffaello shirt was in tatters. This gruff cornfed ol' boy in a cowboy hat standing behind me, ready to wail on my bare, bleeding back again with his heavy buckled belt. The other ruffian leaned on a beam of the unfinished wall of the tract house. This one bopped his head to *The Best of Warren Zevon* playing on his iPod.

"Roland, the Headless Thompson Gunner," Leaning Man mouthed as Hat Boy took another chunk out of me. "Talkin' about the man..." he smiled, absently scratching his threadbare beard. He took another swig of his bottled water.

Hat Boy cocked back again like Roger Clemens goofy on the juice and let another one go. The leather sizzled on my flesh, and the edge of the buckle dug another groove.

"Ke-Rist," I screamed into the gag tied around my mouth.

"He looks about primed," Leaning Man said, yawning. He straightened from the skeletal wall, wire conduits snaking through the holes cut into the framing lumber. He removed his earpieces and methodically wrapped them around his iPod. He then placed it carefully on a juncture of wood beams.

"Yeah?" Hat Boy said dubiously. "A few more love taps would make sure." Eager bastard.

"He's got to be conscious when Bishop George gets here," Leaning Man pointed out. "That cocksucker'll skin our hides if sugar lips here isn't conscious."

"I suppose," his compatriot agreed reluctantly. He wiped at his forehead with his forearm; the Vegas heat particularly stuffy inside the raw plywood shell of the house's second floor. Despite this, Leaning Man wore a bulky nylon windbreaker, shades, and a baseball cap.

We were in what the blueprints indicated was the master bedroom. The homes in development on one of the higher plateaus of Red Rock Canyon. On the other side of the ridge, down in the womb of a valley, was an eighteen-hole golf course I frequented. Beyond that was the tail end of Summerlin, this was where my latest operation was bivouacked.

Leaning Man walked over and doused my back with what was left of his water. It wasn't much, but I was mutely thankful. Funny how things work out, I reflected as we waited for the big boss to arrive. Less than two weeks ago, my golf game was improving, my off-shore bank accounts fat, and I was doing, with gusto, I might add, the wonderfully preserved late '70s sex pot Jerri Rocklyn doggy-style. She of the *Ava of the Underground WWII* actioners, wherein each installment included heady doses of sadomasochism and girl-on-girl.

"Thank you, kind sir," she joked as we finished up. Her turquoise skirt and lacy pastel panties were down around her ankles, that gorgeous Nautilus firmed butt of hers bent forward with her torso leaning over my maple wood desk. On the lower right cheek was the mole made famous in the photo layout the real Jerri Rocklyn had done for Gallery, one of the slick skin mags, back in '78. Looking dreamily from that image, I gazed out of my office window, which offered a view of Rainbow Boulevard. Life sure was good.

"My aim is true, baby," I replied as I hiked up my Calvin Klein boxer briefs and Hugo Boss trousers.

Jerri was back in her clothes and sat on my desk crossing tanned, muscular legs. She lit a blunt and inhaled. Her real name was Helen Hobart. She was thirty-six years old and originally from Redondo Beach, California. But for the escapade we'd just pulled, she'd been modeled to look like Rocklyn, who she happened to favor.

"Do I really have to go back under?" she asked, blowing fumes and offering me a toke.

I took the joint, sampled it, then answered, "We can't have the mark spotting you at the craps table, now can we?"

She sighed heavily, getting off the desk with a flourish, those marvelous gel-filled breasts of hers swaying hypnotically. "But I like this look. And so do you." She sucked in more smoke and put the joint on the edge of the desk. She reached a hand down and adroitly pulled it up slowly along her leg until she'd lifted her skirt and was gently kneading that heavenly mound encased in the sheer undergarment.

I stepped forward, and we kissed while she placed my nimble fingers inside those Victoria's Secrets. Momentarily lost in lust, I eventually got back on track. "Doc's ready to go, baby. And we've already agreed you can keep the ta-tas," I murmured as I nibbled her scented neck.

"But," she started, but she didn't finish. She knew I couldn't force her to get re-cut. But she also knew it would mean the end of any future lucrative assignments if she insisted on keeping the Jerri Rocklyn look. For like me, Helen was addicted to those pretty little green ones.

"Fine," she said, giving me a last peck and sauntering out of my office after putting the dead blunt in her handbag. I checked my appearance in the mirror of my tiny private bathroom, making sure my hair was just so and my eyes weren't red from the weed. Then I opened the floor safe beneath the rug upon which sat a cylindrical glass case of sports memorabilia I'd pushed aside. I took out the acrylic encased page from the 7/21/73 program book of the Braves versus the Phillies at Atlanta. I smiled crookedly like Mel Gibson speaking at a synagogue and put everything back in its place. Aluminum attaché case in hand, I left.

Not forty minutes later, I was sitting across from retired dental clinic King Eldon Dudley in the Blue Velvet Lounge on Bridger. In fact, there was a Dr. Dudley Discount Dental facility several blocks away on this street. His big smiling face, circa thirty years ago, beaming down on the abscess-plagued and broken-toothed citizenry from the 3D logo.

"Wonderful," Dudley said, examining the inauthentic certificate of authenticity I'd laid on him. I was especially proud of the hologram work on that bad rascal. The lab in Taiwan knew its stuff. He picked up the encased program page again, savoring the item. On that date in 1973, Hank Aaron hit home run number 700 in his irrefutable quest to best, and eventually surpass, Babe Ruth's home runs. Say what you want about Barry Bonds, Hank did it without 'roiding up while also putting up with racist death threats from jealous crackers. Sure, I was a con artist, but I could appreciate the real thing when it came along.

Scouring as I do antique stores and estate sales, I'd chanced upon the actual program book from that auspicious day. The rest, faking Aaron's signature and the certificate, then working the network I'd established for high-end sports memorabilia, was simply reeling in the right fish.

"Okay," he said, sipping his cranberry juice. "You've got yourself a deal."

"This," I said, reverently touching the artifact, "is not only a wise investment on your part, but a legacy to leave your children."

He snorted. "My grandkids, maybe. "'Fraid my son and I don't see eye to eye," he lamented.

He was like that, regurgitating those clichéd homilies now and then. I said nothing, merely sat back, tenting my fingers as he wrote a check for fifteen grand. The waitress came by our table.

"Can I get you gentlemen refills?"

"I believe we'll just need the check," I said, adding after the right pause, "Noreen, is it?"

Dentist Dudley looked up from his checkbook.

"Yes, it was my grandmother's name." She put on a neon smile and glided away in her skimpy outfit after laying the tab on us. Naturally, I picked it up. Dudley stared after her.

"You okay?' I asked.

"Yes, uh-huh," he said, handing me the payment. "Had she been our server originally?"

I hunched my shoulders. "Maybe her shift just started." I rose and said my goodbyes, reassuring him one more time about the timeliness and efficacy of his investment. I strolled out, sure that he was staring at the waitress named Noreen as I passed near her. She was earning her tips laughing politely at the inane "Girls Gone Wild" level of word foreplay of a couple of 'SC frat boys. I'm sure they were in Vegas to show us hairy-knuckled droolers how to party. I got in my platinum colored 300, put on the factory air and a Celine Dion CD—what can I tell you, I actually like the way that broad belts out a tune. I drove over to the kitchen of a downtown casino to make a pick-up. Then, out to see my man.

Dr. Mathias Stiner was the cat you'd cast to play the Nazi doctor if you were of a mind to make another *Ava of the Underground* flick. He was about medium height, stocky, with good-sized shoulders even at his age. Apparently, back in the day, he wrestled at Dusseldorf U or whatever it was in Germany he attended was called. He wore a pencil mustache, touched up his gray locks, and his fashionable rimless glasses stood in relief over his steel blues. His hands were long like a pianist and it annoyed me to no end that his golf game was better than mine, even though he had a couple'a decades on me.

"I'll have Shauna call Helen. I'll schedule her for the day after tomorrow," he told me in the hallway of his cut shop after his new receptionist had buzzed me into the back.

"Where'd this one come from?" I said, meaning the new receptionist called Shauna. She was a statuesque hottie I took to be no more than twenty-four or five. Once upon a time, Helen had been his receptionist.

Stiner took my elbow and guided me toward his open office. He liked nothing better than thinking about, touching, smelling, and pursuing women. He had an invalid wife. While he was a sucker for female flesh, he did right by the wife when it came to care and whatnot, so he wasn't a total ogre.

"Shauna Cheung. She's studying Economics and 19th Century English Lit at UNLV." We were standing just inside his office, and he gazed around the room as if worried his wife had planted a bug. "She made her college money with one of those websites where you watch her in the morning, rant about her boyfriend, feed the cat, and all that." The tip of his tongue wet the center of his top lip as he grinned. "Of course, she did these tasks mostly in short nighties and silken under- things, earning quite a few male and female subscribers."

He tipped back momentarily on his heels as he conjured up those carnal cyber images in his head.

"You hint to her about our sideline?" I asked, conversationally. Her online thing struck me as someone who had a taste for larceny. Or maybe she was just a stone exhibitionist. Either way, she seemed to be a likely candidate.

"Not yet, but yes, she certainly seems prime material. There must be plenty of these bourgeois fools who have fantasies about the Asian goddess or Dragon Lady."

Stine was a study in contradictions. He justified his arrangement with me as a way to strike back at the nabobs of convention and conformity. Going on about his patients, the vain, jowled men and the sun-aged, vodka-breathing blondes deluded they could defy gravity and time. Yet I also knew he was spiteful that he got the low-rent chin nip or outpatient tummy tuck, with the high-end work those vodka blondes wanted flying out to Beverly Hills to get done.

"Here you go," I said, laying the packet of blow on his desk. That was the item I got from my connection at the casino. Women weren't Doc's only weakness.

He put the dope away, relocking the drawer. Randolph Scott looked down on us from behind him. Stiner was also a movie cowboy aficionado and had several such portraits, Glenn Ford, the Duke, Eastwood, and so on, tacked to the walls. All of them were autographed. I'd sold him his Ford. Hey, Western memorabilia brings in a decent buck.

"Noreen make contact?" We were walking back out of his office.

"Yeah," I said. "I still think it was too dead on to use the name of his dead wife."

"We all want to believe that the second chance can be had," he said wistfully. "The heart forever overrules the intellect, does it not?"

I demurred. Since my research had shown the dentist was into mysticism, it did seem Dudley was more inclined to fall for the bit the more he glommed that this Noreen could be the spirit of his departed. This was the first time we'd done the Kim Novak this nose on, and I hoped it didn't jinx the con.

Shaking Doc's hand in front of the receptionist, it looked like I was simply some sort of pharmaceutical salesman making his rounds. Which, in a way, was true. I gave her a nod, and she returned it with a brief smile that could be interpreted a couple of different ways. Could be Doc had let on more than he allowed. Yes, by golly, she was a candidate.

The slap across my face brought me out of my daydreaming and back into my current unpleasant situation.

"Got your attention now, asshole?" Hat Boy followed his question with a jab from his steel-toed boot into my chest. They'd untied me from the makeshift table and dumped me in a corner. A brief wind rippled the blue plastic covering the cutouts for the windows.

"The Bishop will be here soon," Leaning Man said, pocketing the cell he'd been talking on. He crossed his arms and looked down at my pitiful form. "Then we'll get down to it, won't we, sugar lips?"

I feebly managed to give them the finger. Instead of knocking the crap out of me, which I expected, Hat Boy and Leaning Man laughed like they were watching a Chris Rock routine. Hell, why not? They were holding all the cards.

* * *

I know I should pace my intake. I am a doctor, for God's sake. Once, I was in demand and knew more than some windshield-washing addict what this heavenly narcotic does to you physically and mentally. But the feeling it purveys, that, well, that is almost like sex itself, is it not?

I know too that as I sit here in the womb-like dark of my office, Wagner softly on my stereo, the hum of the thoroughfare beyond a desensitizing lullaby of normalcy, current matters are far from that. And yet a kind of throttle of inertia embraces me as I ingest more powder, my self-image that of the immigrant gangster Pacino played in that movie all those rappers sample. The cocaine gives me a hard-on. The cocaine gives me spine, too.

The coke will give me the *eier* to reach for the pistol in my middle drawer should I need to.

This I must believe because I know my erstwhile partner in the doppelganger enterprise is not a heroic man. I dip my head and partake of more of the powder. *Mein Gott*, it is an amazing substance. I wipe the residue from the rim of my nostrils and lick some left off the back of my index finger. I certainly don't mean to say that he is a coward. You can't be gutless and perpetrate the sort of bold swindles he pulls off. You have to project the veneer that reflects what the person you're taking wants to see, and he certainly has that.

But what am I to him? I, who used to be a surgeon and now create cartoon heart-shaped derrieres for the self-perpetuating, self-absorbed class. I have more coke, and I wait. I could go downstairs and get in my Cadillac CTS with the temperature-controlled seats and the surround sound, the vehicle purchased from the profits I made doing my part, but where would I go? I am very comfortable in my newly obtained condo in nearby Summerlin. And really, as I have more coke and analyze it further, I am an asset, am I not?

Here I was, having driven to his office to tell him the important news I'd discovered about Shauna, anxious as I was not to speak on the phone. Cocaine makes one wary. But then spying that large one in the cowboy hat, taking him away forcibly. The other one I couldn't see so well at the wheel of their car. Together, those Macheaths will squeeze my name and the other particulars of the operation out of him. What if they aren't giving him the works and will simply offer him money? Or drugs? The judicious use of psilocybin or scopolamine that would disorient him or create fright or paranoia, and that could get him babbling as well.

Yet when he does give them my name, why would they give me the treatment? It would seem to me their boss would want to keep me in the picture, assuming he wants to keep the effort going. And why wouldn't he? Whoever was in charge of the hoodlums must be a man of means, a gangster of some sort, surely. Unless it was a personal matter that he was taken away as he was. That might be. And if so, then all my worrying is unfounded, and I should cease my consumption. I will, just after this next line.

* * *

"You do have amusing qualities," Shauna Cheung said bemusedly. She set her margarita down on the pub table and fluffed out those raven tresses. "But why should I kick back anything to you or to Herr Doktor?" She put a finger up. "More than, say, the cost of getting the remodeling done, as you call it, and some sort of finder's fee? Though when you really think about it, why are you necessary at all?"

I pantomimed for two more drinks with a sign to the waitress in the faux moll outfit. The third-floor game room in the Riverhead casino was called Nitti's. Leaning just so across the pool table, Shauna steadied her cue stick, smacked the cue ball dead on, and dropped her solid into the awaiting hole. I appreciated a woman who could work the stick. She walked to the short side of the table, eyeing her next shot.

"It's not just setting the job in motion that matters," I said. "But lining up the marks does take a certain specialty." That had come out more harshly than I'd intended. I couldn't let this chick get ahead of me. "But sure, you're right, you don't need me. Only who's gonna soothe that old croaker sack's nerves when you're off playing slap and tickle with the mark? Riddle me that, Green Hornet."

"It's not hard to find a crooked cutter," she said. "Half of them are sniffing their Xylocain or whiffing their patient's panties…or want to."

The cue ball glanced off the solid seven, and it spun on its axis but didn't have much trajectory. She left me with much of nothing on the table, but I was cool. I positioned myself confidently. "You figure to branch out with my idea, that it?"

She smiled radiantly. "I'm not saying that, homeboy. I could see where you might be an asset."

"Now you're just jerking me to make me miss." I did anyway. My stripped ball bounced off the padded corner.

She lined up her next shot. "No. But I was thinking this hustle could be a two-way thing."

"How'd you mean?"

"There're plenty of lonely widows, you know. Fact is statistically, there's more older broads with some savings than older men." She let loose with her cue stick and, banking her shot, knocked in another solid.

"I'm not taking the denture cream money from some gummy grannies. This is not what this is," I insisted.

"My bad." She gave me that smile of hers again, well aware that it got to me despite my anger. "The point remains you're not tapping your market's full potential."

"Maybe that's where you come in," I suggested. "Lining up some of these beefcake boys for the work."

She seemed to consider that while she sunk her last solid. "Who knows? I might take a semester off and show you how to properly expand your operation." She pointed the cue stick at the middle pocket and put the eight ball away in a smooth stroke. "See you, champ."

I stood watching her walk away, allowing as she did a bit of a swing of those wonderful hips in those designer jeans. Yeah, Ms. Cheung was a real go-getter. And if I wasn't careful, she was going to run me like she did this pool game and get me out of the picture.

* * *

"Really, you don't need to keep doing this."

"It's my pleasure to see that look on your face," I said.

She yawned and stretched on the bed. The diamond and white gold pendant I'd just given her was resplendent against her magnificent bronzed skin. Noreen, and I understood she wasn't that Noreen—the woman I met in those days of want in Tulsa—pulled me closer from where I stood, gazing down on her.

"How will I ever thank you," she giggled, planting a smack on my member inside my boxers. Oh, these modern women. Though I was glad I no longer wore the traditional undergarments. Much too much fuss to get out of. She laid back on the bed again, giving me an eyeful of that young and fit body of hers clad only in the frilly panties I'd bought her. What a self-deluding fool I was. How pathetic I must be to this gorgeous girl who could have her way with any of those snarling boys and their bunching pectorals prowling Vegas to satiate hedonistic desires. Yet here I was, a slave to my baseness.

"What's wrong, baby cakes?"

I sat on the edge of the bed, and she snuggled close. "I'm not so gone that for one minute would suppose you have real feelings for me," I began, touching her hair. "Sending orchids and chocolate bunnies to you at that bar and grill like some teenager." I wiped a hand over my face. "Why did you agree to see me?"

"You have to stop doubting yourself, Eldon. I told you. Men my age have grown up playing video games blowing up monsters and making it with digitally animated babes with balloon boobs. Salivating over how they can get a house like they've seen on MTV Cribs and a car featured on Pimp My Ride."

She kissed my far too rotund belly. "I was and still am flattered a man of your experience would find me of interest." I grabbed her by the shoulders, tighter than either of us expected. "What if I'm crazy, Noreen? I know full well you aren't her; she died some thirty years ago. There's plenty of Noreens in this world, and no doubt a fair share in Las Vegas. And sure, you favor her some, but she never had a body like yours or," and I stopped myself, ashamed and excited all at once.

"She never did this, did she, Eldon?" She pushed me onto my back and reached her hand inside the slit of my boxers, took out my member, and put it in her mouth to pleasure me. She took me to the brink, then suddenly stopped. The top of my skull was somewhere in outer space.

"Eldon," she murmured, "have you ever reciprocated?"

"I don't understand."

"Get on your knees, darling."

I did so. Now, she was leaning back, moaning. Her legs were open, and her hand, with the ring I'd bought her, was rubbing that wondrous mound.

The diamonds on the ring were in the shape of a tooth. Corny, I know, but she'd gushed when I'd presented it to her.

"I'm not sure I'd be any good at it," I stammered. "You don't know until you practice, honey."

And so, at my tender age of sixty-seven years, I was giving a beauty young enough to be my daughter head, as the term goes, I'm told. I believe, too, that's what the article I read in the AARP magazine advocated. To keep your mind active in the Golden Years, every day, you should learn something new to keep sharp. And right then, my nose buried in that heavenly bush, all the neurons in my brain were firing like rockets.

Afterward, as we got dressed for dinner, I asked her, "When you decide to leave me, do it quickly, will you? I've convinced myself I can take it easier like that, as if it were a gut punch, okay?"

"Why do you always talk like that? And why would I leave someone who is so kind to me?" She was combing her hair. As I'd noticed before, she didn't look in the mirror. I suppose I assumed all beautiful women regarded themselves, primed themselves for a night out. But then, what did I know of women such as this second chance Noreen? She patted my cheek and gave me a look that rolled the top of my socks.

Of course, at dinner, like before, there were those ogling, wondering just what sort of relationship we had. Her laughing at my shopworn attempts at humor and me grinning like Tom Sawyer must have when he tricked others into painting that fence for him. They were envious, I convinced myself. Here, I was not particularly handsome nor commanding, yet I was the one who'd struck it rich in Las Vegas. The Wheel of Fortune had spun in my favor.

The next day in my office, as I sat and admired my Hank Aaron prize, marveling at how that transaction had brought me such luck, my private line rang.

"Bishop George," I said upon hearing his voice. "How may I help you today?" I listened. He was concerned about my being with Noreen. Her age wasn't the issue. I knew that despite the public image he cultivated for business reasons, he still practiced plural marriage. I knew, too, that his third wife was seventeen. Noreen's and my age difference wasn't the issue. This call was of a more temporal nature.

"Oh, no, she has not made such an inquiry." I listened some more. Bishop Abel George rarely raised his voice, but he was persistent in his manner. "Yes, I understand she's just a cocktail waitress. What? Why would I do that, Bishop George? I've certainly not been very strong in our ward for some time, as you are well aware. But her being a gentile is of no consequence." He talked, then I said, "It's enough that we make each other happy."

I wasn't a child; I knew that answer wouldn't satisfy him. Indeed, I was quite aware of where his probing was going. Oh, I didn't know the exact details, but I knew that he would extract what he evaluated as his due from me. Hadn't he always?

* * *

That Mormon creep was scary. Good thing he just saw me as a stupid gold digger. He doesn't know I've done *Guys and Dolls* at the Rio and was Big Nurse in *One Flew Over the Cuckoo's Nest* in summer stock. I know how to play my part. He couldn't rattle me, even coupled with his two bodyguards looking all fish-eyed at me like I was young boy prison booty like you could tell they were used to getting. Him asking all polite and slithery with his quiet voice and the way he leans in when he's sitting with his fancy cane and all. Eldon showed some backbone though, talked up for me, for us really. That must be kind'a new 'cause that bastard gave him a stare, that's for sure. Pussy doesn't weaken the legs, it makes a man strong—well that and Cialis.

"You like that, baby?" Knowing full well he was ecstatic. "Yes," he managed, breathing heavily and squirming.

I continued giving him a hummer. I sure was thankful the old fella was a stickler for cleanliness. I kept at it for a while, longer, with Eldon damn near passing out as he finished. He was so cute. So ready for the picking. I then nibbled on the inside of his thigh and damned if his soldier wasn't yet again ready for engagement. He hadn't used any penis pills for over two weeks. I had this farm boy hopping.

I straddled him. And as he entered me and I made all the right sounds, I knew my plan was going to work. Sorry Eldon, but you're just a means to an end. You and that clown who actually believed I was going to kick back a percentage to him like his other girls had 'cause this was his idea, and he'd set the con up. Nothing worse than a bullshitter who started to believe his own BS.

* * *

"Are you familiar with the Mormon Cricket?"

If I could talk without spitting blood, I still wouldn't have answered. When the bishop arrived, Hat Boy figured to rack up extra points with his boss and slugged me when I tried to rise from the corner.

"The Mormon Cricket," he continued, "is not, in fact, a cricket, but a katydid."

Whoop-de-fuckin'-do.

The bishop glanced down at his ostrich skin boots, then back at my battered face. He sat near me, imperial-like, in a folding chair, his large hand gripping his dark wood cane topped with a silver bird of some sort. "They are a large insect, though incapable of flight. They live in and on sagebrush and alfalfa, and I've seen them decimate fields of fragrant Black-eyed Susans and Morningstars. These abominations will even eat their own." He got a misty look in his pale eyes, then refocused on me.

"The first settlement's wheat was saved by gulls eating those damned insects," Bishop George said, glaring down at me like Odin used to mad dog Thor in those worn Jack Kirby comics I read. Back when I was in one of the several foster homes I'd supposedly been raised in.

"Do you not see the significance of that? Here you had birds, sea gulls, that came from the ocean, from California, to save us in the desert in Utah." He pointed his gull-headed cane at me.

I couldn't muster a response. What did he expect me to do, convert?

"The spirit of Joseph Smith was with us then as it is now." Okay, right there, I was real tempted to respond just to mess with him. I've made a study of the con, being as it's my avocation. Joseph Smith had bilked chumps with one of the oldest dodges there was, the gold mine. Of course, that was before he got good with another form of gold, plates written with scripture, and got the Holy Ghost.

"Your Jezebel took money from Eldon Dudley and then disappeared. This was some two hundred thousand in cash reserves he kept tucked away for necessities."

"I don't know what you're talking about." Yeah, that was pretty lame, but I wasn't inclined to give him the satisfaction that I was beaten. Not only had he caught me, but the chick I'd set up as the dentist's Noreen had skipped out on me as well. How sad was that?

Given his exertions at tanning my hide, Hat Boy was wiping his face with a handkerchief. He then gulped down some bottled water Leaning Man had passed to him. Bishop George, a tall sumbitch with a mug like a knot of wood and an Abe Lincoln jaw, smiled. That was gruesome. "You make money by setting up lonely, well-to-do men with women who purport to be their lost loves."

Mostly, he was correct. I did background research on the marks like you do in any long con. But I didn't coach the women to be the dead wife or high school sweetheart, endlessly drilling them with facts and dates. That kind of pretend, and the chump would see through it in no time. The art of my approach was for the woman to remind the sucker of the dead wife or the girlfriend. There were other guys hyped on actresses from their teenaged days. Hell, there was even one mark, a software geekonaire, who had this crush on his junior high teacher. So I had Steiner remodel Helen just enough to suggest her features, and he was hooked. We took him for more than three hundred Gs in stock options he signed over to her to save her supposed ailing son. This setup included a child actor we hired to wheeze and sweat in a hospital bed. His stage mother desperate to get the kid a credit. People.

See, I got the idea for the con watching this Hitchcock flick *Vertigo* on TV one night in a motel room in El Monte, laying low from a grift gone south. In the movie, Jimmy Stewart has it bad for Kim Novak, who reminds him of this other woman he couldn't save because of his fear of heights. Only, of course, it turns out Jimmy's being played. Kim is both women; the dead bit faked to draw him into a psychological trap of sexual obsession. And thus, I created the Kim Novak Effect.

I figured the big dog here must have invested money in Dudley's clinics. I knew from my due diligence the dentist was a lapsed Mormon. "How'd you get to me if my girl lit out?"

Bishop George was smoking a cigarette in one of those old-fashioned cigarette holders. On him, it wasn't gay, just eerie. "Searching for the woman's trail, I worked backwards." He blew a stream of smoke into the still air. "The bartender at the Blue Velvet told me for a hundred dollars, you'd gotten her hired there. Said he owed you a favor over some sort of misunderstanding. One I'm sure you engineered so as to have him in your pocket when you needed him." He tapped ash. "That put me on to you and," he spread his arms wide, "here you are."

"So what do you want?"

"I'm your new partner, partner. And you will pay back the money, with interest."

Shit. "That right?"

The bishop stood, poking my leg with the end of his cane. "Yes, that is so. You will continue to do what you do, the research and selection of the woman." He showed his blunt teeth. "I have no insight into the type of devious female you seem to be able to ferret out for this work. But I do have ideas on certain businessmen and politicians that we will go after."

"Wonderful."

"Get him cleaned up," Bishop George said to his muscle. Hat Boy made to snatch me off the floor but stumbled and then went to a knee, heaving.

"The fuck," he said and keeled over like a felled rhino.

Bishop George stared at this, and Leaning Man said, "Let's go" to me. There was a gun in his hand.

"What's going on here?" the bishop sputtered, gaping at his goon. He squinted, pushing his homely face toward the hood. He started to laugh. "Very good. Very clever," he said.

We left the Bishop in the unfinished room, methodically tapping his cane. Out in the dusk, Leaning Man helped me into the late model Mustang they brought me in, and we rode away from those unfinished two-stories where the bishop was one of several investors in the development. At a motel on 93 near the Arizona border, Helen was waiting for us as we entered a room. She was still hosting her Jerri Rocklyn look. "Guess we've worn out our welcome in Vegas," she cracked, noting my condition.

Leaning Man had already removed the bulky coat and now his shirt, revealing the wrap and sports bra Shauna Cheung wore to hide her breasts. She scrubbed off her fake beard and the glue she'd used on her eyelids to make them temporarily rounder and less of her natural epicanthal fold.

I sat on the edge of the bed. "How'd you two work this?"

"The bishop was asking around about you once he got your name from Burt," Helen said. Burt was the bartender at the Blue Velvet. "This I learned from a girlfriend who works the VIP lounge at Caesar's."

I looked at Cheung, who had stripped down to her underwear. I supposed that whatever she gave Hat Boy in the bottled water to knock him out, she'd done to the hood she'd impersonated. She'd worn some padding to give her quite obvious female physique more of a manly shape. Pointing at her, I said, "You two already knew each other."

"Yep," Cheung answered. "We figured you and the doc needed watching."

That was horseshit. Neither of them would give a fuck about me or the doc. They'd been setting me or Stiner up for something, only the bishop's intervention presented another opportunity. Plus, they let me take a beating to make me grateful when they got me out of it. They wanted me for something.

"We better get down the road." Helen was up and moving. I could have split—or tried to since I was sure Shauna didn't just wave around that pistol for show. I should have gone on and left these two scheming broads to work their juju on some other sucker. But I was the dude who came up with this, and damned if I was going to turn over my most lucrative swindle to them for nothing.

Turns out Helen had been scamming the Leaning Man, the real one, for a while. He was too young to know about Jerri Rocklyn but was mesmerized by that rack she sported. That's why she'd tried to beg off getting re-cut. She'd recently learned from him the bishop had a network of non-Mormon business and elected official types he hobnobbed with, and not just in Nevada.

* * *

Relocated to swell Laguna Beach, California, Stiner modeled me to look just enough like the long-disappeared surfer son of a widow whose Frank Gehry-designed glass and stone pad overlooks the Pacific. I clip her toenails, make sure she takes the right meds at the right time, and give her back rubs with lotion that, well, let's just say, often leads to other duties if you follow my meaning. Ugh.

I couldn't run now anyway. My real name and face were on some kind of Homeland Security watch list, thanks to the bishop. According to a bent lawyer acquaintance of mine, this also put getting to my funds in the off-shore accounts iffy—at least for now, until I figured that out.

Hey, I know the situation's somewhat reversed, but I'm also lining up some of the widow's male friends for the women to do their thing. So, as I sat here on the deck of the old girl's house, as she napped from our rubdown session, I sipped a merlot and watched the sky turn orange. On the sound system, Celine was singing about the Last Plane Out. And I dreamed of being on one someday, no longer trapped by the Kim Novak Effect.

* * *

"The Kim Novak Effect," *Ellery Queen Mystery Magazine,*
2008.
Reprinted in *Between the Dark and the Daylight*, Tyrus Books, 2009, Ed Gorman and Martin H. Greenberg, editors.

Swift Boats for Jesus

udy Garza broke a shoelace as he tied one of his Botticelli's. He held the torn end to his face, glaring at it like a building inspector looking for cracks in the masonry work. It was just a goddamn piece of expensive, coated thick string when you got down to it. A lace that matched the rubbed cordovan of his shoes made of ostrich hide. The silver-haired salesman, his buffed nails gleaming, had patted Garza's hand in a fatherly way he'd insisted Garza simply must buy the extra laces only from his store. "It just wouldn't do to get those mismatched replacements from the local supermarket, now would it, sir," he'd gushed.

"Certainly not cheat you out of the ten bucks more you were able to add onto the bill, oh no," Garza muttered, smiling lethargically. Well, he did respect a hustler. Garza retrieved the new lace from the dresser drawer and finished tying his shoes over his herringbone-patterned sock. He checked his profile in the built-in mirror on the inside of the bedroom door. He'd gone with the dark Ralph Lauren slacks and the camel tan Oleg Cassini sport coat over the flyaway-collar bur gundy Zegna shirt and the Belisi silver silk tie with a matching pocket square.

Garza patted his gut, worried that he'd already had Luis, his tailor, let the pants out. Too many damn gin martini lunches with this contractor or that vendor.

"Man's got to know when to cut back," he reminded himself in a gruff imitation of his long-gone father's voice.

"Rudy," Lettie called from the kitchen below, "can you take Rosie in? I have to be out in Playa earlier than it was originally planned." His wife sold corporate real estate.

"Not a problem," he called back as his cell phone rang. He notched an eyebrow, knowing the familiar number on his screen all too well.

"What you doin' up this early, fool?" he cracked to Jason Prichard.

"Shit might be comin' down, son," Prichard said coldly and efficiently. He was a city attorney in Compton, assigned to the neighborhood prosecutor unit. That meant he targeted gangs and gang activity.

"What's wrong?" He willed himself to remain composed. "I got a tip the feds are sniffing into the Burkhalter business," his friend said. "That dipshit cousin of Jaime's, you know the one I'm talkin' about, the one I almost had to put in check over at the Peacock that time."

"Yeah, I know," Garza said, dreadfully expectant.

"Well, that *pendejo*, got himself arrested coming back across the border carrying some Ingrams with their serial numbers filed off and inserts in the barrels to throw off ballis tics."

"Fuck," Garza swore softly. Then his daughter called up to him.

"I got to go, Papa G. I need to help Amy set up her exhibit for science class."

"I'm on my way, sweetie. Just finishing this quick call."

"You're always finishing a quick call. Don't make her late," his wife warned as he heard the front door close.

"So Homeland Security got on his ass," Garza surmised.

"Naturally," Prichard confirmed. "Way I understand it, Jaime T's primo was transporting for the Crazy Nines. But of course, he wet his pants once he was caught and said anything and everything he could to make a deal to keep from getting put on the Gitmo Express."

"Daddy," his daughter peeled.

Garza started for the stairs. "I'm coming, *mija*. You got your backpack and lunch?"

"Yes," she drawled, as only a put-upon twelve-year-old could. Her older brother had slept at a friend's house.

"Look, I'm running late," he said to Prichard. "Call me back when you know more."

"You make sure there's nothing else lying around to back up the testimony of a lame loser like that cousin, dig? Because I have no desire to get in the wind at my age, my brother." Prichard clicked off.

Father and daughter left. As he drove her to school in the Land Rover, Garza half-listened to Rosie's usual drone about some creepy boy or a squirrel she saw munching a hot Cheetoh. Automatically, he put in a "Wow" or "Really?" at the right intervals. He also assessed how much damage Jaime's cousin, Hector Rivas, could do. He concluded that what he had to say would make those buzzdicks at the Bureau salivate, but Hector didn't have shit in the way of convicting them.

Sure he'd shoot off his mouth about Garza, but Hector couldn't be that scared of the government that he'd roll over on his cuz. Jaime was the leader of the Crazy Nines. Hector had to be terrified that between here and whatever cell he was rendered to, Jaime would reach out and touch him with a knife across the throat.

He kissed his daughter goodbye and watched her saunter into St. Cecilia's with the other children. The Catholic school was a funky assortment of sixties-era buildings contrasted with the new playground equipment that fronted the state-of-the-art computer lab. Both courtesy of a fund drive seeded by a generous donation from SubbaKhan, the mega-developer who'd won the bid for the new complex of shops and theaters being built adjacent to the Happy Trails casino.

Their bid was higher than the others, but Garza had convinced the council that SubbaKhan was worth the investment. The work was done right, usually ahead of schedule, and there was the cherry on the sweet percentage of a local hire and training agreement he'd hammered out on the project. With an under-the-table kickback to him for his efforts, Garza, as Bell Park's city manager, lined his pockets, but he never forgot he was a homeboy who'd fallen into clover.

Not that SubbaKhan would gain much initially by erecting this project here in this part of Southeast LA, where the 710 Freeway cut through. Bell Park was all of six-point-six-square miles with a forty-three-person police force, and it had to contract for fire services from the county. But, the deal with them allowed the developer to own part of the leased land. In the long run, given there was a steady traffic of patrons to the Happy Trails from the other small municipalities in the surrounding area, the swollen coffers of SubbaKhan wouldn't grow any leaner. And a happy international conglomerate was a giving international conglomerate at election time and at special times throughout the year.

On his cell behind the wheel, he tried to get Mayor Sharpe on the line, but it went to message. Garza checked the time on the dash: eight twenty a.m. He veered off the main avenue and drove slowly through a residential section. Dammit. He could see Emil Rojas' people were already out, door-knocking. "Look, Abel," Garza said after hurriedly calling and connecting with Chief of Police Ramirez, "I need you to get some of your uniforms talking up the mayor. Rojas' people are out thicker than cock-a-roaches." He pronounced it just like Pacino did in *Scarface*. It wasn't just juiced-up rappers who liked to sample that movie.

"I will, Rudy," Ramirez assured him, "and I've got some firefighters coming, too. But you better get Don Pedro out of the Pearl Blossom."

"The fuck."

"He's been holed up there since about three this morning." He didn't go on. He didn't have to.

"Why didn't you call me?"

"I didn't know until an hour ago. Shit, you're his keeper."

Garza admonished himself and drove over to the massage parlor located exactly two blocks and a hilltop outside of the city in a DMZ of unincorporated county. Tradition held that if a sheriff found a body here, and the caseload was high—and when wasn't it?—then maybe said body might find itself moved a few hundred yards into Bell Park. Sometimes, it worked the other way around if the city cops could get away with it. After all, what was a corpse among friendly rivals?

He parked on the side of the three-story building. The Pearl Blossom personnel conducted their trade on the first two floors, with the second floor reserved for their renowned specials. The neon sign in fancy script announcing authentic Thai deep tissue massage was off, its tubes dingy and splattered with bird droppings. He knocked forcefully on the back door security screen. Footsteps on the rear stairs, then Fanny Xa opened the inner door and, after a beat, the outer one. She was in sweats and a tank top with a picture of a collie on it. Her graying black hair stood up and out like a fright wig.

"How far gone is he?" Garza asked, moving past the bleary-eyed woman and onto the stairs.

"Good morning to you, too, fuck head."

"Not today, Fanny."

"Whatever," she mumbled, shuffling outside in her bare feet to spit.

Upstairs on the third floor, Garza entered her bedroom, which was painted in purples and black for accents. She had one of those old-fashioned vanities in one corner, its make-up table overflowing with small bottles of perfume, eyeliner, lipsticks, and a tube of Ben Gay, he noted. Mayor Pete "Pedro" Sharpe snored on his back in the bed, his girth tangled among the purple silk sheets and dark lavender duvet. Garza smiled, shaking his head. In the late '80s, Sharpe, a former football and track hero at local Israel Bissell High, had taken his cue from Dylan's song and knew which way the wind blew. He adopted the Mexicanization of his first name when he was running that first time for re-election. The mayor knew from being out and about, let alone from a census chart, that the demographics of Bell Park, once the hillbilly haven of Dust Bowl-era migrants, were irrevocably changing.

The city had seen an influx of African Americans in the '60s, and there had been a resulting power struggle for who got what seat at the table. Sharpe, who was black, emerged from that fight and came to office backed by a shaky coalition. This happened just as the next ethnic wave was coming on strong in the city—Latinos. But it didn't hurt that Sharpe spoke Spanglish with ease. On a Spanish language station, he verbally outmaneuvered his Latino opponent in his first re-election contest. That candidate had been earnest, but he was a *pocho*, a Latino who didn't speak Spanish. He didn't go over well with the new majority.

"Pete, time to rock, baby." Garza shook him and only succeeded in interrupting a snore. Sharpe smacked his lips but didn't otherwise make an effort to wake.

"Like Dr. Phil says, how's that workin' out for you?" Behind him, Xa laughed and hacked. She began searching in a nightstand beneath a shelf with a stuffed red-and-black- feathered rooster before a sun painting. These were some sort of religious symbols reflecting her Muong heritage, Garza knew.

A couple of light backhand slaps to the whiskered face roused the mayor. The whites of his eyes were as red as spoiled apples. "Hey," he managed.

Xa found her half-smoked joint and fired it up.

"Let me hug up on a little of that, will you, my dear?" Sharpe held out a large hand. A ring with a dark gem that sucked up the light was on his pinkie. She handed the joint across, and he took a healthy drag. He didn't cough, and his hand didn't quiver as he blew out a stream of narcotic smoke. He handed it back to Xa, who leaned over and gave him a peck.

"We got to filet gumbo, Pete. You've already missed the breakfast at the old folk's home. But you can swing by there on your way back from the VFW hall speech." Garza wasn't the mayor's campaign manager but knew his schedule more intimately than hizzoner did.

"Ah, what the fuck for, Rudy?" Sharpe pushed himself up so that his back was to the headboard. He folded his muscular arms across his broad chest. "Maybe Rojas should get it. I've had a good run, and so have you. Let's golf and play poker in the afternoons and let Mister Reformer find out just how fuckin' hard it is to run things. Let reality kick him in the ass and smack that rose-smelling piety out of his mouth."

"I'll make some coffee," Xa announced, puffing on her joint as she ambled into the kitchen. "I've heard way too much of this already."

Sharpe was in his late sixties. Rudy wasn't. The older man might be at the end of his string, but he damn sure had more to give and get. Bell Park's mayor and city council were part-time jobs, and the city manager a full-time post. But it was a position that served primarily at the mayor's pleasure, so Garza needed Sharpe back in the saddle this one last time.

"We have certain obligations, you and I, Mr. Mayor. Certain fulfillments that we are direly responsible for their completion, *comprendes*, carnal?"

Wearily Sharpe began, "If you can't eat their food, drink their booze and fuck their women…"

"…and still vote against them," Garza said.

"…then they shouldn't have gotten involved in politics in the first damn place," they finished together. Sharpe smiled, self-satisfied.

The city manager's cell phone chimed again. "Look, you only think you want to laze around and count your liver spots. But that's for old men, Pete. Not men like us. Not men who make it happen on the streets and in the sheets."

Sharpe gave him a sideways appraisal. A slight smile creased his seasoned face. He didn't say it but wanted Garza to go on.

"We can't let this prick Rojas set the terms for when you exit office. He's some kind of headline-chasing substitute teacher who the holy rollers and a few prune-faced pedophilic priests have propped up."

"That's right," Sharpe agreed, getting into it.

"This is trench warfare we're talking about," Garza continued, "this isn't a game for punks and *chulos*, am I right?"

"Hallelujah!" Xa cracked from the doorway. The joint hung from her mouth as she wiggled her fingers.

"Right on," Sharpe added, sitting more erect, wiping a hand across his face.

Garza paced about the room, putting the evangelist into his spiel. It used to be it was only twice a year, usually around the Fourth of July and Christmas time, which was when Sharpe's wife had died five years ago, that he had to give him the rah—rah. But this current campaign seemed to have really taken it out of the mayor. He didn't have the fire in the belly, for it like before. He really was getting on.

Garza stood before the window, backlit by the morning sun as he spread his arms. "So what are we going to do, champ? How we gonna rumble?"

"Rumble like thunder and strike like lightning," Sharpe said. He was sitting on the side of the bed in his striped boxers, scratching his nuts.

"And what are we going to unleash on our enemies? What shall we smite them with?"

"We shall bring them low with the power of our words and mightiness of our deeds." Xa helped him stand on his wobbly legs.

"For who is the captain?" Garza said, silencing his ringing cell phone.

"He is," Xa yelled, slapping Sharpe on the shoulder.

"And does he not lead our swift boats through treacherous waters?"

"I do," Sharpe vowed, giving him a quick salute.

"And do we let slip the swift boats against our enemies simply for our own selfish reasons?"

"No, sir," Sharpe and Xa said in unison.

"For whom do we guide our swift boats to victory?

"The people," Sharpe said solemnly. "Our swift boats are for the people."

"Amen," Garza said. "Now get your funky ass showered, shaved, and dressed, and let's get back in the game, son."

"Most assuredly," Sharpe said as Xa, arm around his waist, led him to the bathroom.

Back on the road, Garza returned the two calls he'd gotten from Sharpe's campaign manager. He told her where to fetch him.

"Don't we need to go over some last-minute strategy?" Cerna Chacon then said, chuckling.

"No doubt," Garza answered. As he drove back through town, he was pleased to see the mayor's volunteers were now out canvassing as well.

"Who are these wholesome young women you have out on Portillo?" he inquired. He knew the regular volunteers.

"Don't you go getting any ideas of inviting one or two of those dewy-eyed females to your Politics 101 sessions, teach," she warned. "They're part of a poli-sci course over at Cal State. Nice, huh? Their professor and I attend the same AA meetings. Fact I'm his sponsor."

"You're such a creative woman, Cee-cee," he complimented sincerely.

"Then you better reward me. I need to relieve some stress having to deal with our man." She sighed heavily.

They set a time at their usual place and Garza headed for the Happy Trails, passing back through part of the north side. The base for Emil Rojas' support had come out of the precincts here. This was where a grassroots group called the Local Justice Initiative, a bunch of community college dropout Che Guevara, had organized members of congregations about the proliferation of liquor stores in that area.

The residents became activated on that issue, getting some ink and results. Indeed, the north side contained more than its fair share of liquor stores. After all, Garza had seen several of those permits being okayed by walking the paperwork over to the council and doing some horse-trading. One of those galvanized residents was Rojas, who, because of service as a medic in the Gulf War, got the attention of the *mau maus* and the sanctified, and it was off to the races. St. Cecilia's was located in one of those northern precincts, but its leaders knew who buttered their bread and had held two pancake breakfasts for the re-election of Pedro Sharpe.

Inside the casino, the SSIers and the day walkers—those old-timers who recharged at home at night to be ambulatory in the sunlight—were already vigorously tapping the keys of the video slots or getting ready for morning bingo. Jules, a former *vato* now working the security detail, gave Garza the high sign. On the side of his neck was a faded tattoo of an eagle grappling with a python. Like the others decorating his body, he was in the process of having them removed via laser treatments. The city manager moved past him and into the outer office of Neil Weaver, the manager of operations.

"His lordship available?" he asked Berta Yanez, the receptionist. As with Jules, he'd gotten her this job at the casino.

"Let me check, Rudy." She buzzed the inner office either for show or as a heads-up. Weaver did like his morning toot. "Please, go on, good sir." She said, smiling, and did a flourish with her hand, indicating the inner door.

Yanez, a high school dropout, had done six and three-quarters years on a ten-year bid for aiding and abetting in the transportation of a truckload of ecstasy. But she was one of the few who took advantage of her time. She not only got her G.E.D., but took coursework that she was now completing toward becoming a paralegal. The fact she'd been incarcerated in a minimum security facility instead of the max lock-down prosecutors initially wanted to send her to was due to Garza's intervention when he was on the city council.

In the office, Weaver, a lanky individual with thin glasses and thinning brown-blonde hair, stood and held out a fist. "What up, homeboy?"

Garza knocked his knuckles against the other man's and remained standing. "We might have a problem on the Burk halter thing." He explained the call he'd received that morning.

"So far, it seems like the feds are stirring the waters to see what floats to the surface. But we shouldn't ignore this," Garza added.

Over the years Bell Park's administration had been the focus of several inquiries by the District Attorney and the Bureau. There was the allegation of their injudicious use of highway checkpoints to bust undocumented drivers so as to impound and sell their cars to raise municipal funds. Or that Crazy Nine shot callers had been tipped-off about impending police raids. These and various other allegations Garza, Weaver and several other interested parties could ill afford to have proven in court.

Weaver asked, "You talk to Jaime T?"

"Not yet, and not likely if I can avoid it," Garza admitted. "I've got an election to secure and don't need him and his crew out and about causing consternation.

Weaver pursed his lips and blew air. "If this investigation gains momentum, I'll have to alert Al."

"That's why I stopped by. We need to make sure he doesn't, you know, go all native on us." Weaver laughed dryly. "Shit."

Alfonso Jardine was a Mexican Jew. His father was from Cuernavaca, and his mother had been a World War II refugee whose family snuck into Mexico, escaping the Nazis out of Poland. Jardine originally made his money in the discount mattress racket and, due to family ties on his dad's side here in Bell Park, had opened the Happy Trails Casino more than twenty years ago. The casino drew patrons from all over and accounted for some two million-plus in salaries and tax revenues for the city. This was not an insignificant sum to the small municipality, and thus, Jardine was a player in local politics as he was a backer of Mayor Sharpe.

Jardine had also dabbled in the internal affairs in Israel, supporting Labor

Party members there, as well as owning land over there. At one point a few years ago, the gang situation was getting out of hand in Bell Park. This was due to the rival Rolling Daltons, a black gang with some Latino membership, encroaching on the Nines' drug territory.

Innocents were getting cut down in the crossfire, so naturally, the residents were demanding action from the outgunned and outnumbered police force. Jardine, from his compound on the beach in Baja, sent a group of mercenaries into town, some of them former Shin Bet and African campaign veterans. It did not go well with these parachute-in, parachute-out types, used to slapping around the populace and letting the Good Lord sort them out later. Even in Bell Park, civil liberties couldn't be that blatantly ignored. Particularly as the media latched onto the story.

"If he gets a mind to send those yahoos back this time," Weaver noted, "he'll have our pictures in their target files."

Garza said, "It's not going to get to that."

Weaver leaned back in his seat. "It can't, Rudy."

Promising to keep him in the loop, Garza was back on the road. The radio ad they'd done for the Spanish language station was running. On the minute spot, the voices of two middle-aged women were talking as if over coffee at the kitchen table.

"Why yes," one said, "that Mr. Rojas seems nice. But with all the abuse problems and the church, why did he have that young girl sitting on his lap?"

"I know," the second one replied, "reading her a story," she snorted incredulously. "*Que lastima*, didn't he know better? What kind of teacher is he anyway?" There was no campaign mailer of Rojas with a child on his lap. Perception was everything.

"Sweet," Garza said to himself as he kept an appointment in nearby Santa Pico, a city even smaller than Bell Park. In a modest stucco home with hand-sewn curtains, he met with the heads of several block clubs throughout the Southeast area. These women, ranging in age from their forties to their seventies, would be on duty tomorrow at several election booths in Bell Park. Each had a son or daughter, grandchild or great-grandchild who

Garza had helped in some way. They had long memories and a peasant's sense of loyalty. These were women like Garza's dead mother, and he was like them.

"Have some tea, *mijo*," Mrs. Almirez greeted him as he stepped inside the kitchen from the side door. She turned to pour from a steaming ceramic pot.

"Thank you," he said, nodding his head and greeting the others, some thirty-seven in all. This was a quick overview of tomorrow's plan. Nothing crude to potentially raise a red flag like misplaced ballot boxes or having the dead on the voting rolls. Through the normal *chisme*, the drama, and the back-fence gossip leading up to this election, plus the use of the traditional phone banking to tabulate how people were voting, these women had been given names of their friends and neighbors IDed as Rojas's supporters.

"We're ready," Estella Rencinos said after Garza finished with last-minute details. Rather than try to stuff the ballot box as Garza had arranged in the past, these women would, when feasible, merely punch another hole in an already punched card of some of Rojas's supporters. An over-voted ballot was as invalid as an unmarked one.

"Now, no one overdoes it, right?" he said to the ladies. "We can't have any of you going to the pokey." That got nervous laughter. The idea here was these women knew a lot of people or were known by a lot of people. The older ones, the neighborhood *tías*, the community aunties, would engage the opponent's voters. The election was predicted to be light, so a backup was unlikely at the polls. Therefore, it was natural that there would be more time for casual conversation.

The person was distracted, talking to the older woman while handing the ballot in its paper sleeve to the younger woman. When this one tore off the perforated top of the punch card for the voter, fumbling a bit to expose that other part of the punched card, they'd use a punch on the end of a ballpoint pen to put another hole in the card, then tap it back into its sleeve. The distracted person, after chatting up the *tía* about her child's progress in school or that recipe for the Christmas *tamales*, would, as required, place that altered card in the sealed ballot box's slot.

Garza had rehearsed the punch move with the selected punchers, and he was impressed at the level of sleight-of-hand these old gals had mastered. They had few reservations about committing larceny in the service of La Causa.

In a close race with low turnout, a one- or two-percent spoilage could be the margin of victory. He gave a finishing pep talk, making sure to crank it down from the sermon with Sharpe, and was off again.

At his desk in his City Hall office, which was a squat, unassuming cinder-block bunker of a structure tucked into a corner of Bolívar Park, Jason Prichard rang him on his cell.

"They found Delia," he said without introduction. "She's living down there in Tucson near the college. In fact, she's shacked up with, of all things, an adjunct professor of late nineteenth-century French fuckin' literature. I guess her thing with Burkhalter turned her on to nerds or some shit," he said contemptuously.

"Fuck," Garza said.

"Double fuck," his friend concurred. "The good news is I learned from another source that she got popped a few months ago on a meth charge, so she's still tweaking."

"And if she's tweaking, she's as unreliable as Hector to a jury."

"Yeah, hopefully. But that might not stop an indictment from coming down," the lawyer noted. "The Bureau has a hard-on for you, Rudy." As was their custom, they were using disposable cell phones. They switched them out every other week.

"True that, my brother," Garza said, suddenly upbeat. He'd received an email and had opened it while they talked. He told Prichard the good news. "The poll we did Saturday has Don Pedro up by five points. When we get over this hump tomorrow, then I can concentrate on how I'll tarnish their images and cause doubt and confusion before the feds can spit-shine their shoes. Don't worry."

"Uh-huh, be happy."

"Exactly."

Telling him he'd report in if there was any other pertinent news, Prichard rang off. For the next two hours or so, Garza did the City's business. From adjusting gaps in the sanitation budget to meeting with the city-sponsored after-school program, he was in his groove.

Then, crossing the parking lot for city employees, he saw a familiar car come around the long way. He couldn't mistake the vehicle for anyone else's as it was a fully restored and fully modernized maroon 1935 four-door Packard touring sedan. It was one gorgeous machine, but Garza wasn't pleased to see it now. The car slowed in front of him, and the rear window slid down on its electric motor. In the back was Jamie Torres, the Crazy Nines chief. Due to a mystical con version brought on while on peyote and getting a lap dance two years ago, he'd taken on the Aztec last name of Teculciztecal. No one, not even Torres most of the time, could pronounce it. So he remained Jamie T.

"My friend," the gang leader said, pointing one of his long black nails at Garza. There were rings on three of his fingers. "I understand we have a problem." He was sitting nearest the passenger window in the Edwardian gear he favored these days, complete with owlish sunglasses. Whatever the hell that had to do with the Aztecs, nobody dared ask him.

Garza explained in a smooth and calm way why he didn't see the Hector and Delia situation as a problem.

"Let us hope," the other man said. "For I am most vexed that this situation my cousin is in may have come from an inside tip. A snitch, you'd say."

"Why do you suspect that?"

"Elemia has seen it."

Next to him was an eight-ball chick Garza didn't recognize. Though he did note her ample breasts strained against her skimpy top. A stylized skull was tattooed on her cheek. Beside her on the car's bench seat was an older woman who went by the Elemia tag. She was Jaime T's personal *bruja*, a witch and spiritual advisor, but Garza knew her when she was Suzanna Rios from the projects.

"Shit," Garza said, looking directly at her, "she couldn't see pale-ass Paris Hilton naked in a room full of Zulus."

Rios had a hand on Eight Ball's thigh. She raised that hand and languidly gave Garza the finger as the car glided away. Jamie T might be all ancestored up, but he did love his three-ways. Back on the streets, he ate two *carne asada* tacos from a cart vendor and headed over to the Royal Viking motel for his assignation with the mayor's campaign manager, Bell Park Police Sergeant Cerna Chacon. She'd texted him to be at the motel at this time. It wasn't their first such meeting at the VK, a few freeway exits further south of Bell Park.

"Don't be shy, stud," she teased. They'd barely entered the room, and Chacon was tugging on his zipper. She was dressed in civilian clothes but had brought her department-issued equipment bag. This she tossed on the bed.

"Please, I do have my standards," he joked, pretending to pull away.

"You better get that standard at attention, soldier." She gave his crotch a squeeze and undid her shirt, revealing a lavender bra and her feathered serpent tattoo that began on her abb'd stomach and disappeared below the belt line of her pants. Soon, she was down to her thong and moving toward the bed, Garza close behind her, naked and excited.

On the bed, they snorted some coke she'd brought along to charge their batteries. The two then got busy with various efforts at exchanging body fluids.

"You like that, baby?" she murmured, nibbling his inner thigh.

"You know I do," he moaned as he reached back to the equipment bag. Given what she was doing, she didn't see him reach inside. He withdrew an old-fashioned revolver with a six-inch barrel. Chacon had her eyes closed, gobbling him up, and he slapped the warm steel against her scrunched forehead.

Startled, she halted and gulped hard.

"Get on your back," he commanded, the gun unwavering on her.

She did as commanded, keeping her legs closed like a chaste schoolgirl.

"Open them," he barked, using the business end of the ancient police special to tap her knee.

"What are you going to do with that?"

"Don't you worry about that. You just do as I say." He rubbed the barrel along her inner leg, moving it steadily upward.

"Please don't," she pleaded. "I'll do anything else you want." She put her hands over the area he was intent on reaching.

Garza's heavy breathing drowned out the din of horns and brakes outside the motel room. The two were in lustful thrall.

She grabbed his wrist, but his other hand was around her throat, and he worked the tip of the gun past the material of her sheer panty and inserted it in her vagina.

She gasped. "Do me, Rudy," she said as she tongued his ear and lobe.

He worked the barrel of the gun in and out of her as she bucked in pleasure, her strong arms holding him tight while she bit into his shoulder. Almost there, she told him to stop, and they came together using the tried-and-true method.

Cooling off, she asked him, "Are you getting in a jam over Burkhalter?"

"How do you know about that?"

"I have my ways." Her cell rang and, noting the number, she answered and listened. "Okay, Pete, I'm on my way." She clicked off. "The mayor demands my presence."

"How's he holding up?"

"He's got the spirit again, Deacon Garza. He's on the warpath. I'm going over with him to fire up the Delta phone bankers." The Deltas were the last black sorority in town.

"As long as he makes it in this last stretch."

"Don't you worry your pretty little head about it, sweetheart." She grabbed for his limp member through the slit of his boxer, giggling.

He returned to City Hall and, after tidying up a few matters, made his rounds. He dropped off campaign literature to the parking enforcement crew on late lunch break, delivered Braille call sheets to the home for the blind, and trays of Pollo Fiero chicken to the soccer club whose members would be out doing evening canvassing.

Somewhere past seven that night, he knocked his tumbler of Jameson's against Jason Prichard's at the Peacock Inn. "Nice work, home," he toasted his friend.

"Good thing I remembered Chambers had retired to Phoenix. He put her on the run." Prichard smiled broadly and quaffed his drink. He referred to Bob Chambers, a former captain with the Compton Police Department, when Compton had its own department before contracting with the sheriff. Prichard called in a chit and got him to drive to Tucson and flash his badge in Delia Gomez's face. He growled that those nice, clean-cut FBI agents who contacted her were the least of her problems. That all sorts of nastiness with this hush-hush branch of law enforcement he represented was about to befall her for narco-trafficking. He'd be back with a warrant, he'd advised her. He'd watched from hiding as she tossed a suitcase in a raggedy Camry and took off from the adjunct professor's house.

With her gone, Hector Rivas could play his tune to the cheap seats, but the feds knew they had nada. Burkhalter had been the comptroller of Bell Park. Three years ago, there'd been another reform push, and the mayor and his allies on the council were forced to fire his crony and hire the stick-up-his-butt Burkhalter. He began to dig up money streams, best left alone. Jardine was unhappy, as was Jamie T and Prichard. Using selective prosecution, Prichard helped clean up the gang problem in nearby Compton, but also kept the Rolling Daltons from expanding. And there had been cash thank yous from Jamie T regarding this.

Fortunately, the forty-something Burkhalter, a bachelor, was a lonely man.

Garza had Delia, an aging neighborhood chick, dress like a square and made sure she bumped into Burkhalter in City Hall. He tumbled, hard. Soon, she had a key to his apartment. One evening, she let Hector in with a replacement computer tower just like his. Only this one contained beaucoup downloaded bestiality images. Naturally, some of the images were leaked to the media. Burkhalter protested, but to no avail. His credibility was toast, as was his investigation.

Prichard talked with Garza some more, then left for a date. The city manager did some politicking in the working-class bar of laborers, copier salesmen, and receptionists. He glad-handed and gabbed, bought a couple of rounds, handed out buttons, and reminded them of their polling places.

Out in the warm evening, walking to his car, Chacon phoned him. He'd stopped near a gardener's old pick-up truck laden with lawn equipment.

"I know you're insatiable, woman, but I've got to get home."

"Rudy," she said in a rushed tone. "Where are you? I'm in my car and coming to get you."

"What are you talking about, Cerna?"

"Jamie T thinks you're the snitch."

"Why the fuck would he think that?"

Two men dressed in working clothes exited the bar. "Because that silly bitch we have undercover was on the hot seat and came up with a story implicating you. She's the one that provided the tip leading to Hector Rivas' bust."

The two working men stood close to the pick-up.

A chill cooled Garza's body. "She got a skull tattooed on her cheek?"

"Yeah. That way, our units would know who she is. But she was able to phone in tonight and told me she was about to be exposed this afternoon and panicked. I was her training officer so she's close to me, that's why she felt she had to get it off her chest in case it caused problems. Problems," she snorted. "That goddamn Elvira, or whatever the hell she calls herself, had a vision that someone close to him was snitching. I've got to get you to a safe house, then we can work this out with him."

The two men closed the gap to where Garza stood with his back to them.

"Okay. I better come up with an excuse for Lettie. I—"

Garza didn't finish his sentence as the first of the fifteen stab wounds entered his body, piercing his lungs and kidneys and stomach.

"No, wait, it's not—" he tried to tell his assassins, but they were coldly and quickly efficient in their mission. They left him curled in his blood on the sidewalk, Chacon yelling into the cell phone in his now slack hand. As they drove off in the pick-up, sure not to stand out like, say, in a lowered ride with spinner rims or the like, Rudy Garza rolled over on his back on the blacktop, his Botticelli's unstained and at attention. He stared peacefully at the stars.

One star in particular seemed to get brighter and bigger, filling his vision.

In the heart of that brilliance, forms materialized. The swift boats were swooping down from the heavens to lift him up and take him away.

Hallelujah.

55

* * *

"Swift Boats for Jesus," *Politics Noir: Dark Tales from the Corridors of Power,* Verso, 2008, GP editor.

Roger Crumbler Considered His Shave

R oger Crumbler considered his shave. On this his fiftieth birthday, he was pleased that while his stubble became grayer each week, he still had a head of hair—and it was still dark.

The face staring back at him in his bathroom mirror had held up fairly decently for half a century. Though not for the first time, he considered minor cosmetic surgery to correct the bags under his eyes, a trait among the men in his family. Was it true that Preparation H reduced the puffiness? There was a kind of logic to that, given that hemorrhoids were what? An enlarged vein, right? But what caused those sacks under the eyes? Fluid? He'd have to google that. It was always good to have something new to learn.

Working the shaving gel into his whiskers, Roger smiled, mentally outlining the day ahead. At the office, he had to do a final review of the Carlson Foundation financials. There had been no major blips on the radar save for some inconsistencies on a pass-through grant from a city agency. The Carlson Foundation funded reading programs for low-income youth, and the City of Los Angeles was a partner in that endeavor. Such inconsistencies were not unusual given the accounting procedures of the bureaucrats versus the private sector. This was a minor concern, and he would resolve it with a phone call or two to his City Hall contacts.

Yet it was because of those inconsistencies that he was able to do what he'd done. For him. For Nanette.

Roger turned his head this way and the other, making sure he'd covered his face evenly as he massaged the warm foam into his pores. At one of those Hollywood Hills dinner fund-raiser parties saving spotted owls, or maybe it was spotted actors, a dermatologist with skin flawless as plastic told him that you should allow five minutes for your night beard to soak properly. He didn't adhere to this advice each morning, but he wasn't going to be fifty every morning, either. This was, after all, a big day.

After reconciling the financials, there would be the regular weekly staff meeting. He'd already written and copied his report earlier this week, so there should be no surprises in that quarter. The company, Nathanson and Nathanson, was a boutique CPA firm that nonetheless commanded more than eight million in billing last year, given a clientele that ranged from old-line family foundations like Carlson to heavy hitters in the film and music business. Roger was senior vice president and was up for partnership.

That in itself was something considering the firm had been started in the '40s, when there were still orange trees on Wilshire. Run and built up by the founder, Sig Nathanson, then turned over to one of the sons, Gabe, and nephew Martin, in the '70s. The only other partner outside of the family had been a member of the founder's temple. Not only was Roger not a member of the temple, for unlike the late Sammy Davis, Jr., he'd only joked after a few scotches about converting. And what about Whoopi Goldberg? She wasn't really a member of the tribe. Was she? Something else to Google.

He dutifully stroked his double blade through the foam. The reassuring sound of whiskers being lopped off were the low notes accompanying the chirping of birds in the tree outside his second-story bathroom window. Post the staff meeting he'd have a light lunch at his desk. He wasn't actually much for diets, but when he'd had the irregular heartbeat detected at age forty-five, he finally quit smoking and resolved to lose the fat.

Roger guided his razor underneath his jaw, taking his time to go over that tough area along the edge. At first, he'd hated running. He'd tried the treadmill at the gym his wife had egged him to join, the one she already belonged to, in fact, but found that boring. There was something about staring at a wall for forty-some minutes that made mush of his brain. And listening to music while he ran, forget it. Because each song, no matter if it was an R&B ballad about a lost love or a jazz instrumental, got him daydreaming about laying around reading the paper or napping rather than running.

So at least when he jogged through his neighborhood, Wilshire Vista the upscalers called it, sans Walkman, he had sights and sounds. And he varied his routes so that it wasn't the same, yet familiar, each time. In the five years of this regime, also putting in some sessions with the weight machine at the gym, he'd lost forty pounds. And for a man his age, his wife and girlfriend both told him amorously, he looked reasonably fit and even a little buffed.

He worked the razor on his upper lip, recalling fondly the mustache he'd also shed five, no, more like four years ago. By then, he'd been seriously into his jogging. That's when he'd met Nanette. And not too long after that decided to be a thief. He stared at the face re-emerging through the lather and smiled.

He finished his shave and regarded his handiwork. Roger touched a rough patch and eliminated it deftly. He dabbed on aftershave and enjoyed the sensation of pinpricks as he stepped back into the bedroom.

His wife, Claudia, was up and moving about. He watched with lascivious interest as she bent over to search in her underwear drawer. Usually, she wore sweats or pajama pants and a top, but this morning, this birthday, she wore only lacy purple panties.

Roger sat on the bed, finding it difficult to cross his legs as he imagined David Niven might in one of those fashionable black and whites. "Have I mentioned how spectacular your ass is, honey?"

"You always know what to say to a woman." She pushed him back and straddled him, nuzzling and biting his neck.

"Glad you woke me up this morning," he said, pulling her even closer and kissing her full on the mouth. He was going to miss her. Yes, he certainly was.

"You didn't do too bad for an old dog."

"Careful, I might have to show you my double play."

She smiled, biting her lower lip. This always got to him, even after decades of seeing it. "I'd like to, baby, but I have to hit that inventory this a.m. You know how Pelecanos gets." Nanette managed a heavy equipment rental service.

"Forget that clown. He couldn't find balls in a bowling alley if it wasn't for you." He slipped his hand inside her panty and caressed that wondrous backside. But she broke free with a kiss.

"Tonight, we'll have all kinds of time, okay?"

"Well, I don't know. At my age, Lord knows I need my rest."

She shook a glossy purple nail at him. "You just be ready and don't drink too much."

He chuckled. "I won't." Damn, she looked good. He got up to finish dressing, and the phone rang.

Claudia moved quickly and plucked the handset loose. "Yes," she said and listened. "Oh, hi, sweetie." She listened some more, looking once or twice at her husband, frowning.

Roger continued to appear languid reposing on the bed, but a spring was winding in the base of his spine and threatened to make his whole bodytaut. That had to be their daughter on the phone, as she was at Cal Berkley up north. If she was in some fix, what could he do? His plans would have to be postponed. And that meant more exposure and chance of discovery.

Be cool, Roger, just be cool, man. Don't let 'em see you sweat.

"Alright, honey. We'll see you tonight." And his wife hung up.

"Why's she coming home? There some problem?"

"Not really," Claudia began.

"Not really?" he said more shrilly than he wanted, "this is the middle of the school year, Claudia." Now, what did he just tell himself? Keep it on low burn, man. Low burn. He rose, clasping his wife's shoulders. "Sorry, honey, I didn't mean to get all tense. You know how us pensioners get mood swings."

Claudia Crumbler-Morris looked preoccupied, tightening the sash on the robe she'd put on. "Janice's coming home because she doesn't have class until Monday and wants to talk to us about something."

Roger wondered aloud, "Dropping out?"

"Or pregnant."

"Aw, hell no." He began to stomp around the room. "We're too damn young to be grandparents."

"No, we're not."

"You're hilarious."

Claudia chuckled. "I don't think she's pregnant."

"She's twenty, and we've both seen how them knot heads with their pants hanging down around their cracks drool at her."

She was heading toward the shower. "She's not attracted to those kind of boys."

"Even boys with slide rules like a little—"

"Roger," she admonished.

"Taste," he declared.

"Heathen." She closed the bathroom door and ran her shower. She wasn't that sure Janice wasn't pregnant. And neither was he.

And if she was with child, then what of his plans involving Nanette and the money? It wasn't like he could pull this off any time he felt like doing it. He buttoned his shirt. It would be casual today: pressed chinos, buttoned-down shirt, no tie, but sports jacket. It was his birthday, and it was expected he'd be taking it easy today once the Carlson file was closed out. Yes, do nothing to raise any concerns among the son and nephew.

Getting his socks on, the ones with the blue hourglasses, he reveled in the simplicity and beauty of the virus he'd planted in his firm's computers more than two years ago. The virus would launch from the receptionist's computer. The Nathan sons outsourced the maintenance on the computers, so it wasn't too hard to hide what he'd done from the IT crew that came in regularly to service the machines. At 9:24 tonight, everything would change.

By then he and Nanette would be heading east, toward Texas, in the used car they'd bought more than a year ago, they'd gotten the brakes fixed, the head gasket replaced and what have you so that the vehicle was reliable for the get away. And most importantly, the final transfer of the funds he'd siphoned off, little by little, had been completed three days ago. The computer crash would cover his nefarious deeds for weeks, time enough to set up his new life with Nanette.

Naturally Roger would be a suspect, but he'd be gone, no forwarding. The cops and the firm would hammer at Claudia, give her a rough going over, but she was innocent. She didn't have a clue as to his caper or his infidelity.

"Roger, what time will you be back home? I know you're going to have drinks with Wayne and the guys."

"What time is Janice supposed to be here?"

"About seven-thirty or so she said. She's driving down. She was already in her car heading this way."

"Alone?"

His wife dangled an earring from her lobe. "Good question, honey." She blew him a kiss. "You have such a suspicious mind."

He walked toward the bathroom to brush his teeth. "I'll be back here no later than eight."

"All right. See you then, sweetie." She gave him a peck, then turned around. She gripped his lower face in her hand and, using her tongue, but keeping her fresh carmine lips off his, probed his mouth. She topped that off with a quick smack. "Love you."

"Love you, too." As she hummed and walked down the stairs, he stood at the railing, watching her go. He remained there, hearing her car start up and fade away. After tonight, he'd never see her or his daughter again. But he was resolved. He was going to spend the second half, well, really, if he was lucky and kept exercising and watching what he ate, the next thirty years with a woman twenty years his junior and some two and a half million dollars in ill-gotten gains. That was an amount a bling rapper like 50 Cent or actor Tom Cruise might sneer at, hardly enough for them to get out of bed. But that amount was sufficient for a humble man like Roger Crumbler.

The down payment had been made through intermediaries on the condo in Port Saint Charles in Barbados. And through budgeting and living within their means, they'd be comfortable. They wouldn't drive Jags or Bentleys, nor vacation on a whim for months in Italy at some mountain villa, but they wouldn't be eating Top Ramen either.

And should the need or notion arise, Roger had also entertained the idea that he might do some money laundering for a select list of individuals.

Certainly, more than once over the years several clients of the firm had hinted at such. Millionaires more than the middle class were willing to take a step or two out of line to hold on to that which they felt entitled to by birth or happenstance.

Wayne Wardlow, the Carlson Foundation's executive director, was not a possibility in that department. But it was Wayne who had spawned this in him.

"Hell yes, I'm tappin' that ass," he'd joked. Referring to a woman, a freelance writer Wardlow had met doing an article about socially involved foundations for Los Angeles magazine.

"Okay, P. Diddy," Roger had remarked to the man whose face should be next to WASP in the dictionary. They were in the locker room getting dressed from their basketball game and shower at the gym.

"I love black pussy, you don't know what you're missing, son." Wardlow knocked him playfully in the shoulder.

"You have lost your natural cotton-pickin' mind, son," Roger said, getting his trousers on.

"Roger, getting some on the side at our age is cheaper than buying a sports car and a damn sight more fun." He then grabbed his crotch like an over-sexed sophomore in high school and bucked his hips.

Okay, it wasn't really fair to lay this at Wayne Wardlow's doorstep. Roger was a grown man. He made the decision to kindle a romance with Nanette, who'd flirted with him that day at the Barnes and Noble in the Grove. A pretty woman like her, browsing in the current events section, able to name the current leaders in places like Turkmenistan and go on about Mugabe's failed policies in Zimbabwe. How could he not be hooked?

His cell phone rang, and he smiled, answering it.

"How does it feel to be a geezer who has two women panting to fuck the shit out of him?" Nanette said huskily.

"You have a way with a phrase; have I mentioned that?"

"Are you hard? Or did the old lady drain you?"

"I want you so bad."

"Me, too."

"Everything ready?"

"Ready and steady."

He hesitated; should he mention his daughter coming to town?

"What? Worried? Having second thoughts? That's understandable; this is serious."

"Don't I know. Everything's fine. I can't wait to see you." Don't say anything; don't put the jinx on this chance you have.

"I'll be thinking about you all day, Roger. I'm wet already. Wish you were over here to find out how wet."

"I will soon, baby."

"You got that right."

He clicked off and nodded his head. They'd even accounted for that. For the last few months, he'd been using disposable cell phones. He had the one that was the duplicate his wife had and was careful to always have that one with him so he could answer her calls. But now as matters came to fruition, Nanette had suggested using the disposables to better cover their tracks. Prior to that, he'd been circumspect and mostly called her from his office phone. So there was a record at the phone company, but that number was to an apartment Nanette had moved out of and a cell phone she'd disconnected. She, too, would be gone no forwarding.

Roger sat in his idling car, looking at the house he was not going to see again after today. It was far from a palace, but they'd lived in this two-story Spanish-Mediterranean since Janice had been three, and housing prices in LA were up there but not in the stratosphere as they were now. The paint jobs, the patching, the lawn that needed re-seeding, staying here while Claudia took Janice to the Valley during the '92 riots—a pint of Jack Daniel's and a revolver he'd never fired his false fortifications. There had been the hole in the roof beneath the tiles that had ruined their bedroom ceiling, those ornery possums prowling in the bushes in the back yard he'd chased off with a golf club, the time Janice learned to ride her bike up and down the block. The house, the touchstone to a vast chapter in his life.

He backed the car out of the driveway and took a slow tour along Curson, taking it all in as if seeing it for the first time. The old timers, the others, the newbies with walls enclosing their front yards, the redone homes with the Southwest flare replete with landscapes of cacti and native plants, how his neighborhood, his part of Mid-City, had changed in the years they'd lived there.

Roger gave a brief wave to Dorothy, one of his long-time neighbors, walking her Chow mix. He choked up, but got it together and went on, there was no time for cheap sentimentality. After making the turn at the signal, he picked up speed going west on Olympic, passing LA High, where he'd gone his junior and senior years, lettering in basketball and track. His folks—his dad worked for the county as a bus dispatcher for the then Rapid Transit District and his mom a legal secretary—had saved enough to move from what they called the east side in those days, South Central now, and bought a tidy one story on Norton just south of Pico.

His father had died in '99, and his mother, still active and working part-time at a senior center, had moved back to Oakland, where she was from. How would what he was about to do affect her? Would it age her? Would she hate him? Blame Claudia? Take it out on Janice? No, his mother was a rational, strong woman. She'd probably denounce him from the pulpit of her church and pray for his lost, misguided soul. There'd be a round of "amens," and shaking of heads, and comforting their troubled sister by the congregation. She'd done what she could to raise him right, some people are just born to be bad they'd commiserate.

To get his mind off his mother's disappointment, he turned on the radio. He was pleased to hear that the forecast was sunny and breezy, a typical day in LA Yes, everything must appear as ordinary.

At the office, he reconciled the inconsistency with the Carlson financial after one phone call and a subsequent fax from his buddy at the County. In deference to his friend

Wayne Wardlow, he'd also stolen money from this foundation. It wasn't too hard, given the continuing bookkeeping discrepancies that organically arose between Carlson and the civil servants. If he hadn't taken any money from the family fund, then Wayne would have come under suspicion and scrutiny. And that might surface his friend's continuing relationship with his paramour and that would surely weigh on Roger's conscience.

"Happy birthday, Roger."

"Thanks, Gabe." The son had stepped into Roger's office. "Just want you to know, it's all downhill from here."

Gabriel Nathanson was twice divorced and fifty-four. "That's what I'm afraid of."

Nathanson clapped him on his shoulder. "I'll see you over at the Bounty. I'll buy a round."

"That's great, Gabe."

"I tried to get the sour puss Marty to come along, but you know how he is."

On cue, Roger dredged up a camaraderie chuckle it had taken him years to perfect. "Yes, I do." Martin Nathanson's idea of cutting loose was putting ketchup on his scrambled eggs.

"And next week, let's you, me, and sour puss sit down, okay, partner?"

"Sure, Gabe. I look forward to it."

"Same here." He left, whistling.

There it was. Roger was going to betray a firm with a reputation for spotless honesty and forthrightness of, well, more than sixty years. Would they recover from the taint his theft would smear them with, or sink under a sea of accusations and blame? That and the avalanche of lawsuits that were sure to come. And though Roger was by far no standard bearer for the race, there was that too. A black man, albeit middle-class and middle-aged, married for over twenty years to a white woman, but a black man nonetheless who gained the trust of his Jewish bosses and, in effect, stole from them. What would be the fallout from that?

And what of his betrayal of his wife and daughter? Wasn't that the biggest crime of all? Running off with a young black woman, fine as she may be. His stomach gurgled as he admonished himself. This was a time to keep your mind focused, Roger, this is not the time for butterflies and second-guessing. Everything was in motion, and you can't drop the ball to mangle the metaphor. He wanted to call Nanette, wanted so desperately to hear her voice tell him how she loved him, how she'd never felt this way about a man before.

He suppressed the urge to call his girlfriend and went about his tasks, forcing himself not to watch the clock, not to mentally count down the hours till he started a new, exciting life. He would not be the same old nine-to-five, mortgage-paying, block-club-going Roger. The hours eked by, and finally, he was sitting in the back room of the Bounty on Wilshire in what was becoming part of the growing Koreatown.

The HMS Bounty was a time-warp steak and booze joint left over from the days of pounding down a couple of scotches over lunch, and cholesterol sounded like the name of a new hair color line. It was where you could find a booth named for LA native Jack Webb, a swing door leading to the bathrooms, and the next-door Gaylord residential apartments with their '30s-era decor. It was across the street from the empty Ambassador Hotel. Once the site of the Coconut Grove nightclub, it was where presidential candidate Robert Kennedy was assassinated in 1968.

Like other old and forgotten buildings in LA, the Ambassador was used now and then for films or TV. It was slated to be torn down, and a high school and shopping complex erected in its place. Though there was talk of preserving and transporting the pantry area where RFK was gunned down to another location.

"Here's to my ace, Roger. May the next fifty be yours for the taking," Wayne Wardlow toasted after they'd sung an off-key but effusive "Happy Birthday." The waitress had brought out a chocolate cake, his favorite.

"Of course, we only used five candles for symbolism's sake since we didn't want to torch the joint." Wardlow joked, getting a round of guffaws.

"Here's to you, Roger," Gabe Nathanson echoed. "Thanks, gents." Roger clinked his glass against the others' and drank. This was his second gin and tonic, and it was going to be his limit. It was seventeen past six, and it was getting harder for him to laugh and seem at ease. There was getting home to talk with Janice, a last intimacy with Claudia. He owed her that, and then Nanette. One foot right after the other, a step into a new you. Roger. Just like walking across the street. Though you could get run over.

"What's up, champ?" Wardlow sidled up next to Roger. "Looks like you got something on your mind."

"Being fifty."

Wardlow had more of his whiskey. "I heard that. But things change, yeah? Don't want to look back and have a trunk full of regrets." He upended his tumbler and signaled for another. "Getting this age, too old to be innovative but just enough juice left in the tank to try something different, it hits you, doesn't it? You can keep doing what you're doing, stay in that rut till you maybe make retirement, and hope you can still manage to wipe your own butt and have enough to buy a few beans and tortillas. Or take a chance on something." He looked off beyond the walls of the bar and grill.

"Exactly," Roger agreed, also projecting beyond the confines of the restaurant. Later, after the goodbyes and a promise to play nine holes with Wardlow and a couple of the others this weekend, Claudia called him on his cell as he headed home.

"Janice isn't here."

"What? She turn around and go back?"

"No. Her cell phone is suddenly disconnected. I couldn't leave a message, and I haven't heard from her."

"You're just now telling me this?"

"Don't yell at me. It's just a little past seven-thirty, the time I figured she'd be here."

"You're right, I'm sorry. Think she's at one of her friends' houses? Could she have stopped on the way, and maybe she dropped her phone and broke it?"

"Then why didn't she use their phone to call?"

"Look, it's not dire yet or anything. We should be calm."

"I am, I'm just, you know, could it have something to do with why she came down?"

"I don't know. We have some of her friends' numbers. Girls from high school."

"I'm going to call them."

"Okay. I'll be home shortly." He hung up, and he called Nanette to fill her in.

"Why didn't you tell me she was coming to town?"

"I didn't think it was going to be a big thing."

"So what are you going to do?" Nanette asked.

"I can't take off till I know what's going on with Janice."

"I know that, I'm not the unfeeling ho," she barked. "That's not what I meant. I can't stop the virus. There's no way I'd get near those computers now anyway. Everyone's gone home; it would be my code and time stamp registered if I went to the office."

Her tone softened. "What about the money in the accounts? We can access the funds any time, right?"

"Theoretically, yes. But once the hard drives are probed, I can't be sure there won't be traces. You know, once they attempt to resurrect the files, they dig deep. The virus was merely a way to give us the time we needed to get to the islands."

"Then find your daughter, darling, and call me back. It still won't make a difference if we leave tonight, tomorrow, or next week. Those computer files won't be recovered that fast. In fact, when they go down, and you're around being all concerned, that will be even better, less attention on you."

"Okay. Talk to you soon."

"Okay, baby."

Roger arrived at his house and was surprised to see his wife's car wasn't there. She called him on his cell as he unlocked the front door. "Janice had some car trouble, I went to pick her up. Should be back in half an hour."

"Fine, I'll be here." He went inside, checking the time and gauging his next moves. The virus was starting its attack. Now, all of it was real. He felt great as a power, a mastery he for once had over his life surged through him. Roger felt his hard member as he fantasized about the money and his woman. Giddy, he took out his BlackBerry and punched in a code. The results on his screen sobered him right up. He put in numbers, again and again, and got the same readout.

Like being winded by a heavyweight's blow, Roger dropped to his knees, fighting for air. There were two accounts in Swiss banks and one in the Caymans. The accounts were empty. There was only one other person who knew about them. He rose, a man with a mission.

Not fifteen minutes later, Roger Crumbler was surprised when Nanette answered the door. She lived in a duplex near Motor, where he'd helped her rent under a false name.

"Hi, honey," she said as he rushed inside.

"Well?" He pushed the BlackBerry toward her face. "Well, what?"

"The money, Nanette, the goddamn money I risked everything to steal. For us."

"I don't have it. Obviously."

"Really?" He stomped around the apartment, not sure what he'd find or do as he looked in the bedroom and the closets. "You're bullshitting me. You must have the money. No one else knew about the accounts but you."

"Keep your voice down, Roger."

"Fuck that." He was breathing hard, sweat glazing his brow. He glared at her, his fists balled. "You're playing some kind of game on me, aren't you? Think I'm stupid."

"Roger, if I had the money, why would I be here waiting for you?"

He grabbed her arm. "You tell me."

"Let go." She jerked free. "So let me get this straight: you're claiming the money is gone all of a sudden? The money from the accounts you set up, the money from the accounts you created passwords for? That money?" She fixed him with a glare of her own.

"Oh, I see. Very clever. Make it seem like you're the innocent here. Like you don't know what's going on when it's perfectly clear you're trying to pull some shit on me.

Or what about this, asshole. What if you planned this all along, come storming in here pretending you can't find the benjamins, and be all outraged and get me sucked in. Then send me off to look for the money some kind of way, and you take off with all of it. Shit," she said, disgusted. "Without me giving you the backbone, you'd never have stolen that money. You'd keep being a glorified bookkeeper until you got your gold watch and, a once a week hand job from your wife."

"Shut the fuck up. I need to think." He wanted to grab his head. He wanted to grab her head and pound the truth out of her.

"You shut the fuck up." She shoved him. "And get out of here. Now that I see how fragile you really are, I wouldn't go to the corner liquor store with you."

He was shaking in anger. "Now you hold on."

"Get out of here before I call the cops on your crazy, useless ass. You probably got all nervous and hit the wrong key, sending our money to some South American dictator's account or something." She laughed hollowly. "How the fuck could I have seen a future with you? You're pathetic, Roger."

"You're not getting rid of me. We're going to find that money you say you don't know where it's gone missing." His voice rose in heat. "This is my big chance, Nanette. And I'm goddamn sure not going to walk away quietly."

"You're unstable." Nanette stalked to the door and held it open. "Get out of here, I told you."

"I'm not leaving until I get my money." He came toward her. "My money, understand me, bitch?"

"Oh, okay." She slapped him hard across the face. "Now get to steppin'. I don't want to ever see you again. We're through, get it, motherfuckah?" She yelled. "We're through. Fuck you, your money, and your sorry little dreams."

He popped her on the point of the jaw, and she rocked back. Dazed, he grabbed her shoulders with both of his hands and shook her. "I want my money," he screamed.

She lunged forward and bit his ear as he turned his own face away. He yowled in pain as she chomped on his ear, and he had to reflexively let her go to free his hands to beat at her. But Nanette was fast and got a screwdriver with a long shaft out of a drawer. "Get the fuck out of here or so help me, Roger, I'll gut you." Red washed her teeth and mottled her lips. The lips that all day he'd longed to taste.

"Look, let's—"

"Hey," a voice called from below. "I've called the police on you two." An approaching siren punctuated the warning.

"Get out of here," Nanette repeated. "What are you going to tell the cops?"

Her eyes were pitiless. "Get going, Roger."

He ran from the duplex and tore away in his car. The downstairs neighbor was out on his lawn, watching Roger go. Blood clotted his eardrum, and there was some of it on his jacket and shirt. His cell phone rang and, feeling the need to do something normal, he answered it.

"Daddy," his daughter said.

"Janice. Where have you been?"

"Waiting for you and Mom at the house. Aren't we supposed to go out to dinner with your friends?"

"What?"

"Mom called me this past Wednesday and said it would be good if I could come down this weekend because it was your fiftieth birthday, and she was having a party for you at this fancy restaurant."

"She…" he began, but didn't finish. "You didn't have car trouble?"

"No," Janice said quizzically. "Mom told me to be home around eight-thirty. I got in town earlier and went and saw Ruthie and them, you know. I called her earlier and told her that."

Roger looked at his watch. It was 9:01. "And your mother's not there?"

"No. I called her first, but her phone's dead. Nothing. Maybe she broke it by accident."

"Or on purpose," he mumbled.

"What'd you say, Dad?"

"Nothing."

"You on your way home?"

"Yes, dear. I'll see you in a few minutes." They severed the connection. Roger was heading toward his house but pulled over on Venice and parked. He called their mutual friends. Nothing. Hadn't seen or heard from Claudia. He called her friends. Again nothing. She was gone. He was sure of it. Took the money he worked so hard to steal. Roger got out of his car, dizzy and disoriented. He retched, vomiting into the gutter.

He sat on the curb, head in his hands, almost in tears. All his planning, his dreams, his chance, gone. Claudia must have found out or suspected he was having an affair. She'd have searched through his Blackberry, looking for a name or phone number. The passwords to the accounts were in the PDA. And it wouldn't have been too hard for her to figure them out as she'd chided him more than once that he used his mother's maiden name, his favorite movie, or his father's nickname way too often.

He sighed, and it seemed as if anchors were dragging on him as he trudged back to his car. Driving aimlessly, he realized he wasn't going home. He didn't think that Nanette would tell the cops much since she risked trouble if he was arrested. But that nosy neighbor probably made a note of his license number. And for all he knew, the LAPD uniforms were running his plate now.

Of course, with his wife having left him, what did the cops have? She found out about his seeing another woman and took off in a huff after clobbering him in the ear. But they'd ask where she went. They'd talk to his daughter, and she'd have this other story that didn't fit. Roger could ask Janice to lie, but how long would that hold up? And then they'd be back in a week or two, easy-going, conversational.

"Say, pal," one of them would start, "you hear from your wife? No, huh? That's funny. Usually, couples that break up have to talk, you know, to split up their possessions, the house, what have you." Then they'd give each other that knowing cop look. "Like we said, that's funny."

What if Claudia had a boyfriend? What if she'd run away with some young stud she met at the gym or that class she took at UCLA last year? Had she played him for the fool all along? He hadn't written down when he was going to run away with Nanette. But the money was gone. His wife must have figured he was going to leave her once he turned fifty. Nanette's numbers were in his PDA. She'd been smart. Not giving away anything. She'd waited until he'd amassed enough and then took it from him like a pirate sacking a village.

If he could just go to work, pretend like he knew nothing. But that goddamn neighbor. He slowed down near the 10 Freeway and Fairfax Avenue. Roger rehearsed what he was going to tell his daughter. Purposely, he hadn't let himself imagine how she'd react once it was suspected he'd stolen money and run off with another woman. She'd hate him, naturally.

But now he could be the hero. At least he could have that over Claudia.

"Your mother has done us wrong, Janice," he told her after calling her at home. He'd crawled through the hole in the cyclone fence to get down to Ballona Creek. It was an old tributary of water dating back to the days of the ranchos in this once-small pueblo. But like everything else in this city, the creek was walled in with concrete. Ballona ran under the Fairfax Avenue overpasses from the freeway and meandered west for nine miles or so to the Pacific.

"What are you talking about?" She then gasped. "Dad, a man saying he's the police just knocked at the door. What's going on?"

"Tell them everything if you have any idea where your mother may have run off to and with whom—"

"Dad, what are you—"

"It's okay, sweetheart. She'll get hers. I'm going to find her. I'm going to make sure she doesn't get away with this." He hung up and dropped his cell phone into the water. There were ways of tracking you with those things.

He jogged, a cool breeze invigorating him. There was a bike path that paralleled it, starting not too far away in Culver City. He and Claudia and Janice had ridden to Marina del Rey several times. But now it wasn't for recreation that he was taking it, it was his life line—the sea shore his safety. He picked up his pace.

A plastic bag of toiletries in hand from the 7-Eleven he'd stopped at, one hundred dollars in twenties from the store's ATM in his wallet, all that it had left, a determined Roger Crumbler kept going, arms pumping, legs churning.

The banks of Ballona Creek weren't as steep as the other concrete rivers of the Southland—the LA River and the Arroyo Secco—so it wasn't hard keeping his feet dry. The sounds of night and the city were in sharp relief to his senses, and up ahead, in the dark of the bend of the cement ribbon, there was something.

But he didn't slow down. Be it a four-legged animal or the most dangerous of predators, a two-legged one, he didn't care. He wasn't going to be stopped. Roger once again had purpose. He'd hunt Claudia down and get his money back. He was not going to be denied.

In the morning, he awoke in the stale motel room with its walls bleached of color and greasy cracked windows. Overhead, yet another plane rattled those opaque panes as the tumult of aircraft arrived or left LAX. But this was of passing notice to him. In the few pieces left of the broken mirror over the sink with its rust stains, he studied his face as he lathered it. Wasn't there more gray in those whiskers today? The bags more pronounced? And wasn't that some gray edging into his temples? No matter. He had big things to do. Razor poised, his lather lubricating his stubble for the requisite five minutes, Roger Crumbler considered his shave.

* * *

"Roger Crumbler Considered His Shave," *Los Angeles Noir,*
Akashic Books, 2007, Denise Hamilton editor.

The Man for the Job

"No, how the hell could I be Wilson Pickett?"

"Oh, right. Sorry," the square mumbled as I stepped out of the cab. He went down the street the way he'd been heading when he stopped to ask me that bullshit after seeing me step to the pavement.

"You sure this is where you want me to let you?"

"Ain't no sweat, man, I can handle it." I peeled off some pounds and handed them to the driver. On the back seat was a folded newspaper and an article about that bald chick, the singer, Shanay, Sinbad, whatever the fuck, and how she'd joined some kind of Catholic cult and was calling for the Pope to renounce Beelzebub. Hilarious.

"Enjoy your stay, sir." He touched his cap and put his hack in gear. The car was just like the kind I'd seen roving 'round London, only there wasn't as many of them here. You'd think they'd be stacked up at the hotel I was stayin' at, but the doorman hipped me to hoof over to this O'Connell Street where I found them lined up.

I snuggled my upturned collar closer to my neck and put the zipper of my leather jacket all the way up. When you got the crawlies like I had, everything is like constant heated pins poking from beneath your skin. Plus, the goddamn cold, which I wasn't a fan of, to begin with, this gloomy weather was all up in my ass. I looked across the section of the park and could see the projects or estates, as they called them, over here, just beyond.

Walking head down, hands tucked away, I knew way down but wouldn't fess up that I was two steps from being certified a fool. I could have been back in my comfortable hotel room, hands roaming all over Molly, Mary, or whatever the fuck was the name of the honey who'd started conversin' with me in that pub after the game at Lansdowne.

"I've seen you play before," she said, her liquid browns steady on me.

I'd been givin' her and a couple of her girlfriends the glance. They'd been whispering and giggling to each other after me, and some of the others from the Dragons and the Claymores had strolled into the joint. The teams had come to Dublin to play an exhibition game at the stadium normally used for rugby and soccer. Now, the stands weren't nearly as full for us as it would be for their homegrown run and stick, but the curiosity factor and that football, my kind of football, involved its own slamming and swearing got some of the natives out to see us. What the fuck, slappin' heads was slappin' heads.

And where you had muscular dudes grappling and tearing at each other, you had the type of woman who dug that kind of action—and not just to watch.

"When was that?" I said, moving some to give her space at the bar. She leaned in.

"In Chicago. I lived there for a while. Had a job selling dog products."

"Dog products?"

"Flea control solutions, chewy treats, that sort of rubbish." I liked her toothy smile. Well, okay, I also liked the fact she had some guns straining that sweater she was wearing.

Those bad boys were calling my name. But damn, she knew I was looking. She was too. "So you saw me on TV?"

"Live and in color," she said, making the moment of assessing me up and down like a coach figuring out if I was first string or pine rider. "Soldier Field. The Falcons against the Bears, before they were in the Central Division. You had two touchdowns for Atlanta." She paused, considering something, then said, "I believe you shook your arse at the crowd after that second one."

I gave her my gee-whiz Urkel bit. Babes like a mothafuckah to be self-effacing and shit. "Just trying to keep the fun in the game. Say, did we—?"

"No, Zelmont, we didn't. All your women blur in your mind, do they?"

She'd lit a cigarette and let the smoke float between us.

"It's not that. It's just, you know, when you're on the road during the season, shit just gets jumbled. 'Course, it's not like I'd forget you."

She knew it was bullshit, but it wasn't like we were carrying a romance like in one of them whack Merchant Ivory flicks I'd been forced to watch once. She knew the score.

And, not an hour later, we were doing it freestyle in my room, and I had my hand and lips all over her gorgeous ta-tas. "I know this is going to sound off," I said later as we lay in bed, my hand rubbing her firm, what'd she call it? Arse.

Hilarious.

"You're crazy mad for me and want me to journey to your mansion in America with ya?" She said it in that kind of exaggerated Irish accent they used to do in those old black and whites where some stooped-over gray-haired dame played Jimmy Cagney's mother.

"Right," I said, gently squeezing one of her breasts that got a moan out of her. She put her hand on mine. "Do you know where to cop some crack? Get some, I mean."

She laughed down in her throat. "Good thing I was in the States. Over here, crack means to fart, and the Craic means, well, means the good life. Which," and her amber eyes crinkled at the edges, "I guess is a kind of way of looking at it. Though lately, that slang has found its way here, meaning what you mean."

I had no goddamn idea what the fuck she was talking about. I was needing, but had enough sense to know it was best not to go off and probably screw up what might be my only connection, but any chance of doing the nasty again before I had to light out tomorrow.

She reached across me for the phone on the nightstand, those wonderful titties mashing against my chest. "Let me make a few calls, darling."

And that's how I found myself staring confused at a sign. I figured the burning in my head had bored a hole in it, and the crack cravings had me seeing mirages and whatnot. But then I remembered that Connolley, our backup quarterback, had been over here before to see some cousins and had mentioned that it wasn't unusual to see signs in Gaelic, he'd said, the Irish language.

I sniffed, resisting the urge to scratch my itching, the invisible ants marching up and down my arms in sneakers that were on fire. I tried to get rid of the image of hundreds of those tiny pincer jaws taking little chunk after little chunk out of my flesh. There was a sign in English just to the left of the Irish one, but the only reason I'd stopped was not to locate myself, but to get psyched. I was on a field I hadn't played on before and had better be on my J.

Mariah, yeah, that was her name, had told me that this place, Ballymun, was going through renovations. There was a main street running through the middle with brown and gray buildings on either side, with three main tall towers standing out. I didn't grow up in the projects but had been in more than a few in my time for one reason or another. Lately, though, it had been for the reason I was here now, even after getting my walking papers from the real NFL for failing a random drug test and getting bounced here to the European league.

And it ain't like I was 24-7 on the pipe. I wasn't no weak-kneed dope fiend. It was just that my gimpy hip had been giving me fits again, and I'd been hiding that precious detail from the docs. But if I asked for more than the usual allotment of painkillers, they'd know something was up. Hell, if you played ball for more than two years, you just naturally needed some kind of legal narcotic cocktail to dull the constant throb of that sprained ankle that never had much of a chance to heal or the tingle you never lost in your hamstring when you had to cut sharp downfield. That was expected. The League's croakers knew what to give you for that shit; that was the ordinary.

But my on-again, off-again hip had started to pain me something fierce after I'd been tackled by this wheat-smellin' Russian fuck playing for the Monarchs two weeks ago in Wembley Stadium. Bad enough after that, I'd started cutting the pain with crack, knowing it would hype the demand in me and if I wasn't cool, and I could be the monkey dancing on the string like I'd been in the past.

The fuck? Enough of that inspectin' myself humbug. This wasn't no excursion to somebroads' college, and I was working to get some muff-diving professor and her prize pupil to come back with me to my room. Had to stay on point. I crossed behind a bulldozer that was on the low end of a mound of torn-down brick and wood and glass. There were a couple of figures moving over the mound, picking at this and lifting that in their search for plumbing pipes or porcelain to sell I assumed.

I went past them and checking the directions Mariah had written for me, found the doorway I was looking for in the night. Not too surprisingly, there were some kids bivouacked in front of the building I'd been told to find. A couple of them were passing a joint, and another bopping to a boom box blazing a Tupac number, "Dear Mama." The aroma of their chronic drifted to me as I got close. Their blunt popped and sizzled, too many seeds in the cheap shit they were toking on, to get righteously blitzed.

"Hey," one of the kids said, spying me as Shakur growled, "I reminisced on tha stress I caused, it wuz hell huggin' on my mama from a jail cell."

"You a boxer, that it? Come to show us hooligans how ta put our energies and urges to good use?" He did a quick flurry, hands and feet movin' and groovin' all the time his eyes never leaving mine.

The others cracked up. The oldest of them couldn't have been over thirteen. Since yesterday, it had been hard as Chinese chess for me to understand their accents. But now, with the jones all over me like poison ivy, I was getting every word.

To the one, they all looked hungry. Not for a burger so much as that something they couldn't get growing up around here. Say what you want about anything else, but that was a condition I knew something about 'cause it was how I'd come up in South Central LA

"Gotta do some business." I flashed a ducat.

"Yeah," the one who'd called me a boxer said. "Like 'em young and tender, do ya?"

"Sound like I'm cooing like Michael Jackson?" Not that I believed for a second these little shits wouldn't have taken me around the corner and laid a busted chair leg or rusted muffler upside my head in a heartbeat. I pressed the money into the kid's chest, and he took hold of it. I pointed at the door behind him.

He snorted, and, making a show like he was Jeeves, stepped aside, bowing and indicating for me to come forward. What a surprise, the door wasn't locked, and I entered the tower called Pearse, whoever the hell that was.

As the door closed behind me, my radar bumpin' in case one of them got a notion, I heard a clop-clop. I looked back through the safety glass and got sight of another kid in a watch cap and torn windbreaker galloping up to the others on a spotted nag. The horse's belly was sagging, the hind legs barely thicker than my arms, but damned if those kids didn't gather around it, petting it and nuzzling the sad beast. Maybe they'd use the scratch I gave them to feed the thing rather than waste it on weed. Yeah, maybe.

I went up the stairs, the hallways were pretty clean and there were few busted lights considering it was public hous ing. I got to the fourth floor, an older lady all bundled up coming at me from the opposite direction, humming a tune. She lifted her head and then stopped singing. Her eyes went wide then, breathing all funny 'cause she wasn't sure what to make of me prowlin' about.

"What's this then?" she said while I stepped past. "You going incognito for the Guardia?" She smelled of cigarettes and crushed flowers, and I got to the door I'd been directed to after Mariah had made her third call.

"Now, mind you, you're an able lad, Zelmont," she said, her hand down between my legs, "but you want to stay sharp, right? They'll be more scared of you, what with you being big and black and delicious," she kissed me, "but they grow 'em tuff over there too, right? Just because this isn't the South Side or Harlem, doesn't mean they'll all curl up and cry."

"Thanks, baby," I'd said, kissing her back. "You just order up a roast beef sandwich or potato pancakes or whatever the hell y'all eat over here from room service, and I'll be back soon for round two."

"You better," and she put some flutter in her lids while she locked her hand around my johnson, sliding her grip up and down its growing length. But I had the cravings so bad I didn't let her finish and left her snug under the blankets and me flicking icicles off my nose.

"What?" came a voice from inside the apartment after I knocked on number 435 a second time.

"Ian said I was cool." That was the name Mariah told me to give.

"Did he now?" I didn't hear any feet scuffling.

I felt like hitting the door with the blunt end of my fist to let him know I wasn't fuckin' around but didn't want to jump wrong on turf I was clearly out of my element in. "Look here, I don't want to conduct my business in the street." The pensioner was still glaring at me. She wasn't going nowhere until I did.

"Who did you say?"

Fuck. "Ian, what I talk like I got feathers in my mouth? Open this mothafuckah up, man, c'mon on. I got the cheddah," I spat close to the wood. "Got dollars if you want."

The door hinged back. "Oh, well, that's different then, isn't it?"

I couldn't see much of the room beyond and didn't much care. I pushed through if only to keep the old girl from giving me more of her vulture's stare. She was getting on my nerves, which were already, at that point, about to shoot out of my pores, tingling as my sweat dripped over their raw ends.

"You a long way from home, my brother."

"You ain't never lied." The one who'd opened the door was lanky with a dainty potbelly like you saw on cats who liked their apple pop tarts too much. He wore a pullover shirt and pants made out of cotton so goddamn thin I wondered how he didn't freeze his nuts off when he went out in them. He was barefoot but had on a plaid snap-brim hat pulled low over longish hair.

"And you're in need, yeah?"

"That's right." We'd each taken a step back from the other. I knew I could take his skinny ass, just like I knew it wasn't only me and homeboy in this crib. Which wasn't jacked up, no holes in the wall, the furniture, while there wasn't much of it, wasn't busted up and there were no panes missing from the windows. There was even a TV on low with that big-headed Al Gore on it answering questions about him getting his campaign for the Dems nomination underway.

"So what is it you want, sir?" He smiled, lifting his chin some even though he was pretty much my height.

I was holding a few folded bills. "What I want is some crack."

He cocked his head to one side.

"But I'll settle for some snow," I said, putting a finger to the side of my nose and sniffing. Mariah had explained to me that rock cocaine wasn't that big over here like it was in London, but that I should be able to purchase some flake. I figured at the hotel, I could find some ammonia and cook it down to the shit I wanted.

"Ah, well, you've come to the right place, my American friend." He made to take the money from my hand.

"Don't play me for no chump," I said, holding onto them Benjamins like I was guarding grandma's teeth.

He snapped his fingers. "Right, you are. Barbara," he said, adjusting his hat. To my left, where I guess the bedroom was, a thick-shouldered but pretty in a rough way chick with dirty blonde hair stepped into the doorway. She had on tight jeans and a loose shirt, heavy boots on her feet. She jiggled a plastic baggie with a measure of white stuff in it. Maybe she figured I'd make like rover and start panting. Did I look that messed up?

"Hello," she said, being too friendly.

"Hi yourself." The way I was positioned, I could drop her boyfriend with a kick and spin and catch Barbara just right on the jaw. Between the two of them, she'd be the one to give me trouble. She didn't move, and neither did he. Fuck it.

I walked toward her, one hand out and the other extending the bills. Mariah had told me I should be able to get a hit for roughly forty-five American. She took the money and gave me the shit. I opened the bag, worried the powder was more yellow than white. I sampled a taste on my pinkie, my face scrunching up.

"This is heroin."

"Yeah, what of it?"

"Did I say I wanted H?"

"Look, Sonny Jim, that's the way it is, yeah? You come for your high, get mellow as you rugged inner-city types say, and we've accommodated." The dude was peddlin' backward, no doubt to fetch his persuader.

I was hurtin', but I wasn't gonna be bitched up, especially by some foreigners. Naw, that kind of shit don't happen to me. "Give me back my scratch. We ain't got a deal." I tossed the bag on a chair.

"We're not Dunnes, understand? All sales final." The chick stood her ground, ready to throw down. She squinted at me.

"You're that hard man, aren't ya? The one that was mouthin' off on the telly last night about how you'd come to the land of Lucky Charms to show us how to play real football."

Usually, I got a twang in my dick when a broad recognized me. Not tonight. "My money, huh?"

"You say he's famous?" the man said, now positioned next to a low cabinet with a lamp on it. "On a team, is he?"

"Yeah," she said, her tongue cavorting. "And he used to be something over in the states."

"Still am, baby." Now, these mothafuckahs were clownin' me.

"Right, he's worth something to somebody." The man said as he whipped open that cabinet's door and reached inside for his gat. I'd already turned, stepped, and leaped. I plowed into him, and we knocked the lamp over, breaking it apart and making the room shadowy. The chick was also in motion, and she jumped on my back, rockin' and sockin'.'

"Spence, for fuck's sake, get him down," she hollered as I bent my arm back and got it around her neck, and threw Barbara off me and into her boyfriend. Problem was she wasn't without reflexes, and she'd grabbed hold of me and took me with her. It was like some kind of fucked up Abbott and Costello movie with the three of us wrasslin' and yankin' on each other.

I got a grip on Spence's upper arm to keep him from planting that piece, which wasn't much of one, in my grill while Broomhilda rode me like Laffit Pincay and punched me good in the lower back and the kidneys. I pushed back to the wall to put my weight on Barbara and still had to keep a grip on Spence. I managed to tag him with an uppercut, jarring his eyeballs in their sockets.

"Come on, be fair. We'll share what we make on you," the blonde said.

I couldn't figure out whether to laugh or cry. Wasn't no cone in the NFL or Pop Warner, for that matter 'bout to put together a buffalo nickel to ransom my sorry self. We tumbled to the floor, all tangled up.

I was socking Spence again, who was straddling me, but, home girl, who was underneath me, got her arm around my neck and hammer-locked the shit out of my Adam's apple. I had to let go of the man, and he crashed the muzzle of his gun down against my temple. But like I said, it wasn't much of a gun; it was a derringer, like what Jim West used to pop out of his sleeve to scare Dr. Loveless shitless in reruns of *The Wild, Wild, West* TV show.

For a hot minute, the black lights had me, but I couldn't let 'em. I couldn't

"That's it," I heard her say as if she were deep in the ground below me. "Put him under."

Spence clubbed at my head again, but I got my shoulder up, and that took most of the blow. I drove an elbow into her ribcage, and that got her gasping and sputtering. I shook loose from Barbara and came up, arms wrapped around Spence and taking him over in a tackle. I was quick enough that by the time he tried to level his pea shooter, the back of his head made contact, loudly, with the thin carpet on the floor, dazing him.

Girlfriend got her arms around my legs and put her choppers into me like my thigh was prime rib. "Fuck," I screamed and used my fist like a club to work at the base of her neck. That got her jaw open, and I straight right crossed homegirl, making blood spray.

Spence fired his derringer, but I'd grabbed the hefty chick for a shield, and he'd pulled his aim up, shooting the ceiling. We were still on the floor, and I lashed out with my foot, catching him just right alongside his cheek. He bowled over and shoving the woman away, I jumped on Spence and commenced to wail on him like he stole from my baby's mama. He lay still and I got up, putting the derringer in my pocket. That toy wasn't much of a threat.

"Come on," I said to her, a jagged piece of the busted lamp steady on her eyeball.

"You gonna have your way with me?" There didn't seem to be a lot of fear in her voice. Maybe Barbara, the blonde, sized me up to be a replacement for Spence.

She got off the floor, and I made her give me their stash. It was H and some marijuana. I had a plane to catch tomorrow afternoon, and what was the chance I'd be able to parlay this stuff into the coke I needed before then? Fuck it, though. They had to offer decent recompense for inconveniencing me. I fooled with the idea of doing Barbara, big-legged women had serious effects on me. She was giving me that look. Of course, there was Mariah waiting for me at the hotel, and the chronic would cut some of my hype. I mean, pussy was pussy...

"Well, shall we, sport?" She started unbuttoning her shirt. I watched a thin trail of sweat dribble between her braless breasts. She smiled, showing overlapping teeth.

I uppercut her, dropping her like a sack of cement. "I can't shake the feeling that you'd slip a blade between my ribs just for fun."

I left her blinking at me, sitting on the floor. I stepped over the beaten Spence and left with my plastic bag of thrills. I got back to the hotel. The fight and fatigue had spent some of my craving. With a little weed, some blasts of the scotch I'd bought earlier, and hopefully mucho head from my visitor, that should keep me tight.

"Darlin'," she said. She was lying down, a patch of light across her form from the slightly open door to the bathroom.

"They didn't have any crack."

"Oh, don't give out. Come over here, and I'll make it up to you." She squirmed, that gorgeous ass waiting for me to do something to it.

"You better."

I was slipping my shoes off when she came from beneath the covers. The gun she had on me was right proper, as they say over here. Not at all like that pop gun of Spence's

"That's the lad." She got out of bed, fully dressed. She grabbed the shit I'd brought back, me sitting there frowning on the end of the bed watching her, the gun dead on me.

"I'd hoped those eejits would get froggish. I think the term is, right, baby? Try to cheat me, would they?"

"And what would have happened if they'd jammed me up?"

She patted my face, doing a kissy thing with her lips. "I had no such worries. You're too much of a stud to let them do that."

She was at the door, looking back, halfway into the empty hallway. "I told you I'd been following your career, Zelmont. I knew all about your problems with drugs, how you got exiled over here. And like all of you pampered sportsmen, you can't imagine a woman not swooning because you have sleek muscles and a lovely dick. Which you do have, darling. I must give you that. You did live up to your reputation."

"And for being stupid."

"No. I'd say you're too much a slave of your own base desires. That's going to get you in real trouble someday, love, if you're not careful. But for my purposes, you were certainly the man for the job." She left, closing the door quietly behind her.

I curled up on top of the bed, the crack crawlies convulsing my body. I downed half the dam bottle of booze and sweated it out as fast as I took it in. Somewhere around six in the morning I got to sleep and at nine I woke up and couldn't get my eyes shut anymore. I cleaned up and was ready when the bus came to get us for the airport.

Walking through the facility, I spotted a dude reading a *Time* magazine. There was an article about an expansion football team starting up in Los Angeles called the Barons. LA hadn't had a pro team since the Raiders left. Now, that was something. Maybe I had one more chance at the bright lights, just one more shot. Could be last night was a kind of warning.

Get it together, Zee, and there could be the roaring crowds and sweet honey again, the smack talkin' interviews on ESPN, and the million-dollar endorsement deals pimping glorified grape juice. Yeah, shit yeah. I was going to show Mariah and all of them I was the man for the job. Shit.

* * *

"The Man for the Job," *Dublin Noir: The Celtic Tiger vs. The Ugly American,* Akashic, 2006, Ken Bruen, editor.

II

BAD JUJU

The Investor

The three walked through the refrigerated rear section of Limoli's Quality Cuts, passing hung sides of beef and pork. Past the carcasses, Jill McCory turned her head at the whine of a band saw. One of the butchers was cutting into a slab to make individual ribs for barbecuing. She grinned weakly at her boyfriend, Reny Paulski, and he squeezed her hand for reassurance. Tal Shanko, the third member of the trio who walked behind the other two, continued to scan the surroundings, his face impassive. They cleared the work area, and to their right was a set of swing doors with smeared windows they went through.

"What can I get you guys?" the pleasant and pretty twenty-something woman who greeted them asked. She was dressed in low-rise, hip-hugger jeans and a light-weight sweater top with a modest neckline. She was fit, no muffin effect of fat flopping over her pants' waistline. It was warm in this part of the shop. Seen through her tangle of dark brown hair, one of her ears had several silver studs of differing styles.

"Nothing, we're fine," McCory said.

"I'd like coffee if you have it," Shanko countered. "Black, please."

McCory turned in profile to show him her annoyance.

Paulski worked his jaw muscles but remained silent.

"Sure," their greeter said. "Right this way." She turned and walked to a closed unmarked, grey-colored door. She opened it and said, "They're here," to the two men sitting inside the office. She stepped aside, and the trio entered.

The inauspicious office was of the home improvement store wood-panel variety complete with framed reproductions of race horses and a LeRoy Neiman print of the Foreman-Frazier fight in Kingston, Jamaica in 1973. There was also a flat-screen TV mounted on a wall.

Joe Gentenilli sat behind the sole desk in the room, and he looked from the man sitting across from him, Rafe Barata, to the three who stood. His eyes momentarily rested on Shanko as he noted the other man regarding the Neiman work.

"You into boxing?" Gentenilli asked.

"I like it fine," Shanko said flatly. The young woman returned with the coffee in a Styrofoam cup and handed it to him. "Thanks." He took a sip and looked at McCory who they'd agreed would lead the negotiation. Given there were only two chairs in the room, and those seats were occupied, it didn't seem to him the two others in the room expected a meeting of give-and-take. He was right.

"Mr. Gentenilli," McCory began. "We want to work out an understanding on this biodiesel matter. It's not now or in the future our intent to cut into your rendering business." She smiled thinly, making a gesture with her hand. "There's plenty of grease for everybody."

"That some kind of ethnic slur?" Barata cracked, pointing at her. He had a diamond ring on his little finger and another gaudy ring on the finger next to it. There was a heavy gold link bracelet around his thick wrist.

McCory frowned. "Of course not."

"Just funnin' you, girly," Barata chuckled. He was a heavyset man in his fifties, and he shifted his bulk in the over-sized chair. It creaked.

Paulski touched McCory's arm, a signal for her not to react to the remark. He said, "Okay, we came here at your invitation to work this out, not get into trading barbs."

"Then how do we keep you off the street?" Gentenilli said in an even tone.

"What?" McCory said.

Gentenilli went on, "You started out a couple of years ago collecting grease, for free, I note, from the shops not in our association. Donut and fast-food chains around here," he tapped his index finger on the desk.

"We get our used grease from all over," Paulski corrected. "Even over in

New Hampshire."

"Whatever," Gentenilli said with a curt chop of his hand through the air. "The fact remains you were, but it was just converting the stuff for your own use in your cars. Fine. But now, all of a sudden, you got people talking about manufacturing biodiesel."

"You're not," Shanko pointed out.

"Who are you?" Barata said, moving his heft around again, aiming his jowls at the interloper.

Shanko said, "An investor." He had more of his coffee. He liked the brew. It was good coffee.

"That's what I'm talking about," Gentenilli said. "Now you're making some kind of Mother Earth-friendly heating furnace, that it?"

"Yes," McCory said. "We're concerned about the environment."

"We're concerned about our environment, too," Gentenilli quipped. "Our economic one, understand?"

"I'm not following you," McCory said. "Ultimately, what we're doing is going to be good for your business and our business. On average, something like two-point-four million gallons of fuel oil are consumed each winter in the New England area. You have contracts to collect the grease, and you turn around and sell what you render. We're trying to make and market a new type furnace that can utilize a heating oil with a greater percentage of biodiesel content since traditional furnaces aren't designed to handle that kind of fuel."

"Fact is we're creating a market," Paulski added.

"See, that's the problem," Gentenilli said, glancing at Barata. "We're forward thinkers, too."

"Exactly," Barata echoed.

Paulski made a face. "You're going to make furnaces?"

Gentenilli looked aghast at such a prospect. "Hell no."

"They're setting a bad example, that it?" Shanko said.

"You're who again?" Barata challenged. McCory and Paulski were in their early thirties; Barata and Gentenilli, in their fifties. It was hard to tell about the compact, loose-limbed Shanko. His grey-white hair was brush cut precise, his boots scuffed and weathered. He could have been forty-five or he could have been sixty and then some.

His expression remained staid, and he didn't respond as he enjoyed more of his coffee.

"My father and Tal were," Paulski began.

"Friends," Shanko finished.

"Listen, we don't have a problem with you three being jolly green or whatever the hell you call it," Gentenilli said, leaning forward. "But for all concerned, it would probably be better if you maybe saved the trees some other way."

Paulski and McCory exchanged glances. "You can't threaten us," she said.

"I didn't hear no threats," Barata said as if testifying on the stand. "Who the fuck is threatening?"

"This is simply a conversation about business," Gentenilli added. "Colleagues, I note."

"Well, we're not doing anything wrong or interfering with you," McCory said.

Gentenilli looked at her blandly. "Appreciate you coming," he said.

McCory started to respond, but Shanko cut her off. "Thanks for the coffee." He walked over to the desk. Though there was a waste basket next to it, he placed his empty cup on the desk. Gentenilli and Barata glared at him. Shanko turned and walked back to the younger couple.

"Let's go," Shanko advised. The three departed the Quality Cuts office.

"So what the hell was that all about?" Paulski asked when they were walking to their van parked on a pay lot. Painted on its side in stylish letters were the words, "Maple Leaf Furnace Factory.'" Leaning on the "Y" was an anthropomorphic smiling turtle holding a wrench resting on the shoulder area of its shell. They got in the Toyota van and drove away.

McCory nodded toward Shanko. "What Tal said. The way they see it, if we're successful, then others might be inspired to use the mainstream framework, imitate us."

"So?" Paulski said.

"We're collecting the grease for free, Reny," McCory said.

Paulski came to a red light. The French fry smell from the converted van's tailpipe tantalized pedestrians in the crosswalk as they passed by the vehicle. "Oh, right," he muttered. Across from them was the partially finished shell of a mixed-use development in what had been redubbed the Newmarket District by the tony crowd, but was still called the Meat Market by old schoolers and the boyos in Boston.

Paulski continued when the light changed, and he drove forward. "They get a certain price for the rendered grease and want it to stay that way. More green tech means less demand for their services and their product."

"Yes," McCory agreed. She glanced back at Shanko. "But we're the small dogs when it comes to WVO." She used the shorthand for waste vegetable oil as this was how the used oil was referred to by the enviros. She and Paulski had rehearsed not to use jargon at the meet.

"They reached out," Shanko noted. "They wanted to send a message."

Paulski said, "Going green is getting co-opted like everything else in this country, Tal. These old-time castoffs from bad mafia movies can't hold that back. Gangster capitalism is always absorbed into white collar capitalism."

"Usually not without casualties," Shanko observed quietly. McCory grimaced.

* * *

The following week, Lilly Densmore, who attended MIT to study mechanical engineering and worked part-time at the Maple Leaf Furnace Factory, was driving in Somerville after making a repair call. She'd driven out in the company van to recalibrate a dual set of their furnaces installed in a lamp and lamp parts supply warehouse. She was listening to a Massive Attack CD when she turned off Middlesex Avenue, heading back to the shop, and slammed on her brakes. A red child's wagon suddenly rolled into the roadway in front of her. The car behind her also had to brake hard and slammed into the van's rear bumper. A toolbox flopped over and noisily spilled its contents.

"Aw, shit," Densmore swore. She looked back and then got out of the van.

The other driver was out, too.

"What the hell, huh?" the other driver, a tallish man in a shirt and tie, said. He still felt the warmth of his Benz's heated interior even though the temperature was in the mid-twenties.

"It wasn't me," Densmore said, pointing toward the front of the van. She looked around for kids playing but didn't see any. She walked over to the wagon, and her eyes got wide. She said "Shit" again.

In the bed of the wagon was a large turtle on its back with a hunting knife plunged through its underside.

* * *

Two weeks after this incident, the Maple Leaf Furnace Factory, a former bicycle sales and repair converted storefront near Cambridge Square, was firebombed. Two potential customers, a lesbian couple who owned and operated a sandwich shop, were being shown the company's new industrial furnace. A man in a winter coat and gloves entered. He was a bland-looking individual with thinning brown-blonde hair and glasses.

"Be right with you," McCory said to him, talking to the sandwich shop owners. She was the only staffer there.

The man shouted, "Take the hint, cunt." He took his gloved hand out of his pocket and threw a grenade-shaped device onto the floor. This exploded in sparks and flame as he ran out. McCory, fearful the heat would ignite the biodiesel fuel in its metal drums in the rear equipment and processing area of the shop, dashed for the fire extinguisher.

One of the other women, who'd been taking Muay Thai, mixed martial arts lessons, ran after the arsonist. She didn't get a chance to test her skill but did get a partial plate number as he left in a new, dark-red Cadillac CTS coupe driven by another man.

Inside the shop, McCory got the fire out before the fuel went up. Later, after the fire department had come and gone and there was a conversation with the insurance carrier, she and Reny Paulski talked matters over at their apartment. They sat at their kitchenette table.

"Aren't we being hypocrites, Jill?" Paulski rubbed his jaw with a calloused palm.

"'Cause we're tree huggers, we're just supposed to pucker up and take it?"

"I'm just sayin'." He smiled weakly. She put a hand on his. "I know."

Though hesitant to do so, the couple decided to call Tal Shanko, the major investor in the Maple Leaf Furnace Factory.

* * *

"The fuck is this?" Robert "Squid" Sparda mumbled when he came out of the Pink Slipper strip club on Bower Road in Quincy. He'd gotten a blow job in the VIP Room, so was in good humor. Now propped on the windshield of his dark red Cadillac CTS coupe was a teddy bear. Had one of the girls in the club left it? He picked it up and could see a note card attached to the stuffed animal. Curious, he read it: "I got this for you to snuggle with, faggot. Leave the kids alone."

Shaking the teddy bear in his hand, wondering what hump would have the nerve to have left this, he then noticed his four tires were slit. Roiling inside, cold air hissing from his flaring nostrils, Squid Sparda twisted the bear's head off. The thing exploded with a flash and a bang, temporarily blinding him. The stuffed toy also released a dye pack like what was used by banks to booby-trap their canvas money bags. Purple ink was sprayed on his face and expensive, camel-hair coat, ruining it.

"Motherfucker," Sparda screamed, stomping and groping about on the icy slush coating the parking lot. He lost his footing and went down hard on his backside. He continued to swear and promise reprisals.

* * *

"The girl," Barata was saying, "we don't know much about. Hell, there's a half a dozen McCory's up and down this block. But one of the old soldiers over at the hall told our guy this Paulski is the kid of Mike Paulski from the boiler-maker's local."

Gentenilli asked, "Paulski, the father, I mean. He around?"

"Naw, he made enough on the Big Dig to retire, him and the second, younger wife, not the kid's mother. Someplace out in California is the way I heard it."

Considering this, Gentenilli sipped his coffee and brandy. Since the exploding teddy bear the day before with Squid Sparda, the Maple Leaf Furnace Factory was closed and secured. The two young proprietors had not been seen around there or at the apartment they shared in Dorchester.

"The tough guy, the one that inked Squid," Barata began, aware of the irony, "we got squat. He ain't from around here, but the Paulski kid says he was friends with his dad."

"Yeah," momentarily, Gentenilli worried his bottom lip.

"Must be some California connection."

"Must be," Barata agreed. "You want Squid and Dink to make a house call?"

Gentenilli had more of his spiked coffee. "Do that. Mike Paulski needs to be reminded how things work. He can set his kid straight."

Barata nodded quickly and got busy on his cell phone. The chair creaked under him as he moved his bulk.

* * *

"Place don't look like I figured," Squid Sparda remarked, looking out the passenger side of the rented Lexus. The dang Jap car had more legroom than he'd imagined.

"Look at that one," Francis "Dink" Hullson said behind the wheel, nodding in the direction of another McMansion. "Swank," he monotoned, admiring a large home on a small lot that looked to be a mélange of French Chateau and Cape Cod in design. Two Priuses, white and black, sat side-by-side in the driveway. A bumper sticker on one of the cars read: "Stop the War," though wasn't specific about which one or whose.

"This town wasn't even on the goddamn map we got from the airport," Sparda said. They'd flown into San Francisco International and knew from the internet to drive to Redding. From there, they got directions at a café to Northpitch, some seventy miles to the west of Redding. "But it looks like they got money around here. Is this where actors or those computer fucks are moving to or something like that?"

Dink Hullson, more contemplative than his fellow soldier Sparda, said, "I don't think that's it."

"Well, it's something." He looked at the paper again, the one with the address they'd obtained from their guy at the union with Mike Paulski's address on it. This was where he received his pension checks. He pointed, "Here's the street." Hullson made a right, and the two found themselves on a cul-de-sac. At its end was a modest abode, at least by comparison to the other houses they'd seen. There was a worn pick-up truck parked in front.

Hullson parked the rental in the empty driveway, and the two got out and walked to the front door. Sparda knocked. He'd used various face creams and astringents and had managed to fade the dye splotch on his face and neck. But there was still enough color on his skin that it looked like a runaway birthmark.

At first, there was no answer, and he knocked again. A male voice from inside said, "Come on in."

Sparda grinned wolfishly at Hullson and entered the house. The aluminum bat swung by Tal Shanko went right across Sparda's chest, knocking the wide-eyed hoodlum back. Before he could recover, Shanko stepped forward from where he'd positioned himself beside the doorway. He whacked the end of the bat on the side of Sparda's jaw, cracking the bone in two places.

"Christ," Sparda exclaimed as he went sideways, stumbling into and upsetting a stand with a vase of freshly cut fire witch and sunflowers in it.

Dink Hullson had stepped back out of the way and now had his gun in hand. He shot twice at Shanko, who, upon seeing he hadn't knocked Sparda into him as he'd intended, had run and dived through an interior open doorway.

"Get up," Hullson blared, reaching his free hand out and helping Sparda to his feet.

"Cocksucker," Sparda said, putting a shaking hand to his damaged jaw.

"Worry about that later," Hullson advised, already heading the way Shanko had gone. "We gotta get this civilian."

Sparda followed, and the two went through a study outfitted in the latest in-home entertainment gadgets, including a video game paused on the flat-screen TV. A lone controller rested on the coffee table before the screen. The game was something about knights and fire-breathing dragons, they noted absently.

The two soldiers went through a large kitchen with an island to spot an open back door. This let them out onto a deck containing a built-in barbeque grill and uncovered hot tub. There was also a small guest house at the far end of the thick green yard, bordered by a cinder block wall.

"Where is that bastard?" Sparda had his gun out as well. The anticipation of inflicting painful revenge on his attacker ameliorated his own agony.

Hullson made his way toward the guest house. Sparda fell in beside him. Behind them was a splash, and they both turned toward the hot tub but saw no one in the water. In contrast to back east, the temperature was in the high '70s. They eased closer, the idea having come to them that maybe Mr. Baseball was hiding under the water. Closer, they saw several avocados floating in the hot tub. They looked up to the leafy branches of an avocado tree overhanging from another yard.

"Fucking Californians and their goddamn vegetables," Sparda said, talking, causing him to wince.

Hullson didn't correct him that avocados were considered a fruit. As one, they turned and rushed to the guest house, using their shoulders and body weight to crash through the light-weight door. They could see where Shanko had gone through a rear sliding glass window over the bed. He'd moved the bed aside and had climbed on a chair to reach the opening.

"Fucking guy," Sparda muttered between tight lips. One side of his face was swelling.

On the chair looking out, Hullson saw that the guest house butted against a portion of the back wall. Beyond was an open field where several abandoned and rusted hulks of farm machinery resided. Oddly, the grassy field was tended and not overgrown, though it seemed the useless equipment had been purposely left in place. To his left, heading for a stand of trees, he spotted Shanko's retreating form. He ran at a steady clip. Hullson described what he'd seen to Sparda as they exited the guest house.

"He's like sixty or something, isn't he?" Sparda remarked as they saw a way to the field between the houses once they were out in front. "Probably eats that damn tofu and shit," he said derisively. "Motherfuckin' rabbit."

Hullson wondered what else they didn't know about this Shanko but kept it to himself. They took off for the field on foot. There was no way to take the car in there as it was hemmed in mostly by low mountains.

"At least it isn't snowing like back home," Sparda whispered as the two entered the leafy area. He could barely open his mouth over clenched teeth. Where they were wasn't so much a forest as it was trees sparsely separated and a lot of brush. There was a distinct aroma in the air.

"Hey, that's weed," Sparda declared quietly.

"That's what it is about this town," Hullson said in a low voice. "All those damn new big houses around here."

Sparda snickered, then grimaced due to his jaw. "Everybody's in pocket around here."

Hullson glanced sideways at his partner. "That's what I'm worried about."

The two continued their search, heading in a direction toward the mountains. The smell of flowering pot plants intensified. Walking several paces apart, Hullson paused at a sound to his flank. He held up a hand and pointed for Sparda's benefit. They went through the undergrowth and came to a series of razor wire fencing enclosing a cultivated field of crops neither foot soldier could identify. Though they knew the squat plantings weren't marijuana.

Suddenly, a German shepherd appeared on that side of the fence, barking at them.

Sparda stuck his gun out at the dog. "Shut the hell up," he lisped.

His footfalls on the dry fallen leaves and brush masked by the barking dog, Shanko came within the orbit of the two men quickly. He brought the bat down full force on Sparda's gun arm. Shanko broke his wrist, and

Sparda yelped as he let go of his piece. Hullson was about to shoot him, but Shanko had pulled free the mouth of a soaked paper bag tucked under his belt.

He threw it underhanded smack into the gunman's face. Hullson shot his gun, but his vision was blocked, and he missed the fleeing Shanko as he gagged. There were cow droppings in the burst bag, and some of the waste had gone into his mouth.

The logo of a fast-food outlet was on the paper bag.

Sparda held his damaged wrist as Hullson spat and wiped at his mouth using tufts of grass he plucked from the ground. "I'm going to kill that comedian," he grumbled.

Squid Sparda picked up his gun with his left hand. If he didn't hurt so much, he would have laughed at Hullson. Instead, he asked, "Now where?"

The dog sat on its haunches, looking quizzically at them, then got up and trotted away.

"Anywhere," Hullson angrily replied, still wiping at himself. He went in a direction, and Sparda joined him. They weren't in control, clearly on someone else's playground, and the unease of the situation bothered both men. A moroseness descended on them. Sparda was used to Hullson being dour, but he found it a gigantic drag.

"Maybe we should hold up, get ourselves cleaned up and what have you, and call in reinforcements. We got friends in the Bay Area."

Hullson put glittering eyes on him. "No goddamn old hippie is gonna get the best of me." He stomped forward.

* * *

Back in deep brush again, the two heard the whine of an engine, but then it cut off.

"Was that a motorcycle?" Sparda muttered.

Hullson kept quiet and alert. They came out of the brush and into a clearing. Around them were the stumps of cut trees, and the smell of fresh wood permeated the air stronger than the essence of pot plants. The two gaped at the structure before them. It was as if they'd stepped onto a new Las Vegas-themed destination.

"That's the Raj Hall," Sparda said. "Taj Mahal," Hullson corrected. "Yeah, like the one in Atlantic City."

Hullson, splattered feces drying on his face and sports coat, glared at Sparda. "That's a casino with a few minarets in front. This looks like the one from the pictures."

Before them was a modified replica, down to the reflecting pool leading to it, of the famed 17th-century architecturally arresting mausoleum in Agra, India. The building before them was four stories high. There was scaffolding framing the central structure, and several ATVs and pick-ups were parked about the area. Nearby, the two could see several cottages mirroring the main building's style, with other sections marked off in the dirt with wooden stakes and twine.

"Some kind of resort," Hullson guessed.

No workers could be seen or heard. The nearly finished faux Taj Mahal and the stonework bordering the reflecting pool gleamed bright white in the sunlight. This copy, with its dome minarets and wall engravings, was concrete and stucco rather than the marble of the original.

"I don't like this," Sparda said. Everything on him ached, and he wanted a drink.

"Too late now," Hullson said, heading toward the front.

Standing at the entrance before a set of carved double doors, Sparda wondered, "Maybe we're supposed to say open sesame."

Hullson snorted, then looked wide-eyed when the doors swung inward. He and Sparda raised their guns on Tal Shanko standing in the darkened interior, his hands on the door handles.

His composed features gave them pause. Shanko smiled crookedly. The two representatives from Boston looked around at the sound of splashing, like at the hot tub. Only this time, it was not an innocuous occurrence. Emerging from hiding in the reflecting pool were three individuals, two men and one woman. They wore snorkeling masks and breathing tubes and aimed assault rifles at the two North Shore mob emissaries.

"Fuck me," Sparda managed, his jaw so swollen, one of his eyes was shut.

"I want it categorically understood I'm not happy with this."

"I know, Joe," Vincent "Swan" Argostino said. He broke off a piece of one of the chocolate chip cookies on the saucer and chewed it slowly, contemplatively. "But this decision is bigger than you or me." He sipped some of his espresso. The two sat at a small table in the Golden Strike Bowling Supply and Trophy concern in Charlestown.

"What kind of message are we sending here?" Gentenilli said.

"That we're not about to commit time and resources over bullshit." He had another bite of his cookie.

"I'm just sayin', is all."

"Look, weed is a money maker." He pointed out beyond the walls. We don't grow it, but every damn mook under forty around here smokes it, plus you got the aging whatchucall Baby Boomers toking, too. All through the New England area.

"I don't need to remind you," he added, breaking off more cookie, "it's not an enterprise we get any action off of. Yet."

"That means getting in bed with Shanko? He's reached out, hasn't he?" Gentenilli said.

"It means since the FBI patted themselves on the back for running that scumbag snitch Whitey Bulger out of town, we've been sitting sweet. We don't need the DEA or any other government alphabet running around sniffing up our asses."

Gentenilli wasn't quite sure how to interpret that, but he was clear he was to lay off the little shits of the Maple Leaf Furnace Factory. He'd also been informed that Tal Shanko was a player among the pot growers of the so-called Emerald Triangle, the area encompassing parts of Humboldt and Mendocino Counties of Northern California. Marijuana was a business earning millions. And the man sitting across from him, Sawn Argostino, was an underboss who liked earners—and the potential therein to earn.

"I suppose then I gotta accept this…peace," Gentenilli relented. "Dink is, well, Dink. But Squid, you know."

"He's not to be a problem," Argostino declared. Gentenilli spread his hands. "He won't be."

Argostino finished his espresso. Gentenilli left. A sudden shift in the wind made him look around quickly as he stepped to his car. A hint of burning marijuana had come and gone and made him leery. The other thing he'd learned about Shanko was he'd been in Vietnam, one of these crazy bastards they called tunnel rats. Soldiers sent down into smelly and scary Viet Cong tunnels after Army engineers blasted them out—their thankless tasks to clear them out. Never knowing when a spike was going to spear you in the eye or get gut shot in that crawl space, bleeding out while Charlie hacked your balls off for fun.

Fuck, Gentenilli reflected. Shit like that did something to your outlook. Mike Paulski had been in 'Nam, too, though just a grunt. But that's where he'd met Tal Shanko. They'd been in the same platoon, it turned out.

Frowning about Shanko, about how he could have killed his soldiers but didn't so as not to escalate the situation but made it plain he could have, got Gentenilli muttering.

"I note this fucking guy is going to be a real pain one day." He drove away, a light flurry starting up, dusting his car pristine white.

* * *

"The Investor," *Damn Near Dead 2: Live Noir or Die Trying,*
Busted Flush Press, 2010, Bill Crider, editor.

The Snow Birds

Now, one time, it comes on Thanksgiving or rather two days prior, and we were standing on the sidelines in the midst of our permutating as the Silver Slicers of Bowler Street went at the Cruze Cru of Avenue J. Sidelines is a relative term when it comes to street polo as it was of necessity that we and the other onlookers had to, at times, quickly move about to avoid say a smashed toe or bruised shin. The lads and lasses zoomed back and forth, to and fro, on their steeds of battered alloy, whacking the bejeezus out of a croquet ball with their homemade plastic mallets while adroitly slaloming their bikes, most of the time barely sluicing past one another, on the field of play.

We stood upon a one-time overgrown lot that had been the graveyard for discarded refrigerators, accessories from chopped Benzs and Mustangs, hype needles, and used condoms. Now, it was a cleared, leveled, and green cityscape upon which the various organized and loosely affiliated street polo teams competed and honed their skills.

"Watch out, fool," a youngster who went by Droop intoned as he rambled past on his bike.

Droop was not so heady into the contest that he would address us in that manner. Oh, no, we had more stature than that. He was keenly aware that such temerity would earn him a stern rap across the knuckles, or some other part of his body, from my companion.

I, of course, am not referring to Li'l Vet, whose feline-like indifference to most matters physical and psychological is renowned, but to the other member of our trio, one Laticome Malloy Burris affectionately known in our environs as the Sour Apple Kid. The sobriquet, having arisen from when he was no more than a mere crumb snatcher ambling about the numbers emporium, his dear old widowed mom maintained— hidden behind a false basement wall no less—to the delight of its neighborhood patrons. Even as a little shaver when he helped her keep track of who was betting what number, graduating from writing this pertinent information on flash paper to retaining the various bets in his voracious memory, he sucked on sour apple candy. And to this day he has continued that avocation.

Droop bore toward the goal then suddenly back-pedaled furiously, as these bikes they rode are termed fixed gear, no brakes. Simultaneously, he swung that mallet with a Tiger Woods-like élan and drove the ball through the truck tire that had been cut in half and stuck partway into the ground to form an arch.

"Ye-hah. What's my motherlovin' name, chump?" Droop trash-talked his opponent again, named Mando, belittling his inadequate defense.

Mando did not take this jest in the spirit of sportsmanship in which it had been delivered. He lashed out with a foot, scuffing one of his new kicks, a classic Chuck, against Droop's chest. At this juncture I'd be remiss if I didn't mention that there was an ongoing riff between the two as, one might suspect, it involved a dame. In this case, it was a lovely young woman named Annakosta, who'd come this close to gracing the pages of a King magazine thong special.

Subsequently, she dropped Mando for Droop. To her, Mando had not demonstrated proper commiseration when she, sniffling and teary-eyed, recounted to him how she'd lost the opportunity to expose her wondrous backside to the paid, and significant pass-around circulation, of said publication. King was not called the illest men's magazine ever, for nothing. And so there it was.

The two were aloft on their bikes, maintaining their balance as they squared off against each other while their respective teammates urged them to take their beef elsewhere. There was, after all, a game afoot.

The Sour Apple Kid looked from the potential dust up to me. "We'll vamp on the shipment tonight. There'll be four refrigerated bobtail Kenworths."

He took a toke, then passed the blunt to me, the pungent contents packed into a cherry-vanilla-flavored wrap. Despite partaking, The Kid was alert, seemingly no worse for wear after his redeye flight arriving from Miami this morning.

"That's a quality truck," Li'l Vet ventured.

"Indeed," I concurred, inhaling and passing the joystick to him.

Out on the field, the polo match had resumed. Mando had ridden away to be replaced by a chap we all called Ferengi because he was ugly and small, like those aliens introduced on *Star Trek: Deep Space Nine* that I enjoyed as a youngster. Droop took no pleasure in the other's departure as he knew Mando kept grudges like 'tween girls kept love letters— forever. There would be disproportionate payback or at least the attempt at such. Droop would have to be mindful, which did tend to crimp one's style when you were out on the town with your girl. It did help, though, that Annakosta, the former lady friend of the affronted Mando, knew how to handle the gat she kept in the knockoff Gucci bag she sported. Such was life here in the Tri-Quarter section of the city.

"I realize this goes without saying," I began, "but there are four trucks with two men in each and only three of us," I mentioned this knowing the Kid had certainly calculated this rudimentary math, yet I was curious as to his answer. We knew that these aforementioned rigs rolled with a driver and a guard, that both were armed with the latest in firepower and were more than happy to demonstrate their knowledge of these weapons. For these wastrels were in the employ of Sid "Dragon Eye" Ludlow, the Kid's rival in certain sundry endeavors.

Li'l Vet offered the Kid the blunt, but he eschewed any more chronic. Instead, he popped a sour apple hard candy in his mouth. He wrapped his tongue around it and illuminated, "Due to the holiday season getting underway and what with the number of drunk driving incidents from last year, there will be at least one if not two check points along the highway to town."

I was beginning to get the picture, but Li'l Vet was not quite obtaining focus. "What the fug does that have to do with our caper?" he inquired testily. Understand, Li'l Vet was not special in a special class way. But he was a meat-and-potatoes sort of guy and always strove to be one hundred percent clear on a job before undertaking his appointed tasks. That certainly made for fewer mistakes as he had never been sent to the hoosegow, and did not intend to break precedent.

The Sour Apple Kid dislodged the candy from inside his cheek to address Li'l Vet's concern. "Dragon Eye Ludlow will have his drivers take the old Windhaven Road to avoid the checkpoints." The road he spoke of was in places no more than a narrow lane that allowed for only one truck's progress at a time. Indeed some of that road wound through scenic country like a bucolic scene fronting a Get Well card you'd send your baby's mama if she had a cold or threw out her back doing a hoochie dance for a rap video.

Li'l Vet nodded his head in light of this clarification. "When those bobtails get through Linsburgh, that's where we'll hit 'em," the Kid said. Linsburgh was one of those recent suburban developments that looked like it was designed by that huckster who cranked out those syrupy sweet paintings of Smurf-like houses and landscapes. I still could not fathom why so many seemingly rational people were gaga for his stuff. To each his own for sure.

"Yes," I said, duplicating the head motion that Li'l Vet had displayed. The Kid's idea was sound. There was a piney woods section between Linsburgh and here, and it made sense to hit the trucks there. "That also means they'll be on edge, ready for an attack," I observed. I, too, liked to cover all the angles before these after-hours undertakings.

"I know," the Kid said but did not continue. Soon enough, the Silver Slicers won two out of three games, and the Kid was in a jubilant mood. For not only had he utilized his pull among the local pols to get the lot cleared for street polo, but was also a financial backer of the Slicers. That and the Cruze Cru was backed by Dragon Eye, so we interpreted our victory as an omen of things to come. Said gent was not in attendance, but a few of his lieutenants were, and they shouldered the loss morosely and silently.

These neighborhood intramural contests were a proving ground for a soon-to-be-established semi-pro league of street polo players the Kid was lining up a coterie of downtown swells to back as an athletic program for at-need youth or whatever the current in-vogue term was to describe the raga muffins from our area. The Sour Apple Kid examined all the angles and played quite a few of them in the process.

Not long hence, as the team enjoyed their pizzas and red soda water at Good Time Mary's eatery, we huddled in a rear booth reserved for the Kid, wherein he outlined the rest of the plan to us. Our lingering doubts were assuaged.

And so that night, actually around two the following morning, we were in place as a light snow flurry dusted the landscape. The wintry effect had been unexpected until the bubbly weatherwoman on the local eleven o'clock news proclaimed, "Gosh, folks, it looks like our Doppler Radar readings are showing the front has about-faced, and it's bringing parka time with it." She smiled big shiny horse teeth into the camera while dispensing this update.

I'd smiled back at her as I broke out the proper gear.

Myself, I like big-toothed women.

Dressed warmly, we were now hunkered down along either side of a bank of fresh snow. In the near distance, we heard the trucks get closer to this quiet, isolated part of the woods.

"Ready?" The Kid asked over the two-way.

"Fo' sure," Li'l Vet affirmed for he and I. As one, we adjusted our night vision goggles.

The first Kenworth rumbled past, then the second behind it. They kept a little less than a two-car length between each vehicle. As the third went past, the Sour Apple Kid rose on his side of the roadway and me on ours, and we primed and threw our homemade phosphorescent grenades. The three of us closed our eyes tight as they flared.

It goes without saying that in addition to dressing correctly, we'd also brought along the right equipment for this mission. As an example, these grenades gave off little sound but did burn with a brilliant, blinding light courtesy of ignited aluminum and magnesium particles. The attack caused the driver in the fourth truck to swerve radically and smash into a conveniently stout tree, sending the passenger slash guard's head into the cracked windshield. Seat belts. Always wear your seat belts, I say.

Eyes wide open, Li'l Vet, being a rather fleet-footed individual, popped up with his weapon and swiftly gained his position. He fired the tear gas launcher; he aimed with practiced ease. At this juncture I should mention Li'l Vet was called this not because he'd served in the military but due to his love of his pit bulls. He raised these dogs for the purposes of gaming—of the sort a certain ex-NFL quarterback was sent to prison for doing as well.

But where the QB treated his animals cruelly, Li'l Vet, for veterinarian, was the soul of compassion when it came to the ones under his wing. But a debate on the merits or lack thereof of this underground so-called sport is best reserved for a later time. The important thing here is that Li'l Vet's projectiles hit their marks.

He bombarded trucks three and cracked up four. The stuff wafted back on a gentle night breeze, seeping into the trucks' cabs. It was not tear gas he'd unleashed but knock-out stuff. Actually, that was a misnomer, as the chemical we used was an opiate in vapor form and was designed to disorient our targets. Obtained, I mention on the QT, via a prominent anesthesiologist who owed the Kid a favor for once getting his wayward daughter out of a jam.

It was my assignment to then use one of the street polo mallets to incapacitate the ruffians stumbling out of their trucks. One chap emerging from number three had his nine lose but found he couldn't pull the trigger due to the effects of the gas. I sent him to dreamland with a deft whap and tap.

The hooligans from the second truck were proving worrisome. They'd diverted their vehicle into an opening in a copse of trees and were now out of said carriage and shooting at us. Just beforehand, Li'l Vet and the Kid, utilizing the Glock his dear mom had bought him one birthday, had taken care of the driver and guard in the first truck. They lay nicked but alive and bound on the side of the road, where we also took cover.

"Your jammer on?" The Kid inquired, squeezing off a shot for effect.

"Yes," I replied, removing the instrument from my pocket and showing him its green light aglow. We'd purchased these cell phone signal jammers from a foreign country via the internet. We each had one on our person, as well as several scattered between us and our vehicle deeper in the woods.

I said, "So they can't summon reinforcements, but how do we curtail their bullet melody?"

"Yeah," Li'l Vet piped in, "even out here, we can't keep this racket up without the highway patrol or some nosy cop making an appearance."

"That is so," the Kid said, reviewing options silently. "Getting into a firefight with these mugs is bound to garner unwanted attention, let alone the chance one of us gets plugged."

I gulped at the suggestion.

"But they're between us and our whip," Li'l Vet pointed out. "So we got to get through them to get out of here."

The Sour Apple Kid then loaded a grenade in the RPG-7 he'd also brought to the party. The grenade launcher was of the variety originating in the former Eastern Bloc. The Kid won the weapon a few years ago at the conclusion of a successful poker game with some Russian mafia gentlemen of his acquaintance. He'd been holding onto it for just the right occasion.

"I propose," he announced, "we do something to get the cops here on the double." Without waiting for our vote, he crouched and fired the explosive charge not into the wooded area from where Dragon Eye's boys were bristling, but at abandoned truck number three. Words fail me on how best to convey the paroxysm of sound, light, and fury that erupted as that diesel-powered conveyance was powerfully rent asunder. Metal, wood lining, and molded plastic whooshed everywhere. Suffice it to say the three of us were knocked down by the concussive wind even as our mouths hung open.

"My, my," the Kid uttered, gaining his feet and helping me to do so as well. A singed turkey fell next to my foot. Several more turkeys and their parts rained about the landscape, and we put our arms up for protection. Fortunate, too, as we turned just in time to a groan as one of Dragon Eye's men, apparently having somehow slipped his bonds, was zeroing in on us with his heater. But it seemed a descending turkey had struck him in the head and knocked him senseless.

"Hey, look," Li'l Vet proclaimed, pointing and running over to the split-open turkey carcass that had saved at least one of our lives. He bent and then straightened up. In his hand was a blackened packet wrapped in translucent material of a familiar size and shape. A certain prepared powder trickled from a small hole in that brick, as it was nicknamed.

"Well, I'll be," The Kid said as we neared our compatriot.

"Dragon Eye Ludlow's smuggling blow in the turkeys," I announced.

The Kid inclined his head in the direction of wailing sirens. "Time to make our departure."

"Indeed," Li'l Vet agreed. We three ran to our van, the rival gunman already in the wind ahead of us, and departed. The Kid's retired mother lived out this way in a house he bought for her some years before. He'd also some time ago reconnoitered this area in case the gendarmes should happen to be chasing him, and he needed an escape route. Thus, we were able to avoid the fuzz and get back to town intact.

At light that morning the local news was filled with speculation as to what had transpired in those woods outside of Linsburgh. It was known the trucks had been stocked with frozen turkeys. There was a rumor these birds were intended to be centerpieces in a turkey dinner giveaway for the indigent and unfortunates in the Tri-Quarters section. Some of those plucked fowls, it was breathlessly added in the accounts, were stuffed not with pre-packaged giblets but Bolivian Marching Powder. The loaded turkeys were marked with a slash on the left leg.

It was further alleged the gobblers and the weasel dust belonged to Sid "Dragon Eye" Ludlow. But he was unavailable for confirmation or other comments to the newshounds camped out in front of his swank townhouse. He was doubtless elsewhere. The men captured at the scene remained mum.

* * *

Thanksgiving in Tri-Quarters was a splendid affair. The down and outers, the addicts, the boozers, the recovering, the enablers, the streetwalkers, the under-employed and the non-employed, the folks who helped these folks, and the Kid and his crew, including dear old mom, enjoyed a fine meal of turkey—fried, soaked in brine or traditionally prepared—and all the fixings. Tables and chairs had been set upon the cordoned-off street polo field. This was the third such shindig the Kid had put on.

When he'd received the tip that Dragon Eye was looking to steal some of his thunder by putting on his own Thanksgiving feed, the Kid had been beside himself.

"He can do Christmas or Easter or Chanukah, but not Thanksgiving," the Kid had bellowed. This day, you see, was the date his brother, a social worker too enthralled with the bottle and too burdened by the plights of his charges, had passed out drunk and perished from exposure. He'd broken out of a classy rehab facility The Kid had placed him in, and not for the first time. The Thanksgiving feast was his way to honor him and give back to our neighborhood.

All along, the Kid and us had wondered why Dragon Eye was going so far out of town to get his turkeys? Sure, his scheme was to have his dinners prepared on the down low as all the soup kitchens and homeless pantries in Tri-Quarters were lined up to cook the meals the Kid was bankrolling. But until that tom broke open, we didn't have the answer as to why Dragon Eye had procured his fowl from afar—killing two birds with one stone, as it were.

"Here you go, Mom," the Kid said as he handed the gravy bowl to his mother.

"Thank you, son," she said, beaming with pride.

Li'l Vet tapped the Kid's shoulder as a black Lincoln glided to a stop along the avenue. He started to reach for his roscoe under his coat, but the Kid stalled that with a look.

The smoked back window of Henry Ford's finest went down part way, and outglared one large bulging orb nestled in burnt, scaly skin set next to a squinting one. Dragon Eye Ludlow took a few moments to take in the festivities, and then the window went back up, and the car started off.

I breathed again and took a sip of my brandy. The Kid had flown to Miami as part of the plan. On the sly, he obtained a monogrammed cufflink belonging to a brigand who'd threatened to muscle in on the Kid's and Dragon Eye's action in the past. I shall not go into detail as to how this item was obtained, but it involved a lady who is the spouse of said kingpin, but who, it's asserted among some, has an affection for the Kid.

The cufflink had been deftly and strategically left in the cuff of the khakis, of one of the tied-up malefactors of truck number one.

Early on, Li'l Vet and I tried to tell the Kid if we did intercept the turkeys, even though we wore masks and gloves, Dragon Eye would be awfully suspicious that cufflink or no, it was he and not the Miami bent nose behind this. But the Kid was insistent on doing this, and so the presence of the snorting snow added verisimilitude to the frame we'd meticulously constructed.

The Lincoln was heading in the direction of the airport.

* * *

"The Snow Birds," *Once Upon a Crime: An Anthology of Murder, Mayhem, and Suspense,* Nodin Press, 2009, Gary Bush and Chris Everheart, editors.

Sportin' Men

Be careful, Junie, you ain't old enough to handle that yet."

"Don't sell the boy short, Brim. Remember how you were at his age." Mercer Cooke and the other men at the table laughed. The teenaged Glen Murray, called Junie, had been caught gawking by his uncle at one of Miss Zenobia's party girls.

Cooke held out a couple of dollar bills to the teenager. "Mix me a Jack and Coke, would you, youngster? And fetch me a ham hock sandwich, too, son. Slap some hogshead cheese on it, too." He saw and upped the raise by ten dollars.

"Okay, Mr. Cooke," Junie said, his cheeks still warm. The liquor and such was on a sideboard, and he took care of the drink order. Then he went off toward the kitchen in the antebellum-restored colonial mansion. This meant leaving the parlor where the game was going, dealer's choice. This also meant having to pass by the girl he'd tried to peek at on the sly when she walked past. Well, she must be at least four years older than him, he figured, which made her twenty and, he supposed, a woman. For she was certainly more experienced than he was.

"How come they calls you Junie?" The girl he'd been transfixed by asked when he entered the area off the parlor that Miss Zenobia called the foyer. A fancy ballroom chandelier hung from its ceiling. And this space was bigger than what Junie had for sleeping at his uncle's place.

She and the other one, whose name was Tanya, were sitting on a couch in the room containing the two pool tables and the plasma TV. They were playing the AlienQuake II video game on the set. Tanya blew a megadroid's head off, earning her bonus points. Both of them were dressed in silky undergarments and short, untied, satiny robes. They looked like honeys fresh from a BET rap video. How could he not peep at that when she'd walked into the parlor to whisper something to Valentine Lewis, one of the players?

"'Cause you was called junebug when you were small?" the girl-woman asked, invading Junie's reverie.

"My mother and older brother were both born in June," the smitten teen answered.

"And so were you?"

He got lost in her eyes. "No. September."

She frowned and chewed a little on her lower lip, and a rainbow of lights popped inside his head.

"This is Missa. She just started this week," Tanya said, her thumbs furiously working the control's toggles.

"Glad to meet you," he managed without stammering. "I've got to get something," and he scooted away. He could hear them whispering as he went, and they laughed that laugh that fine females do when they know they're messing with a dude's mind. At least his cheeks weren't warm again.

In the kitchen, he deftly separated the meat from the shank to make Mr. Cooke's sandwich. Miss Zenobia entered as he started out. She'd just come back from some business she had to attend to and was wearing one of her crowns, one of her flamboyant hats, the kind that black women of a certain age wore to church. This one was a volcanic eruption of peacock feathers and rhinestones. Junie was sure Miss Zenobia hadn't been to church in many years. But he'd seen a deacon or two in the poker game, who headed upstairs afterward with one of the heavenly honeys, as Uncle Brim would crack.

Behind Miss Zenobia was her driver and number one of two bodyguards, the crosstown bus-sized Peteypeet. He was trying to be cool while eyeing the prize Junie was carrying on a saucer.

"How are things, young man?" Miss Zenobia asked. "Fine, ma'am, just fine." He wanted to get out of there, but there was no way to simply ease past them. The madam was of some size around, and Peteypeet was like an anchored battleship at the open swing door.

"Aren't you already a junior?"

"Yes, that's right. I turn seventeen in about a month."

She smiled and removed some folded bills from her protruding bosom. "Put that toward your college fund." She handed him the money. "Brim is alright for who he is, but you've got imagination, Junie. You can go somewhere and not wind up here."

"Thank you," he said, getting by the two of them. Junie looked at the money; it was two one-hundred dollar bills. Oh, man. Now he was not only nervous, but feeling even worse about what he and Uncle Brim were about to do. He was sure glad he hadn't checked the wireless remote he'd previously plugged in behind the refrigerator.

"I guess I'll have to throw my gat on them," Uncle Brim had said when he told Junie what he intended to do.

"There's a better way," the young man advised. They went to the public library, and online, he showed his devious uncle a site about remote control homes. At Circuit City, they bought a radio frequency device that controls lights.

"If it goes black at the right moment, then getting away shouldn't be that hard while everybody runs into each other."

"Good to see you get something out of school, nephew," he'd said, shaking his head appreciatively. "Damn sure more than just filling a seat like I did."

And tonight was the night. Uncle Brim owed some serious money to some impatient types. Junie didn't know what all for, but what else could he do? His mother, a crack addict, had sunk into the netherworld. His father had died years before in a prison fight, and Brimfeld Lee, his mother's brother, was the only family to take him in. He was going to do the robbery regardless, Brim had told Junie, so he had to help and hope that nobody got hurt. Junie knew if he did nothing, Miss Zenobia wouldn't believe he wasn't in on it. And he couldn't snitch on his uncle, so he was stuck.

The two hundred weighed like iron in his pocket. He placed the snack at Mr. Cooke's elbow. Miss Zenobia had been good and fair with him.

His uncle had gotten him this job of keeping the players supplied with their refreshments and running the occasional errand to the store. He worked Thursdays and Fridays after school and on weekends. If it came to rough stuff involving a drunk or a "belligerent second-floor patron," as Miss Zenobia would say, Peteypeet or Hiram took care of that.

And now he was going to not only spit on her kindness, but do this crime that would change his life forever. His uncle had to leave town. Junie wasn't stupid. He knew his uncle wasn't about to pay these others he owed—others he was even more scared of than Miss Zenobia. What would he do about school? And where would he live? His uncle only mumbled incomplete sentences to these questions. The robbery was the only thing commanding his attention.

The game wound down and it got to be time for the last hand.

"Omaha, high-low, eight or better for low," stated the dealer Valentine Lewis, who owned a used car lot.

"I can only play two from my hand?" Morris King asked. With his sister, he ran the family's funeral parlor and was considered an expert embalmer. Uncle Brim picked up stiffs for him now and then for extra money.

"Right, the cards speak," Elliot Harris said. He was a small-boned, light-skinned black man who managed a popular seafood restaurant and had taught mathematics at the university level. It was rumored that he was a silent partner with Miss Zenobia in her establishment.

The four down cards to each were dealt, Junie watching the faces and bodies of the players for their tells, the unconscious giveaways that indicated good, bad, or so-so cards. As usual, his uncle, Mr. Cooke, and Mr. Lewis' faces were like ancient masks on display in a museum. Sometimes, just to get in the heads of the others, his uncle would smile broadly when he had no chance of making anything. The embalmer sniffed, and that meant he had something decent, a pair or an ace. And Mr. Harris might as well show his cards, given his sour look. He folded on the first round of betting.

On the flop, turning over the first three cards, Mr. Lewis gripped the back of his neck and cracked it. The action wasn't a tell, an unconscious giveaway as to whether he had good or bad cards. He did that routinely, the stiffness a byproduct of getting T-boned a few years ago in his Caddy by a cheerleader in a Trans Am paying more attention talking on her cell phone than driving.

His uncle raised and raised again when the bet came back around to him. The others knew that didn't indicate he was holding anything of value as Brim liked to bluff, often recklessly. "You better know they hang low on me, baby," he was fond of bragging to Junie and anyone else he could regale. "I ain't scared of no motherlover in this world or the next."

The turn, the fourth card over, was a ten of clubs. There was a nine of clubs, a jack of hearts, and a three of diamonds already exposed.

"No low possible," Mercer Cooke announced.

Betting resumed. Junie's uncle bet strong, putting twelve dollars in the pot. What did it matter to him? He was going to take it all anyway. The fifth card, Fifth Street, the river, was a jack of clubs. Mr. Cooke bet the maximum. Uncle Brim and Valentine called. The undertaker threw his cards in.

"Pot's right," Mr. Cooke declared. There was three hundred and forty on the table. The players showed. Valentine Lewis had a king-high flush with the clubs.

"That's beats me," Mercer Cooke said, showing his two jacks to give him three-of-a-kind.

"But not me," Uncle Brim said, beaming. He showed an ace of clubs, giving him the highest flush. "That's a good sign," he breathed as he raked in the chips, winking at Junie standing nearby.

"Well," Mr. King sighed, looking toward the doorway where Missa waited. "I'm tapped out." She retreated, snickering. "For cards, that is."

As was the procedure, the bank, which was Miss Zenobia, cashed out the players after taking her customary cut. She'd been away when the game started, and Hiram had initially gathered the buy-in monies. He reappeared. Hiram was tall, long-limbed to Peteypeet's stocky width. He'd been a jailer in the past and was known to favor knives as his choice of inflicting discipline.

Everybody stood and stretched. Junie moved toward the archway. Miss

Zenobia was probably upstairs, but he didn't know where the hulking Peteypeet might be. If he was in the kitchen fixing himself food, that would cut off their escape route and access to the stash. Once, when the water heater had busted, Junie had spied Miss Zenobia lifting a loose board out of the kitchen floor to take out a healthy stack of bills. This was underneath the standing cutting board. That was the real goal of Uncle Brim. Why had Junie been such a big mouth and told him about that?

"Sweet dreams, gents, till next week," Uncle Brim said after getting his money, and goodbyes were said all around. "I've got to squeeze the lizard." He headed for the bathroom that was situated at the end of the foyer and thus closer to the kitchen and his goal.

Junie began cleaning up the parlor and counting in his head. Hiram drifted away. Mr. Cooke and Mr. Lewis were hanging around, chatting with Tanya and Missa. They were married men and never journeyed upstairs. "They're window shopping," Uncle Brim would say. "Old whiskers like the attention of young things, but their hearts couldn't take the strain if they really tried to do anything," he'd laugh roughly.

Junie counted to a slow forty and pushed the button on the electronic tab in his pocket. The lights went out, a bulb popped, and the shouting began.

"Pay your electric bill, Zenobia," Mercer Cooke joked. Junie called out, "I'll check the circuit breaker."

"I'll go with you," the gruff voice of Peteypeet said.

"Sure," he said to throw off suspicion. "Where are you?"

"Over here," the bodyguard said, flicking on his lighter.

Junie came over to him. They headed toward the kitchen, then there was a crash of a body and cursing. Junie had carried one of the chairs with him, placing it in the way of where he remembered the men had been talking with the females. At various times during the last two weeks, he'd practiced going from the parlor to the back of the house with his eyes closed to memorize the layout.

"You better see about that," Junie suggested to the large man.

Peteypeet's pissed look was illuminated by the tiny flame of his plastic liquor store lighter. But he knew if he didn't go back and one of the customers was hurt, he'd get chewed out by Miss Zenobia. "Stay put," he ordered and turned around. The little light bounced from side to side with the bruiser's gait and disappeared into the archway. Junie was already at the backdoor off the rear stairs once used by the maid.

"What's up," a voice called, and he almost fainted. Missa came close, and he could hear her satiny robe fluttering open.

"I've got to go."

She put a hand on his arm. A current shot through him. She smelled wonderful. "What are you two up to? I know Brim just lit out of here. I couldn't tell directly, but by the light of the moon, it looked to me like he was carrying something."

"I don't—"

Missa put a finger to his lips. "I get a share, or I yell."

"If I'm caught, you won't get anything," Junie whispered urgently. He could hear Peteypeet rumbling closer.

Her head down, Missa smiled crookedly up at him and said, "How can I trust you?" And then she kissed him. Kissed him like he'd seen in the movies, and so much better than the couple of girls he'd kissed in school.

"The Eden Motel," he breathed and jumped over the back steps. He dived into the open back window of his uncle's old school '74 Pontiac Catalina with the panties hanging from the rearview mirror. Uncle Brim righted the boat of a car, and they tore off toward the highway in the humid night.

Looking back, Junie saw Peteypeet bang the rear screen door so hard it busted loose from the top hinge. He just stood there staring, a sweet little ugly smile of determination on his sweating face.

After two hours on the road, the two thieves arrived at the Castle Rock Motel off Route 40 across the county line. Junie had been thunderstruck, but not so naïve he would tell Missa where they were really headed.

"Not as much as I hoped," Uncle Brim complained after re-counting the nine thousand, seven hundred dollars, a thousand two hundred of which came from the poker game. "Zenobia must have had to make some payoffs lately. I know the new District Attorney has been making noise about cracking down." He paced, hands on his hips. "I can't get far enough on this fast enough." He looked around and then pawed through the equipment bag he'd previously packed with clothes.

Uncle Brim threw a pair of his boxers at the bed in frustration. Fuming, he looked at Junie's bag. The teenager was lying face up on his bed, trying to imagine his future.

"What you got?" Uncle Brim demanded. "Nothing."

The older man was already going through the young man's bag. He took out a box like the kind used for jewelry, felt-covered, only larger. "You got this. I can get something for this."

Junie snatched the box back. "No."

"This ain't no time for sentimentality, Junie. We're on the run, don't you understand?"

"Whose fault is that?"

"Junie." His uncle held his arms wide in an embracing gesture. "We're the only family each other has. We have to stick up for each other."

Junie was sitting up now. "Then how come I don't get half the money?"

Brim's eyes went agate, and he reached back into his bag. The one item he wasn't considering pawning was the Glock pistol Junie knew his uncle had packed. But was he about to put it upside his nephew's head?

What he pulled out instead was a deck of cards. "We're sportin' men. Let's play for it."

If he said no, would his uncle go crazy off? "Okay."

"None of that TV jive. Just straight up five-card stud. You and me, youngster. Let's see who has the biggest ones."

Junie stood, and his uncle handed him the deck. There was no desk, so the two marched into the small bathroom, and Junie put the lid down on the toilet for a surface to shuffle the cards. Then they returned to the other room and stood at one of the twin beds.

The nephew dealt one down to each, then back and forth, four to each player face up. There was no bets, no bluffing, no tells. This was pure luck of the draw. His uncle had two queens and he had two deuces showing. They hesitated. A truck on the highway rattled the walls, and blues singer Etta James' splendidly tortured voice seeped in from one of the nearby rooms. Each turned over their hole cards.

"I'll be damned," Brim hissed. "Trip twos beats my pair of ladies." He glared hard at his nephew.

"That's 'cause you rely on women too much," a female voice suddenly said.

An open-mouthed Junie watched Missa walk in the unlocked door. She was dressed in hip huggers, a black T-shirt, and some fresh Air Jordans. She kissed Brim. "I drove Mama's car like you said," she told him.

"Good." Brim put the cards and his boxers away and zipped up his bag. He threw the keys to the Pontiac right on top of Junie's winning hand. "You rollin' with us?"

Junie considered what that meant. The next town, the next con or take down. Always on the make, always one step ahead. "I'm straight."

"Go on with your bad self." Brim put an arm around Missa's waist, and they started out. She stopped him.

"Give him his due, Brim. He didn't panic and didn't give up where you'd be. He did right."

Even though her kiss was just a test, Junie liked her.

"We gonna need this money to stake us in our next action," Brim complained.

"Sign the pink to your car so he can at least sell that."

"I don't have it with me. And anyway, it ain't exactly legally in my name."

"He did right," she insisted.

Uncle Brim blew air through his puckered lips and counted out five hundred but made it a thousand after the withering glare she laid on him. He handed it to Junie. "I'll see you around, huh?"

"Yeah."

On their way out, Missa blew the teenager a kiss.

Junie sat on the bed and opened the box. In it was the bronze-colored medal his brother had been awarded in Iraq—posthumously, they'd called it. His name and rank was inscribed on the back of the thing. The white van with the two marines had pulled up to their apartment, and his mother had collapsed, right there on the porch. After that, though having been clean some five years, she got back on the pipe, and, as far as Junie knew, was still riding it hard. He shut the lid, tucked it in his bag, and with that in tow, left the motel room, buttoning up his jean jacket against the wind and cold.

* * *

"Sportin' Men," *Full House,* Putnam Juvenile,2007, Pete Hautman, editor.

Beginner's Luck

Chainey awoke with a headache. She smacked her lips and wiped at the side of her mouth, wet from drool. She sat forward and felt woozy. Then, a bolt of nausea lanced through her, and for a moment, it seemed she might vomit. The throbbing beneath her skull and the rising heat bearing down on her compelled her to sit back and slump down. She squeezed her eyes shut and tried to assemble chunks of random memory into sequential events.

A door slammed. A car door.

A man shouted her name. No, he didn't yell; he'd spoken in a tone as if he was a friend or at least knew her in some way.

Close, he stood close, smiling, conversational.

Turning, sunlight glinting off a polished hood, the man before her, asking her a question quietly.

Then a burning mist fogging her eyes. Bastard sprayed her with pepper spray? No, something else, something nastier.

Sky upside down, sun behind her eyes. Mooch, what about Mooch?

A cell phone jingled. Chainey sat up again, aware that she was on a bus bench, traffic going along. Pedestrians walked by, used to drunks or druggies sleeping off their highs in public. Anything goes in Vegas. Then the cell phone went off again. The drowsy woman realized it was in her jean's pocket and removed the instrument.

***

"How do you feel?" The man asked pleasantly.

"Like shit. I'd appreciate the opportunity to return the favor."

His chuckle was mirthful, suggesting a person of expansive humor. "At another time, Ms. Chainey. But right this minute, you have a more important task to perform."

An RTC bus chugged up, and Chainey waved it on. "And what would that be?" Her annoyance was quickly becoming anger and it was dulling the hammer blows inside her temple.

"That large envelope-sized accordion folder you were supposed to deliver to a certain party in LA."

"If you know about that, then you must also know it's in the safe." Anxious, she chewed her lip. She had a bad felling what was coming next.

"Yes, about that," the man on the other end said. "Mooch is a stubborn cuss."

There it was. "I want to speak to him."

"Your boss is unavailable at the moment, Ms. Chainey. So you see, it falls to you to obtain that envelope for me and deliver same not to the city of oranges and palms, but to me." His tone had remained upbeat, but the implication behind his words was clear.

"Only Mooch has the combination," she said.

There was a gulp as he drank. "Yes, well," he said, clearing his throat, "as I mentioned, Mr. Maltizar is determined to be non-compliant on this matter, and really, there's little time or patience I can ill afford to waste."

"Look, there's nothing I can do unless you release Mooch."

"Oh, don't be so modest. I know a little something about you, and you're plenty resourceful." He paused to take another sip. Fucker was probably having his morning latte, Chainey reflected.

"And you don't have much choice. None at all if you don't want what could happen on your pretty head."

Chainey was up and walking around. "Let's say I can get the envelope, and I'm not promising that."

"But let's say you can." The voice lost part of its casual veneer.

"Where do I deliver the package and get Mooch back?"

"You're in no position to demand a goddamn thing, missy. What you better do is get that sweet ass of yours in gear and back to your office to get my money."

"Why aren't you at the office? You had the drop on both of us." She'd been in the parking lot below the second-story set of offices that Ira "Mooch" Maltizar maintained as Truxton, Ltd., a licensed and bonded courier service. And though the company, named for a racehorse owned by the seventh president of the United States, Andrew Jackson, did generate decent revenues conveying such freight as law firm's briefs to the courthouse or the occasional platinum watch to the showgirl from the smitten sharpie, it was Truxton's "off the books" endeavors that had earned the company its real swag.

"Quite observant of you, Chainey," the man replied. "That's why you're needed."

"Who's watching it?"

There was that laugh again. "I can't for one hundred percent say who, but if you press me to lay odds, I'd wager one of the men on duty is a good-sized gentleman, six-five or six, head like a four-slot toaster, chest like the back end of a Peterbilt truck."

No use complaining. It wasn't going to change anything. "You've got to give me time to work this out. It's Sunday, and—"

"Sorry, my dear, but the clock is against us. You will have to be at the McDonald's on the food court floor of the Excalibur by one forty-seven this afternoon. Be at the table with the 'MC' carved into it."

Her watch read three minutes after eleven. "Hey, you're the one that needs this file, man. Seems to me setting an unrealistic timeline is counterproductive. Might lead to mistakes."

He sighed. "I realize haste in a situation such as this is fraught with unpredictability, but so be it. My time is not my own, and neither is yours, Chainey. For the moment, you hustle when I blow the whistle for the good of Mooch. You can dispense with the cell phone you're using as there will be another one waiting for you at the Mickey-D's. Just in case you have the ability to trace these things." The line clicked off.

Chainey didn't waste time trying to figure out who the asshole was. That would come later if she completed the job. It didn't matter to her what was in the file. For all she cared, it could be Long John Silver's lost treasure map. And now, one part of this equation was desperate enough to commit a kidnapping to achieve their ends.

The problem that nagged her was there was at least one large individual representing another interest babysitting her office. She assumed that he would at least have somebody with him. But what about the chump who was making her jump through hoops? Did he have help? Did he have a partner too?

Chainey was on Fort Apache Road near the twenty-four-hour Albertsons. She walked across the street to the store and hailed a cab. Two blocks from the unpretentious mall where Truxton was located off the Strip and not far from North Vegas, black Vegas, she got out and paid the cabbie. Her enemy was unknown to her, and she had no way of gauging if he would truly hurt or kill Mooch. If, she chillingly amended, he was still alive.

Walking closer, she tensed as she passed a van, but there was nobody in it, at least not in the front seats. But she didn't think a couple of gunmen would be hunkered down in a family van, but you never knew. In the lot of the strip mall where the office was, six cars were parked. As this was Sunday, only Kleopatra's Nails and the video store were open for business. Technically, Truxton didn't have set hours, the need to move unreported monies demanded 24/7 service.

Chainey had come to the office because Mooch had called her. Over the phone, he'd mentioned that a matter had come up suddenly, and he needed her on the double. And it was a sad testament to the current fallowness of her love life that she was alone and available this Sunday morning.

Two of the cars on the lot she could ID. One was her late model T-Bird, the other Mooch's Cadillac Eldorado. The others, strangers to her, could belong to anyone. She watched from across the street, alongside a narrow passage beside the closed Cosmic Cube comic book shop.

A woman with two small children left the video store and departed in one of the cars on the lot. Chainey had focused on a shiny Jaguar S-Type tucked in the far corner. From this distance, she couldn't tell if anyone was in the vehicle, but then her hunch was confirmed. A hand came out of the passenger window. Probably a guy flicking ash off his cigarette.

Okay, that's the players. Time to get busy. The design of the mall was such that the steps and storefronts all faced the parking lot. There were rear service entrances on the backside of the shops, but only on the ground floor. There was only one way to the second story.

One option was to draw the men in the Jaguar out of the car or distract them long enough for her to sneak into the office. It happened that Chainey was acquainted with several working girls, as they were always good sources of underworld information. She could rally a few of them, work out the price, and have them show up and descend on the occupants in the Jag. They could offer all manner of sexual favors. Of course, she glumly concluded, that would probably result in one or more of the women getting punched in the face. And if the cops rolled up, they might haul everybody down to the station to straighten out the mess, and she could get in the office unbothered.

It was thirteen to twelve. She needed a better plan. Chainey walked the long way around the block to avoid being seen, hopped her six-foot frame over the rough-hewn wall behind the mall with the aid of a plastic milk crate, and went along the narrow path. She hoped she counted the doors right and knocked.

She put her face in line with the peephole.

"Martha?" Jenny Giap, the owner of the nail salon, said when she opened the door.

"Too long to explain, but you mind if I come in?"

"No, come on." As was customary, her fifty-plus body, her stocky legs still shapely and toned, was clad in a mini.

Chainey entered. There were only two customers inside the shop. One was at the nail table that Giap, in her rubber gloves and face mask around her neck, had been working on. The other woman, her foot in a cast, had her chipped vermillion toenails sticking out. She idly leafed through a Vogue. An oldies soul station was playing "Hollywood Swinging" by Kool and the Gang on the radio.

The watch on Chainey's wrist felt like a hundred-pound weight dragging her down to the bottom of a depthless sea. She didn't want to look at it nor the cat clock on the wall, with its eyes that shifted back and forth ticking far too loudly. "I need a favor, Jenny. No questions, but there's four hundred in it for you."

"You've just said the magic words, girlfriend. What I gotta do?"

Less than fifteen minutes later, Jenny Giap was waving her arms wildly above her head, hollering incoherently, and trudging onto the parking lot in her platform clunkies. The fire truck had arrived without blaring its siren. The crew drove it onto the lot at an angle, blocking the Jaguar.

"The car, the car is on fire," Giap pointed nervously at the Jaguar. "This ruins business. I can't have them burning up my store."

"Now hold on, ma'am," the firefighter who'd alighted from the truck said. "Calm yourself, what are you talking about?"

"Smoke, smoke was pouring out of it." Giap took two steps back from the Jag as if afraid it might combust at any moment.

"What from the engine?" The firefighter looked dubiously at the car.

Jenny Giap said, "All I know is I've seen smoke, and that means fire, don't it?"

"What is this dizzy broad talking about?" The man, the tall man the kidnapper had described, had unlimbered himself from behind the wheel. He was in his forties, dressed in a dark suit and thin dark tie with a clip.

"We're trying to determine that, sir," the firefighter said. "Well, move your fuckin' rig and work this out somewhere else, huh, pal?"

"Be cool, Hal," his partner in the passenger seat advised. The two other firefighters alighted from the truck.

"Why don't you cooperate, sir?" This firefighter was a sizable blonde man with a tackler's shoulders. He drifted toward the belligerent Hal.

"Okay, look," the tall man began, "I'm sorry for any misunderstanding we might be having." He pulled out his wallet. "This is for the fireman's fund, okay?" He flashed a hundred-dollar bill.

"Maybe we should check his car," the third one, a tawny-haired woman, said.

"You're not cops, so stop trying to sound tough." The tall man commented.

"It's no problem to get them here," the first one mentioned. "No problem at all."

"Hey, how about you move your truck and let us out?" Hal's buddy, a brown-skinned man with white hair in a Hawaiian shirt, was now out of the car. "We're late and need to get going. Or maybe your captain would like a call from our lawyers."

The one who'd talked to Giap took a cursory look around the Jag and did a modified push-up to look below it, too. "Okay. Sure," he said.

"I tell you, it smokes, whoosh," Giap said, throwing her hands back in the air and muttering to herself as she returned to her shop.

The fire truck backed up, and the Jaguar tooled out of the lot.

"That was great, Jenny," Chainey said, heading for the front.

"It's all good," her friend cracked. They knocked fists.

At the door, Chainey added. "Those motherlovers will be back in a few once they figure the fire department has bounced. Just to play safe, close up for the rest of the day, alright? I'll tighten you up on the *dinero* this week."

"Shit, a couple of chumps like that don't scare me," Giap retorted, dropping the stilted English act she'd put on for the suckers. "I got something for 'em if they want to jump bad." She snickered.

"Jenny," Chainey implored.

"Fine, for the sake of my customers."

Upstairs at Truxton, Ltd., Chainey hoped that since Mooch Maltizar was past sixty and enjoyed his after-hours Cuba Libres, rum, and coke with his cigars, he would have written down the combination to the safe in case he forgot. But as it was now almost twelve-thirty, she was trying to be methodical and not just rush in looking for it. That the numbers would be in Mooch's office was a given. So, at least the area she had to search was knowable.

The phone rang, and she let the machine get it. Nobody spoke on the other end, so it had to be the two hitters calling on their way back to check if anyone had come in. And the third party, the one that had engaged Mooch, was no doubt going to be pissed that their goods weren't going to reach them. But, Chainey reminded herself, one set of worries at a time.

Fortunately, the blinds hadn't been opened yet by Mooch in his office as the morning had been overcast and the sun had come out late. She started her hunt in his office with occasional breaks to peek through a slat for the return of the watchers. And she hoped none of the other couriers of the company had any business that required them to come in today.

Less than ten minutes later, the Jaguar returned. The tall man, Hal, got out, and Chainey observed him as he walked up to the shops on the ground floor. After a few moments, having no doubt confirmed that the nail salon was closed, she heard his footsteps on the concrete stairs. She remained motionless, one of the office guns, a fifteen-shot Glock 20, ready at her side.

The door handle jiggled. Chainey had reset the alarm. It had been due to Mooch having been hustled out of the place, probably with a gun in his ribs. The tall man's heavy footfalls echoed on the balcony as he prowled back and forth in front of the office. The window shuddered. Chainey figured the frustrated hood had pounded the pane. His footsteps then receded.

It took Chainey longer than she would have liked to find the safe's combination. The crafty old player had secreted the numbers, typed out on his Underwood circa Horace Greeley, on a little sheet of paper he'd cut to a sliver and taped to the underside of the back padding of his executive chair. In the corner of the office, the safe squatted. The thing was a Defiant, a free-standing '50s-era floor model old battle hull of a mother that had been there before Chainey came on board.

She dialed the combination and opened the heavy door. Inside were all manner of items ranging from bundled bills to jewelry boxes. The accordion file had an object wrapped in white sheeting on top of it and she had to remove this to get what she wanted. Curious, she unwrapped the cloth to reveal a weathered machine pistol that had Japanese lettering stamped on the stock. She shrugged, replaced the piece, and shut the safe. Now came the hard part. She had to get to her car.

At the entrance, she took a deep breath, mentally ran through her plan, shaky as it was, and stepped onto the landing. Chainey had reset the alarm and walked toward the stairs, but not fast. This part called for icy nerves to resist running.

Hal, who'd been standing in the parking lot smoking, was striding quickly to the foot of the steps. "Hey, I want to talk with you," he demanded, his long legs bringing him up two steps at a time.

Chainey made sure she'd stopped halfway down. "Who the hell are you?" She tried to sound unaware.

"Don't you worry about that, sweetness." His hand was inside his jacket, locking on the piece she was sure he kept there in a shoulder rig. "What ya got there, huh?" He asked, referring to the file. They were now both in the middle of the stairs, separated by less than an arm's length.

"Oh, this?" She produced the Taser she'd taken from the office, shot the two probes into his chest, and juiced him.

"Fuck," Hal hollered as the volts charred his kidneys, causing his legs to buckle. But he was strong and held on to the rail, the piece slack in his gun hand. "Fuckin' bitch," he slurred, dropping the gun and making an anemic grab for Chainey.

"Nice meeting you, too." She jabbed an elbow into his face, and the tall man fell ass end of the stairs. His pal in the Hawaiian shirt was out of the Jaguar heading toward them, but Chainey had scooped up Hal's gun, an old-fashioned Smith & Wesson revolver, and leveled it. The Glock stuck out of her back pocket.

"Now, look, baby—"

"I ain't hardly your baby. Face down," she ordered. "I'm sure we can—"

"You want to try me to see if I know how to use this thing?"

"I guess I don't." He complied.

Hal groaned as Chainey gained the lot and patted down the man in the flashy shirt. She took the gun he had on his belt and walked to their car.

"We can work this out, you know," Hawaiian shirt said. "Money is the great communicator."

Chainey ignored him and got the hood of the Jaguar open. She pulled out a few electronic pieces connected to the engine, hoping that would incapacitate their car.

"This is only a minor delay, miss. We've got time and resources."

"Aren't you special." Chainey got in her car, and, as she backed up, Hawaiian shirt was helping his stunned partner to his feet. Hal was bleeding from the nose. She zoomed away in the T-Bird.

At the Excalibur, Chainey bought a cup of coffee at the McDonald's in the food court. She was ahead of schedule and walked around the tables. Given the hour of the day, the place was full, and it was hard getting a full view of the table tops because of food trays, extra-large cups of soda, and whatnot. Because she didn't want to look too suspicious, she walked in and out of the section. It would do no good to have security show up to escort the lady, making the kids nervous away. She wasn't having any luck spotting the table with the carved letters. It was now twelve forty-three.

She kept circulating. A man with straggly shoulder-length hair in a T-shirt with the rock band Creed's logo on it, sat at a corner table, slowly munching on his Big Mac. Fries were spread out before him like pieces of a chic jigsaw puzzle. He had the baggy-eyed air of having pulled an all-nighter at the tables and come up short. Way short. He looked up as Chainey cruised past.

"You showgirls think the world owes you the driver's seat of life, don't you?"

Please, she told herself, let this fool be talking to himself. She kept going, but, naturally, he was going to get her attention.

"Gonna ignore me, huh? Spend my money in this pussy trap, get the toothy smile and the free drinks as long as I'm feeding the slots." He was starting to squeeze his hamburger. "All of you are worthless cunts."

The people around him did their best to continue talking and eating amiably, hoping that indifference would make him shut up or at least return to gambling elsewhere. Chainey looked back at his table now that he'd shifted his arms. Sure enough, her initials were etched there. It was twelve forty-six.

She came closer. "Why be so unfriendly?"

One of the man's orbs was shrunk to the size of a dot, the other pulsing and engorged, seemingly contaminated with brain fluids that had leaked into that side. "You know why." He held onto his Big Mac with both hands, the veins rigid on his thin forearms. Pinkish sauce embedded with bits of chopped onion dribbled across his fingers.

"You know," he said again, taking another bite, smacking loudly.

The cell taped beneath the table chimed a tune, and Chainey had to sit next to him to reach for the phone.

"Okay, yeah," the goof bobbed his head agreeably. "All you chicks eventually come around to the dude. Don't milk my lizard too hard, baby." He cackled like a hyena.

Chainey withdrew the phone and clicked it on. She tried to get up, but her new boyfriend had put an arm around her shoulders, staining her shirt with gooey stuff.

"I got your package."

"Good," the voice said on the other end.

"Let me talk to Mooch, or I burn what's in it now."

The goof leaned toward her. "I love black women. You know how to treat your men."

"What?" The kidnapper said.

Chainey stomped her boot heel on the clown's tennis-shoe-clad foot. He didn't yell as she expected, but his face and upper body twitched convulsively like a man attacked by hornets. She rose.

"Quit fucking around. I don't know if Mooch is breathing, dead or incapacitated. But this goes no further until I talk to him." She had to bank on his greed, or desperation, or both. "Go ahead, drag this out. How long do you think before Hal and Mister Hawaiian stud catch up to you, asshole?"

"They follow you?"

"Yeah, I'm that stupid."

"Hold on." There was the fumbling of the phone, the scuffing of feet, and inaudible conversation. Then her boss said in his thick Cuban accent. "I'm here, *chica. No preoccupado. No se—*"

"No Spanish," the kidnapper ordered, snatching the phone back. "Okay, you had your little pow-wow. Now you do as I say, and everything will be just swell."

The goof was once again occupied with his burger. "It better be. Now, where do we finish this?"

* * *

The rear side window looked like a dry river bed crisscrossed with parched lines, then imploded, and hundreds of tinkling pieces rained down. Chaincy crawled forward in the dirt and squeezed off two shots from around the T-Bird's tire.

She didn't expect to hit anyone, just let that joker handling the shotgun know she was still kicking.

That done, she pulled her body back and got up on a knee. It didn't help matters that the sun was now up high and that there wasn't much in the way of shelter in Tender Oaks—there wasn't much of Tender Oaks in general.

The plan had been for Nevada Power to build a coal burning plant in this desert section east of Boulder City butting up against the Arizona border. The rest of Nevada might be static in its growth, but Vegas was sprouting like wild weeds. And as the city and environs expanded upwards and outwards, the beast of a million neon signs had a need to gobble up more and more electricity. The Tender Oaks power station was to be a pristine example of public and private capital working together for the common good and commerce.

Only the transmission lines were blue-printed to travel over sacred Indian burial grounds. A court challenge was mounted by the Shoshones to block the development. And during the process of discovery by the attorneys, a funny addition was revealed. The private sector developer, Rene Hilli brand, disappeared, and the project was stalled in suits and counter-suits.

"Come on, let's join forces. We have the same objective in mind." Hawaiian shirt yelled to Chaincy. He was crouched behind large spools of cable, nearer to the Nevada Power maintenance shed.

"Let's ask Hal," she quipped.

"Fuck her and Fraizen." The tall man and his shotgun were on the far side of the Tahoe SUV they'd screeched to a stop in minutes after Chainey.

"He's just blowing off steam," the one hiding behind the spools said. "He's really a big ol' teddy bear."

"Well, I'm not hugging him," she muttered.

"Chainey," the man in the Hawaiian shirt said, "there's got to be a reasonable way we can come to terms. We want Fraizen, and you want your boss back. They're both in that shack. And Fraizen's a punk. Gun or no gun, he's not going to be a problem."

He knew her name. They worked fast. "And the file?"

"That's our property, you devious skank," Hal bellowed.

"You ain't getting it."

"Shut up, Hal," his partner advised. "I'm trying to work a deal here."

"No," he answered in a tone like a defiant teenager. "You can't trust her. She'll cut you down, first chance she gets."

Hawaiian shirt asked, "So now what? Wait here until a police chopper flies overhead, and we all go to the pokey?"

From where she was, Chainey was pinned down by Hal. But if Hawaiian shirt stepped out toward the shack where this Fraizen and Mooch were, she could tag him.

Fraizen appeared at the window of the shed again, half his face showing as it did when Chainey had first arrived. "Ramos, I got something to trade for my life."

Ramos, the one in the bright shirt, called out. "You suckin' hind tit, Fraizen. Like you been doing all your lousy life."

"The old man, he's got all kinds of shit in that safe. I know they move money for the casino owners."

"Oh, you stupid," Hal began.

"Yeah," Ramos cut in, "that sounds good, Fraizen. Real good. You bring him out, we sweat him, and we all go home rich."

Chainey shook her head. Hal and Ramos were pros. They knew better than ripping off the cold cash belonging to the types that Mooch delivered for. They weren't going to bring that kind of heat down on themselves. But Ramos had to be hedging that Fraizen saw no other way out and believed his foolish offer had weight. They were going to kill him and Mooch, too, in the process if he was in the way.

"Nothing happens to Mooch," she said from her cover. "Things have a way of working themselves out in these funky trickbags, Chainey."

Ramos addressed Fraizen. "Come on out."

"Take care of her first," Fraizen said.

"She won't shoot with Maltizar in tow," Ramos answered. "That's right, Fraizen," Hal added, realizing what his partner was up to. "Besides, she pokes her head up, I'll take it off."

Incongruously, a jackrabbit suddenly bounded into the shooting area. He sat back on his haunches, aware that everyone was suddenly transfixed by his furry presence. The animal twitched its nose, then bounded away.

The door to the shack creaked open, and Mooch was shoved out first, Fraizen behind him. The older man's hands were tied and there was a clot of drying blood alongside his face where Fraizen must have pistol-whipped him. Fraizen, a beefy man in expensive slacks, had one hand on Maltizar, the other pressed into his back. They stopped about a yard beyond the shack.

"He's told me the combination, Ramos," Fraizen said, laying out his insurance policy. He kept Maltizar in front of him, facing the man in the Hawaiian shirt. This exposed his flank to Chainey.

"You pointing him in the wrong direction, slick," Ramos chided.

Fraizen cocked Maltizar toward Chainey and walked sideways, heading over to the grouping of giant spools.

"You're almost there, Fraizen," Hal goaded. "You're almost home free, baby."

When Ramos took care of Fraizen, he was going to have control of Mooch, but there wasn't much Chainey could do at that moment. The file gave her something of a bargaining chip, but a live body was the ultimate trump card.

"We're going to work this out, okay, Fraizen?" Ramos said soothingly. "Money is the great comforter."

Fraizen and Maltizar were at the edge of the spools.

"Okay, Ramos," Fraizen started, "Let's you and me go get the money. Hal keeps the girl pinned down, then we come back and take care of her." Maltizar was positioned in such a way that he was now between Fraizen and the still-crouching Ramos. Part of the heads and shoulders of the kidnapper and her boss were exposed to Chainey. Even if she could make the shot and take Fraizen out, Mooch was still Ramos' prisoner.

Suddenly, Mooch slumped and said, "Oh God." He sagged against his captor, knocking him back a few steps.

"You old bastard," Fraizen screamed, "don't you have a heart attack on me now." The dead weight folded against him, and Fraizen let the body drop. Having a clear shot, Ramos shot him in the gut. Reflexively, Fraizen shot back.

"Ramos," Hal called out. "Hey, man."

"Motherfuckers," Fraizen said. He staggered backwards, away from the spools. "You lying motherfuckers." Spittles of blood flew from his mouth. He had one hand on his bleeding stomach, the other clutching his gun. His pant legs were soaked in crimson, and he was colorless as old parchment.

"You're bleeding out, Fraizen," Chainey said. "You need a doctor."

"No, he doesn't," Hal had stood up, and the blast from his Mossberg semi-auto took most of Fraizen's face off.

Chainey had also popped up quickly, and her round caught the tall man up high on his torso. He spun around, then went down to the ground. She knew he was alive and wasn't going to rush to the spot behind the Tahoe.

After a moment, Hal said, "So where does that leave us, girly? The ones we cared about are dead."

"Fuck you, Hal," she said through gritted teeth. "Fuck you to hell."

"I'm sure that day will come." She heard movement and chanced to look up from the top of the pick-up's bed. Hal was inside the Tahoe and had started the engine. The vehicle was driving away as she ran to where Mooch Maltizar lay.

She stood over his still form as the SUV's motor receded into the distance. Ramos died in a sitting position, his legs straight out, his back against one of the spools. Fraizen's bullet had punched a hole in his heart. Quite a shot for an amateur. Beginner's luck.

"The bad men say bye-bye, *chica*?"

"You goddamn faker." She wiped the wetness from her eyes and helped him to his feet.

"It wasn't that much of a bluff." He was shaking and unsteady, but he was alive. "I was about to, *come se dice*, stroke out, *que no*?"

"Whatever," she said, smiling, helping him to her car. Chainey never did get the full story from Maltizar about the relationship of Ramos and Hal to Fraizen. He hadn't survived since the days of running numbers for Moe Dalitz by being chatty. Though he did bestow a sizable bonus in her bank account for saving him to enjoy more Cuba Libres.

Her friend, Rena Solomon, did an in-depth piece in the *Las Vegas Express*, the alternative bi-weekly where she was a staff investigative reporter. From that and a few segments on the local news, Chainey learned that Fraizen had been the attorney for the missing developer of the Tender Oaks project, Rene Hillibrand. In her piece, Solomon pointed out that Hilli brand and Fraizen had lived lavish lifestyles but had come up bust in both investments in the dot-com fever a while back, and the more recent downturns in the stock market.

There were also, Solomon wrote, allegations that some of the operating capital for Hillibrand's business originated from less-than-Fortune 500 sources. The sort of folks for whom lawsuits might as well be Sanskrit for all the meaning it had for them. They believed in the direct approach in getting their monies back.

Maltizar and Chainey had to provide statements to the police, and the accordion file—containing cashier's checks made to bearer totaling some four million dollars—was turned in. The story she and Mooch agreed to beforehand was that the file of checks was with Fraizen all the time. That he'd kidnapped Maltizar in a deranged effort to force him to get Chainey to deliver those checks to a boat offshore in Baja. Sure, the story was flimsier than a politician's promise, but who was around to contradict them?

Hal never turned up. And Chainey knew better than to persist in asking Maltizar who it was she was supposed to have delivered those checks to originally. About three and half months later, a bit of stink was raised as the checks disappeared from the police evidence locker. This on a weekend when Mooch Maltizar had gone to Scottsdale to relax, he'd said.

And later, Chainey noted a small item in the *Review-Journal* that a man vaguely answering to Rene Hillibrand's description was spotted boarding a transpacific plane at LA International Airport.

* * *

"Beginner's Luck," Shades of Black: Crime and Mystery Stories by African-American Writers, Berkley Prime Crime, 2004, Eleanor Taylor Bland, editor.

Branded

Mark Sullivan's tongue had a spongy feeling and tasted like stale cotton candy. Now that was funny, he supposed, moving his thick tongue around in his dry mouth. When was the last time he'd had that sugary treat? Yeah, he grinned like a gibbon; that's right, he was eating something that had reminded him of the confection last night. Yes, indeed.

Pictures coruscated through his sweltering brain. The images were like loose film fluttering in front of a fixed light source. For the briefest of moments, the likenesses the film had captured were projected on a sun-bleached wall. She was on the bed, her glorious backside to him, panties down, and he was riding her like a jockey going for the Triple Crown.

He opened his eyes, smiling broadly. Then, just as suddenly, a stifling anxiety bolted through the hangover shrouded like a tarpaulin over his pulsing head. The pressed wood nightstand with its peeling veneer and the Googie-style lamp upon it had thrown him at first, but now it all came back to him: the smell of her, the feel of her, and, of course, letting the tip of his tongue cross his chapped bottom lip, the taste of her. Yes, buddy.

Sullivan was getting stiff, seeing her again in his mind, now with only her lacy black bra on, riding atop him as he bucked like a Brahma bull. He touched himself and winced. His penis felt sore. "Damn," he chuckled, "she wore me out."

The hung-over man sat up in the bed, the mattress surprisingly firm and comfortable. Surprising, given he'd spent the night in a motel room off a noisy main drag. He rubbed his whiskered face and groaned loudly. "Oh, shit," he suddenly blurted, then scrambled out from underneath the black sheets. He stood on wobbly legs, allowing his eyes to rove the room. He spied his pants draped over the lone chair in the corner. His shirt was crumpled up at its foot on the floor.

Apprehension and guilt cleared his head enough for him to snatch his pants up and plumb the pockets. "Shit," he repeated. His hand touched change, and what felt like a folded napkin in the front right pocket. And in the left, his keys. Well, he mused, at least those were still there. His wallet, "Fuck," he fumed—his wallet wasn't in his back pocket. But that could be explained, he rationalized as he continued searching.

But there were no other pockets. Sullivan threw the pants down in disgust, his head pounding from the exertion. Defeated, he sat on the air conditioner-heater unit attached below the curtained window. Idly, he noted the heavy drape was purple, the walls a mild fuchsia, and the floor's carpet a Pepto-Bismol pink.

"Jee-zus," he murmured, taking in his surroundings. "Where the hell did she take me?" He leaned back, taking a deep breath that caused him to hack up mucus and tequila. "Damn," he blared, struggling to his feet. As he did so, he got a glimpse of part of the area beneath the bed frame.

Sullivan got down on his knees and was happy to find his wallet. He sat on the floor, cross-legged, and thumbed through his billfold. It all seemed to be there, so that was one less story he had to work out. One less lie. Sullivan got up and almost fell over. The blood draining inside his head made starbursts flicker before his eyes.

He steadied himself and tousled his brown hair. "Never again," he promised quietly while smiling smugly. "What the hell was that chick's name?" Remorse and excitement mingled in him as he recalled the woman he met in the bar last night. She was compact, chunky in the hips, but packed just right. She was dark-haired and wore jeans, platform shoes, and a low-cut sweater top. What had caught his interest, aside from the fact she'd sat next to him on a stool, was the arrow on her breast. It was a tattoo, and the shaft and quill of the arrow stuck out from the edge of her top. It was green against her tawny skin and turned him on like crazy. He just had to see the other end of that arrow. And he had.

"Ow," he said, a sudden pang throbbing along his penis. "Uh-oh," he whispered warily. No, wait, he'd used a condom, hadn't he? Or had he been so drunk he didn't remember or couldn't put it on? Hell, he was surprised he hadn't been too drunk to fuck, the old punk song went. Maybe he had been, but no, he was sure he'd knocked boots. He chuckled, then got serious. This was no time to reminisce about his lustful indiscretion. Had he taken his wedding ring to the bar? No, he hadn't. That was a relief.

First, there was a kidney to tap. As he sauntered into the white-tiled bathroom, he probed his memory in an effort to recall the woman's name. He stood before the toilet, putting the ol' two-finger hold on his johnson, and reacted to the soreness of his member. He looked down and could see the skin had an off-color hue. He sure hoped that wasn't evidence of some new kind of sexually transmitted disease. Naw, that couldn't be.

As he relieved himself, he tried different names. "Mary, no. Roxanne, no. It was short, one of those model/Hollywood kinda things," he mused aloud. There was a mirror tacked to the wall behind the toilet, and he caught a glimpse of himself naked. He smiled. Yeah, the babes still dug him. Shaking himself, the soreness of his penis became apparent again. He looked down, then in the mirror. "What the hell?"

The discoloration wasn't from being rubbed raw due to sexual gymnastics. The tinge on his penis was of a uniform formation. In blackish Gothic letters, tattooed in an arc along the circumference of his penis, were three letters, each an inch high.

"Mia," that was her name, he gasped. And she left it on his penis.

Sullivan didn't move for several minutes, trying to comprehend what had happened to him. "I'm fucked," he concluded correctly as a clammy tremor worked up and down his legs. Each letter was finely crafted along his cock, and each was very distinct—as if a neon arrow were pointed at them, blinking "idiot" over and over. There was no dried blood, but the area where the letters had been applied was the source of the discomfort.

"Shit," he repeated yet again, sitting on the bed. "Oh, man, what the fuck am I gonna do?" Sullivan closed his eyes and rubbed his face, hoping and praying when he lifted his head, he'd be in his own bedroom, the victim of alcohol-fueled pent-up sexual frustration. But such, he intellectually knew, was not the case. He stood, staring at his branded penis as if it were a friend who'd stabbed him in the back.

"It's punishment for sticking it someplace it didn't belong." Sullivan squinted at the letters, trying to come up with a plausible story to tell his wife. *All right, get the ball back, take the high ground and all that pseudo-military, sports macho jargon we throw around at the business.* Sullivan chanted while taking several deep breaths and got dressed.

It was a quarter to eight and he had to do the presentation at ten this morning. He stepped out of the hotel room onto an open-air second-story balcony. Down in the concrete courtyard was a drained pool. A tall blonde in a skirt that, by a whisper, made its way south of her crotch walked its length in clunking platform shoes. She had blue streaks dyed in her hair. Nope, that wasn't her.

The woman he'd been with hadn't stepped out to get them coffee and poppy seed bagels. And then to return all girly-giggly as she happily related to him how he'd been so smitten, he'd begged her to have her name scrawled in ink on his tool.

"Fuck," he bellowed. The anger that had been lying beneath the surface was finally poking its way through the layer of shock. The woman in the awfully short skirt looked back at him, a wan smile briefly ghosting across her hard face. Then she kept going underneath an overhead arch and out to the street beyond.

Sullivan wasn't paying much attention. He made his way down the stairs and put the mind that had made him sales manager before thirty to work. He didn't stop to settle his bill, as he assumed from the appearance and name of the joint, ubiquitously called the Boulevard Motel, that it was a pay-first kind of establishment. Besides, the heavyset desk clerk in her muumuu barely looked at him from inside the tiny glass-walled office.

Out on the street, Sullivan quickly assessed where he was. He didn't know the buildings around him and therefore was not near the Red Pirate Bar. The bar was an upscale joint, and his surroundings told him what he'd already guessed: he was in a part of town where a hot-sheet motel was not out of place. He started walking. The blonde with the blue highlights was across the street, sitting at a bus stop. Her great legs were crossed, and her dangling foot jiggled to a beat playing inside her skull. A beat-up pickup, at least twenty years old, pulled to the curb in front of her. Two men with hats were in the vehicle.

Sullivan walked to the corner to see the street name. Danziger. This put him farther from the bar and his home than work. He checked the time. Okay, Bob Ward, his immediate boss, kept mouthwash and an electric razor in his desk. At least once every two months or so, Ward was kicked out by his third wife for some transgression or another, thus he maintained his emergency grooming supplies. So Sullivan's decision was made for him, it was to the office he'd go first.

There was a pay phone near the entrance of the motel. He went back to call a cab. Amazingly, the phone still functioned.

The beat-up truck had left the curb, the cutie now sitting between the two men. Sullivan was getting the number from information when the truck did a U-turn in front of a coffee shop on the corner, heading toward the hotel. Idly, he wondered if she had a special price for two.

"Yes, I need a ride at," dammit, what was the damn cross street, "ah, it's in front of the Boulevard Motel." The truck pulled into the driveway, but didn't go in. "Yes," he stammered into the handset, "yes, that's right, Danziger and Lewis." The company no doubt made several calls a week at the location.

"Ten minutes, perfect," Sullivan said. The driver and the other man in the pickup had gotten out. Sullivan hung up as the two reached him. Each wore a stylish Borsalino hat, in contrast with their jeans and casual shirts. One had a patch over his right eye; the other had his left eye covered. Their look went with the area.

"It's all yours." He held the receiver aloft for the driver.

The man, thick in the upper body with Popeye-like forearms, hit him in the bridge of his nose. Sullivan staggered back, reflexively bringing up his arm. "What the fuck?"

"Where is she?" the man's partner snarled. "Who the fuck—"

The driver swung again but Sullivan was prepared this time. He clubbed the fist intended for his face with the receiver, breaking it in two. As this one yelped, the passenger went into motion. Sullivan kicked him in the groin. He might be a solid citizen of the striving middle class, but that didn't make him a punk. He played hoops at a court where some brothers from the hood came, and he'd learned to handle his bidnez as they say. And he certainly couldn't afford to be mugged just now.

"Where is that bitch?" the driver demanded again, rushing him. He got his arms around Sullivan and drove the other man back against the motel wall. Sullivan punched him alongside his temple, his hangover having dissipated due to the adrenaline he was pumping.

The passenger had straightened up and he and his pal were crowding Sullivan. "You mean Mia?"

A grunt was his confirmation from the driver. "Where the fuck is she?"

"That's what I'd like to know." Did this guy have her name on his penis, too? "Look, maybe we can sort this out and—"

"Only thing that's gonna get sorted out is your ass after I'm through with it," Passenger proclaimed.

"Not here, it won't." The new voice belonged to Muumuu. She held an old-fashioned six-shooter down at her side. She seemed to have had practice with the piece. "Get to steppin'," she commanded matter-of-factly. "I can't afford any more law trouble."

"Look, Sharnu," Driver began.

The peacemaker's barrel angled up from her massive hip. "What?"

The two attackers weighed their possible responses. Silently, as if sharing an ESP link, they trod back to the trunk. The blonde watched dully. "It ain't over, motherfucker." Driver backed the truck up, and they took off.

"Lady, thanks," Sullivan said hurriedly, trying to get his breathing notched down to normal.

"You just get your ass out of here before Sally Jessy Raphael comes on, you hear me?" She started to walk away.

"Hey, wait," Sullivan started, "do you remember me coming here last night?"

She went around the corner. The cab came, and he left.

* * *

"Come on, what the fuck did you do last night?" Ward had that particular bemused smile of his etched on his face.

His face and demeanor were that of the bastard son of Peter Fonda and Dennis Hopper. He was leaning against the rim of sinks in the men's room. Sullivan was shaving.

"She close her legs too fast or what?" He pointed at the swelling prominent between Sullivan's eyes.

He was on his knees, his hands up her dress as she swayed before him. He shook himself. "Let's just get the presentation over with, shall we?" There was no sense concentrating on too many things at once. Everything had to be dealt with in order.

"Sure, Mark, sure." Ward, a rangy, athletically built man older than Sullivan, took off his glasses. He scratched part of his face with the end of the stem. He, too, tossed the rock at the courts Sullivan frequented. "Whenever you want to talk about it."

"Got an extra toothbrush?" Sullivan inquired, judging his handiwork and ignoring his friend's invitation.

"Got one unwrapped from the stop and rob. When you're my age, teeth are real important."

"Listen," Sullivan said, "when this is done…well, thanks, man, huh?"

"Uh-huh," he sagely replied.

The presentation was what it was. Sullivan had done most of the preparation beforehand, and he and Ward knew what the clients and their boss wanted to hear. It would have been stellar if Sullivan hadn't, despite his efforts at laser focus, been distracted about the letters on his salami.

Twelve minutes later, he and Ward got word the deal hadn't been nailed. "They still want to see how the billboard ads make for the synergy with the banners on related sites." Their boss, a dot-com millionaire younger than Sullivan, gave them his best Kevin Spacey stare. "Let's not lose this in the last quarter, okay, guys?" He removed his Prada-clad body from the doorway he'd been leaning in, leaving the door ajar.

"Doesn't the word synergy make you retch?" Ward snorted quietly through his nose.

Unconsciously, Sullivan was looking down at his crotch. "I've got to go."

"You have short-term memory loss, old bean?"

"It's important, Bob. This has everything to do with my"—he waved in the air— "and what happened to me last night."

"You know he's expecting our synergistic answer, the unfolding connection of the living and the inanimate in the universe, by the morning." Ward peered at him over the rim of his glasses like a professor dressing down a lazy student.

Sullivan was already at the door. "I'll call you tonight. You blue sky some ideas like you're so good at, and I'll flesh them out. Tonight, I promise, man."

"You better."

"Like I got a choice, right?" He walked fast, taking the side exit. Goddamn, he was spotted by that boot-licking clown Crawford, who coveted his job. But there was nothing he could do about it now. If the ass puckerer told the boss, Ward would come up with a convincing lie to cover him.

But no story was going to explain away a woman's name on his penis. He could get away with it tonight; his wife would be tired from traveling and her visit with her mother and older sister. Katherine's older sister Carey, who'd moved back home after a funky divorce, had been wearing her family out with her tales of woe for months. But what about tomorrow and thereafter? Was he suddenly going to become a prude and never appear naked before his wife? Would they only do it in the dark? Would he never let his wife stroke him again?

"Shit," he swore again for the umpteenth time. "Sir?" The cab driver swiveled his head a quarter turn. "I'm sorry, it's not you, just something on my mind."

The cab deposited him where he'd left his car, in the parking lot of the Red Pirate Bar & Grill. Last night, he'd figured that was a sign of luck to find a spot so near a jumping joint like the Pirate. The place was open for lunch, but it wasn't the same crew as the evening shift. He found out those folks didn't come on till four. He drove away.

$$* * *$$

"Sorry, dude," the tattoo artist chuckled, "but there ain't much can be done until you heal up."

Sullivan stood before him, pants and briefs down, in the man's shop. He'd picked the business because it was in the neighborhood of the Boulevard Motel. There was a woman working there, but she didn't seem to mind. At the moment, she was applying a tiger-breathing purple flame to a buffed guy's left pec.

"How long does that take?"

"Depends, and 'sides, unless you want me to make it into a sailboat or something, you gotta see a plastic surgeon, you know, for laser removal of the epidermis." He eyed the woman and snickered again. "And you don't know the chick who had this put on you?"

"No." He buckled up.

"Well, somebody did a real good job of it. Not much errant tracks or whatnot."

"How come I didn't wake up with that thing poking me?" He indicated the constant soft buzz of the woman's pneumatic needle gun as she composed her skin art.

The man shrugged. "Drunk enough or maybe a local anesthetic. I use 'em when they want their old man's name on the curve of their vagina or some cat wants a spider web on the tip of his one-eyed beast."

"Look," Sullivan produced two twenties and tore them in half, "you make a few calls and find out who made a visit at the Boulevard Motel last night, and you get these." He shook the other halves and tucked them away.

"Okay," the man agreed. He stuck the currency in his breast pocket.

"Ow," the man the woman was working on said. She dabbed at the blood dribbling along his arm.

An uncomfortable twinge gripped Sullivan down below. "I'll call you later."

Just as he got out on the sidewalk, the pickup screeched to a halt at the curb. "Hey, we want to talk to you," the man on the passenger side with the right-sided eye patch shouted.

"Damn straight," the driver put in. Between the men sat a passive German shepherd.

"What is the problem with you two?" Sullivan didn't wait for the answer. He was already running toward his car parked farther down the block. Sullivan prayed the dog wouldn't bite him on his whang.

The passenger stepped out and commanded, "Sic him, Bruno, sic him."

Bruno yawned and continued to pant heavily.

"What's up with this dog, man?" the passenger screamed at the driver.

"Fuck I know."

"Damn," the other one said. He got back in the car too fast and knocked his Borsalino off. Bruno looked at him and barked.

"Follow him," the passenger retorted irritably, leaning out the open door to retrieve his hat.

The driver was already gunning the truck, and the passenger fell out, crushing his hat. The driver slammed on his brakes just as a CheapAss.com delivery car was speeding along. CheapAss.com was one of those Internet delivery services you could dial up to have videos, food, and booze delivered to your door within the hour. Their delivery cars were silver Checker cab-type vehicles with a giant angled clipboard listing the stuff you could order on the roof. The Checker loudly crashed into the pickup's fender. The impact tore the clipboard loose from its moorings, and it sailed into the display window of the tattoo parlor. Bruno got scared and bit the driver on the leg. He screamed, and the dog howled in unison.

Sullivan drove off in a haze. The clock was ticking, and his options were limited. That name, that fucking Mia's name, was down there, silently taunting him, laughing at his folly. Oh, women like her liked to play with your balls, tell you how much a man you were to get you, like the chump you were, to willingly put them in a vise. They make with the come-on and tell you what you want to know, but really, Mia has contempt for you and your entire species. She'd given him those bedroom eyes in the bar, but inside, she'd been laughing at his weakness, his all too human desire. She'd practically shoved her breasts in his face. The fuckin' arrow. What a fool he'd been. He loved his wife, for chrissakes. Sure, he looked, window-shopped, as grandma used to say, but he didn't touch. "It's not my fault," he uttered, "that I'm a victim of my own testosterone." He gripped the steering wheel tighter as vestiges of the hangover crept behind his eyes. He couldn't do much else, but he could make her pay.

He headed back to the motel, the scene of the degradation. She'd be around, the one with the blond hair and blue streaks. She just had to be around. He parked across the street and waited. He killed more than an hour, but she was a no-show. Determined to find her, he got out and walked into the manager's office.

"Hold on, Annie Oakley," he said to the muumuued woman.

She was slurping a Popsicle and watching Ricki Lake on the portable behind the counter. She'd tensed at seeing him. "I just want a little information and am willing to pay for it." He produced a twenty and placed it before her.

"What?" she demanded, putting the bill away. "The blonde with blue streaks, what's her name?"

"How the fuck would I know?" She turned her attention back to Ricki. The show was about a group called Strippers Anonymous.

"She's a regular around here, isn't she?"

"Hell, no. Never seen her till this morning and haven't seen her since."

"What about those guys in the pickup?"

She put a blank look on him. "Mister, this is not *Jeopardy!,* okay? I'm not looking to answer questions I don't know or care to have the answer to. Now, unless you're gonna rent another room—"

Excitedly, he blurted, "You remember me from last night?"

"Yes," she said indolently, "are you happy now?"

"The woman, the woman I was with, did you recognize her?"

"She was standing outside while you paid. Hell, I thought you two were legit; she was carrying a suitcase and makeup kit."

Sullivan tried to comprehend what she'd told him as he meandered back outside. He called the tattoo parlor, using the phone out front.

"Nope, sorry, I didn't get squat," the owner said on the other end. "Far as I can tell, nobody made a midnight run, even though I told 'em there was a sawbuck in it for them."

Sullivan asked, "What about someone, a woman, who has a traveling kit?"

"That's nothing special, man. I've done some of those kind of jobs myself."

"She's got an arrow piercing an orange on the top of her left breast."

"Don't ring my bell, and frankly, it ain't worth me making another round of calls for what you're paying."

He hung up, angry the dude was trying to jack up the price and angry for getting himself in this predicament. That bitch had set him up. It was all part of the game for her to ensnare him and do this to him. But why him? Was he just an easy target, drooling, and eyes bugged out at her? Did she do this all the time? "Of course," he snapped his fingers. He got in his car and drove back to the Red Pirate.

His cell phone rang. His heart stopped, but he was relieved when it was Ward and not his wife making the call.

"I'm leaving some notes on your e-mail. You are going to tighten this project up tonight, right, old bean?"

"Naturally," he said distractedly. Ward exhaled audibly. "Yeah?"

"Yes, Bob, I promise. I'm almost done with…the thing I had to take care of."

"As you say."

* * *

At the bar, the evening shift was on.

"I kinda remember her, sure." She was one of the bartenders and had brought him his club soda with lime. "She was sitting there." She pointed at a stool.

"Had you seen her here before?" The clock behind her read five past five.

"Yeah, I did," the woman remarked. "Ah, about a week before, I think.

Seems I recall her having a drink with another woman, both of them dressed nice, you know, businesslike." She went off to fill another order.

Sullivan used his cell phone to call the airport. His wife's plane was due in ahead of schedule. He clicked off, the big hand on the clock seemingly speeding around the dial. The youthful sales manager walked into the gathering gloom. All right, no sex with the wife tonight. That would be simple enough. Tomorrow night, make sure he took her out to dinner, dancing, they'd be tired. He cheered up; this might work.

Then maybe he'd be healed enough and get the name removed with laser surgery. It was an outpatient procedure, so what was there to sweat? He reached his car when it occurred to him—bandages, he'd have to hide them, too. But he could say he got some kind of groin pull playing basketball. Yeah, yeah, that could work.

"Look, motherfucker, stop bullshitting with us."

He'd been so wrapped up in his plotting, he hadn't noticed the eye patch twins parked behind a large SUV. They had him pressed up against the bar's Dumpster.

He was more irritated with rather than scared of these two zeroes. "What'd Mia do to you?"

"Where can we find her?" the passenger demanded again. "We owe her for something she done to our cousin. We heard from people we know around here said she was spotted last night with you. Now I'm through talking; it's your turn."

"Tattooed her name on his dick?"

The driver, who favored his bitten leg, screwed up his face. "Huh?" He looked at the other one.

"Stop playing stupid," the passenger said, shoving Sullivan.

"I leave that to you." He shoved him back. "I've got more important matters on my mind, moron."

The driver swung, catching Sullivan in the gut. He doubled over and leaned against the Dumpster. The driver had his fist raised to strike.

"I don't know, man, you understand?" Sullivan said quietly, straightening up. "I picked her up in the bar, and we went to the motel. That's the first and last time I ever saw her."

"No, shit?" the passenger asked. "No, shit."

The two weighed the sincerity behind his words and then drove off. He checked his watch and drove to the airport.

"Hi, baby." He kissed his wife as she got off the plane. "I'm glad to see you." She hugged him tight, and it caused a lance of pain in his bruised John Thomas.

* * *

On the ride home, after discussing how her trip went, she asked, "Did you get out any?"

"No, no, I had plenty of work to take care of."

"Oh, poor darling." She nibbled his ear. "I missed you."

"I did, too, sweetie."

At home, she became more amorous. She rubbed a hand on his crotch as they sat on the couch. Sullivan just about jumped out of his skin from the raw sensation. He had to pretend he was enjoying the foreplay.

"Aren't you glad to see me?" she teased as her tongue probed his mouth.

"Of course, Kath."

"You seem tense."

"I've been under a lot of pressure, you know, the new account we're trying to land."

"I know what will relieve that pressure." She started to unzip his pants while massaging his tender rod.

He stood quickly. "I've got to use the bathroom, be right back."

"Sure," his wife said, a sly smile on her face.

Sullivan went into the restroom, a cold panic taking hold of him.

"Mark," his wife called sweetly from the living room.

"Yes, dear," he replied from the bathroom along the hall. Come on, Sullivan, think of an excuse to get out of this.

"Did you get my present?" she asked demurely.

His spine went ice. "Present? I was supposed to buy you something?"

Their anniversary? Had he forgotten?

"No, dear." She came into the bathroom. He was sitting on the closed lid of the toilet. "I mean from Mia, my love."

He felt faint.

She crouched down beside him. "You see, baby, she's a private eye. Her core business is in adultery cases, though she handles the robbery or even murder suspect now and then, too."

Sullivan couldn't speak.

His wife batted her sea-green eyes at him. "She did some work for Helen, you know, Bob's ex?"

Ward had been married twice before. In fact, he'd run his own company but had to sell it when he'd settled with his second wife. Now he knew why, and why his friend didn't talk about it.

"Seems ol' Bob had been paying for this young, gorgeous fashion student's downtown loft. Well…" She stood, letting her spread hands finish her sentence. "Anyway, Helen and I get to talking one day at lunch, you know how us women are."

Sullivan swallowed hard.

"She mentioned Mia and her agency. Helen said she was sorry she hadn't found out about her beforehand."

"So," Sullivan began.

"So she lures the properly sauced husband with the wandering eye to a motel room. Using some suggestive techniques, she shows him some porno, whispers in his ear, lets him rub on her, plants the right smell and taste." His wife paused and smiled. "But she assures the client there's no penetration. After all, the tattooing takes time, and who can do anything once that's done?"

Sullivan stared at his wife, who looked down at him. "This is a reminder, dear. Marriage isn't easy, but getting some on the side…" She wagged her finger. "Now, I'm sure you have some work to finish at the office. That is, I know that's where you'll be heading, right?"

"Yes."

"Good. 'Cause you don't want to even know about the amputation and taxidermy skills of her other operatives." She started to walk out of the bathroom, then turned to beam at him. "I'm sorry to have taken this step, but you'll be all healed in a few days and then we can get the tattoo removed. It's just, well," she looked regretful, "you know how you men are."

All he could do was stare into space.

***

"Branded," *Flesh & Blood: Erotic Tales of Crime and Passion,* Mysterious Press, 2001, Max Allan Collins and Jeff Gelb, editors.

Black Caesar's Gold

He had a dream, but it would have made Martin Luther King, Jr. shake his head woefully, Malcolm X tongue lash him severely, and Stokely Carmichael would have pimp slapped him. Frank Matthews, along with the other Frank, Lucas, and Leroy "Nicky" Barnes, were, for a time, the kingpins of the heroin trade on the East Coast. Matthews, the self-styled Black Caesar, was a country boy like Lucas. But once he got to the big city, he went all in. Maybe Barnes could quote *Moby Dick* and *King Lear*, but ascending from juvenile chicken thief in his native Durham to numbers runner in Philadelphia to becoming the first major drug lord in Harlem, Matthews had built an organization his compatriots admired, and the Mob feared.

"That moulie's getting too damn big for that mink coat he struts around in," Godfather Joe Bonanno was want to observe.

For Matthews moved product like no other, a Robin Hood in the community and a terror outside of it. Unlike other smaller pushers in Harlem and beyond, he didn't rely on La Cosa Nostra to keep him supplied. (Generally speaking, they controlled the pipeline.) Matthews had a direct South American connection and brought in H and coke that way, cutting out the usual middleman. He invested in property under various fronts and had cash couriered overseas into tax havens.

One time in Atlanta, Matthews brought together a roomful of big swingin'-dick black and Latino drug dealers to form a combine so as to chill the growing static with the Italian mobsters. Matthews was a strategic motherfucker.

Like Barnes and Lucas, the high-flying Matthews eventually got his wings clipped and was busted by agents of the then-newly constituted Drug Enforcement Administration. But different than those two, he didn't rat out his peers for a reduction of his sentence. Then again, Matthews didn't do time in the slammer, either. He liked to gamble in Vegas, those trips also a way for him to launder more of his money.

As these things happen, he had been in Vegas at the time with a beauty on his arm, losing at the craps tables but not sweating it. His plan was to soon be on his way to LA to catch Super Bowl VII between the Redskins and Dolphins. Yet unbeknownst to him, members of his South American network, along with a lieutenant, had already been arrested. The trap was closing in on him, and at McCarran Airport, the DEA slapped the cuffs on Matthews and his lady friend.

"What took you so long?" he was quoted as saying jauntily.

Incredibly, his lawyer successfully argued for his bail reduction, at which point Matthews got out of jail and then disappeared. That was 1973. From Chicago to Rome, Nigeria to Atlanta, sightings of Matthews abounded. But none of them panned out. He was never found. Maybe the Mafia had him whacked, or maybe Matthews had his face changed and retired to some island with a woman who liked to wear mini skirts and no underwear.

* * *

Chuck Grayson pondered Frank Matthews's fate and history as he pretended not to fawn over the too-sweet 1969 Mustang Fastback with a Boss 420 engine. Grayson had done his homework and knew less than a thousand of these particular Mustangs were produced that year. There must have been modifications to the engine compartment to accommodate the larger motor. A woman in stylish clothes and a wide-brimmed sun hat preceded him from the parking lot, where several vehicles were on display. Along with other potential buyers, they reentered the main room of Stedler and Sons Auctioneers. There was a photo of the maroon Mustang tacked to a padded board with its order in the auction noted. There were other pictures of various items pinned there as well, including vases and an ivory-inlaid cigar box said to have belonged to President Grover Cleveland.

Grayson had come to the auction house because this particular Mustang had belonged to Frank Matthews. Stedler and Sons listed the car as having belonged to Ken Schmecken, a producer and shadowy part-owner of three X-rated movie theaters in the Los Angeles area. Grayson was something of a Matthews aficionado and always on the lookout for items connected to the gangster. He knew that *Schmecken*, an oblique slang term for heroin, was one of the names the drug lord had used in hiding his investments.

Because the car had value as being only one of a limited number, there were several interested parties contending for it when it came up for bid. But Grayson was something of a limited edition himself.

He was a mid-thirties African American male who'd made his money as part of a start-up online entity that got sold for a nice profit to a conglomerate controlling various commercial websites. He and his friends' site was one of the first to cater to the multicultural geek crowd in all things pop culture, lifestyles, and fashion. Turned out people-of-color dweebs, a group of which Grayson was proudly a member, liked to hang together.

The car cost him more than he would have liked to pay. This was due to the woman across the room in the hat who kept upping him. But she'd dropped out when the asking price went past twenty-five grand. One, two…the third strike of the gavel, and Grayson took possession of the car.

The Mustang had been found in Altadena in the garage of a house belonging to a long-retired Department of Water and Power secretary named Deborah Keyson. She'd died of pulmonary failure, and any connection she may have had to Frank Matthews or Ken Schmecken was not known.

The auctioneers had put money into restoring the car, and it had been fairly well-preserved under a tarp, the gas, and fluids having been drained from it back when. Grayson had chanced upon its photo and description while sitting in his dentist's office, paging through a freshly minted Stedler and Sons catalog. He immediately recognized the name Schmecken in the brief write-up.

The paperwork done and money deposited, Grayson drove his prize away from the auction house in Glendale. He couldn't help but imagine he was Matthews at the wheel on his way to cement a nefarious deal as he drove home to Santa Monica. Along the way, his phone rang, and he answered, putting it on speaker and propping it in the opening of the car's built-in ashtray.

"So?" his girlfriend Mora Fleming asked. "Scored it, sweetie."

"I knew that you would."

"Yeah, well."

"Want me to bring Chinese or Indian?"

"I could go for some kung pao chicken."

She chuckled. "When do you *not* want that?"

"I want you."

"Hmmmm. See you soon."

Fleming, without her heavy boots on, was two inches taller than Grayson and outweighed his wiry frame by forty pounds—forty solid pounds. She was a bodybuilding chiropractor and gaming enthusiast. They'd met at the annual gathering at Nerd Central—Comic-Con in San Diego. She'd come with a girlfriend, a fellow bodybuilder, and they'd turned the heads of fanboys and their put-upon fathers—the two women dressed in the fantasy of scantily clad barbarian sword-wielding women.

Standing in line to get into a panel with comic superstar writer Neil Gaiman, Fleming had been impressed with Grayson's knowledge of the *S.T.A.R. Ops* game in phantom mode. That, and he managed to look at her face and not just her substantial chest.

In bed later, cuddling after making love to Fleming in his second-floor bedroom, Grayson saw through the slats of the window the light over his garage snap on. The light was motion sensitive, and normally, it coming on meant one of his neighbors' cats was lazing by. But the Mustang was parked in the driveway, near the garage door. He hadn't outfitted the car with an alarm yet, though he'd put a lock bar on the steering wheel.

Grayson waited for the sound of the vehicle's door being opened. He smiled, realizing he better wake up his girlfriend if there was trouble. But the light went off again, and there were no more sounds of disturbance from below.

The following morning, he was changing out the battery in the trunk when Fleming asked, "Why the heck is it back here?"

"They needed all the room up front to squeeze in the big block engine," Grayson explained, lifting the battery out. He figured the auction house had spent money on the car's looks but not on a more heavy-duty battery. He intended to not scrimp when it came to his new beauty. He was going to use his electric motor Leaf and go to the auto parts store to trade this battery in for a better one. There was a recessed metal shell that held the battery in its cavity. He removed it to inspect the shell for rust.

"What's this?" Fleming asked, reaching a hand into the opening in the trunk's floorboard where the shell resided. She worked for a few moments undoing some tape and held aloft a plastic sandwich baggie that had been secured on the frame below the battery's shell.

The couple exchanged a look of anticipation as Fleming tore the baggie apart and removed a sheet of yellowed paper. Gingerly, she unfolded the stiff note and flattened it on the slope of the car's fastback. On the paper was a sentence in block lettering: *SIXTY YARDS NORTH FROM THE PANZER.*

"Panzer?" Fleming asked. "Like German for tank?"

"Precisely," Grayson said, heading for the house. "Let me check something, but I think we might have a road trip this morning."

"Yeah, where?"

"Why, a bombed-out French village, my dear."

* * *

The village had had various names and had been used in TV shows and movies several times. It was a World War II—era set in Canyon Country that, by the late '60s, had become mired in an ownership battle between its original builder and the children of one of the ex-partners. This made it difficult to rent out. But in 1970, the village was utilized illegally—that is, the producers didn't bother to pay—for a hardcore shoot called *Madam*

Satan of the SS.

"You've seen this epic?" Fleming asked.

"Way before I had the pleasure of your acquaintance. In fact, there was a sequel, but that one took place in a mad scientist's castle. Same woman played Madam Satan both times, Jackie Salvo."

"Uh-huh."

"Of course, purely for research into the wild and varied career of Frank Matthews."

"Of course."

Grayson had recalled that under the Ken Schmecken alias, Matthews had been a producer of a porno set during World War II. He'd confirmed this in a nonfiction book he had at home about twentieth-century gangsters, which featured an extensive chapter on the disappeared drug lord.

Fleming wondered aloud, "Does *heron*, to use the vernacular of the day, retain its potency over decades?"

"You figure that's what he has buried there?"

She regarded the freeway outside the rolled-down passenger window. The Mustang didn't have air conditioning. "You think he buried money?"

"He was a careful dude, Mora. Maybe he was planning in case he had to go on the run and needed to make sure he had enough liquid assets to make a break to Mexico or the Bahamas."

She leaned over and kissed him on the cheek. "My little Scarface."

He squeezed her muscular thigh. "Better know it."

Canyon Country was in Santa Clarita, in the northwest section of LA County. In the last twenty years the area had seen the proliferation of housing subdivisions, but there were still large swaths of underpopulated nature. Using tax records and past articles he'd accessed online, Grayson had obtained the location for the place most commonly called Attack Squad Village, as the set had been used several times in the popular 1960s World War II TV show *Attack Squad.*

Once there, they parked and walked along a dusty street bordered by French-style buildings of the proper vintage, a bombed-out church, and a bar called Millie Marie's among the façades. There was another street;

then behind the false front of an apartment building, in the tall weeds, they found the German tank.

"North is this way," Fleming said. Each carried shovels. Using a tape measure and allowing for human error, they marked off the one-hundred-eight feet from the tank. Grayson used the point of the shovel to scribe a large circle in the dirt.

Fleming nodded and got started. He began in another section inside the circle. In less than fifteen minutes, they'd uncovered a coffin.

"Wow," Fleming intoned. "I didn't expect that."

"We've come this far," he said. They dug the dirt out from around the coffin and together hefted it above ground.

"Damn!" Fleming exclaimed, sweat on her brow.

"Here goes," Grayson said. He used the shovel to lift the lid and let it flop open.

"Oh shit!" Fleming rasped.

Inside the coffin were bricks of gold. Grayson picked up a bar, assessing its weight in his hand—roughly two pounds, he estimated. "How is this possible?" he wondered aloud.

"Gold is good anywhere, Chuck," Fleming observed. "I got that, but it's illegal to own gold bars."

Hands on her hips, she said, "A drug lord isn't worried about the rules, honey."

"I know that, but what foundry would cast these for him?"

"I can answer that," a new voice said.

The two looked around to find three newcomers, two men in sports coats and slacks, flanking a slender woman in a loose top, white jeans, and heels. She wore a feathered and beaded Mardi Gras eye mask. The two men had on pedestrian ski masks. One of the men, slimmer than the other, pointed a semi-auto pistol-grip shotgun at Grayson. A slight wind blew, but the couple didn't notice the breeze.

"How'd you know to find us here?" Grayson asked.

The shotgun man snorted. "Like that purple car is hard to follow."

"What you need to worry about," the woman interjected, "is how you're going to pace yourself loading my goods." There was a trace of an accent in her voice.

The smile below her mask was brittle, like a robot trying to be chummy. Grayson, who figured she was the one in the wide-brimmed hat at the auction, noted a mole to the left of her plump lips. The lines on her face indicated a woman of some years, though clearly in fit shape.

The shotgun still on Grayson, the stockier thug retrieved a white van and backed it close to the loot. He opened the rear swing doors. Resigned, Grayson and Fleming loaded the ingots into the rear cargo area. There were a hundred and twenty-four bars.

"Now what?" Grayson said, using the heel of his hand to wipe sweat from his brow. The temperature had risen past the mid-eighties.

"Now we say bye-bye," the woman answered triumphantly.

Fleming was standing near the rear of the van, at an angle to the shotgun holder. She rushed at the man, hoping to tackle him and relieve him of his weapon. But he was a pro and wasn't rattled.

"Back that ass up, you big bitch," he said, clubbing her with the pistol-grip end of the shotgun.

Fleming went down heavy.

"Mora!" Grayson blared, rushing to aid her. The larger hood produced a stun device and jammed it against Grayson's neck. He convulsed and spittle coated his lips as he, too, dropped to the ground on his knees. A second jolt toppled him, and he lay twitching, his muscles unresponsive to his commands. He wet himself.

"That's a cherry ride you got, bro," the one who'd shocked him said. "I'll look good driving that bad boy." The hood removed the keys from Grayson's pocket, easily knocking away Grayson's feeble attempt to stop him.

"Is that necessary?" the woman said.

"It's a perk, baby," the man shot back. He and the shotgunner laughed harshly. The woman said something in Spanish, and the three left in the two vehicles.

Mora Fleming moaned and rolled onto her side. She then got herself up and helped Grayson to his feet.

"That was exciting," she said dryly.

"How're you feeling?" Tenderly, he placed the flat of his hand on the side of her face.

She touched the back of her head. "Some painkillers and intravenous tequila ought to remedy the situation."

He looked beyond her. "I hate getting beat," he declared. "Not to mention, that was a serious haul of gold. And that bastard took my car."

"Maybe we should be happy to be alive, Chuck."

He had an odd smile on his face when he addressed her. It wasn't an expression she'd seen before. "Maybe they shouldn't have left me alive."

Despite him just standing there with the front of his jeans dark from urine, Fleming got nervous.

* * *

There were hardly any photos of Frank Matthews aside from booking shots. But Grayson found one of him at a club in Harlem taken by the black-owned *Amsterdam News,* as the white press at that point didn't know who he was. Using a magnifying glass, Grayson studied the picture that showed Matthews smoking a cigar, holding court with a tableful of cohorts. Because it was a close-in shot, not all the faces were distinct. He wondered if there were other shots from the club.

Through the microfiche records at the New York Public Library, Grayson was able to narrow his possibles to two photographers who worked for the *News* then and who might have taken the uncredited shot. One was dead, and the other, Tim "Cheaters" Pleasy, was still alive. He was seventy-six and taught an extension photography class in Sarasota. Grayson promptly got him on the phone.

"Yeah," Pleasy said after the exchange of pleasantries, his voice clear and young-sounding. "Ol' Frank fancied himself the big shot all right. Passing out twenties to the kids on the streets like free lunch, buying color TVs for the senior center…Yeah, he was something."

Grayson let the old-timer drone on some, then asked, "You remember a shot you might have taken of him at the Montreaux Club? Him at a table of people having a good time?" He described the scene in further detail.

"Naw, young man, that don't ring no bell," Cheaters Pleasy said. "I'd bet Garmes took that shot." Davis Garmes was the deceased photographer.

"Any idea where his outtakes got to? He have family? I wanted to see if he had other shots showing the faces clearly."

"You sure seem to want to go through a lot for your book," Pleasy observed.

"I might have an uncle in that shot, and I want to know for certain," he lied.

"I got you," the older man said. "I'll check on that and will get back to you. I might know where some of his old photos went."

"That would be great, Mr. Pleasy."

It didn't take the photographer long, as he and the late Garmes had stayed in touch. He was able to locate the man's photos left in the possession of an ex-wife he also knew. Garmes's photos were in various film boxes designated by years. She found two other shots Garmes had taken that night, had them scanned, and eventually, they reached Grayson via e-mail.

"There she is," Grayson said to Fleming. They sat at his kitchen island. He tapped the magnifying glass against his opposite hand. "That beauty mark, mole, whatever you want to call it, gives her away. She's at the table here with Matthews."

Fleming folded her arms. "And she's the one playing Madam Satan in those two pornos he produced?"

"Yep. Jackie Salvo, but that's an alias."

Fleming frowned. "Okay, let's say you find out her real name, which isn't hard, then what?"

"Get our shit back."

She put a hand on his. "Darling, we go see action-adventure movies and read comic books. But unfortunately, I'm not Wonder Woman, and you aren't the Punisher."

He winked. "But we've role-played them."

"I'm serious, Chuck. This woman ain't playing."

"We've handled guns," he countered.

"Shooting at targets at a firing range isn't the same thing as blasting a human being, and you know it. We might be geekazoids, but we're solid citizens, baby. We pay taxes, have businesses, homes—in other words, unless you're willing to give all that up, I say drop this."

"Let me just identify her. Just that, for my own satisfaction." She folded her arms again, a questioning look to her. "Don't think you're slick."

"Me? Never."

* * *

Finding out the real name of a woman who starred in two X-rated cult movies from the '70s was easier than buttoning a shirt. Once he had that information, Grayson was able to document the up-and-down career of Pilar Ortega Renaud De La Fontana. She'd gained notoriety back then from the Madam Satan films and graduated to starring in a few grade-C horror and sci-fi movies. She had some TV roles, too, and in the '90s, hosted a cable access show where she made smart-ass remarks and one-liners throughout whatever turkey she was showing.

Naturally, there were a couple of fan clubs devoted to her among nerddom and getting an address for the woman wasn't too tough either, given Grayson knew who to ask what. At a coffee shop on Olympic Boulevard, he met with a man who De La Fontana twice had imposed a restraining order against.

"It's not like I meant her any harm," said Fred Summerville, an underemployed box store clerk. He nibbled on the second Rice Krispies treat Grayson had bought him.

Grayson sized up Summerville as the type who got off on some peep action, and heaven would be sniffing De La Fontana's panties. But he said, "I feel you, man, where would these celebs be if it wasn't for us keeping their names out there?"

"Exactly," Summerville agreed happily, bits of his treat exploding from his mouth.

More commiserating included Summerville warning Grayson about a fifty-some-odd-old boyfriend of De La Fontana named Boris who'd done time for strong arm robbery. He didn't know the last name of this bruiser, but what the restraining orders couldn't do, Boris had done when he'd come into Summerville's store and calmly broken his hand.

"I stayed away after that," the former stalker stated flatly, looking down.

The hundred and fifty in cash Grayson offered elevated the man's mood and produced an address. She lived in a modest Craftsman in East Hollywood not too far from the large Kaiser medical facility on Sunset and Vermont.

On the second night of his stakeout in his Leaf, Grayson saw the Mustang arrive, and a stocky man in his fifties exit the vehicle and enter the house.

Fleming was right. Grayson wasn't about to storm in there armed with an AK and a bandana on his head, demanding the gold and his car back. But he'd be damned if he was going to get taken advantage of and not do something. Driving back to Santa Monica, he came up with a plan and discussed it with his girlfriend the next day in her office.

"Oh, man," she said finally. "That's a shitty idea, Chuck."

"It could work."

"Or we could spend several years in prison, if we don't get killed. And if it's the former, I couldn't stand the thought of a booty bandit wearing out that fine ass of yours."

"Good to know," he said. "Anyway, it's not we, just me."

"Bullshit. He's my patient, and you're not doing this without my help. Besides, I don't want you going to the next con talking about how I pussied out on you."

They both grinned broadly.

* * *

Grayson wanted to obtain a kilo of black tar heroin—those tense opening teasers of many a *Miami Vice* of cool crooks and sweating undercover cops flashing through his mind. He owned the complete box set on DVD. But trying to buy that kind of weight also meant making connections beyond

Fleming's patient. And this meant gaining the acquaintance of certain individuals who'd cut out your intestines and sell them back to you as a scarf. So he settled for two small glassine packets with a blue devil head stenciled on them.

The patient Fleming was treating for back alignment problems was very much into holistic health and organic foods, which he gladly talked about extensively. Yet when you work on a person's body up close and personal like she did, the conversing invariably covered a lot of territory—like one's past.

Todd Jessup, the patient, had been a pharmacist who got hooked on the drugs he dispensed. He lost his license and, in his descent, encountered various unsavory individuals. He'd subsequently rebuilt his life, and it took some coaxing, but he came up with a few contacts from the bad old days. Thereafter, Grayson and Fleming bought the blue devil packets from a hardass runaway teenager working for her pusher pimp boyfriend in the Valley. The one-time pharmacist verified the authenticity of the packets.

Staging the accident came next. Boris, no-last-name, was driving the Mustang back to De La Fontana's house from Vons supermarket, blasting the Eagles on the aftermarket CD unit. Grayson almost cried as he purposely bashed his Leaf into the left front fender of the classic vehicle. Boris was out in a shot, yelling.

"The fuck is wrong with you, man? You blind or something? Hey, it's you," he said, recognizing Grayson.

"Your mama's blind, bitch," Grayson responded.

Boris rushed over, and Grayson jabbed him in the face without hesitation. This earned him a left to the stomach and a right to the chin. He was younger than Boris by more than twenty years, but the other man was far more experienced with his fists.

"What, figured you'd try and get your car back, punk? Well, come on."

He laughed and again hit Grayson, who rocked back; he ducked the next blow, but the inevitable was upon him. A crowd gathered, cheering the combatants. By the time the motorcycle cop arrived, there was a cell phone video of Grayson getting his ass kicked up on YouTube. Though at one point, down on all fours, Grayson had managed to get ahold of his tormentor's calf and bite through his pant leg. A couple of people watching clapped at that.

As Boris Stallings had no paperwork for the Mustang, nor proof of insurance, the car was impounded and searched. Stallings was arrested for possession of heroin, planted under the floor mat on the passenger side by Mora Fleming as her boyfriend took his beatdown. The door had been locked, but when Grayson got the car, he'd been given two sets of keys. She'd argued she should be the one to plow into the Mustang as she felt she could handle herself better against Stallings.

"Dammit, woman, you've already seen me piss myself.

"What pride do I have left?" Grayson had said.

She'd kissed him. "A man must do what he must do."

* * *

It took a week to recuperate at home from his encounter with Stallings. His face was still tender. The Santa Monica PD notified Grayson about his car once the LAPD contacted them. Grayson told the police he had been in the area to shop at Skylight Books and was shocked to see the Mustang that had been jacked from him the week before. He'd lost control of the car, and that's when this horrible Stallings person went wild on him.

He also saw on the news that De La Fontana had been found shotgunned to death in her house, though no ingots were mentioned. A known associate of Stallings was said to be a person of interest.

Among the online fan club, there was talk that De La Fontana had family ties to one of Frank Matthews's South American financiers. It was speculated that she and Mathews had been romantically linked at one point. There was also a rumor about her being the mistress at age seventeen of a general who'd absconded with treasures from his country's coffers.

In a chat room, Grayson read the suggestion that maybe she'd done Matthews in after he ripped her off and that she must have been on the hunt for the gold for a long time. But her killing him didn't make sense, since she would have needed him alive to reveal where the gold was hidden. Though could be she got carried away having him worked over, someone else offered, and so it went, back and forth. All this merely conjecture among her fans.

Grayson got the Mustang repaired and painted a sedate color. Now and then, behind the wheel, Mora Fleming humming to an oldie on the radio beside him, he wondered whatever became of Black Caesar's gold.

* * *

"Black Caesar's Gold," *The Heroin Chronicles,* Akashic, 2013, Jerry Stahl, editor.

III

BOTH OF SHADOWS AND SUBSTANCE

Can't Be Satisfied

He rested the semi on the bleached gravel among a row of similar vehicles at the truck stop off the highway. Shutting the rig down, he re-checked the pressure gauges assuring him the refrigerated trailer was working properly. The driver rubbed a hand on his tired face, dried sweat and road grime working its way into his stubble. Roosevelt Hopkins took a quick glance at his features in the rearview, idly flicking a finger at the baubles dangling from it.

He got out of the truck, stretched, and walked toward the diner called McKinley's Manor, home of fine eats and cold beer. He entered to the smells of the business of feeding strangers. Hopkins took a stool, nodding down the way at another trucker he recognized from this route. Perusing the menu, he was pleased the café had smothered pork chops and greens. He'd love to eat heavy, something satisfying on his hollow stomach, but he had to make the port by six in the evening, so no time for a nap after such a meal.

"Get you something to drink while you make up your mind?"

Hopkins looked up at the waitress. She wasn't a kid, but she was pretty in a way a woman past forty could be. Darker than his complexion, she had full breasts beneath the military-pressed white shirt she wore, the diffuse presence of a black bra evident underneath.

"Water would be just fine."

She pointed with the eraser end of her pencil over her shoulder. "We've got a barbequed half chicken as the special today, and that comes with sliced carrots and candied yams.

Now look, this is real Q, sugah, not a roasted bird with store-bought sauce splashed on."

Her voice had him imagining a smoky club, laughing low, sharing drinks and tongues. He spun back to reality. "Cool. I'll figure out what I want."

She smiled briefly with practiced ease and scooped ice chips into a large plastic tumbler. Hopkins studied the menu and settled on a tuna melt and fruit, tempted as he was to have fries. Not for the first time, he lamented being old enough to worry about his waistline and cholesterol.

"To be young again," she said, putting the water and ice before him.

For a moment, he wondered how she knew what was on his mind, then understood she was looking at a man and woman cuddling on one of the benches in a booth by the door. Both not too far past the legal age for drinking, tattoos decorating their bare arms.

"You ain't ready for your rocking chair yet."

The smile again, but, this time, it seemed less automatic reflex. "Aren't you sweet."

He chuckled and gave her his order. Today's folded sports section had been left on the counter. Hopkins read the ball scores and about athletes' woes until she returned with his food.

"This is your first time through here, isn't it?" she said.

There was no name tag on her shirt.

"Had to do my friend's run," he said. "Play cousins we are. He's having some elective surgery, but he's got to pay the bills like the rest of us. The time or two I've been through here before, it's been at night."

"I work the night shift a couple of times a week. Funny, we never synced up." She went away as more customers arrived.

Hopkins enjoyed his lunch, playing out various pleasurable ways he might "sync up" with the woman. Could be this was merely harmless flirtation on her part, just something to pass the time during the days of the same. But it beat worrying about some baller's knew going out.

Afterward, he put his money down, and she said, "Come on back, okay?"

"Will do." He walked outside, regretting not pushing himself to ask her which nights she worked, but it wouldn't have been the first time he misread the vibe, and he didn't want to look like a chump. For all he knew, she was a part-owner and wanted to sucker him back only in regards to having the cash register sing the ca-ching chorus. Stepping away, Hopkins heard two men coming around the near corner of the diner.

"That's a sweet sled, that's for damn sure."

"Yeah," his companion agreed, working a toothpick between his teeth with gusto. "It'll need some work, but could be nice once it gets going."

The two walked away talking about the car, and curious, Hopkins went around the way they'd come. Behind the diner were wood pallets stacked by the screened back door, a half drum for the 'queing, a locked dumpster, and some plastic buckets that once contained allotments of industrial strength butter.

There was a short cement path leading to a circle of cement bordered in overgrown grass and weeds. An old-fashioned car port, virtually bereft of its paint, was over this. Reposed under the carport was a two-tone, white on blue, 1957 Plymouth up on blocks. He got closer. The car's color was dulled, but his cursory inspection of the body indicated little rust or dents.

"You've been a good ol' wagon, daddy, but you done broke down."

Hopkins turned to see the waitress he'd been talking to standing in the rear doorway of the restaurant. She was smoking a cigarette and came down the short steps to walk over to him and the car.

"One of the Eighty-Eight series," he said. "HyFire V-8's in 'em they were called."

"Rocket 88. You know about cars?"

"I know about ones this vintage." He squinted at her as some of her smoke drifted by his eyes. "Whose is it?"

Hand on her hip, her other fingers around her cigarette. "Mine, slick."

"You keep it out in the open like this?"

She took a puff. "No, most of the time in the last eight years or so, it's been in a garage and under a tarp." She pointed at the interior. "Take a look."

He opened the door and, looking in, the aroma of leather preserver hit him, triggering a pleasing sensation. "You've kept the seats and dash in good shape," he complimented, straightening up.

She lifted her brows while taking a last drag on her cigarette. She exhaled and flicked the butt onto the concrete pathway. "A friend was working on it, but he had to stop a few weeks ago. Clarence, the owner," she jabbed a thumb at the diner, "let him work on it here 'cause there was the room, and my friend had removed the tires and chained it up."

She paused, then, "Friends are something, ain't they?"

Hopkins frowned and, looking under the car as she indicated, could see a heavy chain wrapped around the rear axle leading to a stout iron ring embedded in the circle of cement. A padlock gleaming off-yellow affixed the chain to the ring.

Hopkins said, "Can't leave a fine car like this."

"My friend made some progress before he took off with the tires and the keys to the locks."

"You broke his heart, huh?"

"I do it all the time." Both hands on her hips now, head cocked to one side. "Why you care?"

"I like to put my nose in all sorts of tight places."

She showed strong teeth. The café's owner, a heavyset man in rolled-up sleeves and suspenders, came to the back door, scowling.

"I'd like to take a look at the car if I could."

She was walking back to work but stopped, turning her head partway around. "Be back Thursday, 'round nine at night, the Scimitar Lounge, down the road a'piece here." She went back inside, and he watched the sway of those hips as she did so.

Hopkins had a hard time taking the grin off his face as he powered up his friend's rig and drove away.

* * *

The bar she told him to meet her at was on Sixteenth Street. Hopkins strolled in and was surprised there was live music in the form of a lanky youth with his guitar and portable amp on a small, raised stage off to one side of the place. He was doing justice to a rendition of an Albert Collins song, "Cold, Cold Feeling."

He spotted the waitress sitting at the bar in a simple dress, legs crossed, showing a conditioned thigh. She was talking to the bartender, a tall, lean individual with an old-fashioned bowler perched on the back of his head.

"What's your poison?" she asked, touching his arm when he sat next to her. She wore a luminescent peach-colored lipstick that complimented her dark skin.

There was just enough plunge to her neckline that, in the half-light, made her breasts seem larger than he remembered. If he wasn't careful, he was going to break out in a sweat.

"Vodka tonic, the house vodka is fine."

"That's the only kind we got, pardner," the bartender said.

He smiled good-naturedly at Hopkins and made his drink. "How you doing, you make your delivery on time?"

"I did, thanks for asking. How's your work?"

She made a sound. "Work, you know."

His drink was placed before him. He clinked his glass with hers as she held her drink aloft.

"Here's to not being satisfied." Hopkins reacted. "That's a crazy toast."

"Yeah?" She sipped from her drink, eyes on him like a waiting jaguar. "You don't want more?" Her foot was out of her shoe, and she rested this on his lower leg, moving it around some.

"I want plenty," he said huskily.

"I know you do." She moved her foot higher on his leg, digging her toes in.

Later that night, they were in the Rocket 88, up on blocks. It was a cool evening, but they were generating enough warmth. She lay partly against the rear door on the back seat, her legs open and dress pushed up. She rubbed her midnight blue nailed hand on her mound. She slipped a finger inside her pale panties and rubbed her clit, moaning.

"Do you want me, RH?" she said between breaths.

"My head's about to explode, baby." It was roomy in the rear of the car, and he had no trouble unbuttoning and removing his shirt.

"Which head?" She took her finger from between her legs and placed the tip on his willing tongue. "You better get over here and fuck me."

"Yes, ma'am."

It was almost light before the two excited the car after their thrashing and sleeping in the vehicle. She was barefoot.

"Doesn't that hurt?" He asked her as they walked away, she carrying her shoes, over her crooked fingers of one hand.

She turned into him and put her free hand on his withered member inside his pants. "Not as much as I hurt you."

"I need more of that hurtin'." She kissed him.

That weekend, Roosevelt Hopkins had to do a haul with his friend's truck again but was able to make it back to town the following Tuesday. He'd brought his tools and went to work on the Plymouth. Some time ago, it had been explained to him, the gas left in the tank had been dumped and the fuel lines blown clean.

Old gas tended to become gummy and had to be disposed of in the process of rebuilding an auto. A reconditioned engine block had also been installed by the last mechanic working on the vehicle and Hopkins located the heads for the car in the trunk. Those, he had to send out two towns over to get redone. But locating a mechanical fuel pump, alternator, and so forth wasn't too hard, given the internet and the number of old car clubs and enthusiasts out there.

He and Clover, that was the woman's name, Clover Stovall, were going to get in the car when he got it running and take off down the highway. Since being laid off more than two years ago from the brewery where he'd driven a delivery truck, Hopkins had made do with hustling freelance jobs like filling in for his buddy.

Hopkins didn't want to get sucked down in debt at his age trying to finance his own rig, but this catch as catch can approach to making a living was wearing thin as well. He needed a change, and so did she, Clover had told him.

"I don't care where we go, as long as we put miles between this place and the next and the next after that." They lay spent in her bed; night sounds rustling through the compact bedroom in her compact apartment. They were on the second story over the Shelby Domino and Tonk Parlor, an unofficial after-hours joint.

"Your boy just got twenty-five on the bones," Stovall said, caressing and licking Hopkins' chest.

He laughed at her joke about the domino game happening below. They could hear the muffled excitement of the players through the floorboards.

"You gonna be ready?"

"Like I got something holding me here."

"That car's gonna be our ticket, Clover." It gave him a chill to say her name.

She had her hand around his member, going up and down slowly and surely as he stiffened. "I was going crazy until you got here, RH. You know how much this means to me?"

"I know how much you mean to me. I needed this second chance."

"Hmmm," she murmured, taking him in her mouth.

Head thumping against the headboard, heart hammering, Hopkins looked down at her bobbing head and put both of his hands gently on the back of her head.

She decreased her rhythm momentarily and whispered, "Go on, RH. Put it deep in my mouth like you do my pussy." She increased her actions again.

"Ughhh," he exclaimed and thrust his hips as she noisily gobbled him. "Oh, yeah, shit…"

Hopkins was consumed. Down below, the domino player who was in the third house, ahead in points, pushed his hat back some with a touch of his long fingernail to the underside of his brim. He smiled a rattler's grin as he plopped down another tile for fifteen.

"Damn, son, you can't do no wrong tonight," an old man, a regular, groused as he considered his hand.

He spread his arms. "What can I say?" The game went on, but soon, the outcome was clear as the winning player poised a tile over the lopsided cross on the table of the previously played dominoes.

"Get it over with," the old man said.

His hearing, keener than any man's or woman's, picked up Hopkins, who joyfully announced, "I'm comin', Clover, I'm comin'." He slammed down his winning domino at the same instant Roosevelt Hopkins loosened in his lover's mouth.

"That's game," the victor pronounced to a round of groans and cussing.

* * *

On a hot Sunday afternoon, a breeze billowing the fabric of the light summer dress she wore, Clover Stovall handed a rusted key to Hopkins. "Unlock our future, Roosevelt."

He took the key and, crouching down, grasped the lock and, surprised, let it go. He looked up at the woman.

"What's wrong?" She rubbed her fingers in his short naps. "Felt...felt like it had a pulse."

She clucked her tongue. "Don't be silly."

"Yeah," he half-heartedly agreed. He reached out, hesitating, then took hold of the lock again. It was warm in his hand but certainly, he told himself, not alive. He hadn't paid much attention to the padlock while getting the car back together. But it now occurred to him up close it wasn't done up in imitation gold plating but was the real thing. Nor was there a smooth, machine finish to the lock. Rather, it appeared to have been forged and shaped long ago. Not that he was an antiques expert, but this shadowy notion flooded through him.

"Damn," he muttered, inserting the key in the lock's key slot. Behind him, he didn't see his lover putting a hand to her stomach, anticipation afire on her pretty face. As Hopkins turned the lock, Clover Stovall responded by licking her bottom lip, her hand going lower.

Hopkins stood and undid the chain from around the rear axle.

"Start the engine, Roosevelt. Start this goddamn car." Stovall demanded, wide eyes fixed on the Plymouth.

"I will," he said, "but we gotta do it right. I'll turn the motor over to pump the fuel and oil out of the sump. Have to do that for several cranks to make sure—"

She latched on to him and kissed him fiercely. "Just do it. Shit."

After his precautions, the car running like a sewing machine, they took the Plymouth for a test drive.

"Front end could stand an alignment," Hopkins noted, taking a curve onto a country road. "But we can worry about that later."

"That's right." Clover Stovall sat close to him on the bench seat, her hand on his thigh. She turned on the radio, catching a news program in mid-broadcast. She turned the knob and found an oldies station.

"When I start drilling, I'll have to give you Novocain," Dinah Washington warned in her sirenic voice on "Long John Blues" from the dashboard speaker.

Her hand rubbed his thigh and then rested on his zipper. Spellbound, Hopkins looked from her to the end of the road where it narrowed down among a mass of poplar and maple trees. Coming out from under a leafy overhang was a man in a bowler Hopkins at first couldn't place—then did. He slowed the car.

"What's he doing here? What's going on, Clover?"

"We better get out." Her body language matched the sudden arctic tone of her words.

Hopkins shut the engine off and got out. The woman scooted out on the driver's side as well. She had her shoes in one hand and went to stand next to the bartender.

"Explain this to me," Hopkins said, more hurt than angry. "Hard to sum up in a few ticks, pardner," the bartender began, gesturing with the bowler in his hand. "Old folks hoodoo tales they spouted in their rocking chairs from way back when. Conjure ways handed down and down, intricacies inside of other intricacies," he said, his long fingers proscribing a symbol in the air between them.

Hopkins advanced. "You're not taking her or this car from me."

Clover Stovall shook her head from side to side. "'Fraid it's not for you to say, sugah. This is all been writ before you and me came along."

The bartender smiled slyly and put a hand around her trim waist. "Ain't she something?"

Hopkins made to strike out but was forced to grab at his chest as a lancing pain attacked his heart. He got wobbly on his feet, his vision blurring and breathing as if his windpipe was now the size of a straw.

"You used me to break some kind of spell," he managed to wheeze at the pair.

The bartender hunched a shoulder in his suit coat. "Well, yes, see it could only happen at a certain cycle of the earth and Beelzebub yank my toe, you happened by during the, what they call it, window of opportunity."

There were others before him, Hopkins realized. Because of particulars of the spell ,he had no knowledge of, the men before him had or could only complete part of the task. Who knew how many years she and the car had lured fools like him.

The bartender and the woman laughed, and Hopkins, now on his side in the dirt, didn't have the strength to stop her from plucking the solitary key from his numb fist. Impotently, he watched the two embrace. The bartender made a show of putting a hand under her dress, then they departed in the car intended for his escape and rebirth.

He rolled over on his back, hearing the Hy-Fire V-8 rumble away as the car took the two farther and farther away. His edging toward death's shroud lessened as the wielder of the power over him left. He was already forgotten by the two schemers he figured.

Hopkins was glad his friend was superstitious. He kept a crow's foot, black cat bone, and purported piece of the box that held Stagolee's revolver hanging from the rearview mirror of his truck. When, in an off-handed manner, Hopkins had told his friend about this incredible woman he'd met who liked to go barefoot and about the make and model of the car, his friend had convinced him to keep a charm on his person. It was on a small chain he'd given Hopkins.

Hopkins had scoffed but to placate his play cousin, had attached the piece of silver, shaped like some sort of flower he didn't recognize, to his key chain. Soon he was able to rise and dust himself off and walk back to town.

Soon too he was on the road in a borrowed vehicle, looking for the man who a few old ones who still kept the old ways he encountered said was maybe Rawhead Rex, others swore he went by Uncle Monday.

No matter. He was going to find him, her, and the car. He was going to be satisfied.

* * *

"Can't Be Satisfied," *Too Much Boogie: Erotic Remixes of the Dirty Blues*, LL Publications, 2011, Cole Riley editor.

Incident on Hill 19

"Why can't they put those spades where they belong? Stick 'em in the 24th."

"Yeah, them colored boys get shot at, and their eyes get large, and they blubber so bad they wind up shooting one of us," his buddy joked.

"Seems to me I seen you shake a time or two when those 82s opened up, Pullman."

"Figures you'd be a nigger lover, O'Neil. I guess up there in New York, you had yourself a darkie girlfriend tucked away in Harlem."

Pullman and Hickey cracked up.

"Stow it, you mutts," Lieutenant Franklin said, walking up to the three as they greased their M-1s with anti-freeze to keep the parts from icing up. "Keep that kind of talk to yourselves."

"We were, Lieutenant," Hickey responded, stifling a giggle.

Franklin breathed clouds close to the corporal's face. Slowly, he said, "You know what I mean, soldier. What you did before you got here and what you'll do afterward does not concern me. What does is this unit functioning at tip-top shape. Understand?"

There was a moment, then Hickey managed a "Yes, sir."

"That goes for you, too, Pullman."

"I get it, sir."

Franklin walked off, and the three exchanged looks. "Glory boy." Hickey wrung out his rag and wiped down his rifle's breech. "He just wants to be kissy-kissy with the press because he wants to run for office when he gets back to the States."

O'Neil checked the action of his M-1. "What are you talking about?"

Pullman piped in, "You didn't hear our junior MacArthur there talking to that reporter from *Life* who was around last week?"

"I guess not," O'Neil said.

"They were here to take pictures and get stories of how happy us'ins all is to be fighting Joe Chink," Hickey added, smirking. "Like we all sit around the mess eatin' fried chicken and mashed potatoes. Turns out Franklin's father was a senator in Philadelphia or some such. And the reporter asked him was he going to run for his daddy's seat once he got home."

"Yeah, so?" O'Neil inspected his handiwork.

"So he's already running, don't you get it?" Pullman groused. "Last month, we had that colored broad from…what's the name of their colored magazine?"

"Jigaboo Monthly," Hickey commented. "*Ebony*," O'Neil corrected.

"That's it," Pullman said, snapping his fingers. "All this attention on the integrated front line units because Truman gave in to those loud mouths and Jew trouble makers left over from FDR's time."

"The NK's bullets don't know color," O'Neil remarked. "And a corpse is a corpse."

Pullman and Hickey could only shake their heads as they finished up.

Between a set of Quonsets and across a tuft of frozen ground from the GIs and their maintenance, Lieutenant Mark Franklin entered command's tent.

"Captain." Franklin gave the seated man a crisp salute.

"At ease," Captain Thomas Westlake said. He pushed a pack of Lucky Strikes toward Franklin. "Be my guest."

Franklin lit one and savored the aroma. "What's the skinny, Captain?" He'd observed the prints of aerial shots to one side of the man's ivory inlaid table. An item they'd commandeered along with chairs, canned food, a box of metronomes, and a portrait of Pope Pius XII from a bombed-out Catholic school.

"Take a gander at this." Westlake's thick fingers shuffled through the prints and arranged three of them for viewing. He held a magnifying glass that Franklin used.

"What am I looking at?"

"That's what G-2 wants to know. These are fresh photographs from our jet jockeys passing over the north-eastern section of the Taebaeks less than forty clicks from here. Not far from the border, I don't need to remind you."

Franklin bent again to peer through the glass at the images the Sabers had captured flying over the mountain range. "NKs or Chinese regulars?" Franklin asked, regarding the men marching up a trail in one of the shots.

"One of the details you and a light detachment will find out."

Franklin nodded slightly. The second shot again showed the enemy soldiers along the hill. In this one, they were reacting to something out of frame. Moving the glass back onto the third, he again regarded the object that had prompted his initial question. "Is it a downed MIG?"

"Doesn't seem to fit that configuration. At least the part that the white coats back in Tokyo can make of it." The captain tapped the third photo. The aerial shot depicted the top of the ridge where an oblong object was stuck in the side of a pyramidal rock formation, thrusting up from a portion of the hill's apex. The image was blurry due to the jet's speed, and Franklin couldn't hazard a guess as to its entire shape.

"Maybe it's part of a bubble on some kind of drone spotter plane. Of course, there would be debris around, and there isn't any."

Captain Westlake held his hands apart and leaned back to absorb more of the warmth of his portable heater fighting the cold. "You shove off at 04:20. I'd say pick no more than six to go with you. Small enough to move fast, but enough men to handle a situation should it arise." He produced a leather folder and handed that across to the lieutenant.

"There's some exact coordinates delineated on a map, landmarks indicated, and notes on what's been troop strength in that area. The brass has designated the hill you're after as Number 19. This is a recon mission, Lieutenant; only engage the enemy if there's no back door open.

"Alright, sir." With the toe of his Mickey Mouses, one of his snow boots, he ground out his cigarette and turned to leave.

"And, Mark?" Westlake was standing now, rubbing his hands.

"Sir?"

"Do you plan on taking our Negro men with you?"

"I planned on taking the dogfaces that can help me fulfill the mission, Captain. Why? Is there going to be another reporter waiting when we get back?"

His superior considered the pack of cigarettes, then put them aside. "I took you to be a broadminded man."

"I don't follow you."

Westlake came forward, clapping him on the side of his arm. "This is about morale as much as it's about information."

"Now I see."

"U.N. forces had to cede Kimpo Airfield, and Inchon has been abandoned. Right now, Ma and Pa need to hear how unified our fighting forces are when they sit down to the radio after supper, Mark. How these setbacks will be overcome when we regroup."

"This is just a lousy recon mission, sir."

"But one that we can play up a lot of different ways, especially if we can have a picture of smiling black and white faces of our men in an edition of *Stars and Stripes*. This damn police action is getting to be one large mudhole that we can't sink any deeper into. As an officer, as someone looking to build on his war experiences for later, you know what I'm saying."

"And," he continued, "I'm sure you want to put to rest that talk that the colored soldier is only suited for rear guard detail." He paused, smiling, "I believe Negros vote where you come from."

"Very well, sir." Franklin saluted again and left. A bitter wind had kicked up, and it matched his mood. He did consider himself a fair man, a man willing to judge another based on what he did and not what he looked like. But when that goofball, that reporter, asked him about his family and his plans, how could he pass up the opportunity? It was sobering to finally realize that he was as ambitious as his father and older brother.

"Sergeant Pickett," Franklin said to the colored man hunkered down with a private by two cans of burning sterno.

"Lieutenant," Dawson Xavier Pickett snapped to, setting aside his C-ration of corned beef hash. The private also stood and saluted with his cigarette dangling from his mouth.

"Word with you, sergeant."

"Yes, sir." He stepped over to where Franklin had positioned himself next to the fender of the Quad 50 half-track. "What's up?"

"You and a man you choose are with me and three others before sun up."

"Advanced patrol?"

"Sort of. We're to do some scouting and report back on what we see in a particular section of the mountains due east of here."

"How about we bring Holmes along?" Pickett indicated the man who'd resumed eating by the low fire.

"Anything special about him?"

"He used to help his uncle, a shutterbug in Detroit. He worked for the local Negro papers and politicians there. Holmes has his Nikon he loves to use."

The officer frowned.

"This nip camera. Pretty good, I'm told."

"Why not." Franklin agreed. "It couldn't hurt to take some shots." He told him what time to be ready and departed.

"What was that about Ex?" Holmes asked when the sergeant returned.

"Looks like we get to do more than hauling mortar launchers and putting up huts?"

Holmes displayed wide teeth. "Maybe it's because the Army has lost so many ofays at Inchon, they don't have any choice but to use us, too."

Pickett, a sturdily built individual over six-two, stretched and gulped down an amount of warm water from his canteen. It had been set near the fire to prevent freezing. "Get some shut-eye and no apple jack."

"Sarge, you know I—"

"Who you trying to jive, gate?" His bemused expression said it all.

"Okay, chief." The private said and hunkered down to take in all he could from the dying fire.

Before the sun was up over Whitehorse Ridge, the small squad of men moved out. Hickey, a corporal, was one of D Company's BAR, Browning Automatic Rifle handlers, had the point with the lieutenant close behind. Private Pullman and Sergeant Pickett were next, and the others filled in.

"Eyes front, Hickey," Franklin said, referring to the point man regularly looking back as the soldiers advanced.

"Just want to make sure there's no gooks coming up on my flank, sir."

Franklin pointed ahead. "Keep moving. If the reds show up, we'll send you a telegram."

A little past 09:32, they were walking along the perimeter of a small village called Sohbo-ri. Several scrawny chickens pecked about. The cornstalks the huts were constructed from were like brick, the freezing wind having solidified the last vestiges of the moisture in them from the humid fall.

"Where you going, Pullman?"

He put an index finger to his lips and snuck down to a clay pot suspended in front of a hut. Taking his glove off, he used the back of his hand to feel the pot. He continued on until reaching a hut midway along the clearing. He rejoined the others.

"That pot was used recently," he whispered to the lieutenant. Previously, they knew the village had been deserted.

"Pickett, take two over there to cover us, and we'll see if we can flush our guests out."

"Got it." Pickett turned and tapped Holmes and Hickey on his way past.

"Hey—" Hickey began but followed the other two, unlimbering his Browning.

Holmes said, "You okay?"

"I'm fine. Just don't get in my way."

"Wouldn't think of it."

As those men went to the left and a slight incline, the three withFranklin converged on the hut in question. There was a crunch of straw, and suddenly, two North Korean soldiers in heavy coats and fur hats ran from the hut, hands up and hollering in Korean.

"Reds, reds," Hickey shouted and dropped, peeling off rounds from the Browning.

"Hickey, no," Sergeant Pickett yelled. "Stop firing."

"Holy smoke, holy smoke, he's reaching inside his coat," Holmes blurted while he opened fire on the enemy soldiers.

Pickett grabbed Hickey's arm and yanked hard, causing the BAR man to turn with his rifle.

"Look, snowball—"

Both were gritting their teeth, condensed air issuing between the spaces.

"That's enough," Franklin ran up while O'Neil and Pullman went to check on the NKs. "That's enough, I said."

To Franklin, Pickett said, "Watch him." And he double-times over to the two on the ground.

"Who the hell does that dinge think he is?" Hickey's tightening hands made the Browning's casing creak.

"You have to respect the stripes, Hickey."

"Aw, come on, Lieutenant."

"This is not some bar or counter at your favorite café. This is war, and either there is a chain of command, or there's anarchy. It's that simple."

Franklin glared over at Holmes. "That goes for both of you."

"Yes, sir."

Pickett crouched over the bodies. The left side of one man's brain was now splattered on the hut like a hurried paint job. But the other one was gurgling blood, air seeping from the gaping wounds in his chest.

"*Haneul eh suh ssol ah ji neun bool,*" he repeated several times. In his hand was a piece of paper that he shakily held up to Pickett. Their eyes met, and then the enemy soldier expired.

"I guess he was praying, huh?" Pullman opined to no one in particular.

"He was saying, 'Light or fire from the sky.'" Pickett rose and, unfolding the paper, looked at the drawing on it.

"What do you have there, Sergeant?" Franklin asked. "Don't know exactly." Pickett handed the blood-stained scrap to the officer. Holmes got his camera out and captured the enemy in their death poses.

After a moment, Franklin offered, "This supposed to be a meteor?"

Pickett's eyebrows elevated. "It looks like this fireball in his drawing crashed into these rocks. I guess that's where we're headed."

"Yeah, well," the lieutenant drawled, "there's only one way to find out."

"I found their rifles, Lieutenant," O'Neil called from the doorway to the hut. "They had them leaning against the wall in here."

Franklin didn't want his men dwelling on the fact the NKs had run out purposely unarmed. "Okay, let's move out," he ordered. Absently, he put the paper in his breast pocket.

After they'd cleared Sohbo-ri, Franklin made a point of walking next to Pickett along the trail.

"Where'd you learn Korean?"

Pickett shrugged. "In Oakland, there's a Korean community, actually over into San Francisco, too. Of course, everybody figures they're Japanese. Anyway, the neighborhood I grew up in I came into contact with them. Even worked awhile at the ice plant with a KA who taught me a little."

"KA?"

"Korean American."

Wind flitted through the trees, and they walked on.

"Did you really think that Hickey would shoot you in the back?"

Pickett didn't answer right away. The soft crunch of the packed ground was all that could be heard. "It wouldn't have surprised me. There have been incidents in other squads among the colored and the whites."

"You think that little of your fellow GI?"

"He thinks that little of me."

By late afternoon, the detail had arrived at the foot of the mountains. A light snow had also started.

"Grab some chow. We'll take twenty," Franklin said. "My dogs are killing me," Pullman complained. He sat down and taking off his boots, massaged his sore feet.

Franklin consulted his map.

"That's it, right?" Pickett was beside him, looking through a pair of binoculars.

"Yes, Hill 19," Franklin said, having put on his rimless glasses for a better look. He regarded Pickett's expression. "I had perfect eyesight before I started getting shot at."

The sergeant chortled, and the two puffed on their smokes simultaneously. "Don't see nothin', but of course, that doesn't mean anything."

Franklin took a deep drag and exhaled. "Look down from the peak, to the left, and there's another small rise. At a kind of valley area between the two."

Pickett said, "That a balloon? You know, like they used in World War I with a spotter to track enemy movements."

The lieutenant asked, "You a student of history?"

The non-com took the binoculars away from his eyes. "Had an uncle in that one. They called him by his middle name, Nefarious—which fit him. He was part of the Harlem Hellfighters who fought with the French." He didn't supply that was because the black American troops were never allowed active duty by their own country.

"Huh," the lieutenant said, "That's something. Whatever that thing is up there is what we're supposed to find out, then hustle back to base to make our report."

In the packet the captain had handed Franklin, there was a brief report from the pilot of the F-86. He wrote that when he made the second pass over the object, his engine stalled, and he lost all radio contact but was able to relight his engine. He didn't relay that to the sergeant.

Franklin announced, "All right, men, we keep low and keep sharp. Those two in the village came from somewhere, and G-2 says there might be Chinese troop presence as well.

But we need to make that crest." The snowfall was increasing. "What's up there, Lieutenant? Some kind of gook outpost?" Pullman flicked a smoked Chesterfield away. "You'll know when we get there. Saddle up. Hickey and Pullman, you two up front."

"Those slant-eyes are gonna make us out too easy," Hickey complained, ascending the hill. "Those tar babies stand out real good against this damn snow."

"You're too much," Pullman commented.

"I'm just sayin', that's all." And they trudged on. Ahead were O'Neil and

Holmes.

"Can I ask you something, Holmes?"

"What?"

"You enlisted, didn't you?"

"Yeah, so?"

More snow and more walking. "Not much else for you back home?"

"Aw, you know, boss man," Holmes began in a Kingfish accent, "we's gots to do what we can for our mamas and babies." He laughed dryly.

"That's not what I meant."

"I'm just having fun with you, O'Neil. Don't take it seriously."

Past the mid-way point, the lieutenant, who'd moved to the head of the line, signaled a halt, and the men crouched down on the leeward side of a ledge of rocks. He scanned the terrain ahead.

Hickey leaned close. "I feel it. They're up there, aren't they?"

"Can't say for sure. That's why I had us stop to check." The lieutenant considered whether the object was some kind of experimental Russian jet, and there were troops up there guarding it.

"So what should we do, Lieutenant Franklin?"

"We need to—"

"I'll scout ahead. One man should be unnoticed."

"You?" Hickey shook his head. "You see how white it's getting out here… Sergeant?"

Franklin grimaced. "Got any pineapples on you?"

"I've got one." He tapped a small pouch on his belt.

"Give him yours," Franklin said to Hickey.

"Huh?"

"You heard my order, private."

With a look on his face, like he'd swallowed sour milk, Hickey handed over his grenade. "Don't drop it."

Pickett moved off, staying as low as he could to the snow-covered earth. He slithered over rocks and through spare stands of shrubbery. It was behind one such outcropping of bush that he peered through the binoculars toward the rise where the object was, then started up again, slowly.

"Come on, Ex, come on," Holmes muttered.

They waited and watched, the snow continuing to fall and crystallize on their lips and eyelids. Pickett got closer until he stopped again, suddenly diving into a natural trench.

"Up at the top, I see somebody," O'Neil said. "But do they see Pickett?" Holmes said.

The sound of a Tokarev's whine answered that question. "All right, men, let's pour it on," Franklin yelled as he leapt over the ledge, the enlisted men's M-1s cranking out shots around him. He pumped his legs, the soles of his winter boots sinking, then lifting out of the snow. Over the top, he could see the commies on their bellies shooting down at them. There was a blur of motion to his right, and suddenly Pullman was staggering backwards, his rifle in the air as his heels gave out from under him. The ragged hole in his abdomen was the size of a dinner plate.

Stepping over the body, Holmes aimed, but Franklin was too busy scrambling while bullets careened off rock, and he could feel a burning in the side of his rib cage. He went to a knee; he was having trouble breathing, but he kept shooting.

Up there, he saw that Pickett was fighting hand-to-hand combat.

Rifle up, sighting down the barrel, working the trigger, Franklin's father filled his head. It was one of those times the two were out in the thickets hunting quail.

"The men of this family have strived to make our forbearers proud," he said, putting his orator's strength behind the words.

Usually, the younger Franklin was tired of hearing about great ancestor Benjamin and the burden of that heritage. But on that cold, dry morning in the brush, he accepted his calling.

"I understand, Dad," he'd said. And he did.

Lieutenant Franklin looked forward to fulfilling his family's wishes. A bullet cracked, and he didn't feel the round that slammed through his five-pound helmet and rattled around the back of his steel pot after exiting his head.

Up the hill, the knife in the enemy's hand had carved a chunk out of his shoulder, and now it was hovering near Pickett's breastbone. The blade would have been buried in him, except he'd crossed his wrists and blocked the other man's thrust. The sergeant then took a step back, and the commie soldier assumed he had an opening and lunged forward.

Pickett's fist caught the NK flush just below the cheek while his other hand grabbed the wrist of the knife hand. And pulling hard, he yanked his opponent off-balance, making him stumble. The sergeant got his sidearm out and shot the other man dead.

More gunfire forced Pickett down into the trench. The enemy was bunched at the top of the ridge, near the object they'd been sent to identify. Whatever that was up there, the communists wanted to protect it.

An NK stuck his head up to get a bead on him, but he had to duck down as the whine of M-1s whistled past Pickett. Back on his belly, the sergeant crawled forward inches from his cover, aware that at any second, one of the reds would poke up again and blast his head off. He pulled the pin on one of his grenades, holding the lever tight so it wouldn't detonate.

There was a scream, and he prayed it wasn't Holmes or even Hickey, for that matter—they were on the same side, weren't they?

Sucking in air, scared but having no choice, Pickett counted to five. Echoing in his head were his DI's admonishment from basic about the ten-yard killing radius of a pineapple. "Two…Three." That was the explosive part—the shrapnel could fly for some fifty yards or so.

"Four…five," and he stood up and threw the grenade into the soldiers clumped together on the ridge. The thing was out of his hand when a bullet pierced his body, driving him down into the snow-compacted ground. The grenade exploded and body parts pirouetted in the air, and the shooting stopped.

"Ex," Holmes called, "Ex, how bad are you hit?"

"I'm still breathing."

"I'm coming for you, man."

"Hold on, they may not be done."

"They got Pullman and the lieutenant. You're in charge."

"Then do what I say and keep your carcass where it is."

He tried to move, but it caused blood to seep from his chest wound, so he got still again. Moaning drifted toward him from the ridge, but that could be a ruse, or their buddies were laying low and hoping the anxious GIs would saunter up there and get slaughtered.

"Hey, can you hear me?"

"What is it, Hickey?" Pickett said.

"Since you're also knocked off your pins, that makes me in charge."

"No, it doesn't, corporal. You will follow my orders, or you will be court-martialed."

"If you or us get back to base, don't you mean?"

"Don't press it, Hickey. This ain't the time." Grinding his teeth, Pickett turned his body in such a way as to peek over the top of his trench. He tossed a loose rock he'd picked up, but that got no response. He settled back and considered what to do next.

"I say we move out," Hickey yelled up to him. "We've done what we can. We need to get you to a MASH."

"We haven't finished the job." He coughed blood and wiped it away with a grimy hand. "O'Neil and Holmes, work your way to me. Hickey, you lay down cover if you see a head pop up. And I'll do the same."

"But—"

"Do it."

There was no answer, but soon the two soldiers were belly crawling, and running hunched over to the trench.

"You think there's some reds up there playing possum?" O'Neil blew on his hands, then put his cotton gloves back on. It continued to snow.

"Between us, we must have polished 'em off," Holmes said. "Those two in the village must have been deserters."

"I was wondering about that," Pickett mused. "Could be it was a patrol like ours, small and light sent out to guard their plane or whatever it is up there."

"But that might mean others are on their way," O'Neil added.

"Means we still gotta get up there for a look-see. And this has to be taken care of soon," Holmes tore off part of his sleeves and pressed the cloth against the wound.

"I'll be all right. Get going, you two."

The privates exchanged minimal nods and started their climb.

The pain hadn't let up, but that didn't matter because Pickett couldn't allow himself to pass out. He was in charge, and he knew what would go around if he couldn't muster up.

"Hickey," he hollered.

"What?"

"Get up here." As he expected, the corporal didn't budge. "Now, mister."

"Okay."

Running in a zigzag pattern, Hickey bowled into the trench and flopped down, his Browning trained on the ridge.

Holmes and O'Neil, moving, halting, and listening, and repeating that, were almost to the top.

Pickett, too, had his rifle aimed but wasn't sure if he could bolt forward if he had to.

Hearing his ragged breathing, Hickey asked, "You gonna make it?"

"You just worry about the men." It surprised Pickett how small his voice sounded.

O'Neil gained the top of the ridge, and the sight that greeted him was the insides of a man's stomach spilled over the ground. He retched. As he dabbed at his mouth with his shirt front, Holmes joined him.

Before them was a tangle of three bodies and their disconnected limbs, including the one with the missing stomach—this the result of Pickett's grenade. Beyond them was a dead man on his back. Part of his head was shot off, and they assumed he'd been picked off by one of them from below. His eyes gazed into the beyond.

Buried in the side of the pyramid-like rock formation was the object. Both men approached it cautiously, rifles in hand.

"It's like a giant metal egg." Holmes reached for the milky gray metal surface but didn't have the nerve to touch it. The thing was at least forty feet tall at its highest point.

"Some kind of bomb?" O'Neil said.

"It's big enough to blow up the whole damn peninsula if it is," Holmes responded. He slung his rifle over his shoulder and, taking a few steps back, snapped some pictures.

O'Neil was walking around the other side of the object. "We better," and then he stopped talking. He could only blink and try to process what he saw. "Holmes," he rasped, "come here."

Holmes stepped around and almost dropped his camera. "Holy crud," he exclaimed.

On a flat expanse of snow-blotted ground were two more NK soldiers. A creature was squatting on one of the soldier's chests, one of its tentacles wrapped around the man's crushed throat, his eyes bulging out of their sockets.

"That egg is a spacecraft, Holmes."

"That a Martian?"

The alien was about the size of a foot locker, though shaped more like an octopus with six tentacles and a gelatinous body. There were two bullet holes in the still creature. A dark fluid had emptied through the holes and mixed with the snow that now partially covered these two.

The other dead soldier was a radio operator. He was laid out near his instrument, both of his arms had been torn off. Neither GI noticed the transmitter was on.

Holmes took more pictures. O'Neil went back to Pickett, and he and Hickey had to carry him up the hill to the sight that awaited them.

"It's dead, that's for sure," Hickey announced after poking the thing with the barrel of his rifle. "I guess we hit the jackpot, fellas. We're going to make the cover of all the magazines."

"Maybe not," Pickett said. He'd managed to stay upright by leaning against a boulder and had been using his binoculars to look across the other side of the 38th parallel. "Three jeep loads of soldiers are on their way. Chinese, I'd say. And three of 'em are in civvies, serious types."

"Scientists." O'Neil was already heading toward the ledge, the way they'd come. "We've got to move out."

Holmes said, "Not without Ex."

Hickey blared, "You crazy, he'll just slow us down."

Holmes tossed his camera aside and reached to loosen his rifle, but Hickey was on him.

"If you want to stay with your colored pal, fine. But me and O'Neil are getting back to base." He pushed him, and Holmes fell. Hickey was about to kick him when Pickett yelled.

"That's enough." His .45 was pointed straight at Hickey's heart. "All of you move out, get back, and report what you've seen. You've got pictures, so maybe they'll believe you and not slap you with Section 8s. I'll keep them busy with me as long as I can. Leave me a few clips for my rifle."

Holmes was on his feet. "Ex, you've got—"

"Get going, soldier, that's my order. And Hickey, stop acting like the peckerwood you are and somebody who is a

U.S. Army Corporal. Get your men back alive."

O'Neil shoved Hickey's shoulder. "You heard our sergeant."

"I'm not having this," Holmes protested. "Them white boys can leave you, but I'm staying."

"No, you ain't. If the Reds get past me, it's going to take each of you watching out for the other to make it back." Snowflakes dotted his wet forehead. "What we found today is like something out of *Flash Gordon*. And our side has to know about it 'less we let the enemy use this somehow. You got a duty, Norman, and so do I." He put a hand on the man's shoulder. "We've got to show them we didn't bug out in a fight."

Holmes handed Pickett a couple of extra clips. So did O'Neil. Hickey just looked at the ground. The three made to leave when a portal, where there was no indication of one, suddenly opened like a camera's shutter in reverse. The hole was in a lower portion of the egg, and a being in a silver space suit stepped through it. He was tall, the suit he was in seemed to be of some silken material and there was an oblong helmet covering his head affixed to a metal collar. There was no visor, but it was evident he could see from the other side of the helmet.

The being held his hands up to show they were empty to the soldiers, and then he, as it was the shape of a muscular man, walked to the dead creature with the tentacles. Hands on his hips, the helmet was tilted down for a few moments. He then put a hand on top of the creature and petted it.

From where the cosmic traveler stood, he could see the approaching convoy. Particularly given the vision amplification apparatus built into his helmet, but the earthmen didn't know this. Already, one of the jeeps had stopped, and the soldiers were advancing up the hill.

The spaceman touched a portion of his collar, and a nodule of a peculiar design sprouted from the top of the egg. The nodule, which had no apparent bearings or hinges, undulated like a snake and, once in position, shot a purple ray from its nozzle. The nodule repositioned itself and shot another ray blast.

After that, the nodule merged with the casing of the egg.

The spaceman walked back toward his ship. Holmes and O'Neil looked down the hill.

"What is it? What do you see?" Pickett wheezed. He slumped against the rock.

"He froze them, Sarge," Holmes said. The ones walking and the ones still in their jeeps. It's like they were living photographs."

The visitor from the galaxy re-emerged from his ship and came toward Pickett.

"He's going to attack us." Hickey leveled the Browning. "If he wanted us dead, we would be. Put it down," Pickett braced himself.

Hickey hesitated but complied. The spaceman, who'd halted, continued toward the sergeant. Facing him, he held up a small rectangular device that had lights of various colors swirling across it. He made a few circles with it around the area of Pickett's wound.

"You all right, Ex?' Holmes asked, worry straining his face.

"Yeah. In fact, I feel much better. It's like he dissolved the bullet. There's no burning anymore." Pickett pulled back his shirt and saw that his wound had been closed as well.

The alien paused before the sergeant, the GI's reflection cast in the helmet's shiny surface. He then turned and went back into his ship. The four watched as the portal started to close. At the spaceman's feet was a bounded creature similar to the dead one. This thing wrapped a tentacle around his leg, much the same as a dog or cat would nuzzle its master.

Just before the portal sealed, the traveler removed his helmet, revealing an individual with mahogany-colored skin, a wide nose, and close-cropped, kinky hair. Then, the egg was once more one seamless piece of milky gray metal.

Speechless, the four were mesmerized as the egg began to vibrate. Large chunks of the stone it was embedded in began to fall away, and the men backed up. The egg broke free and was stationary in the air, hovering before them. And then three tail sections shaped like curving spiked heels sprouted in the fat end, equidistant apart. The ship turned, shook, then zoomed into the heavens.

Holmes took the camera away from his eye and, like the others, silently filed down the hill. The snow had stopped.

On the way back to base, they all agreed to say nothing of what they found. The four concluded that the visitor must have crash-landed and had to repair his ship.

Sure, they had the photographs, but Holmes would have to give the film to the captain, who in turn would have to send it off to be processed. Once that happened, who knew what would happen to them? Maybe the brass would hail them as heroes, or maybe the G-2 spy boys would want this to remain hush-hush. Could be they'd be quarantined or put in separate rubber rooms for who knew how long.

They reported their engagement of the enemy and that the object at the top of the hill was a radio-controlled balloon rigged with a camera for tracking troop movements. And that the film that Holmes took got fogged.

A few years later, after the war, while walking along Broadway in downtown Oakland, Dawson Pickett passed a newsstand. The cover feature of *Weird Science Tales* magazine caught his attention. The story was entitled "The Space Man of the Hills" and depicted an illustration very similar to the traveler in his suit and full helmet. The alien was bending down, aiding a wounded GI, while shooting his ray gun at advancing commie soldiers.

Leafing through the magazine, the name on the story was credited to a

Mark Norman. Pickett bought two copies of the issue. He was going to save a copy for his infant daughter to read when she got older. The Montgomery Bus Boycott was in full swing, and one day, he hoped, she might go to the stars and meet the man who saved his life.

* * *

"Incident on Hill 19," *Retro Pulp Tales*, Subterranean Press, 2006, Joe R. Lansdale, editor.

Disco Zombies

Wild Willie stumbled backward, knocking against the rickety kitchen table, sending the two plastic bricks of coke somersaulting to the floor.

"Goddammit, Spree, pay up." Wild Willie wrenched hard to get the six-shooter free from the other man's grasp.

"Fuck that, Willie," Spree Holmes blared. "I did." He had both of his hands clamped around Wild Willie's gun hand, his fingers tugging on the barrel of the revolver even as Willie beat the shit out of his arm with his free fist. "You fuckin' reneged, man," he added, gritting his teeth.

Holmes sprung from a tip-toe position so as to maximize his weight bearing down on the heavier but flabbier Wild Willie. It worked, and the two went over and down onto the worn linoleum. They slid against one of the lower cabinets, busting off its handle.

"Shit," McMillan hollered from the doorway, ducking and diving beneath the wind of the samurai sword Crider swung at the top of his thinning hair. McMillan flopped onto his stomach in his vintage Hawaiian shirt atop the ratty shag carpet. But for once, he wasn't worried about keeping his clothes neat. He twisted around onto his back, kicking and flailing his legs like an angry turtle, just as Crider chopped at him with the blade. A section of McMillan's heel was sliced off, and he instinctively shut his eyes as if he'd been gored in the heart.

"Ugh," Holmes grunted after Wild Willie yanked the gun free. He'd been partially straddling him but flung himself sideways as the other man righted the piece. Desperate, Holmes reached out and latched onto anything he could off the counter. With brutal force he slammed alongside Willie's head a glass container used with a blender. Its impact caused Willie's shot to be misdirected and singe past Holmes' head—but not into it.

"Motherfucker," Wild Willie swore. A thick piece of glass was embedded in the meaty part above his eyebrow and he had no choice but to grab for it to relieve the pain. As he did so, Holmes shoved the heel of his hand into the shard, driving it deeper. Willie's legs twitched in agony as he tore off another blast at Holmes' chest.

In the dining room McMillan keenly registered the shot but was concentrating on throwing a porcelain statuette of a trumpet player he'd plucked off a shelf with as much shoulder as he could put behind it.

"You throw like a little girl," the silver-toothed Crider taunted. A cut had opened up on his face as a result of the miniature musician hitting him. He was on one side of a round dining room table and McMillan opposite. Crider held his gleaming sword in both hands, the bulk of it poised over the table.

"Which you want to lose, man? Hand or ear?" Crider made a quick back and forth with the steel, letting it whistle in the stifling air of the little house.

"You ain't man enough to take me without your chop suey prop," McMillan said, inching to his left.

"Come on, I'll make it nice and clean and fast." Crider made a vicious swipe that caused McMillan to tense but not be so stupid and start running and get the back of his neck severed.

Holmes and Wild Willie tumbled out of the kitchen, entangled. When Willie had shot at him the second time, Holmes was in the process of lowering his upper frame, and as the bullet funneled into the bone of his shoulder blade, his momentum carried him forward, and he'd rammed into Wild Willie's chest, stunning him. Batting tears and doing what he could to ignore the stars exploding behind his corneas, Spree Holmes had pressed the fight, knowing if he let up, the next shot from that old Colt would blow his guts out.

Instinctively, Crider had bounded over to the wrestling forms to give his homeboy Willie a hand. He turned to refocus on McMillan, who was now pushing the dining room table toward him. Crider dodged to one side, but McMillan followed his movement and upended the table onto the sword man's feet.

"Bastard," Crider yelped. He got his left foot free, but the right foot, in its snakeskin boot, wasn't so easily extricated. McMillan held onto the edge of the table, lifted it up quickly, and then brought it down again on the right's instep. Crider gritted his teeth and wielded the blade toward McMillan's hand. The other man got his hands out of the way and the sword sliced into the table's rim and held fast.

McMillan laughed and, putting effort behind it, shoved the table, sending Crider into a wall as he attempted to free his weapon. "I got your girl," McMillan said and plowed a fist into the opposing man's nose as the sword came loose.

At that same moment, Holmes and Wild Willie were digging into each other's faces with their fingers. Holmes' thumb was gouging into the corner of Willie's mouth when he shifted and bit down on that thumb like it was fresh steak.

"That ain't gonna help you, Willie," Holmes said, leveraging forward and causing Willie's head to rattle against the doorjamb. He reached for the six-shooter, which was now lying on the kitchen floor, but Holmes wasn't about to allow that to happen. Holmes took hold of what material he could of Wild Willie's T-shirt and, jerking him up, head-butted him, opening the gash wider over Willie's eye.

"Ke-rist," Wild Willie screamed and tried to scurry away. Holmes was on his feet and stomped on the escaping man's side like he was a bothersome cockroach. He pressed the barrel of the gun onto Willie's thigh and shot him.

"That ought to slow you down," Holmes said over Willie's whimpering.

Behind him, Crider had his sword but was also keeling over from a rocking blow delivered via the dining room chair hefted by McMillan. The chair was rusting metal tubing, and a torn leatherette-covered seat, but it served McMillan well as a shield. Like a lion tamer from an old Saturday morning serial, he had it up and was using it to fend off the blows from Crider's sword.

"Put it the fuck down," Holmes ordered.

Crider and McMillan stared at him. McMillan grinned broadly, stroking his goatee with his long-nailed hand. "Shoot him," he said.

"You heard me." The Colt in Holmes' hand didn't waver even though the burning in his shoulder intensified.

Crider made a guttural sound and pivoted toward Holmes. The sword was at his side, the blade pointing outward—a Mississippi samurai in pointy-toed cowboy boots and worn Lee jeans.

"I'm not fuckin' around, Crider."

"Smoke his ass," McMillan repeated. He still held onto the chair.

Crider cocked his head to the side, waiting and wondering.

He grasped the sword with two hands on its hilt. "Get the shit."

"On it." McMillan scooted into the kitchen, not letting go of the chair until he was in there. Wild Willie was curled into a fetal position and moaned softly, his leg leaking profusely.

"Something broke?" McMillan teased cruelly as he scooped up the two keys of flake. "Or is it indigestion from trying to cheat us, you cheap fuck." Spittle dotted McMillan's graying goatee. "Huh, Willie, that it?" He leaned over, feigning like he was listening for a response.

"You…" the man on the floor began.

"You what, you fuckin' Shylock." McMillan planted his two-tone Nunn Bush's in Willie's stomach, making him wince and gurgle crimson. "You gonna try and play us, man? After the business we done together, making your thirty percent state disability retard self fatter than you deserve to be?"

Holmes called from the dining room. "Come on, let's get on the road."

"Yeah, yeah. Can't have no more fun." He kicked Willie in the ribs, a bone giving way. As McMillan started to walk out, Wild Willie suddenly gyrated his body and reached for the exiting man's pant legs. McMillan reacted but still got tangled up as the man continued to paw at him, and he fell forward.

Holmes knew better than to be distracted and look at his partner while he went timber. The problem was McMillan whirly-gigged his arms to stay upright, and this caused Holmes to reposition himself, and Crider took his opening.

There was a flash of silver, and the sword swiped downward at McMillan's tilting head. "Oh, fuck me," the goateed man exclaimed and put a hand to the side of his head.

Crider turned on the balls of his feet, bringing the sword level like a batter going for a sliding pitch. Holmes cranked off a round even as he peddled backward to ward off being hacked. His shot blasted into the swordman's forearm, and he dropped his weapon.

McMillan was on his knees, his eyes saucers from fear. "Finish him, shit, finish him, Spree."

"We're done here," the calmer Holmes declared, already heading toward the front door. He carried the samurai sword, the peacemaker tucked into the hollow of his back. Redness soaked into his shirt, and blood dripped onto the carpeting.

"You sure?" McMillan stared at Crider who was crumpled into one of the other chairs at the space where the dining room table had been. He was holding his useless arm by his opposite hand. The .44 slug had entered at such an angle that it exited through his elbow, shattering the joint.

"What's he going to do," Holmes said derisively, "call the cops?"

"Still," McMillan ventured.

"I gotta get patched up. And I'm hungry, and I'm hurting." It occurred to him that the money they'd brought wasn't in his hand, so he looked around for it. No sense leaving it now, it wasn't like there wasn't going to be hard feelings between him and Wild Willie.

He found the small gym bag beside the couch and picked it up, tucking it under his arm like a football. With that, Holmes made for the front door, not particularly concerned with whether a nosy neighbor or the local law was on the other side. It was getting on toward dusk, and he wanted to be out on the highway away from Wild Willie, Crider, and this shitty town of Greenwood.

"You think this is over, Holmes? You know it's not." McMillan pointed at Crider. "Shut up."

"Scared, McMillan? Scared I'm going to put my red magic on you?" Crider said, his sunken eyes swallowed up as if his face were caving in on itself.

"I told you to keep your mouth shut." McMillan smacked the wounded man with the plastic Circle K shopping bag he'd placed the coke bricks in. This upended Crider, and he crashed to the floor, wailing as he landed on his exposed bone.

McMillan laughed and couldn't resist standing over the whimpering man. "You know, Crider, I never did cotton to you.

Holmes said from the vicinity of the front door. "Stop fucking around." McMillan grinned at him and looked back at Crider. A burst of a sparkling brown cloud engulfed his face.

"Hey," McMillan said, hitting Crider hard, twice in rapid succession as he lay on the floor. Crider went limp, but he wasn't unconscious.

McMillan put his angry face close to the still man. "Why don't I just shoot you?"

"I'm leaving, Mill." Holmes stepped through the door and into the coming darkness.

In the car, plowing across the gravel of the driveway and onto the residential street, each assessed the other's damage.

"How deep is it?" McMillan looked but didn't touch the wound atop Holmes' shoulder blade.

"I can feel the bullet grind when I move my arm." Despite this, Holmes was at the wheel. He glanced sideways. "How about that chunk Crider took off?"

McMillan blinked, then opened his mouth wide as he felt along the top, or what had been the top, of his right ear. "Ain't that some shit? I got so excited I almost forgot about that." He leaned so he could see his lobe in the rearview mirror as he gingerly fingered the flesh. "Can it be sewn back on?"

"Sure, want me to turn around so you can get the piece?" McMillan gave him a lopsided look. "Shit," he finally said.

"So where to, drive across the border to Arkansas? I used to know a cat there in Little Rock who can help us out." McMillan was reaching into his back pocket for his cell phone.

"Too far, and even though we ain't gushing out, I don't want to go that long without attention."

McMillan nodded, understanding his meaning. "You just lookin' to get your dick wet."

"Ain't you? We just scored enough coke that once it's broken down to crack in the 'hood will keep us in dead prezs for months."

McMillan indicated the trunk where their cash kept company with the snow. "And the discount we got it at. I still can't believe, after we'd already agreed to the price beforehand, that Wild Willie tried to jack it up once we got here. What the fuck, huh?"

"Exactly," Holmes said, heading toward Highway 49. "Probably some static from his supplier. But that's his worry, not ours."

McMillan clucked his tongue. "Man didn't want to listen." He sneezed and coughed. "Goddamn ju-ju powder Crider blew on me. What was that about, huh?" He plucked at his nose.

Holmes tried to shrug, but his shoulder was already stiffening. "Some kind of Indian thing, I guess."

McMillan looked blank.

"He's part Choctaw," Holmes illuminated. "Crider was always into hoodoo shit, casting spells and chanting and all that to protect him when we were about to do a job."

"You two used to run together?"

"Yeah," Holmes said but didn't go on. He gave a number to McMillan, and the other man handed the phone over when the line connected.

"Uh-huh," Holmes said after saying hi and listening for a bit. "I know I have some nerve, Janey, but I'm hurtin' baby, and I need a safe port in the storm." He didn't dare look over at McMillan or he'd start laughing at how thick he was slathering it on and blow it for sure. "Baby, I know, but I promise you we'll make it worth your effort."

He listened some more as Jane Corso chewed him out, but he could tell she was softening. What they had once was too strong and too real for either of them to pretend otherwise—and being able to help her with car and utility payments was certainly an added incentive. She was a practical woman, after all.

"And, uh, if it's not too much bother, maybe you could ask whatsherface, you know, the one with the green flamingo to help you out."

McMillan brightened and considered just where Corso's friend had that flamingo tattooed.

"Okay," Holmes said after another minute or so of negotiating. He hung up. And even though his shoulder was starting to burn worse, he winked broadly. "We're set, man."

"Righteous." McMillan settled back, wondering how much reconstructive surgery would cost.

In less than an hour and a half, the two reached Jane Corso's modest frame house, inherited from her grandmother, in Clarksdale, not too far from the Sunflower River. It was in a dead-end lush with overgrown shrubs and set down the slope from a medium-sized hill. Its location along an unpaved street gave it a semi-rural feel and, therefore, less busy as the nearest house was half a block away.

Corso and her friend with the tattoo, Ella Fernandez, worked at the Diamond Stud Casino over in Tunica. Corso was a dealer, and Fernandez a waitress.

"Like old damn times," Corso said, working the probe in Holmes' exposed shoulder area. She'd numbed the wound as best she could, using a paste made from some of the coke and Lidoderm for cold sores she found in the medicine cabinet. Holmes sat rigid and gripped the sides of the chair's seat, grinding his teeth.

"You know I—"

"Hush, Spree," she said, a suggestion of a smile on her face. She kneaded her bottom lip with her teeth while she dug for the slug fragments in him.

It wasn't merely nostalgia or simply a longing to see her that had brought Holmes to her abode. Jane Corso had been a nursing student at one point—before acquiring a taste for the nose candy and shady men like her current patient. "Ah," she said, removing the probe with part of the bullet that had fragmented. She held the tweezers to the light, examining her find. "If you could finish up before I pee on myself, Doc, I'd appreciate it," Holmes said, sweat wetting his face and chest. Corso's sometimes pale green eyes lightened with mirth.

"Best be cool, or I'll really put you under and do a Loraine Bobbitt on you."

"You tell him, girl," Ella Fernandez encouraged. While Corso was in street clothes, Fernandez wore her casino uniform given her shift had ended after the men had arrived. It was a short version of a cowgirl skirt that barely covered her ample rear and a fringed leather vest with a revealing scoop. She and McMillan were sitting on the couch, and he was regaling her about his real and exaggerated criminal exploits. They rested against an Afghan comforter spread against the back of the couch.

Fernandez had already snorted up three lines of blow from the glass-topped coffee table. There was a current *TV Guide*, a discount store 1.75-liter bottle of Jack Daniels, a few plastic cups, a pack of Kools, and a Zippo on the coffee table, too. Corso had heated the ends of her tool with the lighter.

More digging and more discomfort, and Corso extracted the remaining piece from Holmes. She stitched the gash closed. After that, she handed a grateful Holmes a plastic cup with a dose of Jack Daniels sloshing in it. McMillan's wound had also been sewn shut.

"You always gotta do it the hard way, don't you, Spree?" She rubbed the side of his close-cropped graying hair.

He grinned thinly at her. "Bust my balls, why don't you?"

"I intend to." She took his hand and led him from the living room toward her bedroom. On the couch, McMillan had slathered coke on one of Fernandez's nipples as she held it aloft for him. He was busy licking off the powder, the green flamingo on the topside of her breast filling his vision.

Near two in the morning, Holmes and Corso lay awake in each other's arms.

"You heading for New York or LA?" Corso put a leg over his.

"LA"

"Give that heartless city another go, huh?"

He didn't answer right away. "That's where we were going to make it," he finally allowed.

"We almost did, Spree. We sure gave it a good run then."

He pulled her tighter to him and kissed her, lost in what could have been. They soon started to doze off.

"Funny that song would be running through my head," Corso muttered, her head on his chest.

"'I Love the Nightlife,'" Holmes remarked. "Alicia Bridges."

"How'd—" she began.

"You're not dreaming it," Holmes said, "I hear it, too."

Just as he said that, there was the loud retort of wood splintering and the crash of the front door being ripped from its hinges.

"Spree," McMillan yelled over Fernandez's scream from the front room.

Holmes and Corso had already scooted out of bed. He put on his boxers. She tossed the six-shooter to him, which was on the nightstand next to a rolled-up dollar bill. He tore into the living room, expecting that somehow, muscle sent by Crider and Wild Willie had found them. There was no way he could anticipate what was waiting for him.

"The fuck," he breathed.

"Do something, Spree," McMillan pleaded. He was naked and pinned against the wall. Fernandez was clad in her panties and lying half off the couch on her back, her eyelids fluttering. A bruise welled on her jaw.

Holmes extended the gun and shot one of the things that had invaded the home. The bullet punctured the creature's eye socket, and that should have dropped any normal man, but as Holmes was rapidly grasping, these were not normal beings.

"Zombies," Corso gasped from behind Holmes.

The one that had its hand around McMillan's throat was dressed in tattered clothing of an unmistakable vintage. He had on a dirt-stained silk shirt with billowing sleeves, once-tight bell-bottom slacks, a belt with a huge lettered buckle, and platform shoes. The other creature was dressed in what had formerly been a white suit with a matching vest and blue super fly collar point shirt open to expose a bony chest that blind earthworms crawled in and out of. This one had a raft of gold, now moldy green chains and medallions draped around its neck and the remnants of a puffy afro full of leaves and twigs. He held on to the two bricks of coke.

The feculent odor rising from the two zombies was over-powering and caused Corso to gag. Holmes was more concerned about his dope. Medallion zombie had turned toward the door, and Holmes shot him in the knee. The bone popped, and the creature stumbled as if it had stepped into a pothole. Holmes ran forward, but bell-bottom zombie threw McMillan, and he had to prone out to avoid being struck.

"Thanks for breaking my fall," McMillan groaned after colliding with the chair Holmes had sat on previously.

"They're taking our powder," Holmes yelled, launching himself and tackling the bell-bottomed one. The monster made a guttural sound and hit him so hard behind his neck that Holmes was knocked to the floor, dazed.

"Coke," Afro zombie growled to his buddy.

"Ughh," the other one said, smiling. Dung and beetles spilled out of his maw.

The two shambled out of the hole they'd made, ripping off the door. Afro zombie walked lopsided, due to its decimated knee cap.

"Spree, Spree, get up." Corso shook him.

Holmes got up to a knee like a fighter taking an eight. "Come on," Corso said, heading out, wearing pajama bottoms, her pump shotgun cradled in her arms. That was the other thing that Holmes liked about her; she always had his back in a scrap.

The two zombies were heading up the hill behind her house and Holmes and Corso went after them, joined by a limping McMillan who'd tied the comforter around his waist.

"Wait a minute," Holmes said to Corso, who was taking aim with the scattergun. "Bad enough, we've been shooting off pistols, but we're not that isolated around here. You start using that sumbitch somebody's bound to call the law. We've got to follow them."

"To where?" she asked.

"Where they can snort up the shit." He trotted after the pair, clad only in his boxers. The two creatures were nearing the top of the rise.

"Greedy motherfuckin' zombies," McMillan exclaimed. He looked around and spied a rock about the size of his fist. He picked it up and threw it, hitting the bell-bottom zombie in the back.

The thing turned around, growling and flailing his arms. He charged at them, and Holmes grabbed the shotgun out of Corso's hand and swung the stock at the thing's head. This knocked loose skin and dry grey flesh, but it kept coming. Holmes made to swing again, and the creature caught the weapon and snatched it out of Holmes' hands. He broke it apart by banging it against a thick tree trunk. As this was going on, Afro zombie made it over the top and disappeared.

"Get the coke," Holmes directed McMillan. We'll take care of this undead shithead."

"Don't have to tell me twice." McMillan went wide as the zombie lunged for him, but as its muscles were atrophied and its joints long since dried out, it couldn't move with the attenuation and speed of a live person. He got past and went up.

Holmes shot the zombie again, and it turned toward him, snarling at the continuing irritation of Holmes putting bullets into it. "I need an axe or something to cut the head off or burn it," Holmes said.

"I won't leave you, Spree," Corso declared.

Momentarily, they exchanged a look, then the thing was upon them, clawing and snapping its jaw. Holmes was down on his back, and he drove a fist into the creature's rib cage.

Some of the brittle bones cracked but it was taking all of Holmes' effort to keep the monster from biting into his head. He had both hands pressed under what was left of the zombie's clacking jaw, the rancid breath making his eyes water. The stitches on his wound ripped, and he pumped red from atop his shoulder blade.

"Get off," Corso screamed, jumping on the zombie's back and pummeling him.

"Coke," the creature intoned. It reached around and pulled Corso off by her hair and flung her away. It got its bony hands around Holmes' neck and squeezed, causing him to gag. The zombie's jaws open and unhinged, and the zombie bent down to eat the man's face off.

"Hey, shit breath," Ella Fernandez hollered. She brought the Jack Daniels bottle down on its head. The thick glass broke apart, causing a dent in the side of the creature's skull. The alcohol spilled over its upper body.

"I got something for you, dead bitch." Fernandez avowed as the zombie started for her. She lit the Zippo and threw it on him, lighting his head on fire. The zombie wailed and stomped about.

"I guess it doesn't like fire," Holmes observed in his grass-smeared Fruit-of-the-Looms. The zombie was running around in a circle, screaming. It bumped into a tree and knocked itself down. But it didn't have enough presence of mind—or enough brain left—to roll to try and put out its now totally aflame body. It got back up and screamed some more, accelerating the fire.

Corso helped Holmes to his feet. "Or it's the way he died," she said.

Fernandez breathed deeply, her heavy breasts rising and falling, the flamingo contracting and expanding. She was still only dressed in her panties.

"Good work, Ella," Holmes told her. He asked Corso, "What do you mean?"

She started to run up the hill. "We better get up there."

"The ya-yo," Holmes remembered as he and Fernandez also took off. At the top, it was a regular zombie jamboree. Eight more of them had crawled out of their graves, and all were dressed in disco regalia.

There was a female zombie in what was left of a mini-skirt. She wore torn fishnet stocking over charred legs and a stretch velour top hugging a worm-infested chest. Another was in a spangled-studded Safari suit and broad-brimmed pimp hat. Part of his entrails hung from a gap in his safari shirt. Yet another was in hot pants, thigh-high platform boots, and her angel sleeve blouse was being ripped off by another zombie in a poncho, Gaucho pants, and dingo boots.

The zombies were growling and snarling and tearing at each other to get to the cocaine.

"Holy shit." Holmes held his head, ignoring his freshly opened wound and marching around in total befuddlement. "What the fuck?"

Corso gulped. "They're the ones who were killed in the fire."

"What are you talking about, Janey?" Fernandez asked. "New Year's Eve, 1980."

The mini-skirted zombie had pulled the arm off of the one in the Gaucho pants and was beating him with it. "Coke, coke," she repeated as she drove the other one to the ground.

"Some local talent built a club down here, inspired by Donna Summer, Studio 54, you know all that," Corso said.

Holmes stopped pacing about. "There used to be a disco here?"

"Yeah. It was called, and this would prove to be ironic, the Disco Inferno. From what I understand, it was a popular place from 1976 when it started to the night it burned down."

"The Bicentennial till the death of disco," Holmes gasped.

Not a religious sort, he nonetheless sent a prayer up that the sky would rain gas and that the Lord would then add a few lightning bolts to set the zombies ablaze.

Fernandez said, "You must have been a kid then."

"She was old enough," Holmes grinned wanly, grabbing some foliage to light with the Zippo. He had to save his score. "I'd already run off, wound up in LA. Got involved with a creep that strung me out and pimped me out to this porn fuck. Even better that I was underage." Despite the humidity, she wrapped her arms around herself. "That's when I met Spree. The man in the white Charger—with a four on the floor."

Holmes gazed at her through the small fire he'd started with his crummy torch. "It was your ass that mesmerized me." He ran into the thatch of zombies, but they were fevered and ignored his pathetic flame as they tore and ate into each other. He found McMillan on the ground, shivering.

"Aghhh," he grimaced when Holmes tugged on him. "Fucking freaks broke my arm." He got up, staring. "We're fucked."

The zombie in the thigh-high boots had jumped on the back of another who wore a torn gold lame cape. The cape man had gotten a hold of one of the bricks, or what had been the brick. He dipped his face into the powder, snorting madly like Pacino in *Scarface*. Thigh-high ripped the top of his head off and bit into his pulsing brain. She gobbled up pieces of the matter. The two shambled about, in stoned nirvana.

Holmes' flame petered out. "This ain't right," he lamented. "We gotta save our shit."

"Forget it, Spree," Corso advised, joining him. "These monsters will tear you apart if you get between them and their coke."

"It's not theirs," he cried. "It is now," Corso declared.

"'Fraid she's right," McMillan agreed, holding his busted arm. "Crider's spell or mojo or whatever the hell it was has us whupped good."

One of the zombies teetered on its feet, snow powdering its decomposed face. It ran into a tree and started to bang its head against the trunk so fiercely that it broke its face open. It continued hitting its head against the tree, smearing gore over the bark.

"Shit," Holmes swore. "Shit." He stomped about in frustration.

The zombies fought and scratched and snorted and mutilated each other until body parts were littered among the overgrown grass. Even legless, zombies crawled their torsos over to any patch of flake on the ground to snort. The moon shown pregnant, and brilliantly yellow against the warm night air.

Watching this, the four were soon witness to the last two zombies left standing. One was the creature with the nasty Afro and the other the ghastly one in the mini skirt. They each pulled on the end of a piece of plastic; a clump of the white stuff clung to the material. They stood among the battered and deformed heads, smashed eyeballs, torn-out tongues, broken teeth, ripped-off fingers, cracked mood rings, ankh and cross ornaments, and knit caps of the walking disco dead.

Several of the disconnected heads mumbled, "Coke, coke," over and over again, as a few of the severed hands crept across the ground in search of any fine white crystals left.

Meanwhile, mini-skirt had an arm around Afro zombie's neck and was gnawing in his ear as he ignored this and snorted his treasure of blow. He then turned and bit into her face, and the two bear-hugged each other and rolled down the opposite side of the hill to a tributary of the river. Their bodies broke against a cropping of rocks, yet they continued to claw and rend each other.

Holmes wanted to cry. Corso consoled him as the four trudged back to the house, each step toward there they grew more elated and pumped having survived a vicious zombie attack.

"Come on, baby," Corso told a brooding Holmes back at the house. "I got something that will make you forget all about those funky zombies." And they made loud, rough love that left them both satisfied and weak as was the same for McMillan and Fernandez.

In the morning, they ate well, and Holmes and McMillan talked over other sources for some blow, given they still had their cash. Corso had declined any money.

"I'll call you."

"Liar."

"No," Holmes said as they stood outside her house in the morning. "We connected again."

She kissed him.

Holmes and McMillan started for their car. Wild Willie shambled from around a corner of the house. That he was dead was obvious from the hyper-extended eyes, grey flesh, and festering leg with flies buzzing around it.

He sprayed bullets from his AK, all the while grunting, "Coke, coke, give me my coke back," as the Trammps could be heard singing, "Burn that mutha down," from Disco Inferno.

* * *

"Disco Zombies," *The Cocaine Chronicles*, Akashic, 2005, reprinted 2011, Jervery Tervalon and GP, editors.

Rio Blanco

The bruja, the witch woman, pinched her thin lips and eyes closed in her craggy countenance. She rocked back and forth on the chair, kneading her hands together and reciting her incantation in a low, whispery voice like powder on the wind. Her trailing white hair hung straight from her head and was almost to her waist. While her clothes and shack were unkempt, that hair seemed to glimmer with inner lights as if in receipt of a source of nourishment separate from its owner.

"What is it, you old devil? What do you see?" Her questioner leaned forward across the table, his sinewy forearms causing the poorly made item to creak. The flame of the lump of a candle between them licked at the bottom of his greying van dyke.

Her agate mestizo eyes crinkled open. She stopped rocking and sat upright, letting her hands grasp the opposite shoulder as she sat sideways to him. "Boots and ropes," she declared in Spanish.

In his Tennessee-accented Spanish, he said, "What the hell are you talking about, bitch." He gripped the sides of the table, his arms shaking with the effort.

The old woman, stout and shapeless in her faded black dress, rolled her head toward him, spittle bubbling on her bottom lip. She laughed hoarsely, spraying the man and the candle. "Where is my money, *puta?*" She asked, mostly in English, then laughing again at him.

"I ought to snap that evil Mex neck of yours," was his reply. But he didn't take his hands away from the sides of the table. His knuckles stood out like bleached ridges.

Those eyes, flat and unknowable like a raven's, remained on the man before her. They dared him to strike her, aware he would do nothing to her. "A black rider on a black horse is coming to White River." She smiled a cruel child's smile. The bruja flopped a hand, palm up, on the table between them. Her fingers were curled open, a plant of flesh waiting for its meal.

The man stood and angrily knocked the candle away. "You've got to tell me more than that, you goddamn harpy." The candle had been snuffed out when it struck the buckled floorboards. In the nether light that engulfed the cabin, their forms seemed to be carved from the pitch itself.

"Is he coming with others? How many ride with this man?"

"Many," she said. "Many *sombras*." She snickered at her own joke.

"You fucking crazy witch," he bellowed. He put his hands to his face, and momentarily, it seemed as if the earth were moving out from under him. "What's his name?" he demanded.

"Does it matter? When did it ever matter to you?" She stuck out her hand again, letting it slowly rise toward him.

He scowled at her contented expression, and it seemed he'd just as soon cut that hand off as satisfy the greedy cow. But he did what he always did after insulting and threatening her to mask his need for her. He reached into his pocket, and, doing a hollow laugh of his own, tossed twin double eagle gold pieces on the floor.

"How about that, you snaked-skinned hag," he spat in English.

The seer let her tongue slide over her lower lip again. If she was younger, it might have been sensuous; as it was, there was a lurid, deviant quality to her action. Then, a column of light flared. The candle was back on the table, and its wick burning hotly. She rubbed her bony hands on her upper thighs, arching her head and shoulders back. The candle sizzled and popped like hot grease in a skillet, and he balled his fists up as he pressed his back against the wall. Next to him was one of the dried animal heads she'd tacked up. This one was a jaguar, and its orbs had been replaced with jade.

"What the hell," he panted. Sweat was boiling off the top of his head. More than anything, he wanted to feel his big, knotty fists colliding with the horrors she was calling up inside him. "You better quit messin' with me.

I paid you your goddamn money, you red nigger."

"What's wrong, Captain Stoddard? Are you seeing those boots dangling from the leaves?" She held her hands aloft, the fingers pointing downward as she fluttered them. The candle's light coruscated around her long fingernails.

"Shut up, old woman, or I'll beat you into the ground."

"He knows about those boots," she advised.

The light subsided to its usual glow. The thumping of his brain ceased. His face and shirt were clammy from sweat, and he breathed hard as if he'd been running after a wayward horse. "When will he be here?" He wiped at his forehead with the flat of his hand.

"When he gets here."

Stoddard turned to leave. He was through with her games, at least for now. But as he tugged on the latch of her door, he couldn't resist asking. "You say he'll be wearing all black?"

Her peal, like a hyena's, made the back of his neck go cold. "It's not even a real horse," she said boisterously. He stepped out of her cabin into the sticky night. Down below the village was a tomb. And even the laudanum he drank that night couldn't make him sleep for more than ten or fifteen minutes at a stretch.

Two days later, two men had themselves tucked away under an outcropping on a rise overlooking the village of Rio Blanco. One wore a heavy woolen coat and the other a jacket made of horse hair. This second garment gave off the unpleasant aroma, in summer and in winter, of its unwashed predecessor.

The man who chose to wear this particular garment, seemingly inured to its gamey smell, took a perverse pride in his nickname.

"I sure wish your grandma was here, Horseshit."

"Yeah, why's that, William Lee?"

"She can suckle on a man's balls like no other woman I ever met. And nasty and windy as it is this here night, I sure'in could use the attention."

Horseshit was busy sealing a cigarette he'd just rolled. He snuggled his tobacco pouch in his vest. "Help me light my smoke, funny man."

"My good pleasure." William Lee Sykes rested the Sharpe's with its scope against a rock and cupped his hands close to his friend's mouth.

The other man had a match poised and waited until there was a lull in the wind that had been gnawing at them all through the starless evening. On his third match, the fire held, and the cigarette was lit. Horseshit blew a thin bluish stream around his head. "Maybe your sister could come along, too. I like the way she lets you poke her from behind while she holds onto the hitchin' post."

"Yes, sir," the other man said agreeably. "She learned it good from Ma."

Both men laughed in their throats. They didn't want to make too much noise and give their position away.

"Hey," William Lee said abruptly.

His companion was busy trying to blow triple smoke rings like he'd seen this fairy actor do in Kansas City once. "What?" he uttered languidly after William Lee said something indiscernible.

"Shhh, you hear that?" William Lee admonished Horse shit.

The clip-clop of shod hoofs was faint but growing in clarity. The animal would be coming along the main trail that led into town. That's why the men had been posted where they were.

Horseshit looked closely at the pocket watch he kept on the other side of his vest. "It's nye on three-thirty."

"Must be the one the Stoddard's all atwitter over. Hardly nobody else comes this way, and it sure ain't no trail hand waltzing into here this time o' the morning."

"We 'spose to bushwhack this billy goat?" Horseshit got himself set. He took the glove off his right hand and blew on the ball of his fist before unlimbering his Colt .44.

William Lee plucked his Sharpe's from where it was leaning and sighted through the scope. The moon was flat and bright like a freshly washed china plate and afforded light on the trail. "Cap'n says he wants us to bring whoever it is to him if'n we can." After a moment, the ambusher declared, "That cain't be."

"Huh?" Horseshit, whose real name was Remmy Nolan, not only needed advice on clothing but was in sore need of glasses. The one vanity he indulged was going without an aid to his vision. He felt spectacles made him look too old. He leaned over, ready to fire then saw what the other man had said. "Huh," was what he said again.

"Come on," William Lee. The two got from underneath the outcropping and went to their horses tethered to a sickly jacaranda on the blind side of the hill. The pair rode down onto the main street of the village. The trail led into town and became the central artery through the village.

"A donkey, by hisself." Horseshit pointed at the beast that had seemingly wandered into Rio Blanco. The creature was now standing at a puddle, lapping at the water before it all turned to mud.

"It's a mule," William Lee corrected. "Big, too." He dismounted and approached the creature. He put his hand on its side, examining its flanks and sniffing at it.

"You want me to leave so you two can git better acquainted?" Horseshit chided.

"This ain't no plow mule," William Lee pronounced. "I can see where the saddle's been cinched on him, and his hair has been washed and groomed not too long ago."

"Yeah, he sure is a pretty," Horseshit concurred. "He's so black and glossy like one of them paintings."

"So where's the cowboy that was on him?" William Lee wondered aloud.

"Maybe he got thrown. The saddle come loose, and he fell and cracked his head open."

"What about the bit and the reigns?"

"How do I know?"

"Let's take him to Stoddard."

"Are you loco, William Lee? He wants us to bring him a man, not a goddamn donkey."

"Mule."

"Shit."

William Lee put his rope around the animal's neck and led him to the La Reina Cantina. The establishment was located at the other end of the short main street. Eli Stoddard kept a large portion of the second floor of the cantina for his personal quarters. They tied up the mule and went to inform his boss.

Stoddard wiped at sleep in a corner of his eye. He'd come downstairs, and the three of them stood near the cantina's bar. "No markings or nothin' on it?" Stoddard fooled with the belt to his robe but decided to let the thing hang open over his long johns.

"Walked into town, easy as you please." William Lee thumbed in the direction of the door where the mule was tied outside.

Stoddard scratched at one of his lamb chop sideburns. "It's been regular fed?"

"Yep," William Lee confirmed. "It damn sure belongs to somebody, Cap'n. The question is what happened to the *hombre* that were a ridin' it."

Stoddard shifted his vision to the door as if he were going to walk out to see the animal for himself. But he merely turned his gaze back to his men. "And black?"

"Like coal," Horseshit added.

"That's very unusual for a mule," William Lee contributed. "They mostly run to variations on brown or even grey." He set his hat back from his crunched brow. "Fact, I don't believe I've ever seen one this dark. Nope, cain't say I have."

Stoddard ran a hand over his dry mouth. "I want you two to go back out of town the way this mule came and find the manjack that was on it."

"Now?" Horseshit whined. He'd been envisioning slipping into his bed after two days and nights cat napping among the rocks.

Stoddard's graveyard stare told him the answer. "And take the breed with you."

"Okay." William Lee made to go then, "What about the mule?"

"Shoot it."

"I was hopin' ta keep it."

"Why, it cain't mate," Stoddard answered irritably.

"But it's a fine animal, Cap'n. We could get some money for it."

Stoddard was too tired and too keyed up to sustain an argument. And extra income was always welcome. "Let's see about it when the sun is up, and you've brought me the man who owns it."

"Okay," a pleased William Lee said. It would be a shame to destroy the mule, he mused. He liked animals, found their company generally to be much more suited to his temperament than humans. Men he could kill with no qualms. But even wringing a chicken's neck for Sunday dinner gave him pause. Oh, he'd do it all right; it would just set heavy with him some was all.

They collected the one Stoddard had called the breed. His name was Alvonso Rey, and he was half Mexican and half Commanchero. His cascading hair was bleached of color after so much time in the sun, and he wore calfskin boots and a matching flat-brimmed hat. Thereafter, the three set out from town once they'd gotten a few supplies.

It didn't take them long to come upon the smoke from a small campfire. Rey and William Lee had smelled the singed air before seeing the anemic smoke.

They were about one hundred yards away and could see the slight plume rising from what once had been a Spanish mission. One of many selfless attempts by the conquerors to bring the one true faith to the savages—to not only show them the way, but ingrain in them to be more complacent subjects. The mission had been partially destroyed by canon fire during a junta by Mexican independence forces during the Plan of Iguala in 1821.

"I'll come in from that way," Rey said quietly, pointing to the south. Absently, he adjusted his gun belt, then sidled away. "We'll come at him through what's left of that archway,"

William Lee indicated the path he and Horseshit would take.

The men got off their mounts and headed to where they assumed they'd find a man asleep or passed out from his injuries. What remained of the roughhewn floor of the mission was rent and its stones strewn about as if a great force had bubbled from underneath. Weeds and small cacti sprouted everywhere, and they had to watch their step so as not to trip. William Lee had left his Sharpe's in its scabbard on his horse. He had his pistol out, a Smith & Wesson that he favored over the more popular Colt of the same caliber.

They got to the archway, one on either side of the opening. The campfire was to their right, a saddle and unwrapped bed roll nearby.

"Does this fella really exist?" Horseshit craned his neck in several directions.

"I know. It's like he's—" William Lee stopped at the sound of a foot scrapping over the dry ground.

"It's him," Horseshit breathed excitedly. "Maybe," a cautious William Lee said.

A figure walked from the southern direction. He stopped, then came forward again. The other two showed themselves, their guns on the man.

"All right, mister, there's somebody wants to meet you." William Lee cocked the hammer of his pistol to show the stranger he wasn't foolin'.

The figure gurgled, then they could see it wasn't the rider at all. It was Alfonso Rey, and he had a large skinning knife embedded off-center in his chest in his heart. William Lee and Horseshit started forward as Rey uselessly tried to remove the knife from his dying body. But doing this caused the blood to pucker from around the wound. He stopped trying to take the knife out, gasped, and dropped to the ground like a life-sized puppet whose strings had been cut. He sat slumped forward, one leg folded under him.

"Goddamn," a frightened Horseshit exclaimed.

William Lee was already in motion. "Come on." He started for the relative cover of the mission, Horseshit at his heels.

The crank of a rifle's repeater lever, just as a silhouette filled the archway, caused Horseshit to collide with William Lee in a comical way. But nobody was laughing.

"What'll it be?" the shape challenged. It didn't seem he was offering much in the way of choice.

William Lee got off a shot before several rapidly fired rounds fatally aggravated him. He stumbled back, tripping over Horseshit's leg as the latter ran for safety. "Goddamn is right," he bellowed and died.

Horseshit dove into a clump of brush that included some thick bramble.

His arms and face were cut, and a thatch of his cheek came away on a hooked thorn. Not bothering to dab at the wetness seeping into his whiskers, he peaked through the foliage. "Hey, mister, we just wanted to talk, that's all." It was blind luck that Horseshit had managed to stay alive during the war. He'd been at the slaughter of Chickamauga and had come through with only a little toe shot off. Yet here he was, scooting behind cover that couldn't keep the wind out. And he was hollering, giving his position away. But the certain anticipation of losing his life was more pressing on him than good sense.

"Sure," the no-name man said, "let's talk."

There was flint in his voice, and a down-home quality Horseshit recognized. "Sound like we from the same part of the country. I mean, you know, up north but down south, am I right?" The man didn't answer.

It wasn't clear to Horseshit what to do next. Minutes limped by, and he lay there, sweating and fretting. "Mister," he said again. And again, there was no response. Not even the owls hooted. "Look, mister," he began, "this here quarrel you got is with Cap'n Stoddard, ain't that so?" He hadn't expected the man to say anything and went on talking. "So, how about this? How about I toss out my gun, and you let me git to ma horse?" He got up on a knee. "I ride the hell out of here to Texas and don't look back. Don't that sound fair to you?"

"Sure."

Where was he? Horseshit threw his six-shooter onto the ground. "I'm coming out now, okay?"

"Grab some air while you're at it."

He did as he was told. Horseshit remained standing behind the low shrubs. The man who killed his friend and the breed was tall but not overly so. He had a wrangler's gait that was evident as he walked closer. The rifle he possessed was unusual. Though Horseshit couldn't tell what kind it was, he could see that its barrel had been shortened. Why he didn't know. But that's not what finally arrested his interest.

"You're a burrhead." He then remembered this man could send him to Kingdom Come. "I, uh, say, how about letting me git to ma horse? I promise

I won't be no trouble to ya."

The man stepped even closer. His features were haggard and there was a crescent of a scar starting up on his brow that curved like a scorpion's tail under his eye. "You got to sing for your supper, reb."

Horseshit's stomach clenched involuntarily. This colored boy knew about them. "What do you want?"

"How many men are with the captain?"

"You done kilt the best ones," he replied.

"That's not what I asked, is it?" Casually, he struck the man in the stomach with the stock of the sawed-off rifle.

Horseshit teared up, firecrackers exploding inside his head. He had enough presence of mind not to insult the black man again and make him really mad. A sullen "Five, not counting me," issued forth.

A menacing "You sure?" was his reply. "Yeah. I mean, yes."

"You lost another two in that last robbery your outfit did on the Sante Fe train out of Tulsa."

"You tellin' or askin'…mister?"

"What about my mule?"

"William Lee," he gestured over the taller man's shoulder, "liked that animal. He saved it for you."

If the other man had regrets about killing him, he didn't show it. "Turn around."

"What are you plannin' on doin'?"

"Gettin' my mule back."

Horseshit got a chill, and it wasn't from the cool evening. Not long afterward, the dawn leaked grey into the under-belly of the early morning. And a horse and man came riding fast through town, to the surprise of early morning risers.

"Jesus, Mary, and Moses," Horseshit screamed in agony. The kerosene soaking his clothes fed the flames that swarmed him. His gapping features matched the terror of his horse's as the two careened through town.

One of the villagers ran for the cantina to tell Stoddard. But two of his men were already out in the street, trying to halt the runaway horse. The horse ran into the side of the Flores Gran Almacén just as one of the men, called Blue, reached the two. He was grabbing at Horseshit, who was now loosened from being tied to the saddle. As he did so, two rifle shots cracked over the horse's whinnying, and the top of Blue's head was gone forever.

The other man, Casey, saw this and ran toward the doorway to the tannery. But this being before business hours, he found the door locked. He was about to shoot it open when another shot sounded, and a bullet entered his back and traveled downward, shattering his spine. He collapsed on the planked walkway, alive but unable to move.

"He's on a rooftop," one of Stoddard's remaining men concluded. He strained to see, crouching under the cantina's swinging doors.

"Who is this bastard?" Stoddard demanded of no one and everyone.

"Let's skin him first and ask him later," one of Stoddard's' four remaining gang members announced.

"How you figure to do that, Oakley?" One of the other men, a one-eyed individual named Fenton, asked. "This gravedigger is colder'n a virgin drinkin' ice water. He seems awfully intent on killing all of us."

"Yeah, he does indeed." the third one, Harris, an Irishman originally from Cork, added. He exchanged a conspiratorial glance at Oakley. The two, like Blue, had not been in the Confederate army with Stoddard like the rest. They were distant cousins and had joined up with the gang after hearing about the sweet set-up the ex-captain had down here. Neither had any allusions about blood spilled in battle, making them brothers and all that rot Stoddard would give speeches about—particularly after several glasses of mescal.

"We've got to flush him out," Stoddard said, pounding a fist on the bar.

There was a sound, and the anxious men pointed their guns at the entrance. Horseshit's stallion walked aimlessly in the main street past the cantina and on toward the end of the road and a bunch of hibiscus.

"Get on the roof, you two." Stoddard pointed upward at the rafters.

Oakley and Harris pretended like they were setting off to do as told. One stood at ten o'clock to the other's three o'clock to their leader. "It ain't us that boll weevil is after," Harris, who did most of the talking for the two, said.

"Godammit, Stoddard, is there a bunch of Texas Rangers out there or what?" Josefina, the owner of the cantina, hastened down the stairs. She was a handsome woman, large in the hips with grey creeping like vines through her raven hair. Her dressing gown was loosely tied, and its rosy satin complimented her tawny skin.

"Get your hog leg." Stoddard had his gun out and languidly pointed it in the direction of Harris.

Josefina went behind the bar and freed the sawed-off shotgun hidden there. She rested the weapon on the bar top. One of her heavy breasts poked out, her nipple hard with excitement. "I just had some flattened pesos cut up, too." She patted the shotgun like it was a pet.

Stoddard asked unnecessarily. "What you got to say, Fenton?"

"I'm with you, Cap'n, you know that." To prove it, he got up and relieved the two cousins of their pistols.

"Now git," Stoddard commanded. "Git where?" Harris balked.

He wheezed, "Don't be cute."

"That's cruel, even for you, Stoddard. Give us a chance."

"Like you were going to do for me, Harris." He slapped the man with the barrel of his Colt. "Now you two better hot foot it up there, or we'll cut you down here and now. Come on, Fenton."

Oakley and Harris shared resigned grimaces and began up the stairs, their two captors, men who they'd rode and stole with, behind them.

"All right," Stoddard said at the top, taking hold of Oakley's collar. He jammed the gun into his back. "Get over there, Harris."

Harris seethed. "If I get out of this, I'm going to rip you open, Stoddard."

"Big man. Let's go, Oakley."

Oakley went in, Stoddard pushing him while Fenton kept his gun on Harris on the landing.

Harris faced Fenton. Stoddard had his back to the men. Harris wiggled his index finger, indicating for Fenton to shoot Stoddard. "Do it," he mouthed, hoping the other man, scared and confused, would catch on.

"Come on, Fenton, bring that turncoat in here."

Harris took advantage of Fenton's indecision and jumped him. The two went against the wall, knocking a painting of a bullfighter loose. Stoddard turned and fired, his bullet chipping into the flocked wallpaper. Oakley lunged, but Stoddard was too fast. He pivoted around and used the butt of the pistol to club the man.

Harris and Fenton were entangled, thrashing at each other as they crashed against the banister several feet from the landing. Josefina rushed up the stairs, her shotgun poised. Stoddard stepped back into the hall to shoot Harris, but Oakley wasn't done. His wound made him woozy, but he managed to latch his arms around Stoddard's legs, upsetting his balance. He bent forward just as Josefina reached the top, and she had to sidestep his falling form.

Simultaneously, Harris slammed the heel of his boot into Fenton's forehead and tore off in the opposite direction along the hall. Josefina let a blast loose that clipped the fleeing man in the side and dusted part of the banister. Harris kept running, then stumbled and crawled around a corner. She took off after him.

Stoddard was on his back, and Oakley was on him, his arm holding the gun hand of the man down on the floor. "Fenton, Oakley called, "this is our chance."

"Don't be a fool, Fenton," Stoddard bellowed. "You think that gunhawk out there will just stop with me?"

A dazed Fenton was groggily getting to his feet. Oakley used Stoddard's neck for leverage with one hand, pressing his weight on it as he lurched his body upward. "Fenton," he pleaded. Stoddard bucked but couldn't get free.

Fenton scooped up his gun from where it had fallen on the carpet. He brought it up as the two men continued to struggle, taking aim. Whatever his decision was, he took it with him. The shotgun echoed again. Instantaneously, his guts were festooned on the walls, and the faces of the two were on the floor. Slivers of the pesos halves glistened among his entrails.

Josefina had already jacked in the new shells she'd taken time to place in her gown's pocket, also from underneath the bar.

The double barrels bore down on Oakley. "Let him up." Oakley did so.

"Where's Harris?" Stoddard asked.

"He got out on the roof through my room and rolled off." She came closer to him. "Now what?"

"We get this son of a bitch," he snarled.

"In case you haven't been counting, we're a might shorthanded, *mi amor*."

"Then what's your idea, woman?"

"What does any man want?"

Stoddard gave her a cock-eyed look. "You think you can sport Lea or one of your other girls out there naked on a horse, and he'll be satisfied?"

"Besides pussy."

Then he understood and looked at Oakley.

Soon, Oakley, bare-chested and bare-footed, with his hands in the air, marched out the front of the La Reina Cantina. Josefina and Stoddard held their guns on him, crouching from the doorway.

"Mister," the frightened man yelled into the unnaturally still morning. "Mister, they want to make a deal." He kept walking, turning his head and grinding his teeth as pebbles crunched into his feet. "Mister, can you hear me?"

"What kind of deal?" came a voice. Because of the gunplay, the villagers had wisely remained indoors. The main street was deserted. From the side of the Flores Gran Almacén, the general store, the man stepped out.

Oakley was so nervous. He was only momentarily surprised to note the man's race. "Stoddard's got money; he figures that's what you want."

"How much?"

Oakley frowned. "I cain't rightly say, but since me and my cousin joined up, we've done several jobs, you know, takin' down a train shipment and even a bank over in Nogales. Hell, must be ten, twenty thousand. That'd be a pretty good stake, wouldn't you say?"

The man jerked the odd rifle he was holding for Oakley to step closer to him. He did.

"Fancy shooting iron you got there," he said, trying to ingratiate himself with the stranger. "That's a Henry, ain't it? How come you had the barrel cut down?"

"How do I get the money?"

"Stoddard says he'll load your mule with it and then you can ride out, just that simple."

"Nothing's that simple." The man adjusted his hat, the rising sun starting to slant across the buildings. "You gonna bring my mule back to me with the money?"

"I guess," he said, unsure of the procedure.

"Tell him the price is ten thousand. You bring my mule back to me with the money in an hour, or it's no go."

"Okay." He didn't move, didn't want to anger the man. But he didn't say anything else, so he turned around and started back. "I'm going to tell him now, okay?"

"Where is my mule?"

Oakley stopped, his back to the man. "William Lee took him to the hacienda we bunk at. It's just outside the village, by the dried-up river bed."

The man with the rifle didn't say anything, and Oakley felt as if his watery knees were going to give out any second. He chanced a look round, but the man had already made himself scarce. Quickly, he returned as fast as he could.

Back at the cantina, Stoddard concluded, "He's going to gun us at the hacienda." He glared at Oakley, who was sitting, dabbing at his feet with a wet cloth. "This buck was wearing cavalry boots?"

"Yep," Oakley said. "What else?"

"Nothin'," Oakley said. "Except his rifle, like I told you, too. We wasn't exactly havin' no palaver, Stoddard. He wants the money, and he wants it now."

"Then that's our chance to get him," Josefina said. Stoddard paced, rubbing his hands. "This nigger is smart, we have to be smarter. He's got to be guessing we'll dry gulch him there, but we won't."

"You're going to let him ride out with all that money?"

"Yes. But when he leaves, that's when we get him."

"The ambush idea didn't work too good the first time," Oakley reminded him.

Stoddard shouted. "He's not going to go back through town, you idiot. He's going to go over the mountains; that's what I would do. You didn't tell him about Harris?"

"Nope. But he must have heard the gun shots from in here. He saw me walking out with no gun and no shirt. He knows something's up."

Stoddard waved his comments away. "But he doesn't know how many of us are left," he surmised. He pointed at Oakley. "You get his mule loaded, He's going to be riding one of the men's horses and use that animal to pack. I'm going to give him all the gold pieces in with the paper money. That load would slow him down too much to ride just the mule.

"That makes sense," Josefina concurred.

"So what about me?" Oakley stood.

"What about you?" Stoddard laughed. "You do what you're told, and you get to live a little longer."

Oakley threw the cloth down with force, but there was nothing he could do. Yet.

The hacienda had once belonged to a landowner named Ortiz. He'd had a vision of Rio Blanco becoming a bustling town of commerce and crops, and he, its titular king. But the nearby river that the town had gotten its name from had dried up. And Ortiz had become involved with the losing side in the treacherous arena of Mexican politics. Ortiz was murdered by his rivals on a cattle-buying trip to Guadalajara, thus further precipitating the decline of the town. But making it the ideal hideout for Stoddard's gang.

With Josefina keeping guard on him and helping take the money over by horse, he got several haversacks filed and tied onto the mule. The two waited another hour but the stranger, who in less than a day had totally disrupted the way things had been, was not around.

"What do you want me to do?" The two stood outside the hacienda, the smell of mesquite strong. Stoddard had hidden himself up in the hills, waiting for the man to ride by.

The woman scanned the area as she had been doing. She was dressed in patent leather boots, riding pants, and a man's shirt. "Take the mule back to where you first talked to him."

She switched her shotgun to her other hand and used her right to get on her horse. She grabbed the reigns of the other horse. "Get going. And don't you try to get away. We'll track you down."

Sighing, Oakley got on the mule and headed back through the village. Josefina rode hard in the opposite direction to get Stoddard. As he passed what once had been the livery, his cousin stepped out from inside. He'd tied part of a blanket around him, which was dark from the wound on his side. Hungrily, he eyed the bulging canvas bags.

"Forget it," his cousin warned him. "We got that bloodthirsty nigra on one side and Stoddard and Josefina on the other. An' we ain't got no gun a'tween us."

"That's a lot of money." Harris touched one of the haversacks as if it were a mirage. "So much money."

"You must be fevered, Colin. I've got to drop this off. You go back and hide, and then I'll come back. Together, we can get out of this mess we got ourselves into." He tapped his heels against the mule's side and started off again. Harris trailed after him. "We can kill the nigger, then hole up in the stable. When Stoddard and his whore come back, we take them too with his gun," he chortled gaily. "This is our only chance, Luther."

"No." Luther Oakley wanted to gallop away but mules don't gallop. His cousin grabbed his leg and yanked. Since he was riding bareback, it was easier to make him slide off the mule. The two fell into the dirt of the street.

"Don't be crazy, Colin. We can't do this." He hit his cousin in the jaw.

"No, we worked for that money. I ain't givin' it to no black boy who just happens along." Harris grabbed his cousin round his middle, and the two men wrestled and scratched, dust billowing around their bodies. The mule kept going.

"Colin," his cousin appealed. He got to a knee. "You're not thinking right." He wiped at his bleeding mouth with his sleeve. Stoddard had let him put on his shirt and boots.

Harris's desire for the money was worse than any desire he ever had for a woman. But he said, "Yeah, yeah, what am I doing? We're family, for God's sake." He stood and came forward, holding his hand out as if to help him up.

Oakley took the hand and was pulled hard, his cousin kneeing him in the face. This was followed by him being clubbed senseless after Harris clamped his fingers together.

"You'll thank me later," he muttered, taking off for the mule. He was surprised to find the animal alone near the Flores' store. Warily, he approached the creature. "Mister, mister?" he said. There was no response, and he smiled broadly.

At the other end of town, Stoddard and Josefina rode in. Stoddard said, "That eight ball surely done this." They'd halted, looking down at Oakley, who was groaning. "Come on, we can catch that clever boy."

They got their horses going and caught sight of the mule and its rider up ahead. "There he is," a gleeful Stoddard cried, taking a bead with his pistol.

"I'm not sure," Josefina started but didn't finish as Stoddard rode ahead, shooting and hollering. His faster horse closed the gap, and he shot Harris from behind—who had intended to retrieve his cousin until he saw the two coming. But now he lay on his back on the edge of town, looking up at the cloudless sky.

"Where is he?" Stoddard stood over him, his gun pointed at the dying man's skull.

His response was to cough up blood. Disgusted, Stoddard blew his face off.

The mule munched on a berry bush. Stoddard took the beast's reigns and headed back to the cantina.

"Stoddard," Casey called out as he rode past, "Stoddard, help me, I can't feel nothin'." He looked down and kept on.

"Hey, Josefina," he said, stepping through the swinging door. Oakley was sitting at a table, a lopsided grin, his expression. Josefina was sitting next to him, her hands on the shotgun, staring straight ahead.

"Josefina," he began, then saw the dark stain spreading from beneath her left breast. One thrust from his knife was all the deed had required. Stoddard had his gun out and spun toward the banister, but he wasn't there.

"Who are you?" He had his back to the door, but he didn't have to look around to know that black rainey was standing there.

"Somebody who's taking you back."

"For the bounty? There must be a nice price on my head by now."

"That's ri—"

Stoddard had hoped to catch the man unawares as he turned, flung himself flat, and fired. But the shooter was greased lightning with that trick rifle of his. The .44/40s perforated his upper body viciously. In battle, the Henry could easily put a man down at two hundred fifty yards. This close, the damage was savage. Laying amid the sawdust of the cantina, his essence sagged out of him. One of his last glimpses was of the boots of the man as he stepped over to kick Stoddard's Colt away.

They were cavalry boots, all right. "You were a blue belly, huh? Fighting to free your people," he said contemptuously.

His killer didn't answer. But he stood before him, saying something Stoddard couldn't hear clearly to Oakley. He shuddered. It was bitter cold, like that night so long ago when his men had captured four Union soldiers. They were blacks of the 25th Regiment. Buffalo soldiers the Indians had called because of the texture of their hair like that of the namesake's fur.

They'd had a good time that night, drinking corn liquor and teaching those tar babies a lesson, then they hung the four of them. Only now, his life spilling out of him in a village, not on any map, it didn't seem so goddamned funny. Those boots dangled before him, the faces of the men they'd slaughtered no longer features he could call up. One of those pairs of boots had a plug missing from its toe. The soldier had fixed it with a piece of rough brown hide he'd sewn into place.

Stoddard gulped. He saw that boot like it was now, then realized, just as he began to slip away, he was looking at that same boot right before him. It was on the gunman's foot. "That can't be," he said, "That can't be. We burned those bodies," he wailed hoarsely, and the fog enclosed him for good.

Oakley looked over at Stoddard. "What he say?" But he was asking himself. The stranger was out in the street, having hitched his saddle back on his mule. Oakley stepped out into the street, too, as did several of the villagers. The money sacks were draped over a horse. On the lower part of the saddle were branded the initials O. H. Mimms.

"Mimms," Oakley said aloud. "In Galveston I heard of a black bounty hunter with a specialty in tracking down Confederate war criminals. That you, Odet Mimms?"

"Give me a hand with Stoddard." The two wrapped him in a couple of serapes and placed the body across the horse with the money. There was something funny about that, but neither man chuckled.

"I wish I knew what to say." Oakley hunched his shoulders.

"Looks like you got a few graves to dig." Mimms adjusted his hat. Riding away, he passed by the bruja's cottage on the butte. She was sitting on the porch, watching him. After a while, the black rider, his mule, the money, and the fresh horse disappeared in the sun's haze.

* * *

"Rio Blanco," *Guns of the West*, Berkley Books, 2002, Ed Gorman and Martin H. Greenberg, editors.

IV

HELL BENT

House of Tears

"That shit's bad for you."

"What? You're into tofu and brown rice now?" LZ snickered and took a long pull on his Slurpee.

English Johnny turned the late '90s Astro van left off Garfield and drove slow and steady along a side street. As evening approached, kids were still out on their scooters and bikes, and there was even a knot of girls jumping rope while a boom box blared a 50 Cent song.

"I'm just saying," English Johnny went on, "we ain't getting no younger, and you got to take care of yourself." He scanned from one side of the street to the other as he guided the vehicle forward.

LZ scratched his armpit. "Look, man, I'm happy you ain't no longer sniffin' up your profits in crank, and you're clean and sober as an Oklahoma preacher. But let me worry about my own goddamn vices."

"Uh-huh."

LZ grinned. "Fuck you." He had more of his Slurpee and leaned out the window. "Hey, girl, what you packin' in there?" he said to a young woman in tight, low-rise jeans walking past on the sidewalk.

"Fool, be cool," English Johnny said. "Sit your ass back down."

"Maybe you should be on speed again," LZ cracked, "you're too wound up." He jiggled his shoulders and bobbed his head to the beat that pulsed in him. The beat that had been banging about inside him since he ran away from juvenile hall.

"We need to be focused. That's all I'm saying. Your head's gotta be in the moment like Iverson before a big one." English Johnny took a right and checked the rearview.

"You know I ain't nothin' but game, home," LZ replied.

He pointed through the windshield. "How about that one?"

"That'll do," his partner agreed and pulled to the curb, the van idling on the lonely street.

LZ got out and trotted over to a parked Trailblazer SUV. He crouched down and quickly removed the rear license plate. Looking over his shoulder and, spying no one, he got up and did the same in the front of the car. He then attached those plates in the appropriate places on the Astro van. English Johnny put the tranny in gear and got rolling again after LZ settled beside him.

They rode in silence, the driver taking a couple of turns until he reached Atlantic Boulevard. There, he went left, to the north, passing signage on stores in Chinese, Spanish, and English.

Finally, LZ spoke. "Dude like this ain't got no bodyguards around. A couple of three hundred fifty pound pork chop eatin' square head bruisers all tatted up jus' praying for the opportunity to light into some sneak thieves like you and me." LZ smiled at his imagery, showing teeth he cared for daily. You couldn't get anywhere with the honeys if you had nasty teeth.

"He's a recluse. Danielle says until the stroke, he rattled around in his castle by himself. Maybe had a call girl up there now and then, or some session dude dropped by from the old days."

"Man got to get his Johnson waxed now and then," LZ observed. "Man go crazy if he can't have that. Get all backed up and shit."

English Johnny looked sideways at his compatriot. "That right?"

"I'm just sayin'," LZ nodded at the window. "But he was something in his day, huh? I remember Moms would have her girlfriends over, and after they got to drinking and got all misty-eyed about their teenage years, she'd break out that antique that played those goofy 45s. Then they'd get to finger-poppin' and tellin' more lies while they put on homeboy's hits."

LZ stared at English Johnny. "Bet you had a collection of his records, didn't you?"

"Still do, youngster. *The Slauson Shuffle, The Love You Left, Quicksand...*

man, those were the cuts. If you didn't get a grind on a slow tune like *Heart of Fire*, you must have been one sorry chump." English Johnny looked beyond the windshield, then reeled himself back to the present.

"When was that? High school?"

"Yeah." They were on the border of Monterey Park and Alhambra, and English Johnny slowed to a stop at the intersection with Emerson.

"You finish high school?" LZ, a tenth-grade dropout asked

"Hell, yeah." The other man pressed his foot to the accelerator as the signal changed to green. "Hell, I was even on the football and basketball teams."

"First string?"

English Johnny gave him a raised eyebrow. "You got to ask."

"Aw'rite, brah, cool." LZ had another long sip of his iced soda. "So it's just Danielle up there with him, wiping his ass and chin."

"Apparently."

"And you think he keeps his shit there? In that mansion?"

"Know so."

"Danielle seen it?"

"Practically."

"Practically? What? She have a vision?" LZ chuckled at his joke.

"He's got a room, and in the room is this stuffed bobcat, and—"

LZ halted in mid-sip. "A stuffed what? Like a lion?'

"Sort of," English Johnny frowned. "Well, I guess technically, it's more like a cougar."

"What the fuck, he's a hunter?"

"No, everything I've read says he's afraid of guns. When he was a kid, his old man shot the old lady. The gun flashed right in front of his face, his mother's chest exploding, blood all over him. Traumatized him. In fact, that's how he got into music."

"You've studied up on him."

"Naturally." English Johnny checked his watch; the clock on the dash was broken. They were now heading west on Hellman, and he'd turn north again when they reached Fre mont. The cell phone rang, and LZ plucked it off the narrow dashboard.

"We're almost there," he said after listening briefly. "Sure." He handed the cell to his friend. "Your squeeze needs to hear your voice so she can cream."

"You need to stop." English Johnny put the phone to his ear. "Hey, baby." He listened as he drove. "Oh, yeah, we're set. Is he awake…I see. Okay, we follow the plan, and we're gonna make out like a souvenir huntin' Marine in one of Saddam's palaces." She said something else, and he lowered his voice. "You know it." He clicked off.

"Where you two going after this?' LZ took his bandana off and buttoned his shirt over his breastbone. Absently, he flicked at the oval embroidered with the name "Steve" on the upper left side of the shirt.

"Danielle wants to go to London first because she's only seen it on TV or James Bond movies, and wants to know what it's like firsthand. You know, Big Ben, red phone booths, cobblestones." He shrugged. His nickname had nothing to do with the capital of England.

"Yeah," LZ said, "go to Jimi Hendrix's grave and pay your respects."

"Hendrix is buried here."

"Here? Wasn't he from there?"

"Seattle."

"No shit."

"Nope."

"Huh," LZ reached under the seat and extracted a black Beretta.

"We're not going to need that."

"Safety first, son," LZ winked. And he tucked the gun away in his back pocket.

English Johnny weighed raising an objection but understood the lad needed a security blanket of a sort, so why not? He could take care of things if LZ went off, though he didn't anticipate such a situation. No, this was going to be one sweet operation. This was the setup he'd been on the road to since that time long ago when he stole his shop teacher's bad '67 Camero—one of the limited Yenko's with a 427 engine. This was going to work, and nothing was going to derail his chance at a real payday.

The van took a right and traveled up an inclined street heavy with old oak trees, and from several houses, the air faint with the scent of onions and garlic cooking in butter. They crossed from Alhambra into the hills of San Marino.

"Hey, that was the street," LZ said, knocking the tip of his thumb against the side window.

English Johnny looked past him, straining to see the street sign in the gloom.

"That's it, I'm telling you," LZ repeated. "Where's your damn reading glasses?"

"My eyes are fine," he growled, reversing the van in a three-point turnaround. He started onto the street he'd missed, stopped, and put the automatic transmission into its lowest gear. They lumbered up the hill, the street swaying left and right as they neared the top. Behind them in the cargo area, canisters rattled in their harnesses.

"I've got it." LZ reached around and held onto the tanks.

The van topped the summit, and they saw an opening partially hidden among leafy shrubs to their right. They went through that and followed a driveway that curved and sloped downward to a metal art nouveau-style gateway and arch. The electronic gate was open.

"I can smell it," LZ said.

"Don't start barking yet. I don't want to jinx this."

"It's ours, man." LZ gripped English Johnny on the upper arm. "You know it."

English Johnny's eyes widened, and he guided the van next to Danielle's dark blue '77 Grand LeMans Coupe with the Hopster aluminum rims he'd put on the car for her. He breathed in deep and let the air out slowly.

"Ready?' LZ asked.

"Let's do this." His partner got out the driver's side and went around to where LZ had slid the side door back. They got the two oxygen tanks, heart monitor, dolly, mask and tubing, and a clanking equipment bag onto the ground.

As LZ positioned one of the tanks on the dolly, he glared at some illuminated letters cut into yet another arch leading to a garden. "Fuck's that say?"

"*Casa de Lágrima,*" English Johnny said, straightening out one of the casters on the monitor's cart. "House of Tears. That refers to his first album, which the critics liked, but it didn't sell."

LZ took in the massive Spanish-Moorish structure, complete with turrets. "How many rooms in this mug?"

"Danielle said there are thirty-three."

"Damn." Together, they started up the walkway that jutted through the garden. "You sure this dude ain't Dracula?"

"You know what he spends his days doing? He watches reruns of *Combat, Mannix,* and that goddamn *High Chaparral.*"

"Those were TV shows?" LZ rolled the strapped oxygen tanks along on the dolly.

"Yeah, before your time. He's got all the episodes filed away on DVDs and gives her a list of what he wants played and what day."

"Does he listen to them songs he wrote and produced?"

"No, that's the funniest thing, he doesn't. According to Danielle, he never asks her to play them. And barely listens to the radio. Like he's forever shut out that part of his life." English Johnny pointed at a horizontal sliver of light that grew before them.

"There's my girl."

The men got the equipment through an entrance fronted by wide double doors while Danielle stood to one side. She wore a mid-thigh skirt, and her sweater blouse was opened just to reveal part of her black lace bra.

"Ain't you supposed to be in white or something?" LZ set the dolly with its load against the rough-hewn wall in the circular foyer.

"Practical nurses wear what they want. And anyway, my patient likes the view." She cupped her large breasts in her hands and shook them, laughing.

"Long as he don't touch." English Johnny put an arm around her waist and pulled her close. They kissed, and she wiped her lipstick off his mouth with her fingers.

"He awake?"

"He was dozing," she answered. "Rough day of watching his fuckin' shows."

English Johnny looked toward the staircase, visualizing what lay beyond. "Come on."

The trio proceeded up the stairs and English Johnny was struck with the absence of any evidence that the house belonged to a man considered one of the pioneers of sixties and early seventies rock & roll and R&B.

"Know what's odd," Danielle whispered when they reached the mid-landing. "Today, he started to make some notes."

English Johnny bored in on the closed bedroom door at the end of the upper hallway. "What?"

"Looked like he was jotting down some lyrics," she said. "In all the time we've been planning this, the last six months, this was the first time I've seen him do that."

"We'll give him something to sing about." LZ ascended backwards, effortlessly pulling the dolly and tanks.

At the top, English Johnny gently pushed Danielle forward, his hand on the small of her back. She went ahead of LZ and opened the double wooden doors of the bedroom that matched, though smaller in scale, the main ones.

"Ian," she said sweetly, "the men are here from the medical supply." The room was spacious and made even more so by the paucity of furniture. There was a plasma screen with a VCR and DVD player attached. There was a large portrait in oils of a dark-haired woman with a scowl and sizable hoop earrings partially emerging from her tangle of hair. The painting hung on the west wall, and to the left of that was a raised oak bed atop a colorful throw rug and a sturdy nightstand nearby.

In the bed, reposed the former music baron. The thin man, bald, with a prow of a nose below-recessed eyes and stooping shoulders encased in blue silk pajamas. He lay propped against a thatch of pillows and stared intently at the scene between actors Cameron Mitchell and Henry Darrow on his TV set. On a long, low dresser tucked under a window was a series of foam heads, each with a different style of wig.

"Gentlemen," he said in the slightly slurred speech of a stroke victim.

"We'll just set this up, sir," English Johnny said, already heading toward the bed. LZ fell in step, and they worked efficiently as they'd practiced, getting the tank and monitor into place.

A pad of paper was on the nightstand. English Johnny noted the lyrics the man had been writing. Being a fan, he couldn't resist reading the words.

"I don't think it's gonna put me back on the charts." The man in bed looked evenly at English Johnny. He chuckled hoarsely until he started to cough.

"Now, now, let's let these men do their work, and you rest, dear." Danielle attended to the man, making sure not to look at English Johnny.

"Maybe you should have some oxygen," she offered. "Doctor Sawyer did suggest it would be good at this time of the evening."

"Sure, sure," he rasped, gesticulating with knotted and blotched fingers that were more like the hinged legs of an insect than a human's.

Danielle bent over more than necessary and slipped the oxygen mask with its elastic band around his head. The songman's eyes took in the offered view.

"'Bout finished, aren't we, boss?" LZ gave English Johnny a crooked smile.

"Sure." English Johnny calibrated the dials on the heart monitor. He pushed the instrument toward the side of the headboard.

"The city burns at night past the windows of my four-on-the-floor," the former mogul mumbled into the mask. "I got eight starving cylinders and a hunger to match. Something's inside me, girl, and it's no lark, but in this dark, my name is called..." He drifted off to sleep, the knock-out gas doing its work before he could finish the lyrics English Johnny saw on his writing pad. The song was called *House of Tears*.

Danielle slipped off the mask and shut off the valve. The tank contained Halothane, a general anesthesia.

The three plotters exchanged glances and as one, exited the room. There was a shorter hallway off the long one, and Danielle led them past a set of tall vases filled with even taller elephant stalks. At a T, there was a door with a hinged peephole.

"What up with that?" LZ said.

"I think it was a study at one point, and I guess if the man of the house was into his books or brandy, he wanted to know who was knocking and disturbing him." Danielle produced a set of keys and unlocked the heavy door.

"Goddamn," English Johnny said as the trio stepped into the room and Danielle turned on the lights. The chamber was in one of the turrets, so it was circular, with a high ceiling over their heads. There was a set of stone steps built into a part of the wall that led to a second-tiered platform. A low, rectangular bookcase on the platform overflowed with volumes.

On the ground level, part of the space was crowded with stuffed animals, including a murder of ravens on their perches, a mandrill posed in mid-swing, a snarling wolf, and the bobcat. There was also another section that had bunched together all manner of ' '50s-era toy ray guns in several glass-enclosed cases.

"All this shit means something to him? Or is he just another rich boy don't know what to do with his money." LZ touched a bronze axe among a set of different types of axes grouped along one part of the curved wall.

"That's an Egyptian piercing axe," English Johnny rattled off. The other two gaped at him. "I told you, I read up on my man. There was an interview he did in *Vanity Fair* about sixteen or seventeen years ago and they had pictures to go with it."

LZ was in motion. "Well, that's really fuckin' groovy, but let's get busy."

English Johnny removed his torch from the equipment bag. LZ rolled in the other tank, marked oxygen, but actually contained acetylene. He and Danielle pushed the bobcat to one side. Its platform was made to look like a mountain path.

"That's heavier than it looks," LZ huffed.

The woman got down on all fours, running her fingers in the grout between the pavers.

"Here we go," she said, standing up. She pushed the ball of her foot on a particular tile and depressed it. They waited.

"Ain't part of the wall supposed to open up like in an old movie?" LZ looked around.

"I didn't hear a click or anything. You sure that's how he gets to his vault?"

The anticipation in English Johnny was roiling acid in his stomach—he was neither a happy nor a patient man. He held Danielle firm by the arm.

"Yeah, baby," she insisted, pulling her arm loose. "That time the door to the peephole was loose, and I looked in to see him stepping on that part of the floor, and then he…oh."

"Oh, what?" English Johnny said between clenched teeth.

"He walked," she turned to face the door, getting her direction right. "Ian went that way," she pointed, "toward the stairs. I couldn't see him then, and I didn't dare stay at the door too long."

"The fuck." LZ charged close to English Johnny. "We doin' all this on your practically. This bitch never saw the money?"

"Your mama's a bitch," Danielle told him. "Fuck you."

"Everybody relax." English Johnny advised. He tamped down his temper. "If he went toward the stairs, he went up the stairs."

LZ declared, "This is bullshit."

"No, no, it can't be." Danielle looked up at English Johnny, who was now prowling about on the platform, his hands probing the bookcase. He hooted. "You were right, LZ. It's just like one of those Charlie Chan movies." English Johnny slid away a portion of the bookcase.

LZ ran up the steps, followed closely by Danielle. English Johnny was already in the exposed opening. Stepping on the paver had unlocked a paneled section behind the bookcase.

Danielle asked. "Is there a light?"

"Can't tell, but there's got to be." LZ bumped into something, and there was a crash. "Hey, I've got something."

"All you got is one of his framed gold records. I already saw those. This," English Johnny said, tapping metal, "is what we came for." He swung his penlight onto their smiling, sweaty faces. "Get my tools."

"Bet," LZ scrambled out.

Danielle came beside him, placing a hand on English Johnny's chest. She looked at the standing safe. "How much you think is in there?"

"Enough to keep you in thongs and beamers, baby."

She put a hand on his tightening crotch. "So that's what excites you.

"You damn right." He put a hand on her breast, and they kissed ferociously. They only stopped when they heard LZ approach with the cutting tools.

English Johnny got his rig set up. "You two get up front so you don't get any sparking or metal in your eyes." He flicked down his welder's mask and went to work.

When Danielle told him what she'd seen that day, peaking into this room, the idea had taken root. He looked up anything and everything he could about the reclusive records legend. It was already known that he'd had tax trouble in the past, and English Johnny found a couple of quotes from him attesting to his belief that the government had no right to the money he'd earned. In an article in a crumbling issue of *Teen Beat,* he came across at a flea market, the first of three ex-wives was interviewed. She'd been the lead singer of the Sparrows, the girl group, the legend guided to early success.

"He is one cheap, paranoid bastard," she'd said. "He grew up without and took to heart what his grandmother always told him about how the banks had ripped her folks off in the Depression. The more he got famous, the more he did lines of coke and quarts of booze, the more he felt everyone was out to get him."

The torch's concentrated flame made progress, burning a hole just above and to the left of the handle. The box was an old Mosler, and English Johnny had been weaned on specimens like this one.

More digging into the record man's life had produced his last interview. For a piece in *Rolling Stone* in June of 1992, he'd gone on about the riots that April and May here in LA. The quote that sealed it for English Johnny was the one where he alluded to the safe.

The idol maker's father, a Holocaust survivor and a jeweler back when the Fairfax district was solidly Jewish, had the safe in his shop, as English Johnny learned from a documentary obtained from the library. The impresario said that as he watched the smoke and the helicopters in the distance, he figured if the rioters should make their way up his hill, he'd roll down on them the only thing of value his shit heel of a father had left him.

The interviewer had pressed for clarification and the man answered, "Well, maybe I'll just take some money out of it and toss it over the wall." It was related in the article that he'd laughed uproariously at that.

"How's it going?' Danielle asked from the entrance.

"I'm almost to the pins," English Johnny enthused. Fine metal dust congealed on his mask. He suddenly glommed on something that had been in the back of his mind. How did a stroke victim, a man partially paralyzed on one side of his body, move that bobcat to get to the tile?

Then the lights went out. "Hey," LZ yelled.

"Deal with it," English Johnny commanded. "I'm not stopping. Danielle, use my flashlight. It's in my back pocket.

Shield your eyes and come get it."

"Okay." She came forward haltingly. "I've got it."

"And take this." He'd put the torch on top of the safe, cutting down its flame. Its glow lit them in wavering blues and yellows. He passed her the Glock he'd strapped to his calf under his pant leg. "LZ has a piece. Maybe this is nothing, or maybe he's trying to pull some shit."

She didn't blink. "I can handle him."

"I know you can." She left, and English Johnny went back to work. He didn't like sending her off to do his job, but he couldn't have any delay in getting this box open. The hole was completed. He used the reduced flame for light and set about using his drill, hammer, and pointed chisel on the door's lock pins. Sweat gathered on his face, and he had to stop and wipe the grime from his hands. The only thing he could hear was his tapping and drilling and grunting. There was the satisfying slip of the pin from the rotor, and the auger bore through just where he wanted inside the lock mechanism. Soon. Very soon.

The Pretty Boy Floyd-era Mosler opened silently on well-oiled hinges. And just like the fairy tale this job was—the castle-like mansion on the hill, the hermit, Danielle as his princess—there was the treasure inside the safe. Neat, collated stacks of hundreds the IRS would no doubt be happy to know about were nestled inside the safe.

He reached for one of the piles, and his hand jerked at the retort of a gun. His temples pulsing, English Johnny crouched and listened, his fist tight around his hammer's handle. Come on, somebody say something.

"Danielle," he boomed. "Danielle."

Breathing deep, he scooped the money into the equipment bag and got out of the room. There was minimum light coming through the high windows, and he could make out enough to get back down the stairs leading from the hidden alcove in the turret. If LZ was up to something, wouldn't he have been there to bust a cap in him?

Once more in the larger room, every dark form was a potential enemy, every shadow a place where he could be jumped. The equipment bag banged against his leg, his other hand gripping the hammer. There were no more shots, no whispering, and no movement. English Johnny strained to discern the door they'd come through and walked purposefully to it. He was going home with this money.

Out in the passageway he stopped and listened. He started forward and collided with one of the vases, toppling and shattering it. Instinctively he crouched low, expecting… something, but there was nothing. He moved forward, feeling his way to the T section. He stopped again. There was something, a presence. He put the equipment bag aside, wanting to use both hands and his hammer.

"Baby," Danielle said, the word thick with mucus. "Help me." She moaned. "Help me," she repeated. Squinting into the semi-darkness, he could see she was crawling in the long hallway, the one that led to the master bedroom.

English Johnny frowned, trying to make sense of things. "What happened?"

"He," she started but didn't finish.

Was it a trap? Were she and LZ in on it together? She was young and fine. When the three of them had been out, working on the plan, people usually assumed she was with LZ.

"Chris," she coughed, using his real name. "I know you're there."

Fuck it. He went to her, crouching down, keyed up for anything. She was on her belly, doing her best to drag herself along by her arms.

"What happened?" English Johnny had her face in his hands, her cheek cold like fish flesh.

"He whacked LZ alongside his head when we turned the corner."

"He? You mean—?"

"Yeah. He wasn't knocked out by the gas. I had the light on him and was bringing my piece up when he shot, put it right into my chest. Bastard shot me right in the tit." She laughed and coughed up fluid and blood.

"Where's your gun?"

"Dropped it, back at the door. God, it hurts."

"He's in there now? The bedroom?"

"Don't know," she managed weakly. "I need a doctor, honey."

"I'm gonna get you straight, sweetie. You hold on." English Johnny wasn't going to let some gimp get the better of him. Not now, not having come this far. He rose and walked forward. "Hey, faggot. You think you're better than me?"

"Come on in and find out," the man taunted through the door. "You think because I had a stroke, I can't take care of a bunch of also-rans like your *F Troop* crew? You know what kind of shit I've been through for forty years in the record business? What kind of flesh eaters I had to deal with? You're nothing compared to that." He coughed, then continued.

"Didn't it occur to you I might have your girl checked out? Find out about her record and known associates like you, Chris. You fuckin' loser, penitentiary bitch." He laughed. "Did you know I was a lifeguard when I was young? Still pretty good at holding my breath."

"Big man," English Johnny groused. He positioned himself next to the door, the hammer in his hand. He felt along the door, got set, then banged at the old-fashioned latch to bust it off. Two shots went through the door, but he wasn't stopping. "Come on, motherfucker," the sick man screamed. "You aren't gonna let a cripple beat you, are you, tough guy?"

The latch gave, and the door creaked open slightly. English Johnny went low against the doorjamb, waiting and listening. If he were the other man, where would he be? He visualized the room as he'd remembered it and looked to his left where the big TV was.

"Chris," Danielle called from the hallway.

The thief launched himself, and two more shots rang out as he dove for the bed. One of the rounds caught him in the lower leg, right above the ankle. His momentum took him to the bed, and he scrambled over to the other side, knocking the nightstand and doped the oxygen tank over as he got to the floor. Another shot went wide. His wound was on fire, and English Johnny grimaced in pain. He used the bed as a battering ram. He shoved the heavy frame toward the large TV and the man hiding behind it. More gunshots, wood chipping and a round pinging off a metal surface.

The bed collided with the TV, which toppled over. There was a groan and the clatter of the gun across the tiles. English Johnny moved as best he could, his leg spasming from the effort. He reached his target beside the upset big screen. And was surprised the scrawny man still had fight in him. A hand that had more strength than he would have imagined was around English Johnny's throat.

"You lousy fuck," the recluse said. "You think you can steal from me?"

"I earned this," English Johnny hollered, striking him. Only one side of the man's body had power, and with the blow, he was through. His body collapsed inside his silk pajamas.

English Johnny grabbed at him. "You shot my old lady."

"I'd shot you too if I had the chance."

The once record producer was pale and shaking. He was through, but wouldn't admit as such.

English Johnny was about to hit him again when an approaching siren caused him to pause.

"What's a'matter? Didn't think I'd call them, genius?"

English Johnny shoved the squawking man aside as if he were a child. Straining, he got his feet under him, his leg wobbly. A hand clutched at his pant leg. He kicked the man who'd earned twenty-seven gold and platinum albums in the head and limped quickly away. Danielle had managed to sit up against the wall. She held out her arms.

"Help me up, baby."

He went past her to the equipment bag, bumping and stumbling into objects and bric-a-brac. He got the bag and turned. He'd have to pass her again on his way to the stairs.

"Chris," she wailed, using his real name.

"They'll take care of you, Danielle. They'll get you an ambulance and everything."

"You backstabbing, mothafuckah. Get me out, Chris," she yelled. "Get me out of here. You wouldn't have shit if it wasn't for me." She was in tears. He was at the stairs.

"No," a new voice hollered.

"LZ, wait," English Johnny began but didn't finish as the younger man tackled him, and they went horizontally down the stairs to the mid-landing.

"You ain't taking that money nowhere." LZ was bleeding from his head and sounded woozy.

English Johnny got a knee between them and leveraged his partner off of him. He beat LZ's head with the stuffed equipment bag.

"No, no, you don't," LZ raged, lunging for English Johnny. The gun punched a wicked hole in his stomach, and LZ fell back against the carved banister. English Johnny had picked up the Beretta LZ had brought in against his wishes. When the hermit had hit and dazed LZ, he'd apparently placed the piece on his nightstand.

"Sorry," English Johnny said, getting up and stepping over the wounded man on the stairs. "I'm very sorry."

"Man, that's fucked up. That's really fucked up." LZ's warm blood leaked past, the hand held to his gut.

The siren was coming up the hill, and English Johnny was barreling down the road in Danielle's LeMans. The San Marino cop car, a Caprice with crash bars, crowded the narrow incline. English Johnny went right like he was getting out of the way, then veered left viciously, knocking the cruiser into a parked pick-up. The cop on the passenger side aimed with his nine as the driver straightened the banged-up car. English Johnny decimated their side window with a blast from the Beretta.

As he'd hoped, the two cops ducked, and that afforded him the opportunity to barge past, scraping the side of his car against theirs, screeching his way free. The cops put rounds in his trunk and punched holes in his rear window as he got to the bottom of the hill. There was another cop car coming. But there was another street, and he took that. He wasn't sure where it led, but it was better than where he was. For any street leading down would get him out of the hills.

He tore through residential streets, past high-priced houses behind high walls. He was heading into Pasadena. Which meant a larger police force and more resources. His leg bled into the worn mat. A police chopper searched for him overhead, its spotlight cutting like a laser through the foliage. He kept driving. Panic and fear gurgled in his stomach when he got momentarily trapped in a cul-de-sac, but miraculously, he turned around and finally reached flat land.

The hunted man got himself oriented near the Cal Tech campus and bore westward. He took Del Mar, hoping to throw them off by not taking a major street, but already two black-and-whites were on him. At Los Robles, he got lucky again and managed to beat an eighteen-wheeler heading south. The truck locked its brakes, and the trailer fish-tailed through the intersection as he roared past. This momentarily delayed the pursuit and gave him breathing room. On a side street, he ditched the V-8 and took off on foot.

His leg was on fire, but he knew this was better than trying to escape in the moving target he was driving. In the near distance, he could hear the traffic on the 110 Freeway. He got to a cyclone fence, the freeway on the far side. Below, between him and the freeway, was Arroyo Seco Wash. This being the Southland, it was a concrete river, its bed dry except in the rainy season. Access tunnels were cut into its sloping walls. There was one such opening just across the wash from him.

English Johnny threw the bag over and used what reserve he had left to clamber over the fence, too. He lost his grip at the top and came crashing down on the other side on his back. The whoosh of the helicopter and its spotlight suddenly swung into view, trapping him in its glare. Wrenching himself up, he grabbed the bag and ran, limped, skipped his way toward that hole. The zipper had worked loose, and money began flapping loose from the bag. Caught in the light, the bills fluttered about with a green luminescence.

His side aching, his leg numb, English Johnny kept on. Overhead came the warning through the bullhorn. Run, he admonished himself, run. He was on the slope; he was almost there. He was pushing fifty, and he was going to live like a pharaoh.

The rifle shot sent a high-velocity slug clean through his hip, exiting above and to the side of his knee. He went down as if struck by lightning. But he held onto the bag; he held on to the money. He would never let it go.

"It's mine," he wailed. "Goddammit, I'm way past due." He dog walked up the sloping wall, but the second shot bore between his shoulder blades, exited his sternum, and drove him back to the deck with thudding certainty.

His muscles lost control, and his body ceased to respond to his commands. It was all he could do to focus his eyes. Footsteps and loud voices reached him and with nothing left but desire, he reared up, staring at the tunnel hole. It seemed then, as they put hands on him and a foot slammed into the upper part of his back, shoving him down again, that the slot in the wall grew. His breathing slowed, his heart beat less and less, but he couldn't look away.

That hole loomed larger, telescoping toward him, blotting out the light and pain. Darkness was all about him. English Johnny could now see clearly along that long, dank corridor, a *House of Tears* awaiting him. He clutched his money, running, running with Danielle, never to return.

* * *

"House of Tears," *Black Noir: Mystery, Crime, and Suspense Stories by African-American Writers*, Pegasus, 2009, Otto Penzler, editor.

Chatter

"I'm just walking out now. I parked on the street because I spotted an open meter, and since I was running late, it was faster to do that than go into the parking structure. Yeah, uh- huh. It went as good as it could, I guess. You know whatsher name from the mayor's office? Je-zus, what the fuck crawled up her ass? I've yet to be in a meeting with her on this and see the hint of a smile cross her face. Every fuckin' thing with this woman is like it's down to her and another broad on Survivor Island, and she's gonna bite a chunk out of the other chick's throat to be the last ball cruncher standing.

"Huh? You're shitting me. Her and Morrell from the planning department? He's, like, what, fifty-eight, sixty? And she's no more than thirty-eight, right? What the hell does she get out of doing him? I mean, God bless Cialis, but Morrell is a functionary at best. Yeah? That so? Huh.

"Hey. Shit. No, I'm all right. I was crossing the street, and this asshole in an Escalade swooshed right in front of me. Naturally he had tinted windows and blasting some rap number. Probably juiced on his chronic. Ha. Come on, you know me, live and fuckin' let live, but goddamn, whatever happened to simple civility? See, this is what I'm talking about in this matter, right? Wait, hold on. No, I just got to my car and fumbled my cell phone, getting my keys out, and working the latch.

"Anyway, we've got these do-right, moaning and groaning idealistic and unrealistic lefty organizations going on about, oh what about the poor, the less fortunate, where are they going to live if the only concern is the bottom line? If you developers just build these upscale complexes without setting aside so many units for the low-income…yeah, so their poor unfortunates can hog two spaces parking their Escalades after a hard day of selling dope.

"No, I'm not being racist. But it's true. We could have broken ground on this part of the project by now. We've complied with the Mello Act. We've built in the proper amount of set-asides for low- income units, but no, that's not enough. It's never enough with these people. Christ."

* * *

"Look, I know what the fuck I'm doing. The mark ain't on to me. I just wanted to scope him out, make sure I had the right, gee, you know how I do. Plus, it don't hurt to get the blood up, shit. Get the smell in the air, ya feel me? Hold up, hold up. I'm coming to this light, and there's some po-pos. I gotta be cool. Don't want to fuck this up now. Yeah, I'm turning my sounds down. No, I'm straight. Ain't even got a throat lozenge on me, let alone any weed. Yeah, I'm at the light. Yeah, naw, uh-huh. They're giving me their cop looks. I know these fools be running my plate.

"Hell naw, it's all good. We been over that, man. I'm going to use stolen plates for the job. Just like we're using burners, too, so it can't be traced to us. And I'm gonna be creepin' anyway. Ain't no way I'm getting' made. Told you, this is the shit, my nigga. Watching that black and white that night, with you know, the old dude, Colombo, playing Albert Anesthesia. What? Wait, light's changed. Cops be hanging back, letting me go first so they can try and gank me. Stupid motherfuckahs. Like I don't know what they're up to. Come on, you can't play a playah.

"Okay, they followed me for a couple of blocks, then turned off. Come on, T, don't be paranoid. We got this tight. We taking that Murder Incorporated thing into the twenty-first century, dog. Them fools be trippin' using it for the name of a record label to show how hard they are. Shit. When this goes down, we gonna be set. Ain't nobody going to find out who we are. Everything handled by text messaging on throwaways. Man, we geniuses. I know, I know, you're right, don't get all bent. I got that. Yeah, Huh? What? I lost you for a second going under this overpass. Uh-huh, I can hear you now. Right. Right. Homeboy gets taken out of this world tonight on the dot, and we make our bank and our rep. Man, this is the shit."

* * *

"You cannot believe how bored I am. No, really. And the munchables, weak. Sautéed Portobellos, ahi with dill, that's so last year. And oh my God, Wood's speech. Snore time, I'm not shitting you. How the hell did this man make the money he's made, own a basketball team, and none of that sophistication rub off on him? Mister one note. Here we are among the movers and shakers, where he has the chance to lay out his vision of downtown redevelopment—what? Yes, I know it's the choir, but that doesn't mean you half-ass the work. He has to inspire, not just reiterate the obvious. A goddamn chimp can do that. You've got to lead, inspire. Especially now when there's this scrutiny.

"Yes, of course, I know that. I'm being hyper-critical because this is about real consequences. Not only is there multi-millions on the line overall, but there can be a domino effect should any part of it derail. This means so much more than mere physical structures and the anchor businesses we attract for the mixed-use portion. This is about setting the standard for decades to follow. Yes, that's true. Why do you think I'm being so careful?

"Oh, hello, what's this? No, I'd stepped out to the patio and just spotted this bootylicious honey. I think she's cream and coffee, if you catch my meaning. Ha, yeah, see, I'm down. Look, I'm going in. Let's synchronize watches 'cause it's poon tang time, brah. Okay, I'll call you later."

* * *

"Yeah, he was handsome, but he was way too full of himself. Going on about how he was the man, how he was at the center of this deal to end all deals that was going to revitalize downtown, and what have you. Make us the rival of Manhattan we're destined to be. Girl, he went on about all this with straight-up seriousness. Can you imagine that? Like this project of his was the greatest thing like whenever. Really, it's just fancy cracker boxes with a Target and a supermarket thrown in. One more big, ugly thing is gobbling up more land till there's no green space whatsoever.

"No, I didn't give him my number, I lied telling him that I didn't currently have a working cell phone—which yes, I'm on right now of course. But I did give him my email, and he, of course, gave me his card, writing his personal e-address on it. He's a VP with Wood's company. Then he gets a call on his cell phone, and naturally, he just had to take it being so important. You know, being all hushed and whispering into it like it was really vital.

"Huh? No, I didn't see a ring, but it could have been his wife or girlfriend. Then he said he had to run off to a meeting. Girl, don't I know that. What kind of meeting would he be going to at this time of night, except a booty call? Shit.

"I don't know, maybe. It would at least be entertaining in a sociological way to go out with him, I suppose. But then I'd have to sit through a lot of him talking about himself and me, trying not to yawn or look bored. I tell you, though, it's a good thing—oh, sorry, excuse me. Huh? Yeah, I just bumped into one of the servers from the party while I was stepping outside. He was like rushing off, struggling out of his jacket. Funny, the others are still here, starting to clean up.

"Wow, it's warm tonight. The air smells good after that rain we had this past weekend. So, what I was going to say was it's a good thing he didn't learn I'm temping for Dizaksun. No, I don't think this was some ploy. Girl, please, I surely don't think I'm all that; I'm not getting the swelled head. But yeah, it seemed genuine, him coming over to talk to me and not about him getting some kind of inside dope. And if it was, why me? I'm going to be gone when the regular secretary returns once her ankle heals.

"Oh, so now I'm desperate, for talking to him. Too late, dammit, you can't take it back. Of course, I know Dizaksun is angling for a pretty big stake in this downtown stuff. But I think this guy, ah, Martin, Martin Conrad, was his name, wasn't that smooth or what have you. He wasn't trying to get anything from me other than what any man wants from a woman.

"Uh-huh, uh huh—ah, goodnight, Mr. Browne—yeah, he's the one that invited me. Please. Girl, your imagination is working overtime. Can I help it you couldn't get a babysitter tonight and couldn't come? I am not working anything. Browne and some of the other senior staff invited several of us.

"Okay, now you're just getting silly. You acting like I'm some kind of Sydney. What? You know, Jennifer whatshername, married to Affleck on that show that used to be on, *Alias.* Yeah, like I'm some kind of spy or something. Listen, Mr. Browne is orthodox, understand? Very upright. Been married for eons to the same woman. He's short, and he makes it a point to always look up into my face and not at my chest. The three weeks I've been at the firm, he's never tried to put a hand on me, unlike a couple of others there I could mention. Exactly, Jack Crane is out of control, isn't he? I'm surprised he hasn't been slapped with a sexual harassment suit.

"I'm sure glad he wasn't here. Worry about him, not this guy Martin. He's okay. Yeah, the more we talk about him the more I might just—ah, here. The valet just went to get my car. Huh, that's something. That server I told you about? He just drove past me, going down the hill behind the wheel of one of those nasty SUVs. Nope, not sure what kind it was except it was shiny, black, and big. How could he be blinging like that on his salary?

"I don't know. That doesn't sound right. Yeah, I guess this could be a second or third job, but what does that say about his priorities if he's working just to keep up with payments and gas in that thing? No, that's true. I'm going home and crawl under the covers. Might try to watch Tavis, but the Sandman is calling my name. You need to stop. I am hardly going to a motel to meet Mr. Browne for a quickie. You the one that needs it more than me. You realize that, don't you?

"Well, well, you can dish the dish, but…oh, shit. I'm so busy yakking with you I damn near put a ding in this Porsche coming up while I drive down the hill from Wood's house. Look, I better let you go and use both hands to get off this narrow pass because I can't afford to have my insurance jump up after paying that kind of bill hitting a fancy car. Okay, right, see you in the morning. Let's try that new place for lunch. 'Night."

* * *

"Mom, how can you say that? Yes, I've got you on the headset, cognac on my nightstand, and finishing up tweaking the report on my laptop. But I hear every word you're saying. Really. Cute, very cute. Well, let me tell you, when this deal goes down, they will have my picture next to multi-tasking in the dictionary. Yeah, uh-huh. Hold on. I just need to do this last calculation…yeah, this is the shit…sorry, Mom, just getting carried away. But it's my passion for this project that's kept it on track despite, ah, never mind.

"What?

"Yes, I know you understand business, Mom. You ran the shop when Dad passed. And who was there each summer and winter break? Look, I'm not trying to be condescending. It's just I shouldn't be talking out of school, understand? No, it's fine, really. *Wall Street Journal* article? When was this? About a week ago? Hmmmm. No, you know that's just those jealous humps at Dizaksun trying to muddy the waters. That's an old trick competitors do to sully the winner. An unnamed source alleges there's accusations of us double-dealing, kickbacks, blah, blah, blah.

"Mom, think about it. I'm the VP of community relations. I'm the one that's smoothed this project through with all the pols, hungry for headlines, the tree huggers, and the bomb throwers. Bomb throwers? That means the so-called community leaders who stand around, not producing dick…ulp, sorry…and then they howl and moan supposedly in the name of their people when something positive comes along from the Man. But really, it's just a way for them to get theirs too.

"No, I don't mean anything illegal. But a consultant fee here, a rec center there that employs some of their cronies. It's just how business is done. So there's nothing to worry about. Everything is fine. There's no investigation. Huh? What about next Tuesday for dinner? Sure, that Italian place. I love you, too, Mom."

* * *

"Fifteen-Adam-eighty-three, report shots fired, one-four-nine Ocean Shore

Drive, one-four-nine Ocean Shore Drive, Brentwood. Residence of Martin H. Conrad. Thirty-four male, Caucasian, brown hair, brown eyes. Five-eleven. Repeating information."

* * *

"What the fuck, dog? Naw, I got there. The side gate was unlocked, and the alarm was off like we'd been told. I'm creeping up, Glock ready and shit. I go through the sliding glass door off the pool also like we wuz told, and the mark, Conrad, had already been capped. One to the chest and one dead ass center in his forehead. He's still sitting in his bed, spilled glass of something in his limp hand. Motherfuckah never saw it coming. I could tell he had a laptop in there 'cause I saw the connection, but no computer.

"Hell, yeah, that's why I'm out of breath. Think I just waitin' around there for Entertainment Tonight to fuckin' show up? I bounced out of there like my baby's mama was chasin' after me for Pampers' money. No, I didn't leave no prints. Like we planned, I wore rubber gloves.

"But straight up, my nigga, they trying to punk us. This is some shit, that's for sure. Hey, you hear that? Ain't that a ghetto bird? Man, that's a chopper only I'm straining, and I don't see nothin' over me.

"Aw fuck, it's you, dog, they at your crib. You hard of hearing, mother-fuckah? Run, goddammit, run."

* * *

"I don't know how else to tell you this, man. I had car trouble. I don't know why the fuck it stopped running, but it did. I went to that dude, that Conrad's house, because that's where my car stopped. And the reason, like I've told you several times before, I was in that area was because I was coming back from this bar called the Shanty up there on Sunset. I know you checked that shit, Sergeant, 'cause I know you. And I can't tell you why nobody remembers me. That place was crowded. So if some nosy desperate housewife spotted my south of La Brea ass in her precious Brentwood neighborhood, that's why.

"And I ran because how crazy was it gonna sound that me, who's done time, for a beef you busted me for I might add, and here it was I just happened to stumble on a croaked bastard. Wait, I know what you're about to say. But I can't explain that gun in my apartment no more than I can explain geometry. That ain't my gun, ain't no prints on it. I know what your lab said, that was the gun that smoked homeboy.

"But look here, sarge, you been knowin' me since Eazy-E cut his first record. The fuck would I be doin' sneaking around Brentwood. I got some kind of OJ fixation going on? I'm not crazy."

** * **

"Hi, honey. Yeah, I'm still at the station. I was just replaying the videoed interrogation of the suspect. Huh, I'm laughing because I first encountered this character, Choo-Choo, when I was in uniform, and he was this snot-nosed look-out for the slangers. Yeah...uh-huh. His real name is Antonio Stevens, and I got him for receiving once. Right, and now it looks like I've got him for the Conrad murder, but I don't like the fit.

"Choo-Choo would never be mistaken for a mastermind, but even he's not stupid enough to leave the murder weapon in his crib. From what one of my CIs tells me, it seems Choo-Choo and his running buddy, Twin—huh? No, he's an only child. They call him Twin because he has a habit of always repeating himself. Anyway, it seems they were setting themselves up as hired killers.

"I know, pursuit of the American Dream. So these two numb chunks set out on this new venture, right? But you just can't advertise something like that on the radio. And they want high-end customers who can pay some real money. No rooty-poot shit for them, no sir. So, how do they get the word out? Guess. You'll never guess.

"They go to Pilates and yoga classes, trendy bars and what have you in Beverly Hills and the Westside and leave cards on people's windshields. I'm serious. I've got a few as evidence. Check this out. It says, 'Got a serious problem? One that the normal methods can't fix? Need a permanent solution? Call and leave a text message at,' and they leave a number which leads to a disposable cell phone, a burner they're called.

"Actually, yes, that was kind of clever. Something like that old show, *The Equalizer*, right? Only it's reverse. Sweetheart, I'm not making this up. Twin's saving grace is his computer skills so he's like Mister Nerve Center in all this. And you've got to ask yourself, what moron would actually get in touch with someone who left this kind of notice?

"You know, the more we talk about this, the more it might be that Choo-Choo would leave the incriminating weapon in his place. The Beretta was wiped clean, and except for that and what I got from the streets, that's all I have on him. A uniform found a bowtie and jacket like a waiter would wear in a trashcan a couple of blocks from Conrad's house. And the jacket is Choo-Choo's size, but what does that mean? A disguise of some kind?

"Conrad's alarm had been shorted, and the lock on his gate had been jimmied. I guess, could be that Twin helped his boy do all that, but it just don't fit, honey. There's none of that kind of equipment at Twin's apartment or Choo-Choo's.

"Now you've got me believing what that chump said was true; he was set up. Oh, I agree. He needs to be locked up. But more and more, I'm feeling there's someone else behind all this. I mean, it's not that hard putting two clowns who would leave postcards advertising that they are killers-for-hire into a frame.

"Alright, I'm taking one more run at Mr. Twin, who's so terrified he's given up Choo-Choo, Michael Jackson, and Robert Blake. Want me to bring anything home? Sure. Okay, see you in about an hour, baby doll. Don't worry about that, I'm not that tired. Don't you know doing this detecting works the blood up? Yes, it does…"

* * *

"That's correct, it's me. I know what hour it is, and I know it's your home. I dialed it, didn't I? Before you continue ranting, know that your clutch player, shall we say, has been checked. I find it insulting you didn't think I wouldn't make him. Driving that Porsche, shadowing me from the party. Like I'm going to get played like those two delusional homeboys I set up. When I came down the hill, he tried to be clever, turning around and going the opposite way to make it seem he was just some Westsider returning home.

"Don't cut me off when I'm talking, Mr. Wood. That's impolite. And you already have a price to pay for challenging me. Don't pretend to protest; you're not good at playing naïve, Mr. Wood. You now owe me double what we agreed to since you tried to break your contract with me, sir.

"What? I'm chuckling because you still insist on this bluster as if I'm one of thousands of ubiquitous real estate brokers or developers or what have you seeking your largess. We both know that you will gladly and promptly arrange to have the proper amount of cash, in non-sequential bills, ready to be delivered to me. In fact, *you* will deliver my funds. If you don't, that daughter of yours at that college on Long Island might trip down the steps and crack her skull open one sunny day on her way to biology.

"You see, just as you have so arrogantly proclaimed on TV and in magazines of doing your due diligence, I make it a priority to thoroughly know about my clients. Yes, well, now we're getting to an understanding, you and I. Very good, I knew you were a fast learner. Oh, no, it will not be the place or time we previously discussed. Sad to say, I simply don't trust you. Get the cash together, and you will hear from me where to make the drop, precise time, and what have you."

* * *

"Our top story on Action News is that police are looking into the violent death of Douglas Wood, a key figure in a billion-dollar-plus downtown redevelopment boom. It's been reported that, strangely, he was out walking underneath the Santa Monica pier after midnight. Why he was there, and at that hour, is part of the ongoing investigation. Action News is following a lead that there may be a witness. A Marine just returned from Iraq had been out celebrating with his friends and reportedly was sleeping it off beneath the pier when he may have witnessed some sort of altercation with Wood and an as-of-yet unidentified woman.

"And in what may be a related incident, the murder of Martin Conrad two days ago, a man who worked at Douglas Wood's company, is also under investigation. Action News is following up a report that the Securities and Exchange Com mission had approached Conrad about possible irregularities in some of Wood's dealings. Particularly as it relates to monies involved in the Massive downtown redevelopment.

"But this is unconfirmed as of this broadcast, and we will, of course, keep our viewers informed as we learn more."

* * *

"Chatter," *Plots With Guns: A Noir Anthology,* Dennis McMillan Publications, 2005, Anthony Neil Smith, editor.
Reprinted in *Murder and Mayhem in Muskego,* Down & Out Books, 2012, Jon and Ruth Jordan, editors.

Masai's Back in Town

The shotgun blast partially tore away the side of the bearded man's face. It didn't kill him nor knock him over—though it did embed pellets in one eye, ruining its vision. He screamed profanities and cranked off two rounds from his Glock. But Masai Swanmoor went prone, squeezing the Remington's trigger again. This time, his aim was better, and he blew out the other man's stomach, sending him over backwards onto the coffee table, breaking a leg of the furniture.

Swanmoor landed hard on his torso and rolled. The other Aryan Legion member, a woman with a hatchet face and a weight lifter's body, was coming at him. The hunting knife she wielded, cutting and slashing at his legs as he scrambled about.

"Motherfuckin,' black motherfucker," she wailed, arcing the knife overhand at his groin.

Swanmoor swung the pistol grip stock of the auto shotgun to deflect the blade, then aimed the business end of his weapon. "Put the pig sticker down, you ugly Nazi bitch," he blared.

"Fuck you." She didn't let go of the knife. She backed up several steps and stood hunched over, knife in one hand, eyes roving about the room.

Swanmoor stood up straight. "You're not that goddamn valuable to me. You or one of your other inbred sodomites will be of use." Cowboy fashion, he held the shotgun low, left hand under the pump action, right finger on the trigger. "I'm happy to kill you."

She looked from this to the dead man. The knife fell to the thin carpet.

Swanmoor started forward.

"What, you gonna rape me now?" she snarled.

"Don't think every brother goes crazy for white pussy. Even stank muscled-up snatch like yours." Bringing the rear end of the shotgun up, twisting his torso as he did so, he brought it across her face, eliciting a grunt.

She dropped to a knee, a hand to where he'd struck. She spat out blood on the now-stained carpet and got back up. "I don't know much."

"You know enough." He grinned lopsidedly.

* * *

When Rory Briscoe arrived at the house, he drove his well-cared-for LeSabre past and parked a block away. The distinct smell and background silhouette of an oil refinery was evident. He got out of the car. Briscoe had the snub-nosed revolver in the pocket of his cotton windbreaker as he walked back to his destination. His and her Harleys were parked side-by-side in the driveway. The front door was partially off its hinges, hanging at an odd angle. He looked around, no neigh bors or house pets were out. Even the birds weren't chirping.

He walked purposefully across the yellowed lawn and up the porch and, peering inside, could see two chairs in the front room were turned over. Gun out, he went further into the small house and saw Clauson's corpse on the broken coffee table between the front room and the dining room space.

Briscoe surmised the coffee table had been shoved around some in the fight. On it had been a bong, its glass smoked gray and black from use. This had tipped over when the bearded man' body had landed. The bong now lay resting in the gap of his lower abdomen where his stomach had once been. Blood and organ spray patterned a nearby wall.

In the kitchen, he found the one who he knew only as Gigi. She was bound to a straight-backed chair with duct tape and nylon cord. Two dish towels had been knotted together and tied around her mouth. She glared at Briscoe, who noted her bare feet. Her little toe on the right foot and the big toe on the left had been sawed off. The hunting knife, lying on the kitchen table, had been the instrument of torture used by Swanmoor. The severed toes lay on the linoleum in small puddles of blood. He knew that Lumumba lovin' bastard hadn't left his prints on the blade.

Briscoe undid the gag. "You gave up my name, didn't you?"

"Fuck you," she answered. "That jungle bunny was gonna cripple me. Get me undone. I plan to pay him back."

He put the barrel of the Glock he'd plucked from Clauson's stiffening fingers against her forehead. "Good thing this is the kind of neighborhood where gunshots are common." He blew out the back of her head as she gaped incredulously at him.

Briscoe wiped down the gun, then returned to the dead man's body and pressed those lifeless fingers against the grip. He let the gun lay in the man's open palm. Briscoe then quit the premises.

* * *

Swanmoor downshifted the Benz he'd jacked wearing a handkerchief owl hoot style from a trendy restaurant's parking attendant. He'd picked this car because he'd never driven a Mercedes before and wanted to feel what it was like. The seats were leather. Nice.

He came around the corner via the narrow passageway between the two buildings. The macadam of the former Lamplighter bar parking lot was cracked and bulged upwards in several areas, evidence of the various earthquakes that had taken place since the drinking establishment's closing more than twenty-five years ago. Weeds sprouted from those openings.

The Lamplighter had been their office away from the office. Run by a former pimp and numbers man who was sympathetic to the cause, Swanmoor and the others would hold emergency meetings in the rear storeroom and talk trash with the hookers and hustlers who frequented the front area. This was also where Swanmoor had gotten it on in the owner's office with more than one firebrand sister and a white follower or two from the hills—young women enthralled with smack talk of revolution and brothers, street army tough in black berets and black sunglasses. The bar's latest incarnation was Delgado's Discount Furniture Mart.

He got out of the car, hunching his shoulders against the cold and the incoming fog. In the near distance, the mist glistened in the lights of a billboard. On it could be seen an image of a desk mic giving off a bit of fire. The words, "KZRN Sizzles Liberals with Septima", were next to that.

"Hey now," he said as the driver's door of the silver Prius opened. Out stepped a woman a tick or two close to sixty, but still lithe of build and seemingly effortless in her motions. He also noted the hue of her car matched her hair.

"Damn," he said admiringly.

"Stop trying so hard and hug me, fool."

He did, laughing, his hands tight around her midsection, hers around his shoulders.

She kissed his neck before she pushed him back to take him in. "Are you out of your cotton picking, mind coming back here, Marvin?" She rarely called him by his street name.

"No choice, Leann."

"Bullshit." She pulled her open topcoat closer around her. "You better get on your knees and thank the baby Jesus these crack heads around here are too young, mis-educated, and too far gone to know who you are. 'Cause the price is still on your nappy head, negro."

He blew into his fist. This was his hometown, but his body had gotten used to a warmer climate. "After I'm done, you can turn me in if you want to."

She smirked. "Double fuck you and your macho counter-revolutionary posturing."

"Maybe so. But I wanted you to know Briscoe is also back on the scene, and me and that poor man's Lewis Erskine are gunning for each other."

"Shit," she drawled, "he's older than your monkey ass. Like I'm gonna be afraid of some oinker clumping after me with his walker."

"He's got a goddamn hook-up with the Aryan Legion. I'm not sure how extensive, but there it is. One of them, named Clauson, was checking ancient haunts about me, and I got tipped."

She leveled her gold-flaked ambers on him. Angry or inviting, those eyes still knocked him out. "Fuck the Legion, too. I'm not so soft, and I can't handle a few of them, prison-bred goose-steppers."

Swanmoor smiled. "Now who's posing?"

She flipped him the finger, smiling, too. Then, she took on a serious cast. "What about your daughter?"

"Even if Briscoe knows who she is, I'm figuring, given the people around her and whatnot, he won't make a run at her. Now, of course, I'd like you to warn her anyway." He frowned, and what might have been regret came and went on his still-lean features. "It's probably best I don't come at her direct."

"Probably so."

"Yeah," he replied, letting the word and the emotions behind it linger.

She tugged on his jacket and asked, "You still like that cheap Presidente brandy?"

"It's what the masses drink," he deadpanned.

"Nigga, please. Let's hat before a constituent sees me consorting."

She'd brought a bottle of the brandy and two plastic cups with her in the car. At the Star Burst motel, overlooking a ship container yard, once in the room, Congresswoman Leann Holt shoved Marvin "Masai" Swanmoor against the door and kissed him like she was trying to quench a fever.

He got his arms and hands around her, and it was 1980, and they were young and saying goodbye when he'd gone on the run after being indicted. Only now, Swanmoor had the unerring impression this might be the last time he was privileged to be with this woman…his lover…his comrade. Yet the notion that his grey head would soon be blossomed out from bullets didn't cool his ardor but inflamed him like he hadn't felt in years.

After they made noisy love, they took a break to have a few sips of Presidente and talk. The old-fashioned radiator issued weak heat under the curtained window. Swanmoor had placed the one chair in the room under the door knob. It wouldn't stop anybody, but he hoped it would slow them down long enough to reach the piece he'd placed on the nightstand.

"I want to help you," Holt declared. "You are."

"You know what I mean, home. Fieldwork."

"That's not going to happen. You know it's going to get funky."

She chuckled and kissed his chest, then laid her head on it. "You can't do this by yourself."

"My face is only on dusty clippings, but you, you're ghetto fabulous. Besides, you've got grandkids you need to be around for, counselor."

"You might, too."

He glared at the top of her head, flashing on the mushroom cloud jet black afro from all those years before. "Shit, do I?"

"No, but you get my point, old timer."

"I ain't stove up yet. No pork, no salt, plenty of roughage, and their ghosts are with me."

"Who?"

"Che and Malcolm, Ho and Fred, baby."

"I'd say you were delusional, but you might be right. I want you to be right."

"Hell yeah, I am."

She looked up at him, and they made love again.

* * *

The younger and larger man had his arm around Briscoe's windpipe and said, "You must be mixing vodka with your Ensure,in the mornings, Grandpa. The math you learned in grade school has evaporated from your diseased mind."

He choked him some more to underscore his intent. Briscoe's face was red from effort and lack of breath, his hands impotently trying to loosen the other man's chiseled arms. Finally, he was let go, and he wilted to the floor, choking and gagging on all fours.

"We understand each other now, right?" Clete Willhelm walked to the counter, picked up his open can of beer, and took a lengthy pull. On the floor was an upset can of spilled beer. Briscoe had been drinking from this can until Willhelm attacked him.

Briscoe finally sat and cleared his throat. "I'm not trying to cheat you, Clete. You gotta learn to relax."

"Let me worry about my anger management issues. Two of my road dogs are dead 'cause of this super spade sparring partner of yours. How come he knew to come at them looking for your ass, he supposed to have been out of the country all those years?"

Briscoe held his hands wide. "I'm sure he still has contacts. If it was me, the first thing I would do is find out the lay of the land. There's a reason Swanmoor was high on the Bureau's key agitator index. He's no bench warmer."

Contemplatively, Willhelm opened another beer.

Briscoe went on. "We need to flush Swanmoor out to tell us where the money is—or, more precisely, where he thinks it is."

"Uh-huh," Willhelm grunted, considering his next words. "This isn't a Legion matter, Rory. This is between you, me and a few that I trust. And that list is now a lot shorter."

"Whatever you say. But we need to make some moves, or else we're just running around with our heads up our asses."

"Seems to me you need to be doing your job and targeting his old friends to make him come out and play."

"Probably, yeah, that sounds right. Only if we don't have the troop strength, we need to be selective. We can't go around jacking up worn-out Lenin quoting has-beens. The worse thing would be for Swanmoor to go back underground."

"Huh," Willhelm muttered, tipping his head back and quaffing his beer. "But you must have had a snitch or two from back then still around. Like that photographer who documented the civil righters and at the same time was a rat for your bunghole-loving boss Hoover."

"It's not like turncoats belong to a club, Clete. Don't you think I've been out there beating the bushes?"

"What about, what you call it, an intermediary? One of them burr head preachers all hyped up on keeping the peace and shit. Somebody that wasn't on the payroll but who you leaned on in the past, you know, one of those reasonable negroes." He chuckled.

At first Briscoe was going to make a dismissive comment then got a faraway look on his face. "Maybe," he allowed. "Maybe for a cut."

"Or at least he thinks he'll get a cut," Willhelm opined.

* * *

"My friends, we must keep up the good work. The Lord's work, really. I am so heartened that we are one step closer to winning the culture war and restoring sanctity and values for our impressionable youth and our nation. I applaud your efforts good citizens in shutting down that blasphemous exhibit at the Smithsonian. It was a true waste of our tax dollars."

Masai Swanmoor smiled thinly, shaking his head slightly. He turned off the small digital radio, ceasing the woman's rants. He had to admit, though, the sound quality was amazing. Modern technology. Soon he was walking through the park, having reconnoitered the perimeter like he'd been taught in-country.

Laughing children under the watchful gaze of their mothers or nannies played on the swings and slides. Sitting on a bench under a maple tree was Big Stick Caruthers. After two bouts with cancer, once in the throat and the other time in the stomach, he was a slender shell of his former defensive tackle frame.

"Young blood," Caruthers greeted. He stood, and the two men hugged. "You're looking pretty damn decent. What's your secret?"

"I wish it was big titty virgins and palm oil, but I only got the latter in abundance."

"I heard that," Caruthers said, sitting down again.

Swanmoor remained standing and scanning.

"It's just you and me. I'm the messenger, not the tethered goat."

"Not knocking you, brother."

"Just being on point. I ain't mad at you like the adolescents say."

Satisfied, Swanmoor also sat on the bench near the former owner of the Lamplighter bar. "So what's their offer?"

"The ofays figure you, and them don't need to be in this scorched earth mode. Two dead and—"

"Two?" Swanmoor interrupted. "I left that lumberjack-shouldered broad alive. Bleeding but no fatal wounds."

"That's not what was on the news, but what's the difference?"

Swanmoor smiled humorlessly. "Wheels within wheels, man."

"One race hater dead, two race haters dead, even their mamas probably won't miss 'em."

"No doubt. But they probably came from a long line of sieg heiling fucks."

"Children don't always follow in their parents' footsteps."

"There is that. Briscoe came to you alone?"

"He did. Motherfuckah phoned for me at the senior hall during our square- dancing night, you believe that? Was in the middle of do-si-doing with a cute little widow with some beachfront property. Sheeit."

Both men snickered. "What I believe is he's a greedy, forked-tongue devil. He expects me to do the grunt work and then I just give him a cut being all nostalgic and what not?"

"He calls off the Legion. Says you been green lit 'cause of you dropping members of the calling. The inference being it wouldn't just be you in their crosshairs."

Swanmoor looked off in the distance. "How is it that Briscoe's got an in with them? The Aryan Legion wasn't around in his day."

"We're getting off topic, aren't we, Masai?"

"You've kept your ears open, Big Stick. I can't imagine you've retired that much."

Caruthers made a face, then said, "His daughter. She was a doper, college dropout, ran the streets, the whole bit. Don't know the full story but damn right, I made it my business to keep tabs on friends and enemies alike. She winds up marrying one of these white power studs while he's in the joint. He gets out, they set up house, it's all tattoos and mud people bashing, but they eventually split up. She got born-again."

"It's your educated guess that Briscoe reached out to his former son-in-law once he knew I was back on the scene?"

Caruthers made a small gesture.

A silence dragged by as Swanmoor considered his response. "If I get the goods, they'll kill me. What's my guarantee?"

"Briscoe says he knows who your daughter is. The Legion doesn't know, and he'll keep it that way if you agree to the split. Fifty-fifty."

"Shit," Swanmoor swore.

"He's going to call me later today. What do you want me to tell him?" Swanmoor stared at Caruthers.

* * *

Walking back to another car he'd stolen that morning, a fifteen-year-old beater with a dented roof, he took off his shirt, shaking it and feeling up the material. He knew bugging devices had changed greatly since the days of cassette tapes and wanted to make sure Big Stick Caruthers hadn't planted some kind of tracking button on him when they'd embraced. The former bar owner was a pragmatist, after all. Relieved Big Stick hadn't planted a tracer on him, Swanmoor re-buttoned his shirt over his athletic T and drove away.

* * *

There was a decorative table in a corner of the high-rise office of the Wilder Foundation. Upon its surface was a vase filled with fresh-cut flowers, including lilies and chrysanthemums. Their fragrance subtly altered the area. Yet the fragrance of the studious young woman who came out to greet him was both more powerful and understated simultaneously.

"Ms. Van Meter apologizes, but her call should be over in the next five minutes," the young woman said. "Would you care for coffee or sparkling water?"

"I'm fine, thank you." Swanmoor took a seat in a plush chair and leafed through a recent issue of *The Atlantic*. He was into an article about the origin of the Garamond typeface when a pointed shoe touched his shin.

"Well, well." Alison Van Meter stood with her hands on her hips, head cocked, eyes peering over her designer glasses. Her blonde hair was streaked with white but was shoulder-length and full-bodied.

"Hey, Ali," Swanmoor said, rising.

"Get your ass in here before the black helicopters come swooping down." She pivoted and marched toward a set of double doors. He followed. Van Meter was heavier than back in the day, but he could tell she maintained a regime of exercise. There was a muscularity apparent in the calves visible below the hem of her business skirt.

They entered her large office, and she closed the doors behind them. Pressing him against those doors, she kissed him for several beats before they parted. He could get very used to this, he reflected.

"You know you shouldn't have risked this, Masai. The swag might not be there. You could have sent word. I would have retrieved it and gotten it to you, you know that."

"Sending an intermediary would have been shaky. Notwithstanding, there's a damn good chance one of the construction workers could find the dough."

"I'd have gone personally, chump," she said.

He pointed at her stylish shoes. "Those are Jimmy Choos, aren't they? You wouldn't want to break one of those heels, would you trawling amongst the lumpen?"

"Being the sexist dog you remain, it figures you'd keep up with women's fashion."

"Look, I started this. It's only right I should finish it. Anyway, I was homesick, Ali." As he talked, he walked around her office, holding his hands wide. "Nice."

"Money is just a means of exchange, comrade."

"The extent of the power of money is the extent of my power."

From a mini-fridge she offered him fresh squeezed blueberry and pomegranate juice which he accepted. He sat on the couch in her office and she in a chair near him. Looking past her at the cityscape out of her wide windows, he brought himself back to the present.

Van Meter was talking. "I got you a room at the hotel. Part of the place has been demoed; that's how his handgun was found in the remains of the dumb waiter." A cell phone picture of the gun had been shared among the work crew and by chance Van Meter, making a site visit, had seen the shot. Given the location and its age, she concluded it was the piece she'd obtained for Swanmoor decades ago—the one she knew had been used in the job. She then got in touch with him.

"Now there are some tenants left who are moving out by month's end. It's unlikely anybody will bother you as you prowl about."

She rose and went to a closet, and returned with an equipment bag she placed on the floor near him. "A few items you might need." She sat on his lap. "Now, about the equipment I need," she teased.

"Shouldn't I be resentful being objictified in this way?"

"Shut up." They kissed again.

* * *

Later that day Masai Swanmoor took his room at the Warwick residents hotel. This was in a part of downtown still home to the poor—though they were being pushed out due to the area's stepped-up gentrification efforts.

He stepped into the hallway. Loud rap music issued from behind one door, and an argument through another. He walked downstairs as the elevator had long been out of use. In the lobby, there were a few about, including two old men, one with a walker, involved in a chess game. Van Meter, whose foundation was behind redeveloping the hotel into mixed use affordable housing, had provided a layout to Swanmoor.

Across the lobby and to his left was a door leading to the basement.

"Where do you think you're going," a voice challenged him as Swanmoor put his hand on the doorknob.

He looked over at a pudgy bald man in his mid-fifties with a tweed jacket and cargo pants. He had an iPod in his sports jacket's handkerchief pocket and removed his earbuds.

"Who are you?"

"I live here, you don't." The man frowned at Swanmoor. "I'm inspecting." The door was locked but it didn't take much to get through it, loose as it was in the frame. He went downstairs, using the flashlight Van Meter had included in the supplies she'd given him.

Overhead were sewage and water pipes and heat conduits leading from vintage but functioning gravity heaters. He made his way around, operating on the theory he would stick to areas so far untouched by the construction crew. If the money had been found by one of the workers, Van Meter assumed she would have heard of such.

Aside from the inner workings of the building, Swanmoor found cardboard boxes of discarded clothes, neatly tied stacks of yellowed and brittle girlie magazines and *National Geographics*, and an assortment of sweep brooms of various sizes. More exploring turned up little else of interest.

Back upstairs in his room, Swanmoor lay on the bed, hands behind his head staring at the water- stained ceiling. He reviewed the past, hoping for a clue in the present as to where Georgie Boy hid the COINTELPRO slush funds they'd stolen. The FBI under Hoover orchestrated the Counter-Intelligence Program for over a decade. The Program's one overarching goal was through chicanery and agent provocateurs to disrupt and destroy self-determination struggles from the militant American Indian Movement, mainstreamers, Martin Luther King, to hope-to-die revolutionaries like him, Leann Holt and

Georgie Boy, George Dixon—the three who'd pulled off the score.

Dressed in matching khakis, black turtlenecks, work boots, gloves and full- face ski masks, the three moved precision quick out of the Falcon station wagon parked at a yellow zone. Applying the pry bar to a service entrance sans latch, they forced the door open. A day before, Leann Holt, in disguise of a housecoat, curlers—she'd hot combed her afro straight so as to have it fit underneath her mask—and sunglasses, had come into the unemployment office and clipped the alarm wires to that particular door.

Their movements rehearsed by Swanmoor, a decorated Vietnam vet, they got the drop on the building's two security guards. One was an out of shape, chain smoking former cop with a gimpy leg. The other a hippie who said he dug that they were taking it to the man. The trio bound and gagged the two, shooting Novocain into their legs to temporarily make their limbs numb and useless.

Rory Briscoe was the Special Agent in Charge of the regional implementation of COINTELPRO that covered this area back then. Briscoe was a hands-on kind of Bureau man. Beatings, planting evidence and illegal wiretaps were all part of his repertoire. He also shook down the hustlers and weed and smack dealers in his region of operation. Briscoe had amassed a sweet sum coupled with cash shipments from Washington to be used specifically for bribing snitches and setting up off-the-books operations.

This slush fund was nearly three million which even in today's dollars, had worth. But Briscoe had it bad for this one mixed race street walker named Francie. To impress her one time, after she gave him a blowjob in his secret field office, he'd shown her the stash and told her they could get away, start over as he wanted out of his square marriage. She egged him on but Francie, who did like to brag while on the nod, had let it slip in the Lamplighter about the money.

Briscoe's office was inside the unemployment office building and the monies were kept there in a floor safe. Given they had time, the three peeled the safe door using a heavy-duty drill and a power chisel. The goal was to seed the money back into the community. Splitting after the robbery, Georgie Boy had been tasked with hiding the scratch while Swanmoor and Holt ditched their getaway car and clothes, setting fire to them. They made sure to keep apart but otherwise maintain their regular regimes.

Only in what had to be classified as the gods having a laugh on the mortals, Georgie Boy was eating a fish sandwich, laughing hard as he told friends a story about his dad, an amateur prizefighter. He choked to death on a fish bone. Where he hid the money, they didn't know. They'd told Francie to leave town, promising to send her a cut. Her body was found under a freeway overpass, her neck broken.

Swanmoor's reverie ceased as he smiled knowingly. He remembered what Georgie Boy had said as, fueled on exhilaration, they'd dropped him off at the other getaway car, a VW beetle belonging to his girlfriend, Sharon Mason.

"It'll be cool, y'all," Georgie Boy had said driving away. As a kid, Swanmoor knew Georgie Boy sold newspapers in front of the Warwick.

That night, up on the roof of the dilapidated hotel, near the long-broken air conditioning units, he found the two duffle bags of cash. They'd been stuffed into a crawl space access cavity. The panel to get to this was rusted over and the edges of the panel had been super glued by Dixon, though most of that had worn away. Van Meter had supplied Swanmoor with a crowbar he used to get it off.

"I knew I recognized you," the pudgy man said. "Hell, I gave money to your defense fund when you were accused of killing that undercover cop."

The duffle bags were at Swanmoor's feet. The crowbar was within reach, but that wouldn't block a bullet.

"That's the COINTELPRO score, isn't it?" Pudgy man indicated the duffels with the muzzle of the .45 he held on Swanmoor.

"Yeah."

"Fuckin' urban legend. And it was over my head all this time." He chuckled mirthlessly. "Well, Mister Minister of Strategy, you can have the privilege of taking the people's money downstairs to your car and I'll leave with the goods. I'd help, but my back's screwed up. I'm on disability you understand."

"You ain't having no trouble lifting that gun."

"That's true, blood. I know how to shoot it, too. Civilize the mind, make savage the body, isn't that what Chairman Mao said in those Little Red Books you all used to sell?"

Swanmoor remained silent. "Let's hit it, bro. You first."

A million in one-hundred-dollar bills weighs about twenty- two pounds. The almost two point seven million COINTELRO swag was in hundreds, twenties, fifties and fives. Thus, each duffle was roughly forty pounds. Swanmoor dragged them down the stairs by their cords. Maybe if he was thirty years younger, he'd try something, but he was certain he didn't have the arm strength to suddenly turn and swing one of the sacks at his captor.

On the ground floor in the stairwell, Swanmoor pushed the crash bar on the exit door leading to the street. The bar depressed, but the door didn't open.

"Harder," his new companion demanded.

Swanmoor repeated the motion several times, including leaning against the door.

"Shit. Come on." The pudgy man jerked the gun, indicating they had to go through the other door leading to the lobby. He moved to one side to allow Swanmoor to go first, still dragging the duffle bags.

"Can't you pick those up?"

"They're heavy and I'm old."

"Try."

Swanmoor had his back against the now partially opened lobby door. He let go of one of the duffles, and put up a knee to brace the other duffle bag. He got his arms around this one but pretended it was heavier than it was and stumbled backwards into the lobby area, falling down. He kicked himself further into the lobby.

"Get up," the other man yelled, coming partway into the lobby, too.

"Take it, take all of it," Swanmoor said fearfully, crawling away on his backside, his hands out from his body.

The pudgy man was standing near Swanmoor with the gun in his hand, with denizens of the lobby area staring at the two. The duffle he'd dropped was near Swanmoor on the floor. He'd purposely undid its top, bills spilling out. This particularly got the attention of the gathered, who moved toward the money like wolves to deer. The chess-playing oldster with his walker clumped forward furiously.

"Back the fuck up," pudgy man warned the others. He swung the gun back and forth. When he turned his head to look over at Swanmoor, the bigger man was already beside him.

"Sonofabitch," he managed, but Swanmoor already had a hand on the man's gun arm. With his other hand tightened into a fist, he went at the pudgy man's face like he'd seen Marvin Hagler do in prize fights.

"Ughhh," the object of his anger groaned as he assumed a fetal position on the floor, bleeding freely from mouth and nose.

Swanmoor doled out hundreds to each down and outer and drove away with the slush funds. Using the disposable cell phone Van Meter had given him, he made some calls.

* * *

The tawny-hued black woman tented her fingers as she spoke evenly and forcefully into the overhead mic. Her broadcast, based out of her home radio station, KZRN, was carried across the nation. "Before I go today, I wanted to mention this rumor that's surfaced within the last few hours. Now I warn you this seems to be gaining traction in the leftist elite circles so bear that in mind.

"But there's been scuttlebutt about a retired FBI agent suspected in the shooting of one of those biker types. Normally, this sort of headline I'd leave for your local news, but this particular individual has a history with the so-called black power movement, and you've heard me before talk about how that misguided effort actually set black people back.

"So I'll be watching the developments in this case as it wouldn't be far-fetched to believe this no-doubt courageous law enforcer has been framed by sinister liberal forces. Stay tuned, good citizens."

* * *

Rory Briscoe's arthritis had flared in his left hand, but he ignored the pain while jamming clothes into his luggage. That fucking Swanmoor had fucked him good, but he'd get him back, he vowed.

"The fuck you think you're going?" Clete Willhelm said.

Briscoe looked from the Aryan Legion leader to his gun on his dresser. It might as well be in the next block for all the good it could do him.

"It's all about anger management, right, Clete?" His attempt at a jocular tone failed.

"You know the grief that's on me, man? Questions about you, whispers about the missing money. Was I out to screw the brethren, making a deal on the side."

Briscoe had to huff. "You were making a deal on the side." Willhelm gave him a blank look.

Briscoe continued. "This can all be worked out to our satisfaction, Clete.

We just need to concentrate on taking out Swanmoor. We take a run at his daughter and—"

"Uh-huh. Just what I should do, add a kidnapping charge to my happiness."

"No, you don't get it. She's a fraud." He held up his hands in protest. "All we have to do is threaten to expose her, and this will force Swanmoor to play ball."

"I no longer give a shit, Rory. I don't know if Swanmoor or you chilled Gigi. If I was a cynic, I'd say you were using me to get the money then planned on taking me out, too."

"Clete, come on, we're family."

Willhelm went on as if he hadn't heard him. "Now, with you not around, a lot of my problems go away."

"Aw, goddammit," Briscoe swore, moving as fast as he could toward his gun. Even if he was younger, he wouldn't have bridged the distance.

Willhelm shot his former father-in-law in the stomach and, as he bent over, holding his wound, shot him in the top of the head. He left the dead older man's apartment.

* * *

Father and daughter hugged tightly, each tearing up. "I wish you could stay," Septima Mason said. "Me, too. But we both know better than that."

"We have to go. I've got some smuggling to do," Leann Holt said.

"Bye-bye, Daddy."

He smiled and hugged his daughter again. "When am I gonna get a grandchild?"

"How traditional of you, Father." She kissed him on the cheek. "Please be careful, will you?"

"There is nothing which is not an intermediate state between being and nothing."

"Smart ass."

"You're the one that needs to be careful, Septima. How long you going to keep up this charade?"

"It matters little to the individual guerilla whether or not he…or she, survives."

"Quotes are overrated."

In the car, as Holt drove him away, Swanmoor looked back and waved at the diminishing image of his daughter.

"I guess you three have a plan worked out?"

"Oh yes," Holt said. "Septima's finishing her book, which will be coupled with some juicy hidden video bombshells." She winked at him. "Like a certain ex-governor who, it seems, likes it both ways. She made a pass at Septima at one of those right-wing confabs."

"Say what?"

"You'll see. With Wildfire Foundation backing, we're going to roll out a series of high-profile media hits. She'll be the talk of the nation."

Swanmoor was also glad the COINTELPRO monies would be laundered through the Foundation for neighborhood organizing grants.

Holt patted Swanmoor's leg. "Don't you worry, papa. I don't intend to let any wingnut harm a hair on her head once we blow her cover."

"The title gonna be *I was an Undercover Right-Winger*?" Holt glanced at him. "That's catchy."

* * *

They did use his title. The expose was a blockbuster.

* * *

"Masai's Back in Town," *Send My Love and a Molotov Cocktail!: Stories of Crime, Love and Rebellion,* PM Press: Switchblade, 2011, Andrea Gibbons and GP, editors.

The Counterfeit Comrade

"You better start taking me seriously." She leaned her tennis-tanned frame forward on the bed and bit his inner thigh, giggling.

"Damn, woman, I ain't no piece of steak, you know."

Millicent Fielding rubbed her hand on his thickly muscled leg, his foot propped up on the knotted and soaked sheets. "You sure about that, my bronze Agamemnon?" Like a naughty schoolgirl, she licked the end of her index finger and then let that hand move closer to the new style vent of the Munsingwear boxers she'd bought him at Gimbles. Of course, he hadn't accompanied her when she did. And neither had her husband.

"Careful, you might get more than you bargained for," his four-barrel carburetor of a voice reverberated. He stretched, clasping his tensiled fingers behind his close-shaved head.

"You think I'm a slave to your manhood, don't you, Nefarious?" She reached inside the vent, taking him in her hand with her Park Avenue salon buffed nails.

"I think you're a slave to those harebrained ideas of those Broadway Bolsheviks you like to run around with." He tried mightily not to show any emotion as she continued to fondle him, making him more rigid by the second.

"Need I remind you, good sir, you've been known to frequent some of those meetings our friends fond of the hammer and sickle put on?" She kept working him, making the six-foot-four-inch man squirm with pleasurable discomfort. "And I do believe that's how you and I met."

"I was there to throw my two bits in the hat supportin' them Scottsboro fellas. Plus, it don't hurt those pinch necks like to feed the masses at their talkfests." He showed horse teeth in his whiskered face rock-hewn and mahogany burnished.

He was properly aroused, and she pushed him back on the bed, removing the stripped underwear she liked to see him wear. The older woman straddled him, lifting her negligee. She hadn't put on her panties or girdle, and soon, they were making fierce love in the quiet afternoon heat. The rickety Emerson electric fan clattered in its cage housing as it swung back and forth on a corner table. But its noise couldn't mask their carnal-induced melody as they took their time to reach the finish.

The two then lay entwined, occasionally kissing and feeling the beat of each other's heart as their bodies cooled.

"I better get going." She'd crawled across his prone form and grabbed her wristwatch on the nightstand. It lay atop a current issue of *The Negro World* magazine. On the cover was the boss of the man she'd been sneaking out to see regularly for the last five months. "There's a big rally this Saturday, right?"

"Yeah," he said. He helped her fasten the platinum band of her Bulova. "All the mucky-mucks are gonna be there. The Chief even convinced DuBois to make an appearance. And you know how those two have gone at it like wet hens."

Fielding kissed him on his rippled stomach and got out of the sack. "This is a big deal, my darling. A thousand men named 'George' have come a long way."

"You'd think your pals would be happy for us poor colored folk managing to do something for ourselves." He lay back on the bed, naked and vital and sheathed in a light sheen. She caught herself wondering if she had indeed lost her mind. As if sections of her brain were regularly seeping out of her skull and floating off bit by bit into the outer space imagined on radio shows like the ones her husband's company advertised on the Blue Network.

"Given the way your chief talks so bad about them, I should think the Brotherhood isn't more worried about his safety."

"He is a socialist," Pickett amended. "He just don't go in for those that pretend they're for the worker, but ain't."

Mrs. Fielding went into the bathroom, glad that his apartment at least had its own toilet. How, in the name of Teddy Roosevelt, could she explain her presence in a black man's apartment in the middle of Harlem in the middle of summer if she had to use a communal facility? Particularly when that man was Levi Nefarious Pickett. A man who might not get his picture on the cover of magazines, but had a reputation that reached beyond uptown.

"You can stop all that caterwauling," he called to her, his eyes fluttering closed. "I need to get my beauty sleep 'cause I got me a long night ahead. We got to go over the particulars for the rally and you done sapped me of my strength, woman."

By the time she was dressed and had stepped back into his front room, he was asleep on the Murphy bed. His chest, like something sculpted by Henry Moore, expanded and contracted with the precision of a pneumatic pump. She took him in and kissed his forehead before leaving. She knew from experience not to hail a taxi and would take the 2 train down to 103rd and then cross over. The relative anonymity of the subway line was an aid to the adulterous wife.

Walking with purpose, she passed a telephone pole blistered with several handbills. One announced a rent party that Thursday and the other was about the rally to take place on 125th Street and Lennox Avenue. A hobo, one bony arm around the pole like it was a lover, reeled out in front of her and proclaimed, "Madam Rockefeller, I presume." He bowed as she passed and stuck out his hand.

She dug inside her clutch bag and gave him some change.

"May Father Divine keep you in his special prayers, Miss Lady," the shabbily dressed man said.

"Let us hope so," she replied and went on. Turning onto St. Nicholas Avenue, she decided, since she was in the vicinity, to stop in at the headquarters of the Unemployed Workers Council and say hello to the staff she knew.

The UWC had been started by her red pals, as Pickett referred to them at the onset of the Depression as another beachhead among the Negro people. But like all such enterprises promulgated by the Communist Party USA, it was run from the top down despite their expressed platform to let the direction come from the ground up.

"Look, baby, colored folks know who's got the boot on their neck," Pickett would remind her jocularly, "they don't need them sour pusses in the Comintern telling 'em which way to blow their noses and why they got to have a fifty- page report written first to do so."

The Unemployed Workers Council had been through a see-saw of control between the professional radicals and the locals as to how the organizations could be most useful to the residents. The educated whites who'd been sent in by the CPUSA to help politically colonize the Negroes couldn't match homegrown grit and initiative nor downplay the role field-hardened muscle of some country transplants, including Pickett, had played to keep it independent.

Currently, the Council organized and addressed the issues of its members and not an agenda of some men who may have an abstract understanding of the conditions of blacks in America but were perpetually unwilling to listen to them.

Nearing the headquarters, its "No Work, No Rent" banner stretched below the roof line, she slowed at the site of a familiar vehicle parked at the curb. Drawing closer, she stared open-mouthed at the car, certain it was her husband's La Salle Town Coupe. She walked closer and touched the flying heron hood ornament as if it and what the piece was attached to were a mirage. The forest green metal, the chrome polished to neon brilliance, and the supple grey leather seats could belong to no other than Harley Nathan Fielding. To confirm her summation, she noted the small dent in the spare wheel cover attached to the right side near the door.

"Shit," she swore out loud. Two women who looked to be house cleaners passing by looked at this wild white woman as if she were invoking Satan in the pulpit. Voices came to her from the stairwell leading to the second floor of the Council, and she hurried into the dress shop next door.

"Can I help you, miss?" The pretty, charm-school-erect, honey-colored clerk asked her.

"No, I'm fine, thank you. Just looking," she said, stationing herself at an angle to the plateglass window to afford herself a view. She hoped the mannequins she was partially behind provided enough camouflage. She just had to see this.

Out on the street, her husband and Thaddeus Stokes were talking. Stokes was the director of the Unemployed Workers Council. He was a level-headed colored man who had helped reshape the organization from its internal squabbling factions and fashion it as a viable force in the community. And except for an excursion to the segregated Cotton Club once or twice a year if she could drag him, her husband didn't foray into the "bush," as he termed the area.

The density of the window and the distance prevented her from hearing what the two were saying to each other. Audaciously, she considered popping out to surprise her husband just to see his startled expression. But that would wear off, and she'd have to explain what she was doing here when she was supposed to be admiring the Yuan Dynasty exhibition at the Brooklyn Museum. She'd read enough about the exhibit that if he did deign to ask her about what she saw, and that was unlikely, she could converse on the subject in a relaxed manner.

The two men were talking low, their heads close. Her husband puffed on a Pall Mall, his eyes squinting from the smoke. Really, except for the help, her husband didn't know any Negroes—and particularly not a radical type like Stokes. Where in God's name had they met? And what in the world were they going on about?

"You sure I can't help you, miss?"

"Oh, no, no, I'm fine, fine." She made a show of fingering material on one of the window dummies. She moved her body to indicate she was examining the goods. With her back mostly turned to the outside, she prayed her husband didn't look too closely this way. Her margin of safety was his usual inattention to her. Millicent Fielding hoped he hadn't noticed the linen skirt—which she'd carefully folded over a chair when she'd taken it off in Pickett's apartment—and the matching bolo jacket she'd left the house in this morning.

She chanced a glance around and could see the men parting. They didn't shake hands but committed incremental nods to one another as if agreeing on a solemn matter. Stokes went back into the Council, and her husband fired the car's electric starter, the big straight eight thundering to life. He drove off, and she stepped out onto the street.

"What the hell?" she muttered. Better to not enter the Council offices, she concluded. She walked to the subway stop and took the trains that would eventually get her home to Sutton Place. All along the way, she tried different ideas out in her mind as to what her husband was doing in foreign territory.

* * *

Terrible Totten folded his arms as he leaned against the wall, his sturdy build partially obscuring the poster proclaiming the demands of the members of their union. "They've put up all manner of chicanery against us, brother Pickett," he said, his Virgin Island accent tempered but coating his phrasing. "The Plan for Employee Representation, the lily white Order of Sleeping Car Conductors, stooge associations, all of it we've battled and countered and persevered."

"That is so," Pickett concurred, holding back a grin. Ashley "Terrible" Totten was a good man, but he did like to go on now and then.

"And today we stand close to achieving a day the rank and file assumed there would be snow on the pates of their children until they saw it fulfilled. Isn't that right?"

"Amen, brother."

He wagged a finger. "I'll ignore that since you're a heathen and don't know any better."

"I appreciate that."

"As well you should. Now look here, Levi. This rally has got the white newspapers' and radio interest, see? But you and I and the others," he indicated the men and a few women in the hall as the meeting broke up, "know that doesn't matter. So what if after back-breaking years of struggle, our members threatened, fired, beat up, and set up the union almost bankrupt several times, and the Chief took it all on his shoulders? We finally have recognition from the AFL last year."

"Yeah, I know," and this time, Pickett was serious. It was a big deal for the American Federation of Labor to have finally admitted its darker laborers after trying to scuttle them for so long. What was it about these pie cards, whether they wore their ties in flaming red or green or blue, that they had to be eating five courses while blubbering fraternity and loyalty? "And now this rally is going to be the start of either a bold move or a failure the *New York Times* and the *Daily Worker* are salivating to write about."

"It's your job to worry about the start of the membership drive," Pickett clasped the older man on his firm upper arm. "I'll do mine."

"Exactly," Totten emphasized, poking his chest.

Now, he was getting to it. "You been hearing something I should know about, Terrible?"

"No, nobody's sent us a severed hand or ear lately." They shared thin smiles. You got used to such pleasantries in the mails at the union. "Just that a man like the Chief, a Negro leader that don't buck no guff from white nor black, red nor racist. Well, such a man naturally makes enemies and jealous rivals."

"So, have you heard something I should know about?" he repeated.

He looked off. Thaddeus Stokes was coming over. "Well, brother Pickett, it's not that firm, you see?"

"No, I don't," he growled irritably.

"Nefarious and Terrible," the head of the Unemployed Workers Council greeted. "Man, that's some kind of association with names like that. No wonder the Pullman Company is on the ropes." His laugh was hardy, if in a high register.

"A dream," Totten blurted. "It was a damn dream that the missus had."

"When she dreams the numbers, you mean?"

Totten managed a bemused expression at his own embarrassment. "She did indeed play a certain combination the morning after, but the images were vivid for her like a Sunday color insert. Though, sadly, open to much interpretation."

"What's that, Terrible?" Stokes asked.

"Just reminding Levi that when it comes to the Chief, we have to remain on the ready."

Pickett told Stokes about Totten's wife's fuzzy premonition.

"Was it a beast with the mark of Cain on them as in the *Book of Revelations* that came for him?" The known atheist Stokes needled.

"I will take my leave of being the object of you young fellows' levity. But she was particularly insistent about this one part. She recalled a man who had one face, used his claw of a hand to remove that face and reveal another one." He pointed at Pickett. "And you were shocked at this as you leaped in front of the Chief."

"This was at the rally?" Stokes seemed genuinely interested.

"Not sure, but the Chief had been at a podium floating on a river of black lava or some kind of tar when suddenly this person bubbled up from its depths."

"Tell her to lay off the pig's feet after seven-thirty," Pickett advised dryly.

"That I shall." And Totten pulled away to glad hand a deacon in Reverend Powell's Abyssinian Baptist Church.

"How you be?" Stokes asked. He adjusted the frame of his owlish glasses.

"Good, man, good." Millicent Fielding was sitting only in her underpants from France in his easy chair, and he was also naked and fully erect before her as she gripped his thighs and opened those full red lips that heated the back of his neck. What had that woman done to him? He better get straight before the rally. Trying to sound casual, Pickett said, "Got time for a shot of hooch?"

"You know I'm a teetotaler. Liquor and the black race are not meant to go hand-in-hand, comrade. We need to be disciplined and dedicated."

Lord, why had he said that? He'd just been through three hours of jaw-jackin' and planning, and now he was getting Stokes wound up. "Sorry, Thad, just going over too much in my head."

"Just make sure you're rested and not hungover for Saturday."

"On that, you can bet J.P. Morgan's silver, Daddy. Ain't nothin' happening to the Chief."

"Got some extra hands for security?"

"Fact, I do. Some of the cats that used to be in Garvey's personal guard, some porters themselves, of course, and even," he winked, "a few from my old outfit, the Black Rattlers. The 369th will be front and center on the route and at the staging area. If a cracker should even pick his nose too quick, we'll be on him like Eleanor Roosevelt on a bowl of chitlins."

"As long as you got it covered." Stokes smiled.

"All the way." Across the hall, the Chief, the head of the Brotherhood of Sleeping Car Porters, was in a huddled conversation with C.L. Dellums, a leader in the union. Dellums' was making a point, his hands gesturing rapidly. Briefly, the Chief's head pivoted up and around, encompassing the room. He acknowledged Pickett, then resumed talking with Dellums. That little gesture reminded Pickett that the Chief, no matter how many balls he was juggling, never forgot about you and that we were all in this together. He wouldn't let him down.

Later, he left the speak in the basement of the butcher shop on 136th, not far from the Lafayette Theater. He'd had a couple of drinks of the stuff the fellas were calling King Kong, homemade corn liquor, and he was feeling charged. He was brimming with energy and had to expend it in some way. What would happen if he should turn up at the mansion on Sutton Place and tell Harley Fielding he was there for the chauffeur's job? Say what? There's no such work available? Well, how about you watch me lay my mule on your missus? How would that be?

He walked, unreeling various versions of his private *moviola*. He found himself covering part of the route the march would take before its final point at 125th and Lex. It was to start at the YMCA on 133rd and wend its way south.

"Hey, Nefarious," a sharpie in a box coat called out as he and his woman crossed the avenue diagonally. "I'll be there." Folded under his arm was a copy of the *Amsterdam News*, the rally the front page item.

"Looking forward to it, O.C.," Pickett called back. "And make sure you bring them gents from the pool room along with you." Oswald Clevont Bannister was a gambler of some reputation and could pull in some of his shadier brethren. That might be a good buffer for Saturday, as those boys didn't mind a scrap-up if it jumped off.

Good thing a lot of people respected what the Brotherhood had done to fight for better wages for porters—the men who hustled bags, set and cleared tables, made beds, and, in general, had to be at the service of riders, white riders that was, on the sleeping cars of the Pullman Car Company of railroads. Not everyone was a porter, not everyone had to know how to work a fat train, a busy one, from a soft one. Or how to find the strength to muster up a "yessuh," while some sumabitch had barely looked at you and called you "George" because that's what passengers called colored porters no matter what your name was. Some said the insulting tradition had originated from George Pullman himself, as in "George's Boys." So even though you'd just deadheaded—returned to the depot in an empty car and had to go right back out on a run—you'd better snap to, you'd better be quick with that plate for the butter or the tuck of the bed because your meager salary wasn't enough to get by on unless you got tips. And if that didn't beat all, the Company sent its inspectors, sometimes posing as a normal businessman, to make sure your country ass was following verse and chapter of the porter's performance manual.

And for what the union, after years of uphill struggle, had been able to exact from the Pullman stockholders, well then, it wasn't a wonder many folks in Harlem and elsewhere saw that as symbolic of change in other areas, too.

Coming out of his ruminations, Pickett was soberly aware that in a recessed doorway or a break between a building, danger to the Chief could appear in the form of a man with a knife or gun. Or, certainly, a paid assassin could take a shot from any number of rooftops. There wasn't enough security detail, or even cops in New York that the Chief's friend, Mayor La Guardia, could get to cover all the possibles. The best thing was to make sure the Chief and the others, who would be in the front in the middle, were always surrounded on all sides by his men. He'd station a few on specific roofs with field glasses and pigeons. Like they'd done in the trenches of blood and shit and fear at the Maison-en- Champagne, the pigeons would have their wings dabbed with red paint. If one of them went up, Pickett would see it and know there was trouble.

He yawned as he went along. Pickett determined he was also going to use something else from those days fighting with the French in World War I. The head of security was going to bring his gun, the Colt .44 he'd won off a cowboy in a poker game. If the Chief found out, he'd fire him on the spot, but that was his lookout. He was a man of peace. It had washed over Pickett the first time he'd buried his bayonet in a Hun's neck. To kill another human being was not an act you could take lightly. But when it came to you or him, you'd better not hesitate. And he didn't intend to hesitate when it came to protecting the Chief.

Idly, as he sat at his kitchenette table, listening to a Louis Armstrong solo on the radio while cleaning his gun, it occurred to him that the best way to pull off a job on his boss would be with a diversion. That way, whoever was the torpedo could get in close and do his dirt as he and the others were distracted. But it wouldn't be someone from the crowd, the jam up of bodies would be too unpredictable. If he was planning a public rub-out, he'd have an inside man, someone you wouldn't expect as the regulator. Rotating the chamber of the pistol, he considered such an idea from different angles.

* * *

Millicent Fielding woke in the middle of the night, a few birds chirping even at this hour. Next to her in bed, her husband slumbered. She got up, put on her nightgown, and went downstairs to his study as she'd planned. It was locked, but she'd long ago gotten a key made for herself. You had to allow men their illusions lest the wheels fall off the wagon of male ego.

At his desk, she recalled that the set of keys she'd taken from his pockets and duplicated at an all-night locksmith in the Bronx had been with the notion of discovering if he'd strayed. She wanted to find out if he was poking some young lovely in Queens, with him maintaining her apartment or tuition at City College. How things change.

Among the papers and check ledger, she found two phone numbers in his hand, printing on the back of an ad slick for Fielding coal oil he'd been marking up for changes. She deduced the number she couldn't identify must have been the home of Thaddeus Stokes. The one she did know was the phone to the Unemployed Workers Council. What was her husband up to? What was his connection to Stokes, and what did Stokes get out of this relationship?

As soon as she asked herself that, the answer came to her. Unconsciously, she'd been touching her husband's ledger in the drawer. Money was the root of everything, wasn't it?

"Millie?" Harley Fielding's voice called out from upstairs.

Like a sock to her larynx, the air from her lungs was trapped in her throat. Talk, godammit, say something, she admonished herself, moving as fast as she darted for the doorway. "Yes, dear."

"What are you doing?" He too was moving, she heard the creak of floorboards.

"I had a nightmare and came down for a cup of tea." The light on his desk was on, but she couldn't go back through the study to turn that off and get to the kitchen to get the tea going in time. She was sure he was heading downstairs, and she tried shutting the door as quietly as she could. She cursed inwardly because the wood was swollen with moisture from the summer's humidity. By now, he had to be at the head of the hallway leading to the bend of the stairs. She got the door to click, then took off, glad her bare feet made for swift whispers over their Berber rugs. She went through the swing door, its hinges making a racket.

No time to fetch a kettle, fill it with water, and get it going on the stove. What, what could she do now?

The hinges creaked again as Harley Fielding, dressed in the silk pajamas and matching robe she'd bought him last Christmas, stepped into the kitchen. "I thought you were having tea."

She was bent over, her upper body inserted in the new Electrolux refrigerator they'd bought two months ago. It even had a light that went on when you opened it. "I was, but then decided to have a snack." She removed a plate of chicken covered in wax paper. Daintily, she plucked a tear of meat and skin, then returned the food to its perch.

"You're a funny duck," he said.

She came over to him. "I know." She gave him a greasy kiss. "Let's go back to bed, darling."

"Well." Like he'd seen Clarke Gable do in *It Happened One Night*, he twitched his mustache in pleasant surprise.

"Come on." And she took his hand, leading him out of the kitchen and back up the stairs.

* * *

The man's hog butcher knife speared one of the grapefruits in the basket Pickett had tossed at him. The big man didn't hesitate and used the opportunity of the would-be stabber extracting his blade to bash him alongside his head with a wooden crate of tomatoes. The man dropped to a knee, groggy but still belligerent.

"Nigga, I ain't scared of you. I'm'a carve you like soap," the pig sticker promised, rising.

Pickett drove his heel into the man's face, the crisp crunch of his nose bone snapping evident in the pre-dawn chill. He went over on his side and lay there, his knife near him on the ground, as if he were a rebellious child put to sleep with his favorite toy.

Pickett ignored the torn front of his sport coat and stepped around the second man he'd contended with at the farmer's market at the East River and 102nd Street. This one had been stilled by the splintered wheel of a pickle pushcart Pickett had slammed over his head.

"How," Thaddeus Stokes stammered, pressed against a truck with canvas rigging.

"I've been following Deke for more than a day and a half right to y'alls meeting here." Pickett nodded at the one he'd kicked in the face. The tall man stood directly in front of Stokes. "He's the useless kind of colored man

305

that not only would push his grandma under the train for lettuce but hates his own kind. He's done this kind of work for the Pullman Company before against our members."

Stokes was still trying to put it together. How had this backwoods field hand tumbled?

"Don't exert your brain power, Stokes." He wasn't about to hint that it was Millicent Fielding who'd helped him know about her husband's meeting with Stokes. And from that and the phone numbers, her conclusion was that the only thing the two had in common was the union—in a way. She knew that the Unemployed Workers Council had endorsed the rally and that Stokes was playing a role in shaping it, too.

Once he was in the picture, Pickett started doing some asking around in O.C.'s crowd and found out Deke was back in town.

"I don't care why you sold us out," Pickett spat, his anger cold and focused. The handle of the .44 sticking out of his waistband, cool against his wet shirt. The farmers and middlemen and pushcart operators went about their business of haggling and selling. If Levi Nefarious Pickett was busting heads, there was a good reason for it. And besides, if you got too nosy, it could be you broken up at his feet.

"Money, maybe so you could be the big man, or maybe the puckered-up pale faces at Pullman have something on you so bad they forced you into this. I don't give a shit. You have two hours to pack your things, set it straight with the Council so somebody takes your place and gets going. I'd plug you in a heartbeat, but only it would come back on the Brotherhood, and I can't have that. Now get, comrade."

Stokes gave a forlorn look at the East River and walked away for good.

* * *

That Saturday, Harley Fielding sat in his study, the Philco tuned to a wrap-up of the Harlem rally for Negro labor. He half-smoked his cigar, and though the sun wasn't down, he was already into his scotch. He was particularly incensed as Asa Philip Randolph, son of a preacher and head of the Brotherhood of Sleeping Car Porters, quietly but evocatively called for fair wages for fair work, that the black man and his families had the same rights as all Americans to an eight-hour day and overtime pay.

"That black bastard," he flamed. "That son-of-a-buck has more lives than a goddamn alley cat."

"What's wrong, dear?" his wife said, standing in the doorway of his study.

"Nothing," he groused. "Nothing you'd know anything about."

"Yes, dear. But I'm sure even if that Mr. Randolph and his union should force, I mean, should reach a signed agreement with the Pullman Company, your stock in it won't be hurt too much."

He glared at the door for a very long time after she'd closed it.

* * *

"The Counterfeit Comrade," *Measures of Poison,* Dennis McMillan Publications, 2002, Dennis McMillan, editor.

The Measure

That was a lot of money. More money than he'd ever see in his lifetime—he knew that for sure as his muscular stevedore arms cut into the frigid waters of the Stono River. Fortunately, the half-dime of a moon was tallow-colored and barely cast light upon the ink Robert Smalls swam through. His body was cold, but his senses were alert to everything around him. He gained steadily on his destination; this escaped slave most wanted by the Confederacy.

One of the five slave catchers who'd tried to kidnap him in Beaufort had said he was the nigra he was going to become fat on. Another said happily, as Smalls ducked the flat of the man's short ax, that they would whore and drink away the four thousand dollars offered for his capture. Four thousand dollars was plenty for any man's head. And it signified the depths of hatred Brigadier General Roswell Ripley must-have for him. And they wanted him back alive, thus a tortured end awaited him should the general get a hold of the bold coon.

After all, here he was a slave sent to work the docks of Charleston by his master John McKee. He'd been a lamplighter, then waiter, then apprenticed to John Simmons' boatyard. From there, he became a docker and worked his way up to foreman. There were plenty of men, black and white, bigger than his five feet five. But that only meant he had to work harder and longer to show his measure. Yes, he had to send his wages back to his master, but as even the soldiers around the docks joked, he had it pretty good for a slave.

When Simmons didn't have work for him, Smalls signed on to the various boats ferrying supplies and men up and down the waterways of South Carolina. Robert Smalls had only been given the name Robert to balance the last, which he had added as a tip of his cap to his size. "For a runt, he sure hauls like a full-grown man," they'd rib. He was quite familiar with the coastline's geography when the war broke out. And the longing that had been in him since he didn't know when got to fill him more and more on those nights he'd be resting on a pier, looking out across the black carpet of sea.

Smalls felt the ghostly brush of a jellyfish against one of his legs, and this brought him back to his mission. Cole's Island was looming larger, and he kept stroking toward her. The island lay not too many miles off Charleston and had once been a cannon and arms compound.

As the Union erected blockades at several intervals out from the coastline, the island had been abandoned by the Confederates, or so the Northern forces had been led to believe. But as Smalls was piloting the *Planter* three days ago on a, what was the word Captain DuPont used, re-con-e-sant run, he'd spotted something the other troops hadn't given much mind.

"Yes, sir, Captain, sir, I'm'a sure of it," Smalls had insisted when they'd returned to headquarters at Port Royal. "I seen, I mean I saw, it through the spyglass I borrowed from Sergeant Matthews." His wife had been helping him with his book learnin'.

"You see this, Matthews?" DuPont bit off the end of his cigar and spat the chunk into the spittoon next to his desk.

"Well, sir," Matthews began, "I did see a schooner flying Confederate colors, yes, sir." Matthews, Smalls knew from association, had laid out a career for himself in the Army. He wasn't about to side too much with a darky.

"Was this ship departing from the island?" DuPont struck a match with his thumbnail and lit his cigar. He kept his stone gray eyes on both men as they sweated in the humidity outside his tent. As was customary, he was seated behind his field table.

"I couldn't say that, sir. But she was heading in a direction away from Cole's Island, sure enough. But," he quickly added, "that don't mean she was at the island, sir."

DuPont rubbed blunt fingers in his beard's brown whiskers. "But you say, Smalls, you recognized this particular schooner?"

"That's right, sir. I been on the *Jena* more than once, sir. She's got a hold made to carry heavy guns and rifle racks along her insides. She wouldn't be out lessin' they's usin' her for that reason naw, sir." He didn't like to sound so accommodating, his wife Hannah would say. His life as a slave had been different than working sunup to sundown in the fields, an overseer always quick with the lash. But white men were white men, and you best step lightly 'round their feelings.

DuPont smoked and pondered, then stated, "We have to make sure. As you men know, we're preparing to take our ships and men through the back door Ripley has left unguarded by removing the light garrison that had been on Cole's. Information we confirmed from our balloonists and you, Smalls." He quickly waved with the lit end of his cigar at the smallish black man with the wide torso.

"Yet," DuPont continued, "Ripley knows you are with us, and he knows you know the rivers and back washes like he does." DuPont laughed, and it made Smalls nervous. "Of course, he being a fine Southern gentlemen and planter, he cain't put too much stock that you, a slave, actually have put that knowledge to useful purposes with us."

Smalls noted that DuPont hadn't said "former" slave, but what could he do about this man, or Matthews, or any of the other blue-bellies and how they saw him? He was determined to maintain his freedom, and that of his wife and two children.

Matthews couldn't hide his sly grin. "So we go forward as ordered, sir?"

The captain blew gray fumes across his kerosene lamp. "We send you, Smalls, and an oarsman to find out for sure. There is too much at stake for any kind of setback, Sergeant. Too much. We, like them, are strained to capacity and cain't afford unnecessary losses."

"You mean me and him—" Matthews began, a protest forming on his lips.

"Are to sneak out in a rowboat from one of our light ships anchored away from Cole's Island," DuPont finished. "You will conduct a reconnaissance of the island and thereafter report your findings. This will commence," he consulted his pocket watch, which was open on the table, "at approximately 2100 hours this evening, Sergeant." He stood and puffed. "You have your orders."

Both men saluted though Smalls, as of yet, had not been given any official rank. Truth was his position with the Union wasn't formal at all. Though he did know that when he'd first piloted the *Planter*, the ship he'd commandeered, into Union waters and told of what he knew, DuPont had sent a letter to the Secretary of the Navy, Gideon Wells. The letter, it was rumored, had praised his observation skills and his daring. And fair enough, he'd been paid as a pilot for the joint Army and Navel command, so that was something. But it had only occurred to him now, standing next to these men in their uniforms' dirty and fraying though they may be, that he still wasn't truly part of their fight. Hadn't the Union soldiers helped him fight off the slave catchers? Obviously, he was of some worth to them.

Smalls swirled fresh water in his mouth, the liquid bracing him as he drew close to the leeward side of the island. It was merely a slag of land, though there was a small hill upon it which he remembered seeing kegs of gunpowder and cannonball stocked once. He entered shallow water, and his toes slid into mud. He'd tied his boots around his neck, as he didn't want to be squeaking around in wet shoes. Smalls did his best to minimize splashing and hunched over as he got onto land.

Quickly, he shoved his feet into his boots and got his bearings. If the Rebels were encamped again on the island, they'd be by the hill. It blocked a view, and the cannons had been stored in the one cave in the hillside. The officer's tents and bedrolls had been spread around this. He'd had to bring hardtack and salt pork, by himself, up from the shore that time. All the while, the Rebs were calling him names and threatening to shoot him should he drop any of the sacks or crates. But his back was broad for a man his size, and nary a provision fell to the earth, even though several of the soldiers tried to trip him.

Smalls stuffed those slights away. Anything less than getting his foot chopped off by a slaver or getting lynched for sport by a mob, he considered rice and red-eyed gravy. The first thing he noticed as he crouched in a thicket was a dark mound set back from the beach. He waited and heard nothing except the rustling of lizards in the brush and croaks of frogs. Cautiously, feeling fully exposed in the open space, he dashed to the mound.

The compact man was shivering, but he had a job to do. Heading toward Cole's Island, Smalls knew something was up when Matthews had been the only one to come with him in the rowboat from the *Planter*, the sergeant making him row. They got within rifle range, and Matthews ordered him to swim the rest of the way. When he questioned this, his position was made clear.

"Look, boy, you may have impressed DuPont, but that don't mean chicken dinner to me. Jus' 'cause you memorized what you'd seen and heard good as a white man jus' means you bein' on the docks all that time somethin' was bound to sink in that thick skull of yours."

Smalls was stuck. He knew Matthews had seen him reading a months-old newspaper he'd found. The sergeant had snatched the paper out of his hands and said he'd never wanted to see him pretending like that again. The sergeant, he was sure, couldn't read. It wasn't unusual that he couldn't, but it stuck out more so when it was a black that could.

"Now git your black ass in that river and over ta that island."

"Alright," he'd muttered, barely keeping his temper down. "All right?"

"I mean, yes, sir, Sergeant Matthews."

"That's better...Smalls."

Now, digging into the thin layer of sand, he felt the scratchy surface of burlap. He rugged on the cloth and revealed part of the cold cast iron of a cannon barrel. In the weak light and by feel, Smalls assessed the armament was what the soldiers had called a ten-pounder, referring to the size of the cannonball the weapon shot.

Creeping about, he found several other areas where cannons, Napoleons, and even a few Union Parrotts were hidden. So that was it. The Confederates had correctly concluded that the Union knew about their previous withdrawal from the island and other defenses along the Sonto River. Also knowing the Union was looking for a way to seize Charleston,

Ripley had snuck back and assembled an ambush force. When the Union ships came steaming along the river, thinking they'd sneak in the rear, then the back door would be shut on them—and blue blood would flow into the waters. Smalls did his best to count the secreted cannons, since this was the kind of information the captain would want. Though he had a feeling that Matthews would take the credit, as if he had dared get on the island, with Smalls sitting sniffling and praying to de Lawd in the rowboat.

"Is that you, Remmy?"

Hell, he swore to himself. He'd been easing up the rise, as it would be a good spot for heavy cannons like the thirty-pounders he'd heard about. That's when he also smelled the dying smoke and chicory."

"Yes, uh, yeah," he said, trying to sound like a white man who was a fellow soldier.

"What the hell you doin'?" the voice challenged, feet crunching closer.

"Nothin," Smalls said, standing up fully.

"Remmy?" The soldier asked again, his rifle held guard duty fashion.

Smalls leaped, and the two tumbled down the hill. The Confederate was taller than him, but his limbs were skinnier. They wound up along the side, the spy on top.

"A nigra," his opponent gasped. "You're a—"

Smalls silenced him with a punch to the mouth and another one to the side of the man's head. He lay still, and Smalls scrambled up, running for the shore. That bastard Matthews should be there, should have rowed in to see what was happening. But no, he'd be nice and dry three or four hundred yards out. He was probably worrying about the girl he left behind, humming a tune.

Anger got his legs lifting higher and his heart racing faster. The crack of a rifle shot made that same pounding heart stop as if ice had suddenly formed around it.

"The next one takes that pointed head of yours clean off, mister. You better turn around."

Smalls did as the soldier demanded. There were two of them, and it was gloomy enough they couldn't see he was black.

"Hey, Remmy," a third one shouted, "McMahon has been coldcocked."

"Well, well," Remmy said, moving forward. "'Pears we got us a sneak of some kind. But is he a thief, or is he a blue-belly?"

"They wouldn't jest send one," another man offered.

"What kind of scout party would that be?"

"A quiet one," Remmy answered. He'd advanced far enough to get a good look at Smalls. It was just that the image refused to register with him. "Where's your master, boy?" he said querulously.

"I was jus' returnin' Massa Simmons raf, boss," Smalls replied, slipping into slave talk and dipping his head. At that moment, he was powerful glad he wasn't in a Union uniform.

"Massa Simmons," Remmy questioned. He violently thrust the barrel of his Sharps carbine into the other man's nostrils, causing blood to discharge.

"What in the hell you talkin' about, darkie? John Simmons would no sooner let you have one of his rafts out than General Lee would let you shave him."

"I swears thas so," Smalls embellished, hoping his act would buy him time. Goddamn Matthews must be wondering what was keeping him.

"Kill the nigger," the third one who'd discovered McMahon said. "He attacked a white man, didn't he?"

"But he ain't here by accident," the third one announced cogently. "He must be with the Union. I've heard tell they's drafting colored soldiers."

"With weapons?" the second one asked in utter dismay. "Shut up," Remmy, a sergeant, ordered his men. The rifle was still thrust into Smalls' face. "You been sent to snoop on us, nigger?"

"Naw, suh."

"Uh-huh." With that, Remmy butted him with the other end of the rifle, and Smalls reeled back. His first instinct was to strike out, but he knew that would earn him a bullet in his brainpan. He stood, watching and waiting, his fingers touching the wetness around his mouth.

"He ain't that big, but that buck sho cain take it," the second one said. He crowded closer to Smalls, too.

"Come on," Remmy announced. "This is too important to make a mistake now. We gonna find out what this coon knows and what he's doing here. Neville, you and Sykes git him over to tha platform."

"Okay," one of them replied.

The two men roughly grabbed Smalls and started to take him back toward the hill. Desperate, he broke free from one of the men and swung on the other. He connected, sending this one back more in shock than hurt.

"This nigger's a wild animal," the man he hit blurted.

Smalls had nothing to lose, as he knew death was close on his neck. He started to run, but the third man was quick and landed on him. He clubbed him twice with the butt of his Leech & Rigdow .36.

Disoriented, the Johnny Rebs hauled Smalls between them to their encampment. He couldn't see well and realized it was from being hit in the head and blood trickling into his eyes. He felt himself being lashed against a pole, his wet shirt torn from his body. A widow's veil descended on his head, and there was nothing but bliss. He stirred awake after water was thrown into his face.

"Time for some answers, nigger." Remmy lowered the wooden bucket he'd used.

Smalls looked around him. The other two, plus the man he'd originally fought, McMahon, were staring at him. Each had a hungry look in their eyes. That is except the one who'd said he was here for a reason. This one looked sorry for Smalls. He was roped against a pole that was part of a platform upon which were barrels of black powder covered in tarpaulin. The Rebs had made it that way to no doubt keep the powder dry and off the sand.

"Over here, boy." Remmy stood with a dull pig sticker in his hand. "Git a fire going, McMahon."

"Yes, sir," the man replied with glee as he set about his task.

"You got something to tell us?" Remmy jabbed the point of his Bowie knife into Smalls' belly. The thrust was enough to prick but not go in deep.

His head was exploding, but all he could do was grit his teeth and wish he was in Hannah's arms. The worst was yet to be.

"Ain't had no dark meat in some time," one of them joked.

"Remmy, this ain't right," the only one to show concern said. "General Ripley will want to question this man."

"We gonna soften this hard case up for him, Sykes. Don't you get your petticoats ruffled about it, hear?"

"But—" the other man stammered.

"But nothing," McMahon interrupted, "this here nigger acts like a white man. He's got to be shown it's jus' plain wrong." The fire crackled beside the man as he knelt near its flames, warming his hands. "It's ready." A canine fierceness lit his eyes from within.

Remmy heated the deadly steel at the apex of the fire. No one said anything; anticipation or dread had locked their vocal cords. The sergeant turned and paced methodically toward Smalls.

"What you got to say, boy?" The tip of the knife was releasing steam.

Smalls couldn't speak for fear he'd bust out praying. He'd be damned to two hells if he was going to give these crackers the satisfaction.

The white-hot blade was laid against the skin of his chest, and he cried out in pain. Again, the side of the blade was applied, and Smalls was on the verge of passing out.

"Throw water on him," Remmy said. The one called Sykes did so.

Then Remmy asked, taunting, "Well, nigger man?"

"I'll show you," he gasped, his mouth hanging open as if broken.

"What?" Remmy dipped his head closer.

"I'll show you tha papers, boss, tha repot massa DuPont is 'spose to git."

The Rebs knew who DuPont was. "What papers is this?" Remmy asked excitedly.

"The one I's buried at tha beach. Tha one that they's orders from that Grant fella."

All the Confederates looked puzzled, as he hoped they would.

"How'd you get these papers, nigra?" McMahon piped up. They certainly didn't think he had the intelligence to concoct such a tale.

"Sergeant Matthews, suh," Smalls fibbed. "I was a rowin' his boat, and he was lookin' at your island here through one of them, ah, I don't know what you call 'em, suh."

"Telescope," Remmy said disgustedly. "And then what?"

"Well, suh," Smalls added, making it up fast, "somehow the boat got tangled up on sumptin'. Next thing I knows, we tips over and well, suh, that fine young sergeant done drown."

McMahon laughed uproariously. "This nigger cain't walk straight, let alone guide a boat. He got panicky and got that Northerner drowned, probably flailing all about just to save his black soul."

"Sumptin' like that," Smalls muttered.

Remmy took a swipe with the knife, making a diagonal scar across Smalls' stomach. "And he left you with these papers?"

"He, he prayed to Jesus for me to get 'em to DuPont, yes, suh." The sharp but brief pain from the last injury actually cleared some of Smalls' head. It was like a slap to wake the slumber.

"Where are these papers?" Remmy demanded.

"I got to show y'all. I cain't describe it correc'ly wit words, naw, suh."

"He's lying," the Reb called Neville said.

Remmy scratched the side of his nose with the tip of his blade. "We got to check. The general trusts us to watch things here till he gets the men in place t'morrow. We got to see in case those Union boys is on to us." He grinned devilishly at Smalls. "'Sides, this boy is all through. What can he do 'gainst four of us? Even if one of us is weak-livered Sykes."

The other two laughed.

Sykes got Smalls untied, who slumped. The young soldier helped him stand. For a moment, their eyes met, and then the confederate broke contact.

Smalls said, "It's over where you fount me. I knows 'zactly."

"Come on." Remmy stood beside him as Sykes stood opposite. McMahon was behind, and Neville was in front.

"Hurry up, boy," McMahon declared, shoving Smalls. "We got us some skinnin' ta do."

"Yes, suh, boss, I sure hopes ya don't—" and he whipped to his left, where Remmy was. He got a hand around the man's wrist and summoned the strength that had made him foreman on the docks. In a wink, he toppled over with the sergeant as the others reached for him. Remmy hit him in his seared flesh, but Smalls, gnashing his teeth, couldn't let up. He bore down, and there was a snap.

"My wrist, he broke my—"

Smalls had the Bowie knife and came around and up with the steel. The thing went into McMahon's soft gut, and his breath, smelling of corn whiskey, rushed from his lungs. Sykes and Remmy jumped on Smalls. Neville had his gun out but couldn't get a clean shot.

"Git him up, git him up," the man with the pistol repeated.

"Oh, God. Oh, God," McMahon wheezed, writhing on the ground.

"You're dead, nigger, dead and gone," Remmy promised, grabbing with his one good hand.

Smalls broke free from Sykes, who had his arms around his upper body. That was where he was strongest. He poured everything he had left into an attack on the sergeant. Being black and telling white men what to do on the docks, Smalls had had his share of bare-knuckled contests. He pummeled Remmy into the dirt, his fists striking every open area they could find.

Breathing raggedly, he turned, the barrel of the repeater filling his vision. He saw his mother toiling in the sorghum field, his father taking a lashing for talking back to the master.

"Smalls, Smalls," Matthews suddenly called from the beach. "Where are you?"

The man with the pistol looked at Sykes, then toward the beach. That was his chance. Smalls dove and, using his stevedore arm and hand of his, scooped up sandy earth and threw it. A shot came through the cloud, but he was already up again and hurtling at the gunman.

The two bodies collided as Smalls heard feet pounding toward them. Cold steel was against his rib cage, and a shot was let off just as he twisted aside. The bullet creased him, and he yelped, but he couldn't let up.

"You black demon," the gunman swore. Frustrated, he bit the other man on the bicep.

This enraged Smalls, and in a red fury, he beat at the other man until his hands pulled him off his victim.

"That's enough, enough," Matthews said.

The river pilot was groggy, his whole body alive with hurt. It was an effort to breathe, and something was blocking his left eyesight. It was blood.

"Good Lord, man," Matthews looked around. McMahon was on his back, his arms outstretched, gazing vacantly at the heavens. The knife was like a growth in his chest. Remmy was on one knee, groaning, his hand holding his wrist. Neville was at Smalls' feet, curled up, his form inert as if resting peaceably.

"Let's get back...Mr. Smalls," Matthews said. Vaguely, he waved his Colt at Sykes. "Tie your men up," the Union sergeant ordered his prisoner.

Later, Smalls rested in a rowboat, his head lying against the edge. He longed to see his wife and children.

* * *

A month later, mostly healed, he was summoned to DuPont's tent at Port Royal.

"Smalls," the man said, a cigar rolling back and forth in his mouth. He stood and came around his desk.

"Sir," the escaped slave replied.

DuPont regarded the shorter man for several moments, and then a hint of a smile creased his beard. "You certainly proved your measure on Cole's Island, Smalls. I understand General Hunter is requesting Secretary of War Stanton to immediately raise five thousand Negro troops."

"So I heard, sir."

"Raw recruits. Some of them free-born, and some, like you, who tore their way to freedom. But as long as the South has an army, they won't be truly free, will they?"

"I suppose so, sir."

"Well," he finally drawled, "that's all for now, Smalls."

"All right, Captain." He turned to go.

"Oh," DuPont said, "these new soldiers will need men to train and lead them, wouldn't you say, Smalls?"

"Of course." He started to walk off.

"Stop by the quartermaster and pick up your uniform, Smalls," DuPont called out. "And your Sergeant's stripes."

He turned around, a smile on his face now. "Yes, sir." This time, when he turned, he pivoted soldier fashion.

* * *

Author's Note:

After the war, the real Robert Smalls served as a delegate to South Carolina's constitutional convention in 1868 and was in both houses of the state legislature from 1868 to 1875. He also served two terms in the U.S. House of Representatives. In 1889, he was appointed by President Benjamin Harrison collector of the Port of Beaufort. He held that post for the most part until 1913. He died on February 23, 1915.

* * *

"The Measure," *The Blue and the Gray Undercover: All New Civil War Spy Adventures*, Forge, 2002, Ed Gorman, editor.

The Calling

Wilmington, Long Beach, CA

"You're it, Hank. Who the hell else could I lay this burden on?"

Mark coughs up more blood, and I do my best to comfort my dying friend. He's dressed in a suit I'm quite sure costs more than my parish generates in two months. His leaking blood creates a Rorschach test gone awry on his light blue shirt.

"The ambulance is coming." I say this even though I don't hear a siren. Which is ironic, given there's always a peal around here, in the neighborhood where Mark and I grew up. He smiles up at me with his red-stained teeth. "We both know that they'll be too late. Sit me up, will you, and reach into my pocket."

"I'm a priest. You know it's only young boys I feel up."

"Always the joker," Mark says.

I get him against the oak wainscoting, dark with age. I dig out a set of keys on a ring. The one he intends for me is obvious. It's an old-fashioned skeleton key.

He puts his hand over mine, holding the set. "Let me hear your confession, my son," I say.

Again, a flash of the red-stained teeth. "The Devil knows what I've done, Hank. No sense pretending I have regrets now. You can't fool God."

Now I hear sirens, faintly, an ambulance and the police I believe. Outside and up the block is a wrecked Cadillac CTS with two dead men, mouths agape on the supple leather seats. The car is plowed across the sidewalk, the front end embedded in the brick corner of the Perez family bodega. Good people, the Perezes.

The two in that sweet Caddy were shot dead by my childhood friend Mark Shepperds, who is passing away before me. He's the third casualty of their brief and violent firefight. I wonder had he been on his way to see me when the two caught up to him, or just happened to be passing by? Maybe he'd stopped in at the bodega for a soda or cigarettes.

"The key, Hank," Mark says, tapping it as I open my hand with the set on my palm. "There's a number stamped on it."

His voice is getting weaker, and I lean closer. I should be worried about his eternal soul, but I want to make sure I don't miss a word.

"The locker— " he begins, but starts coughing again.

Not much more time now. "The Lighthouse?" I finish. The Lighthouse— we go in for nautical names here in Wilmington—had been a live venue during vaudeville way the hell back. By the time we were kids, it was a second-run movie house where we'd sneak in to watch streaky prints of *Fist of the North Star* and *Under Siege 2.* Then, the joint went out of business around the turn of this century; hipsters bought and refurbished it to mount hipster plays, but that didn't last. It closed for good about three years ago.

"It's all in there, Hank," Mark says quietly, almost drowned out by the wail of the vehicles outside the door. I mumble the last rites as uniformed officers, their service weapons out, swarm the sanctuary of the Five Wounds church.

"Hands where I can see them and prone the fuck out," one of the cops commands, even though I am wearing my collar. I do as ordered and am frisked by the one who'd yelled.

"Sorry, padre...Ramirez is it?" another one says, chuckling. "Burns here is a Lutheran." This officer, a Sergeant Horne, helps me to my feet while looking over at Mark's remains. "You know who that is?"

"We played basketball together at Sacred Heart." The sergeant regarded me. "I'll be damned."

What he'd meant was we all knew around here that Mark Shepperds had racked up plenty of deaths over his years as a high-priced hitman.

* * *

The photos were taken, the bodies carted away, little yellow tented cards placed next to shell casings, and the other witnesses and I were questioned. Afterward, I headed over to the Lighthouse. It took a bit of doing, but I got in and headed to what had been the area for dressing rooms. I matched the key to the right locker, and bingo. It revealed a compact equipment bag and a thick, leather-bound journal.

In the journal, in Mark's precise block lettering, were victims' names, dates, monies received, and the names of the people who'd paid for the deeds he'd done. Powerful people. Not the sort who would be brought to the bar of justice.

In the bag were the various lethal tools of Mark's trade.

I suppose I should have turned all of it over to Sergeant Horne. But ever since I'd taken over the Five Wounds from my predecessor, I'd been frustrated. How many stories had I heard of the abusive husband given one more chance, the local loan shark charging thirty percent vig while the working poor, my flock, were getting squeezed out of their crappy rentals by the gentrifiers and the speculators—the self-same one percenters who'd employed Mark.

Fire and forget, isn't that what the soldiers and grunts said when I was a chaplain in Afghanistan? The heft of the equipment bag, into which I zippered Mark's journal, felt good in my hand as I headed out to my car. I think I may have an answer to my slow and quiet crisis of faith. The sports club we run for our at-risk youth can offer little else, nor can the moribund job training center we maintain, helping prepare poorly educated immigrant women to cook and clean for the shits in Mark's book. Now I can do some thing more than just nod thoughtfully, expressing empty platitudes as I listen to yet another heartbreaking story.

I can do a lot more than merely nod.

* * *

"The Calling," *Akashic's Monday are Murder*, April 29, 2013.

About the Author

Gary Phillips has written novels, short stories, and comics for the likes of DC, Dark Horse and Boom! Studios. He's penned new adventures of Kolchak, the Night Stalker and brought back Xal-Kor, The Human Cat, a sixties fandom favorite. *Matthew Henson and the Ice Temple of Harlem* was his rollicking retro pulp novel, and he edited the Anthony-winning anthology *The Obama Inheritance: Fifteen Stories of Conspiracy Noir. One-Shot Harry* was named one of the best mysteries of 2022 by *The Washington Post.* He'd also been a staff writer on *Snowfall,* a show streaming on Hulu about crack and the CIA in 1980s South Central where he grew up.

AUTHOR WEBSITE:

https://gdphillips.com

Also by Gary Phillips

Recent Novels:

Matthew Henson and the Ice Temple of Harlem

One-Shot Harry

Ash Dark as Night

Short Story Collections:

Monkology: 15 Stories from the World of Private Eye Ivan Monk

Astonishing Heroes: Shades of Justice

The Unvarnished Gary Phillips: A Mondo Pulp Collection

Recent Anthologies as Editor:

South Central Noir

Get Up Offa That Thing: Crime Fiction Inspired by the Songs of James Brown

Witnesses For the Dead: Stories, co-edited w/Gar Anthony Haywood